THOMPSON

Love Lies Bleeding

NEW
ISLAND

This book is dedicated to all those readers
who encouraged me to continue.
I honestly couldn't have done this
without your support.
Thank you.

Oh never weep for love that's dead
Since love is seldom true
But changes his fashion from blue to red,
From brightest red to blue,
And love was born to an early death
And is so seldom true.

Lizzie Siddal

Then while time serves and we are but decaying,
Come, my Corinna, come, let's go a-Maying.

Robert Herrick

PROLOGUE

His hand skimmed her bare leg, coming to rest on the tender place behind her knee. It lingered there for a moment or two, caressing, teasing, before travelling farther along her thigh. It was the first time she'd done this, and she was very tense. As he reached down with his other hand to unfasten himself, she braced herself for a count of five – hoping she could bear the weight of him on her at this awkwardly contrived angle – then exhaled in relief as the director barked, 'Cut! Thanks, Rory. Thanks, er—' a glance at his clipboard, 'Corinna.'

Her silk petticoats made a rustling noise as Rory McDonagh disengaged himself and rolled off her. 'Did you hear about the cowboy who wore a hat, waistcoat and chaps all made of paper?' he asked, looking down at her with wicked green eyes.

'No.'

'He's wanted for rustling,' said Rory.

Shrugging into the robe that the wardrobe girl was holding out for her, she managed her first genuine smile of the day.

'That's better,' he told her. 'You're beginning to relax.'

'I'm sorry. I never dreamed I'd feel so self-conscious.'

'You're bound to feel self-conscious, darling. I've done this many, many times, but it doesn't get any easier.'

'I've done it too. Well – not this, not exactly. But I have got my kit off for life-drawing classes in art college. I thought I'd be well able to do it in front of a camera, but it's *so* not the same thing.'

'That's because it's skin on skin. People find it hard to believe, but simulating sex is one of the most terrifying aspects of an actor's job.' Swinging his legs off the bed, Rory slanted her a look of enquiry. 'So you're an art student?'

'Yes. A typical impoverished one. That's why I have to take jobs like this.'

'What branch?'

'Painting, at NCAD. I love it.'

'I do a bit of collecting. Maybe one day I'll own a painting by the world-renowned artist Corinna Connelly.'

'Corinna Connelly isn't my real name,' she confessed.

'I guessed it might be makey-uppy. What made you choose it?'

'I didn't want my real name to go on the credits.'

'No, I meant what made you choose the name Corinna?' He was small-talking, she knew, trying to put her at ease.

'My cousin came up with it.' She pulled the collar of her robe up to her chin and hugged her knees for comfort. 'She's dead cultured. Apparently it's a diminutive of the Greek word *cora*, which means 'girl'. And that's all I am in this film. I'm just the girl who stands in for the real star.'

The make-up assistant approached with her powder brush. 'The real star is lucky to have you as her body double,' she observed. 'You've a fabulous figure.'

'Get away! Thank you for the *lovely* compliment, but it's nowhere near as fab—'

'Hair in the gate!' came the call from the studio floor. 'We'll have to go again.'

Rory laid a reassuring hand on her arm. 'Don't worry, sweetheart,' he told her. 'You're doing great. Just close your eyes and think of the moolah.'

Think of the moolah, she repeated like a mantra as she unknotted the sash of her robe with clumsy fingers. *Just close your eyes and think of the moolah.* What I'm doing isn't porn, it's not prostitution, it's not pole dancing. And it's paying me many more euros than posing for life-drawing classes ever could …

The camera assistant took a fresh reading, the make-up girl applied a little more body shimmer and Rory McDonagh positioned himself on top of her, keeping his weight on his elbows like the gentleman he was.

'And … *action*!' commanded the director.

1

Deirdre O'Dare was leafing through a film script. Its working title was *Love Lies Bleeding* and it was to star Rory McDonagh in the role of Jack St Ledger, legendary Irish rake, gambler, roué and founder member of the notorious Hellfire Club.

```
FADE IN.
EXT. HELLFIRE CLUB — NIGHT
A SERIES OF ANGLES.

Pale STARS in the sky. The shoulder of the hill
black against a navy blue sky.
CUT TO:
GLOWING EMBERS OF A BONFIRE

We HEAR the soft HOOT of an owl. MOVE IN on the
remains of a midnight feast. A rug has been
spread. Lucy is lying back against cushions.
Her bodice is agape, her hair dishevelled.
Jack is kissing her breasts. CLOSER ANGLE of
Jack's face.
```

'I take it that the camera cuts straight to the body double?' said Deirdre.

Setting the script aside, she raised her eyes to the famously green ones of her husband. Rory was sitting beside her on the couch in their kitchen, sorting through fan mail, his bare feet up on the coffee table.

'Yep,' he said abstractedly. 'Sweet Jesus, that girl's sent me another picture of herself naked.'

'*Another* one! Let me see?'

Rory handed her a photograph of a bleached blonde lying sprawled on a bed. 'Ew,' said Deirdre. 'Too much information.' She tore the photo in two and dropped it in the waste paper basket. 'Have you met her?' she asked.

'Who? That girl?'

'Don't be daft. I mean the body double.'

'No. She hasn't been cast yet.'

'I'm jealous already.'

'Oh, sweetheart. I'd have thought you'd have learned to live with it by now.'

'I've never learned to live with the idea of you getting naked with other women.'

It was true. Although simulated sex was an occupational hazard in the wacky world of movie-making, Deirdre had never felt comfortable with her husband doing it, and it just didn't get any easier. And there was an additional burden. The fact that body doubles invariably had sick-makingly perfect physiques – to pander to the vanity of the stars who insisted on them – simply made things worse.

'She'll need to be well fit if she's standing in for Charlotte. What happens if you get turned on?' asked Deirdre.

Rory gave her an 'as if' look. 'Oh, come on, sweetheart. You know full well that sex is the last thing on my mind when I have to do raunch – if that doesn't sound too much of a contradiction in terms.'

'What *is* on your mind?'

'Camera angles. Just how erotic do you think it is to fake it while there's a director hovering over you going, "Hey! That's great! Just great!"' Rory did a mean imitation of an LA accent. '"And hold for a count of four – two, three, four. Good! Now slide your left hand down her thigh – two, three, four. That's terrific! Now, thrust! Two, three, four. And … cut! Print it!" It's called acting, remember? You were pretty good at it once.' He smiled at her. 'I'll never forget our first stage kiss. That was *very* erotic.'

'That wasn't acting.'

The smile Deirdre rewarded him with was a slanty-eyed one, full of promise. Unfortunately, Rory's phone rang before she could keep said promise. It was the story of her life. PR people, suits, journalists – everybody but her seemed to be able to grab a piece of her husband before she could: there simply wasn't enough of him to go round.

'Bummer,' he said, checking out the display. 'I'll have to take this.'

He picked up and Deirdre could tell at once by the quasi-flirtatious, quasi-business-like demeanour he shrugged on that he was talking to his agent, the Queen Bee. Since the Queen Bee routinely sucked Rory's cell phone dry, this could take some time. Deirdre's own agent, Blake Parker, called her so seldom that she had started to refer to him as the Secret Agent. That said, he was one of the toughest negotiators in LA.

Deirdre got to her feet and crossed the floor to the sliding doors that separated the kitchen from the deck. A gull perched on the white rails took off as she slid the door back and she watched it soar westward into the big blue sky that hung like a cyclorama over the Pacific Ocean. It was another perfect day in LA. White sand, blue sea, the green fronds of palm trees. It was all so picture postcard perfect it could have been lifted directly from the pages of Condé Nast's *Traveller*.

Deirdre compared it mentally with the view from the small balcony of her house in Saint-Géyroux, in the Languedoc region of France. The Languedoc! Even the name of the region had a laid-back ring to it, while the Orange County just conjured up images of fake tan. How different her two vistas were! In Saint-Géyroux she would wander out onto the balcony that overlooked the rue Lamballe each morning with a *café au lait* and a *tartine* and settle herself on her wicker chair to observe the comings and goings in the village below. She might see her friend Dannie Palmer, sitting on the terrace of the local café enjoying coffee and Orangina with her little girl. Or she might spot willowy Madeleine Lennox heading towards the market, a basket on her arm. Or she might get a bird's eye view of Madeleine's husband Daniel astride his electric-blue Harley Davison, keeping the engine idling while he swapped news with one of the village elders. She especially loved to spot Daniel because he was such an accomplished flirt. Any time he looked up, he would blow her a kiss to catch, and once he had even plucked a flower from Mme Verdurin's window box and tossed it up to her (sadly, after the bollicking he'd received from the redoubtable Mme Verdurin, he had never done it again).

Deirdre *yearned* for Saint-Géyroux – oh, how she yearned! The McDonagh-O'Dares relocated to France every summer because there were far fewer demands on Deirdre there. Their three kids were perfectly happy to just mess about on the banks of the River Hérault all day, whereas in LA she and Melissa, the nanny, were constantly running around, ferrying them here and there to various classes and activities and events.

However, it looked as if there were going to be a couple of drawbacks this coming summer. Rory wouldn't be around: he had movies lined up back to back until the end of the year, with a schedule that would take him zigzagging on dozens of flights to dozens of locations all over the world. And due to the fact that she had recently got engaged, Melissa's days as Deirdre's godsend were numbered. Deirdre had offered the nanny countless inducements to accompany them to France, but to no avail. Melissa had fallen in love and she was staying put in LA.

'Don't get me wrong – I'm not looking for editorial input,' she heard Rory telling the Queen Bee now, on the other side of the sliding doors. He was still lounging with his feet up on the coffee table, one hand behind his head. The hairs on his forearms gleamed gold against his tan and the muscular contours of his chest were etched against the fabric of the T-shirt he wore like a second skin. God, was he sexy! She could understand the impulse that had made that blonde send him her photograph. 'No. No. I'm simply pointing out that the dialogue could do with some polishing.'

Rory's role as Jack St Ledger was a gift, but some of the dialogue in *Love Lies Bleeding* was dodgy and would doubtless prove a bitch to learn. Aside from any issues to do with credibility, bad dialogue was always trickier to learn than well-written stuff. Deirdre knew this from her experience as an actress in the days before she'd ditched the day job to write screenplays full time. *Love Lies Bleeding* wasn't terminally ill, but it badly needed the attention of a script doctor.

Another gull wheeled past, reflected in the plate glass of the sliding door. Her own reflection looked back at her a little solemnly. Solemnity didn't sit well on Deirdre: she was at her best when she smiled, which she did quite a lot. That's why Rory had officially declared Van Morrison's 'Brown Eyed Girl' to be 'their' song.

Wandering back into the kitchen, she retrieved the offending script from the floor and opened it at random. This is what she found:

```
INT. KILLAKEE HOUSE
JACK ST LEDGER'S BEDCHAMBER. NIGHT.
FADE IN


We are CLOSE on Jack's face. He is wearing his
usual expression of green-eyed inscrutability.
As the CAMERA pulls back, we see that Jack is
lounging on the bed with Lucy. Under their
robes they are naked. A definite feeling of
erotic sensuality.

The room is richly appointed. The bed boasts a
counterpane embroidered with thread of gold;
there are tapestries and paintings on the
walls. A side table bears a golden bowl heaped
with fruit, two golden goblets stand beside a
bottle of wine. MOONLIGHT can be seen casting a
shaft of silver through the casement window
onto the flagged floor. CANDLES glow on every
surface. A FIRE burns in the massive fireplace,
logs CRACKLE.
```

JACK: I'm told that you have a tiny scar in a secret place, Lucy.

Lucy takes his hand and lays it on her cheek. She smiles up at him.

LUCY: Who told you?

JACK: Your husband.

Lucy's smile becomes more meaningful.

LUCY: Did he tell you how it came about?

The smile on Jack's face mirrors hers. They understand each other.

JACK: During fencing practice with a jealous girlfriend. I understand you were a hoyden.

He indicates for her to turn her back to him, then releases her hair from the pins that constrain it and begins to unravel the thick plait, lifting her hair and kissing the nape of her neck.

LUCY: I am a hoyden still, Jack. Did my husband tell you where to find this scar?

JACK: No. I shall have to find it out for myself.

He shakes out her hair and turns her to face him.

JACK: I want to learn you by heart, Lucy.

He leans in and kisses her lightly on the lips. Lucy smiles.

LUCY: How do I taste?

JACK: You taste of wine and apples.

They kiss again, Lucy responding with increasing ardour. Jack breaks the kiss and they look fiercely at each other for a long moment, registering their mutual lust.

LUCY: Taste more of me.

The embrace becomes passionate. Jack's hands go to the lapels of her robe.

DISSOLVE TO:

A hand slid round her waist. 'Got to any good bits yet?' Rory had come up from behind her. Deirdre had been so immersed in the awfulness of the script that she hadn't heard him put the phone down to Queen Bee.

'Good bits? The dialogue's pants, Rory. "Taste more of me!" Hell's teeth! Why do they always write sex scenes with you in mind? There's something so … *perverse* about it. I bet the screenwriter has the hots for you.'

'Bollocks. It was probably written by committee. When are the kids due back, incidentally?'

'Not for ages. Why?'

'Because I want you to be a sweetheart and run lines with me.' He lowered himself back onto the couch and patted the cushion next to him.

'Sure I'll be a sweetheart.' Deirdre sat down beside him. 'How's Queenie?' she asked, making herself comfortable.

'Queenie's buzzing, as usual. She says she's going to make sure they hire Chalky.' Chalky White was one of the most respected script doctors in Hollywood.

'Good,' said Deirdre, consulting the script. 'If anyone can clean this mess up, Chalky can. Which scene do you want to run?'

'The one you've just been reading. The one that has the "definite feeling of erotic sensuality".'

'Any particular reason?'

'Mmm hmm.' Rory traced the contour of her ear with a thumb and moved closer. 'I'm experiencing a "definite feeling of erotic sensuality" myself.'

Deirdre raised an eyebrow. 'Darling, either we run lines or we get jiggy.'

'We can do both. It's called multitasking.'

'Are you telling me that you – a mere man – can multitask?'

'I like to feel that I'm in touch with my feminine side, yes.'

'All right.' Deirdre gave him a challenging look. 'Here goes. Your cue, St Ledger, is: "I'm told …"'

'I'm told,' said Rory, looking suitably inscrutable, 'that you have a tiny scar in a secret place, Lucy.'

Smiling at him, Deirdre took his hand and laid it on her cheek. 'Who told you?' she asked.

'Your husband.'

'Did he tell you how it came about?'

'During fencing practice with a jealous girlfriend. I understand you were a hoyden.'

'Ahem. Observe the stage directions, please.'

'With pleasure.' Placing his hands on Deirdre's shoulders, Rory exerted a little pressure. She angled her back to him so that he could release her hair from the velvet band that restrained it and felt a frisson as his fingers made contact with the nape of her neck.

'I am a hoyden still, Jack,' she murmured. 'Did my husband tell you where to find this scar?'

'I've an idea it might be somewhere around … here?' Rory cupped a breast.

'You're deviating from the script.'

'I'm improvising.'

'You were always good at that.'

'Perhaps I might make an artistic suggestion?'

'Fire ahead, St Ledger.' Deirdre felt a surge of pleasure as her husband's tongue trailed languorously along the side of her neck.

'Let's dispense with the dodgy dialogue,' he said.

'Well, I think that scene's been covered from just about every conceivable angle,' said Rory some time later. He was slick with sweat and there were cushions all over the floor.

'My favourite was that last one, the reverse angle reaction,' said Deirdre. 'That's when the camera will move in close on Charlotte and we'll get a load of her trademark swoony expression. How many films has she faked it in now?'

'Dunno. More than Angelina, anyway. More than Scarlett. And better than Meg.'

Deirdre hummed a little tune to herself as she reached for the pullover Rory had removed earlier. It was the first time that she'd had rampant sex with her husband for quite some time. It was funny – she was always reading magazine articles about famous couples who managed to combine brilliant careers and happy families and beautiful houses with fantastic sex lives. For Deirdre, sex had become something that you squeezed in between shooting schedules or when you weren't jet lagged or working to a deadline or running around after the kids. Even sex in the privacy of the marital bed had become something of a rarity since Bruno, their youngest, had started sliding in under their duvet in the middle of the night. She thought back to the carefree days when they had had spontaneous sex virtually whenever and wherever they liked – al fresco, in restrooms, on the kitchen table – and felt a rush of nostalgia. Maybe they should think about scheduling sex, the way she'd heard some couples did? But the sex they'd just had had been fun as well as outrageously erotic. Where was the fun in scheduling sex?

A faint purring sound was coming from the direction of the couch. 'Is that your phone?' Deirdre asked.

'Yep.' Rory delved down the back of the couch, checked out the display, then sent the phone skimming across the coffee table. 'Not available,' he said.

'Who was it?'

'The production company's press agent. To use our Gracie's favourite phrase, he can go eat his shorts.' He stretched and yawned. 'What's on the kids' agenda today?'

'Aoife's at a pool party. Grace is rehearsing the school play. And Bruno's gone to the movies with Melissa.'

'Have you thought about finding a replacement nanny yet?' asked Rory.

'I'll advertise, I guess. And I'll put out feelers with Bianca in Saint-Géyroux.'

'For a French girl?'

'Yeah.'

'I've a better idea,' said Rory, pulling on his T-shirt. 'Why don't we find an Irish girl? Someone who speaks the *cúpla focail*.'

11

'What? Why?'

'So the kids can learn their native tongue.'

Deirdre crowed. 'Are you mad, Rory? They'd hate that!'

'Not if it's made fun for them.'

'Irish? *Fun?* A contradiction in terms, surely? Irish lessons were the curse of our generation's teenage years.'

'I know, I know.' Rory got to his feet and ran a hand through his hair, a gesture that Deirdre always found preposterously sexy. 'But I was speaking to Dad this morning, and he voiced a fear.'

'What's he afraid of?'

'He's worried that living in LA means the kids are being deprived of their Irish heritage. I tried to change the subject, but when I told him that we were looking for a new nanny, he was in like Flynn and suggested we get an Irish speaker. There are no *cuileog* on my dad.'

'*Cuileog?*'

'Flies. Call me a sentimental son of a bitch, but I'd love it if the first thing the kids came out with next time we visit Ireland was a greeting *as Gaelige*.'

Deirdre gave Rory a curious look. 'Hey. You're really set on this, aren't you?'

'Yeah. Could you imagine the expression on Dad's face if he heard them say, "*Dia duit, dadóg! Conas atá tú?*"' Rory looked towards the window that framed the view of the Atlantic. 'I get the feeling he's on his way out, Deirdre.'

'Oh, Rory! Don't say that!'

Rory shrugged, then ambled across the kitchen floor towards the fridge. His demeanour was casual, but Deirdre knew that inside he was raw with homesickness. He hated the ocean that separated him from his father and the rest of the McDonagh clan.

'Fancy a beer?' he threw at her over his shoulder.

'No, thanks,' she said, watching him. He was taking too long rummaging in the fridge: he was covering his emotion. 'Listen, Rory … on mature reflection, maybe you're right. I could place an ad for an Irish-speaking nanny in *The Irish Times*.'

'Cool. Thanks.'

The vulnerable nape of his neck spoke volumes. It was time to talk about something else.

'I was thinking about sending the girls to surf camp this summer,' Deirdre told him. 'They could do two or three weeks in Malibu before they join us in Europe.'

'Good idea.' Rory snapped the tab on his Miller, then turned and leaned back against the fridge door. 'I love you,' he said.

'I love you too,' she replied with a smile. 'By the way, I got a postcard from Europe today, from Madeleine.'

'How's life in the village?'

'It was actually sent from Paris. She and Dannie were meant to be on a cultural visit there, but she said they spent most of their time pigging out in restaurants.'

'She and Dannie? Or she and Daniel?'

'Dannie. It was a girly weekend.'

Rory's phone went off again. Deirdre reached for it and checked the screen. 'It's Queenie again.'

'Tell her to buzz off.'

Deirdre silenced the ring tone with a thumb, whereupon the phone started to whimper at her. 'You're out of juice, honey,' she told him, plugging it into the recharger. 'And there's no more room for messages. You're a popular boy.'

'You pay a price for being popular. It's a real pain to delete them.'

'Maybe you should start paying Bruno to delete messages for you.'

'Why Bruno?'

'Being the youngest member of the family means he's the one most proficient in techno-skills. He's been nagging me for a phone of his own, by the way.'

'That's not a bad idea.'

'What?' said Deirdre, surprised. 'I thought you'd be totally anti Bruno getting a phone.'

'I'm thinking about the photography aspect. He'd have fun with a camera phone, and it's never too soon to learn how to take a good picture. I'd like to think that he might end up with a career behind the camera rather than in front of it.' Rory took another swig of beer, moved to the couch and set the can down on the coffee table. 'You'll be glad to know, by the way, that clever Queenie got a clause inserted in my contract stipulating an agreed number of long weekends off filming.'

'Yay! Legend! Long weekends in Saint-Géyroux, sitting on the terrace drinking wine, spending siestas in bed, swimming in the river, eating cassoulet *chez* the Lennoxes' …'

'Don't forget you've a screenplay to write, *mavourneen*. Didn't you tell Blake you'd have something ready to go by the end of the summer?'

'Thanks for reminding me.' Deirdre drooped. 'He'll be expecting more rom com. I'm getting a bit sick of it. I'd love to do something darker – take a break from the feel-good factor for a change. *Gold Diggers* was starting to do my head in.'

Gold Diggers was the name of a television series that Deirdre had just finished work on. Rewrite after rewrite had been demanded from the powers that be and the writing team had almost mutinied.

'Why not dip a toe into the murky waters of film noir?' suggested Rory.

'Because rom com's what people expect of me, Rory.'

'Break a few rules.'

Deirdre made a face. 'I don't know if I'd be any good at it.'

'Breaking rules? Don't make me laugh. You've always had a subversive streak.'

'No, I mean I don't know how good I'd be at writing darker stuff. I might find it morbid.'

'Dark doesn't have to be morbid. Dark can be mysterious, dark can be unpredictable, dark can be thrilling. You could have fun with it, sweetheart – you could wreak havoc. It's not a bad gig, you know, being paid to be imaginative.'

'Until they tell you "Change the location! Change the period! Change the ending!"'

Rory reached for his beer. 'Beats playing Soduko,' he said.

Later that day, the family – including godsend Melissa – gathered around the big table on the deck for dinner. It was a balmy evening, with stardust sprinkled as liberally as cheerleaders' body glitter all over the indigo sky. From the beach below came the whisper of waves, and crickets rasped their distinctive soothing song. Deirdre had never got used to hearing real, live crickets. For so many years of her life, they had been the exclusive – and exotic – provenance of movie sound effects. Now she heard them night and day, both here in LA and in their house in France.

'Natalie's pool's much bigger than ours,' Aoife was saying. 'But she says they hardly ever use it. Her mom's worried about the effect the chlorine might have on Natalie's skin.'

Deirdre smiled at Rory as he refilled her wineglass. Poor Natalie, she thought. No wonder she always looks so miserable.

'And d'you know something else Natalie's mom told her?' continued Aoife. 'She told her never ever to smile unless it's for the camera, because that way she'll avoid the premature signs of ageing.'

'Did she really use those words?' asked Deirdre. '"Premature signs of ageing"?'

'Yes,' said Aoife.

'Holy schmoly. I thought *that* euphemism was strictly for the ads.'

'Does Natalie really never smile?' asked Grace, clearly fascinated. 'Would she not even smile if someone told her the funniest joke in the world?'

'What *is* the funniest joke in the world?' challenged Aoife.

'I'm not telling.'

'That's because you don't know it.'

'Do so!'

'Bet you don't.'

'I know the funniest joke in the world,' said Bruno. 'Pluto told it to me.'

'Pah!' said Grace. 'Pluto doesn't even exist.'

'He *does* exist! He exists more than you do!'

Pluto was Bruno's imaginary friend. He had arrived

16

shortly after Bruno had learned to talk, and had made his presence so clearly felt that he had become a virtual member of the family.

'Knowing Pluto,' said Aoife with a sigh, 'I bet the joke's about a big butt.'

'Of course it is. Can I tell it, Pluto?' There was a pause while Bruno waited for the answer, and then he said, 'He says not at the dinner table.'

'I wish all my children had such good manners as Pluto,' remarked Deirdre.

'Excuse me? I have excellent manners,' said Grace primly. 'Ms Stone told me so at rehearsals today. She said I lived up to my name. Please pass the parmesan, Aoife. Thank you.'

Rory leaned back in his chair and regarded his daughters. 'I understand you guys might be going off to surf camp before coming to France this year,' he said.

Aoife and Grace looked up from their spaghetti and meatballs.

'Yes.'

'We can't wait.'

'That's some adventure,' said Rory. 'Do you think you've earned it?'

'Yes,' said Grace. 'If you look at our list of chores on the notice board you'll see that they're all ticked off. And Daddy, I even polished your shoes.'

Rory looked impressed. '*All* of them?'

'No. Only the posh pair. In case you need to go to another award ceremony.'

Grace was always pestering Rory to get her an invite to awards ceremonies. She wanted to go on record as being the youngest guest ever at the post-Oscar *Vanity Fair* party.

'OK, little girls. So you've earned your adventure. Let's check out this surf camp on the net.' Rory got to his feet, crossed the deck into the kitchen and set his wineglass on the coffee table. 'Is it in Favourites, Deirdre?'

'Yep,' said Deirdre. 'Under 'S' for Sun, Sea, Surf and Summer Camp.'

'Bummer,' said Rory. 'Their bikini page is unavailable while undergoing a facelift.'

Grace jumped down fom her chair and skidded across the floor to where Rory was manipulating the mouse with a relaxed hand. 'Bikini shmikini,' she said. 'Go back, go back. There! Enter the site and click on 'Parties'!'

'Parties,' said Rory wearily. 'I might have guessed that's the first thing you'd want to check out, Grace. Don't you think you should get your priorities right?'

'What are priorities?'

'Priorities? They're the things that matter most in life.'

Grace gave her father a look of stark incomprehension. 'But parties *are* the things that matter most in life,' she said.

Aoife crossed the room and slid onto the couch, tucking her legs up under her and laying her head on her father's shoulder.

'Did you go surfing when you were a kid, Pop?' she asked.

'I did. But I didn't surf in the balmy waters of the Pacific Ocean, sweet pea. I surfed in the frigid waters of the Atlantic, on the west coast of Ireland. Hey! Maybe sometime I could take you there and you could show off your surfing skills to *Dadóg*?'

'Who's *Dadóg*?'

'*Dadóg* is the Irish name for grandpa.'

'Irish is weird,' muttered Aoife. 'No one ever knows

18

how to pronounce my name when they see it written down. Maybe I should start calling myself Eva instead.'

'No, darling,' said Deirdre. 'Don't be afraid to be different.'

'What's my name translated into Irish?' demanded Grace.

'Gráinne,' Rory told her.

'Ew. I'm glad you didn't call me that. It sounds like some kind of muesli.'

'Or somebody throwing up,' observed Aoife.

'Did you know, you gorgeous girls,' said Rory, 'that the Irish language is very, very difficult to learn? Neither your mother nor I were ever very good at it, and I don't expect either of you young Americans could get the hang of it in a million years.'

'I could,' said Grace. 'I can learn anything.'

'I could give it a go,' said Aoife. 'My French teacher Mademoiselle Beauvais says I have an aptitude for languages.'

'Well, *pogue mo hone*,' said Rory, adding '*Sláinte!*' for good measure.

'*Pogue mo hone*,' echoed Aoife.

'What does *sláinte* mean?' asked Grace.

'It means 'cheers'. It's about the only Irish word I know. Apart from *cúl*.'

'What's *cúl*?' asked Grace.

'In Irish, *cúl* means to score in football,' Rory told them. 'Come to think of it, Irish is a pretty cool language.'

'Then we want to learn it,' said Grace.

'You only want to learn it because Pops says it's cool,' said Aoife. 'That's all you care about, Grace. Cool stuff.'

'That's not true!'

'Shh, shh, shh, girls! What about you, Bruno? Do you want to learn Irish?' Deirdre stretched out her arms to Bruno, who slid off his chair and came clambering onto her lap.

Bruno looked grave. 'I'd better ask Pluto,' he said.

A beat or two of silence followed. 'Well? What's the verdict from Pluto?' Deirdre asked.

'Pluto wants to know who's going to teach him Irish.'

'Her name would be Nani Nua.'

'Nani Nua?'

'Um. That's Irish for new nanny,' hazarded Deirdre.

'What does she look like?'

'I don't know. We haven't found her yet.'

'How will we find her?'

'We have ways and means,' said Deirdre, smiling across at Rory. 'Nani Nua is out there somewhere, just waiting to be found.'

'Will she be as pretty as Melissa?'

'I hope so.'

'Will she be as fun as Melissa?'

'We'd have to make certain of that.'

'Nani Nua,' said Bruno thoughtfully. 'If she's fun and pretty, then Pluto and me are looking forward to meeting her.'

'Pluto and *I*,' corrected Melissa.

'*Pogue mo hone*,' mused Aoife. 'It sounds so romantic. What does it mean?'

'Kiss my ass,' said Rory.

'Cool!' said Grace.

2

'Love Lies Bleedin'. Love Lies *Bleedin'*!'

'It's the name of a flower,' said Greta.

'What is?' Simon lobbed a chocolate wrapper into a nearby waste bin. It missed.

'Love Lies Bleeding. It's a type of flower. Go pick that up, film star,' commanded Greta.

'Love Lies Bleedin',' chanted Simon as he hopped on one leg in the direction of the bin. 'Love Lies *Bleedin',*' he resumed, hopping back to where Greta was sitting on a prop chaise longue in a shadowy corner of the studio. The studio was at Ardmore in the garden county of Ireland, the film being shot was called *Child Harry* and the star of the film was her charge, Simon. 'I'm bored,' announced Simon.

Greta looked at her watch. Key grips and focus pullers had been in discussion for the past ten minutes, and from the intense expressions on their faces, Greta could tell they'd be at it for at least another ten. She could take Simon back to the more comfortable surroundings of his dressing room and read him yet another story, but the dressing room block was miles down the other end of the sound stage, and by the time they'd covered the distance, they'd more than likely be called back. It wasn't worth the hassle. Simon bounced down beside her on the

21

couch with a loud 'Boing!', then stood up and did it again.

'Hey, you, you messy pup. Cut it out and come here to me,' said Greta. 'You've chocolate all over your gob.' She took a face wipe from the packet in the canvas tote bag that she humped around from film set to film set and from location to location. The bag contained all the tools of her trade: face wipes, story books, drawing books, crayons, an iPod, a GameBoy, magazines for Greta to peruse when she wasn't being an all-round entertainer, and her knitting. It also contained shooting schedules and hefty chunks of script and pages and pages of contact details.

'Love Lies Bleedin'. Love Lies Bleedin',' muttered Simon, screwing up his face as Greta wiped his cherub mouth. He was clearly chuffed to be able to use the 'B' word without being given out to. 'It's a weird name, isn't it, Greta?'

'It's a weird name for a flower. But I think it's a gorgeous name for a film.'

Love Lies Bleeding was the title of the film next in line to be shot in Ardmore studios.

'Are you going to be a chaperone on *Love Lies Bleedin'*, Greta?' Simon asked.

'I am not,' she told him.

'Why?'

'Because – sadly for me – there aren't any kids on it to chaperone.'

'So does that mean you've no work after this film's in the can?'

'That's right.' *After this film's in the can!* It always made Greta smile when she heard kids like Simon talk arcane film-speak. This was the third day she'd been employed to mind this particular small boy, and because he'd 'been there, done that' on a big film last year, he was easily as savvy about movie-making as she was. He was familiar with all the lingo: 'rolling', 'mark it', 'hair in the gate'. 'Hair in the gate' was the term Simon and Greta dreaded hearing most, because it meant that the film stock had been spoiled and the actors would have to do a scene all over again, even if the performances had been perfect.

'What made you decide to be a chaperone, Greta?' he asked. 'It's a kinda weird job, isn't it?'

'I didn't decide. It was a fluke, really. Tch! Look at the *state* of you. I'm going to need another face wipe.' She reached out an automatic hand for her tote bag. 'A friend of my ma had a little girl who got a couple of weeks on a TV drama,' she continued, rubbing at a stubborn mark on Simon's chin. 'And she needed a chaperone because she was only nine. So that's when I got roped in.'

'How many films have you been on now?'

'Six. I've been dead lucky – touch wood.' Greta reached out and did just that, then resumed mopping up her charge. 'But none of the kids I've had to look after have been quite as much fun as you, *mavourneen*.' She took one last swipe at him, then aimed the face wipe at the bin. '*Cúl!*' she said.

Simon took a stick of chewing gum from his pocket. 'It's not that cool to throw a face wipe in the bin,' he observed.

'I meant a different kind of cool, Mister.'

'What d'you mean, a different kind of cool?'

'*Cúl* is Irish for 'score'. Don't you ever listen to sport *as Gaelige*?'

Simon gave her a baffled look and popped his chewing

gum into his mouth. 'Why would I want to do that? I *hate* Irish.'

'That's a shame. It's a real useful language to know.'

'Why?'

'Well, any time I go abroad, I always speak Irish with my friends. People are forever coming up to us and asking what language we're speaking in.'

'Why?'

'They're fascinated by it. Most people in the world don't know that the Irish language exists, you know. It's a great way of making new friends. It's kinda hip, too.'

'Pah! I don't care about hip stuff. How come you speak Irish so well?'

'I was born and dragged up in the Gaeltacht.'

'Poor you. That means you're a culchie.'

'And proud to be one, you little city slicker.'

'*Cúl!*' said Simon, lobbing his chewing gum wrapper into the bin as the strains of Greta's ring tone sounded from her bag. She gave a guilty start and lunged for the phone immediately, silencing it with a thumb. She'd invite the wrath of God – and worse, the sound engineer – if Nokia made its presence felt during filming.

'Who was that?' asked Simon.

'That, nosy parker,' said Greta, glancing at the display, 'was my boyfriend.'

'What's his name?'

'Jared.'

'What does he do?'

'He's a drummer with a band.'

'Cool! Is it a famous band?'

She smiled. 'Not yet.'

Jared's band, Rawhide, was currently on the final leg

of an Irish tour. Greta had first seen them when they'd played support to a much bigger act at the Olympia Theatre, and while she knew very little about music, she knew from the minute he walked onto the stage that Jared Kelly had star quality. He occupied the space as if his drum kit were an altar and he some pagan idol to be worshipped, and when he took up a tom-tom and moved downstage, swaying to the rhythm, it was as if he was inciting the audience to adore him. She had never seen anything quite so electrifying: he had left her quite weak with wanting him. After the gig he had come down to the bar, and, to her amazement, he had singled her out with an incendiary smile. He could have had anyone, she'd told herself, he could have had *anyone* – but he had singled *her* out.

'Is your man Jared a culchie, too?' asked Simon.

She laughed. 'No. He's American.'

'What made him want to come to Ireland?'

'He has Irish blood. And he loves Irish music. What makes you ask so many questions? Is your real name Rum Tum Tugger?'

'Who's Rum Tum Tugger?'

'The Rum Tum Tugger is a famously curious cat.'

'Why is he famous?'

'He's in *Old Possum's Book of Practical Cats.*'

'What's that?'

'It's a book of poems about cats. My cousin gave it to me.'

'Do you love cats, Greta?'

'I do.'

'Do you own one?'

'There's a kitten back home in Connemara. He's called Tum Tugger, after the one in the poem. But I can't keep a cat in Dublin, it wouldn't be fair to keep one cooped up in a flat.'

'Tum Tugger,' repeated Simon. 'I want to be Tum Tugger. Will you call me that from now on?'

'Sure.'

Simon snuggled into her, then reverted to curious mode. 'Why d'you think there are no kids in *Love Lies Bleedin'*?' he asked.

'Because it's a grown-ups' film,' she told him.

'Does that mean there's going to be loads of sex in it?'

'Um. Maybe.'

'Yuck. Do you have sex with your boyfriend, Greta?'

She touched a forefinger to the tip of his nose. 'That is *so* none of your business, Tum Tugger.'

Simon chewed his gum in silence for some moments. 'Why are grown ups so mad for sex?' he asked.

'You'll find that out when you're grown.'

'I'm gonna tell Eugene that you have a boyfriend. Ha! He'll be dead jealous.'

'Why would Eugene be jealous?'

'Because he fancies you.'

'What? How do you know?'

'I can tell by the way he smiles at you. His face goes all weird.'

Eugene was Simon's on-set tutor and Simon *detested* him. Greta couldn't blame him. Eugene was a creepy individual with adenoidal problems and bad breath and Greta hated the way he talked to her breasts.

'He doesn't fancy me,' she said without conviction.

'Does so.' There followed more vigorous chewing of gum. 'Are you scared of my mum, Greta?' Simon asked out of the blue.

Greta gave him a surprised look. 'Divil a bit. Why should I be scared of Anita?'

'Because I think Eugene's scared of her.'

'Hmm. That's probably because she's a teacher and he's scared that she might think he's not teaching you properly. Your mum's dead cool, you know, Simon. She's way more easy going than some of the mothers whose spoiled kids I've chaperoned.'

'Who was the spoiltest?'

She thought about it. 'A boy called Jason. He thought he was a bigger star than Tom Cruise.'

'Poo to Tom Cruise. Rory McDonagh's way more of a star than him. It's a shame you can't be a chaperone on *Love Lies Bleedin'*, isn't it, Greta?'

'Indeed and it is. I could do with the money.'

'Ha! I bet that's not the only reason you'd like to be on it.'

'What do you mean?'

'I bet you'd like to be on it because Rory McDonagh's in it. All women are mad for him. Are you mad for him?'

'I am not,' lied Greta.

'Huh! I bet you are, secretly. My mum says he's the sexiest actor on the planet. She met him once.'

'No *kidding*!' Greta looked down at Simon's button-cute face nestled in the crook of her arm and he smiled back up at her, a kind of 'told you so' smile. 'Where did Anita meet him?' she asked.

'In France. We were on a camping holiday. It was crap. My parents just lazed around and drank wine all day.'

'Sounds good to me. Whereabouts were you?'

'In a crappy village up some crappy mountains.'

'What was the name of the village?'

'San something. San, san, san … can't remember.' Simon shut his eyes and snuggled in tighter to Greta.

'You're not to go to sleep on me now,' she warned him. 'They're going to come looking for you soon.'

'But you're nice and cuddly, Greta. And you smell so nice, too. You smell of soap – all flowery.'

Greta smiled down at his curly dark head. The poor wain had been up since the crack of dawn to get to the studio, and there'd been more than the usual hanging around today. Hanging around the studio waiting to be used was more knackering than anything – no wonder Simon was feeling sleepy. So was she, for that matter. She'd had to be up even earlier than Simon, since the driver always called for her first.

Leaning her head against the padded back of the chaise longue, Greta closed her eyes, wondering what Jared had wanted. He was due back from tour next week. She couldn't wait! She hadn't seen him for nearly three whole weeks. She'd asked her cousin Esther, with whom she shared a flat, to let her have the place to herself the following weekend – for obvious reasons. Jared was free that Saturday night, but he'd mentioned something about a gig on Sunday night. Where was it? Vicar Street? Or Whelan's? The Sugar Club? She couldn't remember …

'Greta? Simon?' Greta opened her eyes to find the gofer, a lanky man called Pete, looking down at her. 'We're all set to roll, young 'un,' he said with a smile. But the smile was directed at Greta, not Simon.

Greta tousled Simon's curly hair. 'Wakey, wakey. Looks like you're gonna have to get ready for your close-up, Tum Tugger,' she said.

Simon opened his eyes and sat up slowly. He gave a

big yawn. 'Pete fancies you too,' he stage-whispered in her ear.

Janey! Greta could tell from Pete's mortified expression that he'd overheard. 'Make-up's going to need to do a re-touch. He got chocolate all over his face,' she told him with a smile. But the smile just made Pete turn even more puce.

'Erm, you on top of your lines, Simon?' he asked.

'Yeah.' The mini film star slid off the daybed and started trailing in the direction of the set. 'Greta and me have been running *bleedin'* lines all morning.'

'Hey, you! Gum,' commanded Greta, holding out a tissue for Simon to spit into. He obliged, then followed the gofer across the studio floor to where the crew stood waiting for him, intoning his favourite new mantra, 'Love Lies *Bleedin''*.

Love Lies Bleeding. Great title, great subject matter, thought Greta, smiling at Simon's retreating back. *Love Lies Bleeding* was based on the life of Jack St Ledger, who had been a founder member of the infamous Dublin Hellfire Club back in the eighteenth century. Easily as sexy as Casanova, Mr St Ledger had ripped more than his fair share of bodices in his time, and rumour had it that the actress starring opposite Rory McDonagh, Charlotte Lambert, was insisting that a body double be engaged to stand in for all her sex scenes.

Greta checked her watch, then took her knitting out of her tote bag, wishing the light was better. She unfurled the swathe of cobalt blue wool from her canvas bag and ran her hand over it. There was something so very sensuous about the feel of the stuff that she was almost sorry she'd promised the shrug to her mother as a birthday present.

But cobalt wasn't Greta's colour: she guessed she was more Monet than Matisse. She'd love to be able to wear dramatic colours the way her flamboyant cousin Esther did, but she just looked clownish in them. Esther was rangy and angular, like Stella Tennant, while Greta was soft and a little curvy: old-fashioned looking, she supposed.

Cousin Esther was a successful theatrical designer. She had been the one responsible for encouraging Greta in her dream of studying at NCAD. 'Aim straight for the top,' she'd told her two years ago. 'You're going to the *National* College of Art and Design.'

'But there's no way I can afford to live in Dublin!' Greta had wailed.

And when Esther had answered, 'Being my favourite cousin, you can have the spare room in my flat for a token rent,' Greta had wanted to prostrate herself in front of her and kiss her cousin's foot.

Picking up the pattern, Greta consulted it, squinting in the half light that spilled through the gap in the wooden flats that encircled the sound stage. Beyond the flats she could hear the murmur of dialogue as the actors rehearsed their lines, Simon's reedy voice in contrapunto to the velvet tones of the actor playing his father. She hoped her charge was dead letter perfect.

Greta slipped into a rhythm, sliding the fine wool from the left needle onto the right. She had taken up knitting on her very first engagement as chaperone because she'd read in *Heat* magazine that loads of actresses had taught themselves to knit as a way of keeping occupied during the endless hours spent hanging around film sets. It was easy to understand why. It was an ideal way to pass the time, since it was both soothing and productive. Charlotte

Lambert had even set a boho trend by wearing the rather *outré* shawls she created from spun silk and chenille to red carpet events.

The sound of steps ringing out on steel made her look up. Someone was descending from the gantry.

'What are you doing here?' said an amused voice. 'I could have sworn I saw you on Sky this morning, immortalising your handprints in the cement outside Grauman's.'

Greta put her hand up to shade her eyes against the residual light from the arc lamps. The man looking down at her was instantly recognisable – although his eyes were even more greenly disconcerting in real life.

'I'm sorry?' she said.

The eyes gleamed greener for a moment. 'I beg your pardon, sweetheart,' the man said in his unmistakable Galway drawl. 'I mistook you for someone else.'

'Oh?' said Greta, feeling wobbly suddenly. 'Who did you mistake me for?'

'I mistook you for Charlotte Lambert. Has anybody ever told you,' he said, raising an eyebrow at her, 'that you and Charlotte are very alike? In fact, you're so very alike that you could almost be her double.'

And Rory McDonagh unleashed his trademark lethal smile upon her before turning and strolling away across the studio floor.

Greta gazed after him, pensively.

3

'Oh, Jesus – this is agony. I've got to stop, Madeleine.'

'Just a couple more minutes. We'll stop when we reach Chez Maurice.'

Dannie Palmer and her friend Madeleine Lennox were power walking through the village of Saint-Géyroux, accompanied by Madeleine's dog, Pilot. Dannie felt like a right eejit, striding along like a CGI – and she could tell by the expressions on the faces of the people they passed that they thought she was an eejit too. Who in their right mind would go marching around one of the most picturesque villages in the Languedoc instead of taking their time on the terrace of the local café, shooting the breeze over a pichet of local red wine? Especially since it was the first fine day of spring, and especially since both women had the luxury of time off, their daughters having been dispatched on a school trip to the Musée Fabre in nearby Montpellier.

Dannie swung along the serpentine rue du Jujubier, crossed the rue Lamballe and emerged onto the market square hot on the heels of Madeleine. Thank God! The local café, Chez Maurice, looked like an oasis, its green awning shading a verdurous stretch of AstroTurf. A beer! Dannie would kill for a beer. Muscling onto the terrace like a marathon runner hitting the finishing line, Dannie greeted Maurice as gratefully as if he were her trainer.

'*Bonjour, Maurice. Un demi, s'il vous plaît.* Madeleine?' she asked, turning to her friend. 'What'll you have?'

'I'd love a beer, but I really ought to stick to water. All the toxins—'

'Feck the toxins,' said Dannie. 'A beer it is. *Deux pressions, Maurice.*'

'*Tout d'suite, Madame Palmer.*'

Maurice disappeared through the door of the café, Dannie collapsed onto an aluminium chair and Pilot searched for a shady spot before dropping onto the AstroTurf. Madeleine sat down opposite Dannie as gracefully as an actress in a period drama.

'Look at you!' said Dannie crossly. 'It hasn't taken a flitter out of you. You're fit, Madeleine! Have you been practising secretly?'

'No. I've just been doing laps of the pool. Don't you love the endorphin buzz you get from exercising?'

Dannie gave her an 'as if' look. 'The only endorphin buzz I want right now is the one that a big swig of beer delivers.'

It had been Madeleine's idea to go power walking and it had seemed like a fun thing to do earlier in the day, when she'd suggested it over coffee in Dannie's house. But Dannie knew now that power walking was just *so* not her. 'I'm sticking to gardening from now on,' she told Madeleine. 'It's the best form of exercise there is. And it's productive, too. I feel like a total tool doing power walking.'

'We could go power strolling, I guess,' said Madeleine. 'No better place for it than this laid back little *ville.*'

'Power strolling sounds good. *Merci, Maurice.*'

Maurice had arrived with their beer. He set the two glasses on the table and said with a smile, 'You are welcome, Madame. That is how they say it in English, *n'est ce pas*?'

'It is.'

'Now I will be more English still, and talk about the weather. It is a jolly clement day, is it not?'

'It most certainly is.'

'The spring is here at last. *Bonnes bières, mesdames!*'

'*Merci, Maurice!*'

It really *was* a jolly clement day in Saint-Géyroux. Anyone viewing the planet on Google Earth might be tempted to zoom straight in and take a virtual tour. Saint-Géyroux was picture postcard pretty, and today she looked as if she'd dolled herself up in her best bib and tucker. There had been a festival recently to celebrate the four hundredth anniversary of the *Mairie*, and the imposing edifice on the main square was bedecked in red, white and blue bunting. Cherry blossom was scattered like confetti on the terrace, birds were being rambunctious and window troughs on the sills of the buildings opposite the café were bristling with spring flowers.

Dannie stretched out her legs, knowing that they'd be sore tomorrow. 'Arra, we're jammy bitches, really, aren't we Madeleine? A fine thing it is to be able to take our ease in glorious weather, when all round the world people are BlackBerrying and texting and Skype-ing.'

'All stressed to the nines.' Madeleine reached for her beer and took a sip. 'And stuck in gridlock. D'you know something, Dannie? The best thing I ever did was to swap my city girl heels for espadrilles. Hey! That rhymes. Maybe I could get a sonnet out of that. I haven't written one in ages.'

'You write poetry? I'm impressed.'

Madeleine shrugged. 'I used to write sonnets, as a kind of hobby – the way some people might do crosswords. But I'm out of touch with my creative side. Being a full-time wife, mother and web designer means I've no time to potter about with poetry.'

'Not to mention being a muse.'

'True. Being a muse is *bloody* hard work.'

Dannie smiled. 'So it's not about lolling around on divans eating grapes?'

'Damn right it's not. It's more like being a housewife.'

'A housewife?'

'Yep. Artists are selfish bastards, you know. Daniel would go to pieces without someone to take care of him. And nag him. Any time a business letter arrives, I have to nag him for weeks to reply to it.'

'Isn't that funny? I'd never think of Daniel doing anything as mundane as writing business letters.'

'There's a lot of crap talked about the art world, you know,' Madeleine told her. 'Lofty, esoteric stuff. But artists need to earn a living, the same as everyone else. Where's the fun in starving in a garret, painting pictures no one wants to buy? While the creative imperative is a truth universally acknowledged, to misquote Jane Austen, the ultimate muse is money.'

Dannie raised an eyebrow. 'Isn't that a bit cynical?'

'No. Paint costs money. Canvases cost money. Exhibition space costs money. Models cost money. Daniel's been paying a small fortune to that Dutch girl who's been sitting for him.'

'The hitchhiker he picked up?'

'Marjan. Yeah.'

'I thought artists' models were usually paid a pittance.'

'Not Daniel's girls. He has no truck with exploitation.'

Dannie was curious. There was something she'd wanted to ask her friend for ages. 'Can I ask you a personal question, Madeleine?' she said.

'Fire ahead.'

'Would you describe Marjan as being Daniel's muse too?'

'Definitely. He's got an entire series of nudes of her. They're exquisite.'

'But doesn't it feel, well, a small bit strange to be living under the same roof as a nubile young thing whose job it is to undress for your husband every day?'

Madeleine shrugged. 'It felt strange in the early days, yes. But I guess I've got used to it. Painters' wives have lived with it for time immemorial, after all.'

'But couldn't you, as his chief muse, call a few shots, Madeleine? Couldn't you insist that the girls keep their clothes on, for instance, or—'

Madeleine crowed with laughter. 'You really don't understand, do you, Dannie? That would be a bit like you insisting to Jethro that he edits out the sex scenes in his films.'

'Oh. OK. Point taken.'

Dannie's husband, Texan film director Jethro Palmer, commuted between LA, Saint-Géyroux and whichever location he happened to be filming in. He was probably right now BlackBerrying and texting and Skype-ing simultaneously while conducting an interview with *Variety*.

'I just have to trust Daniel,' continued Madeleine. 'He came up with a good analogy once. He described himself as being like a chocolatier.'

'A chocolatier? Why a chocolatier?'

'A chocolatier is surrounded by delicious sweets all day, but that doesn't make him want to scoff them all. Jethro's in a similar position when you think about it, surrounded by all that LA totty. But why would Jethro *ever* be arsed chasing painted ladies in Hollywood when he has a totally gorgeous wife waiting for him at home?'

'Totally gorgeous?' Dannie indicated the cut-offs she was wearing, the trainers, the sweatshirt. 'Don't make me laugh. I'm a kind of liability – like Mr Rochester's mad wife in the attic. If any of Jethro's LA colleagues were ever to visit Saint-Géyroux, it might be a good idea to ask you to stand in for me, Madeleine, and pretend to be Mrs Palmer.'

'A wife swap!'

'Yeah.' Dannie took a swig of her beer. 'D'you know, I wonder sometimes how two such very different people as me and him wound up together.'

'Don't be daft. You really *are* gorgeous,' insisted Madeleine. 'Daniel wouldn't have painted you if you weren't. That's why he so rarely accepts commissions – there's no sense of spontaneity about them.'

'But aren't commissions dead lucrative?'

'Damn right they're lucrative. Marie-France was always nagging him to do more because of the obscene amounts of money he could charge.'

'Sure, he hardly needs the money. Aren't his paintings worth a fortune?'

'The early stuff's fetching a lot at auction. But Daniel doesn't get a penny of that, you know. And his agent takes fifty per cent of his new stuff. And Marie-France gets virtually fifty per cent of what's left.'

Dannie knew not to ask Madeleine too many questions about Marie-France, Daniel's ex-wife. The first Madame Lennox had cemented a deal through her divorce lawyer that had made headlines at the time: she'd taken Daniel for everything she could get and had happily gone through life discarding wealthy lovers ever since.

'*Bonjour, Madame Palmer! Bonjour, Madame Lennox!*' Madame Bouret, doyenne of the village gossips, was passing with a basket on her arm.

'*Bonjour, Madame Bouret!*'

'Yikes,' said Madeleine in an undertone. 'It'll be all round town in no time that we were lazing around in the middle of the day, swigging beer like a couple of lushes.'

'Pah! Who cares? At least it's not absinthe.'

Dannie sometimes wondered what the locals made of the two Irish blow-ins to the village. Madeleine, whose father had been French, could easily be mistaken for a local herself, since she was quintessentially Gallic-looking. She had inherited a sallow complexion, high, prominent cheekbones and an elegant, aquiline nose. She moved with the grace of a dancer, wore her sleek hair in an artfully artless-looking chignon and favoured a boho chic look, courtesy of an exclusive boutique in Montpellier.

Dannie, on the other hand, had an earthier look. She had a wide, upward-curving mouth, a dusting of freckles on her nose, eyebrows that slanted diagonally above dancing conker-brown eyes and a thatch of unruly hair, which she had recently taken to cutting herself because she loathed the hours spent making small talk in hair salons. Dannie was smaller than Madeleine, and curvier, and she never bothered much with fancy clothes – apart from underthings. The one positive thing about Jethro's trips to LA was that he never came home without something stunning from Victoria's Secret or Fredericks of Hollywood. She wondered what he'd bring her next week, when he was due to jet back from the première of his latest movie …

'Do you ever regret leaving your life in the fast lane, Madeleine?' Dannie asked out of the blue.

'What? Where did that come from?'

'I was just thinking about my workaholic husband.'

Madeleine shook her head. 'No. If I were still living in Dublin, I'd probably have been made redundant by now.'

'How so?'

'I'd be too old.'

'Get away out of that! Sure, you're nowhere near forty yet.'

'That's the down-side of the advertising game,' Madeleine told her. 'Only one out of every four people in advertising is over the age of forty, and it's worse for women. It's a young turk's business. I'm much happier now that I'm working freelance.'

'I envy you your work, Madeleine. I sometimes wonder if I put enough thought into it when we moved here. I had some romantic notion that we'd settle down, maybe buy a vineyard or start a market garden or something – live a low-key lifestyle high in family values. Ha! I'd been reading too many feckin' Sunday supplement features about families downshifting to Provence and Tuscany. I was completely delusional.'

'What about another baby? Would that help?'

Oh, God. Would that help? Would that *help*?

'Hey look, there's your Dutch girl now,' said Dannie conversationally.

On the other side of the square, a striking-looking black girl was standing outside the *pâtisserie* talking to one of the local youths. She waved over at Madeleine and Dannie couldn't help noticing that the wave Madeleine returned was more cordial than enthusiastic.

'It was her final stint today,' remarked Madeleine. 'She's all painted out.'

'Painted out?'

'Yeah. She'll be taking her leave of us tomorrow and going back to Holland. Daniel's finished the series.'

'Does that mean he'll be on the look-out for a new muse?'

'Yep. And he'll be difficult to live with until he finds her. Oh – *bonjour, Valérie!*'

Valérie Poiret, a girl who worked in the local *boulangerie*, was passing. The tight T-shirt she wore showed off the proud swell of her belly and she exuded that aura of radiance that pregnancy confers upon some women. *'Bonjour, Mesdames!'* she called back with a cheerful salute.

'Daniel was very keen on painting her,' Madeleine remarked. 'Said he'd get an entire series out of her changing shape, but she said no. She looks great, doesn't she?'

'Here comes Bianca!' interjected Dannie. 'Time for our fix of gossip.'

Dannie was very glad indeed that it was her turn to change the subject for the second time in as many minutes: as far as she was concerned, Bianca couldn't have rolled up at a more auspicious moment. Because Dannie was desperate for another child, she didn't remotely want to talk about Valérie Poiret's baby: the swollen bellies of other women only served as a reminder of her own repeated failure to conceive. Since the arrival of her daughter Paloma several years previously, Dannie had conceived on two occasions but had miscarried both times. Dannie wasn't just hungry for another baby – she was ravenous.

'Madeleine! Daniella! Hi!'

Bianca Ingram swooped down upon them and the two women braced themselves for the air-kissing ritual – 'Mwah mwah! Mwah mwah!' – then, smoothing the folds of her fluid white palazzo pants, Bianca plonked herself down at the table. 'Dora Maar! Sit!' she barked at the fluffy white dog that accompanied her wherever she went, much like Mary's Little Lamb.

Dora Maar was sniffing around at Pilot's nether regions. Pilot opened one eye, regarded her laconically, then shut it again, whereupon Dora Maar trotted over to her mistress and sat down at her feet, assuming an almost identical stance. That theory about dogs looking like their owners certainly applied in this case, thought Dannie. Dora Maar was quite puffed up with self-importance.

'How are you both?' asked Bianca. 'Well? Good, good. And how are your adorable daughters? Still joined at the hip?'

'Pretty much,' said Madeleine with a smile.

'Maurice!' Bianca raised a peremptory hand at the waiter. '*De l'eau Evian, s'il vous plaît.*'

'*Tout de suite, Madame Ingram.*'

Bianca Ingram was as near to a socialite as it got in Saint-Géyroux. She was a keen organiser of parties and

41

dinners and cultural evenings (she called said evenings her *salons*), and while her affectation was regarded as something of a joke, without Bianca there would be no social life to speak of in the village because everyone else was too lazy to organise anything.

'I have news!' Bianca announced now. Bestowing a Sphinx-like smile on her companions, she leaned her elbows on the table and adopted a conspiratorial tone. 'My first Creatives are installed,' she told them. 'They arrived last night to take up residence in my Sanctuary!'

Bianca's 'Sanctuary' had been set up to accommodate artists and writers who were in search of some inspirational laid-back living. She had converted the outbuildings of her very des res into studio apartments where creative types could chill and wait for The Muse to descend (Bianca was inordinately fond of using capital letters).

The Muse was a pretty frequent visitor to Saint-Géyroux, which was why the village had become a Mecca for arty types. Over the course of the past couple of years, myriad painters and writers and film-makers had come snooping around in the hope of finding their dream holiday home – much to the irritation of Daniel Lennox, who had been the first to discover the place.

'So your Sanctuary's finished, is it?' said Dannie, diplomatically remembering to put in the capital letter. 'I thought you were having a shite time with the builders.'

Bianca gave a little wince at Dannie's choice of phrase. 'I *was* going through the *merde*, rather. Coincidentally, so were my first Creatives. That's why they've booked themselves into my Sanctuary. Their own home is being renovated and it'll be several months before they can return. But I was determined that nothing should stand in the way of welcoming such an Illustrious Literary Personage as my first Resident. When I received her Petition, I insisted that the builders work twenty-four seven to finish.'

Bianca sat back in her seat with a smug expression, clearly waiting for their next question. Madeleine and Dannie duly obliged. 'Who is it?' they asked in unison.

'It is,' said Bianca, 'a fellow countrywoman of yours. A Very Famous One.'

'She's Irish?'

'She is indeed, Dannie.' Dannie noticed that Bianca's upper crust British accent had assumed a hint of Hibernia. 'She is *quintessentially* Irish. The very first artist to seek Sanctuary *chez moi* is – Colleen!' Bianca's smug expression had been replaced by one of triumph, for Colleen's renown was such that she needed no surname – a bit like Madonna or Britney – although artistically speaking, Colleen was as far removed from those two gals as it was possible to get.

'Colleen?' said Dannie. 'Well, isn't that a turn-up for the auld books! I know her.'

'You *know* Colleen? *Incroyable!*'

'It's not as *incroyable* as all that. Sure, don't we both hail from the same neck of the woods – Kilrowan in Connemara? She's a gas character, so she is.'

'Gas?'

'Yeah. You know – wacky.'

'I would hardly describe such an august figure as Colleen as 'wacky', Daniella.' There was a hint of reproval in Bianca's voice.

'Eccentric, then. Is Margot with her?'

'Her partner, Margot d'Arcy, the poet, has accompanied her, yes.'

Dannie laughed. 'Jayz, I'd *love* to see Colleen again! Why don't you invite me round some time?'

'A superfine idea!' said Bianca brightly. 'Would this evening suit for aperitifs? Will you come too, Madeleine? And bring Daniel, of course. I'm sure that Colleen would be delighted to make the acquaintance of another Artist of International Repute.'

'That's very kind of you, Bianca, but I'm not sure that Daniel will be able to come. He's working flat out on a series.'

'*Dommage*,' said Bianca as her Evian arrived. She inspected the ashtray on the table to make sure it was clean, then set it down at her feet and poured the water into it. Dora Maar set to with gusto – the ultimate lap-lap-lap dog. 'Perhaps Jethro is available to attend, Daniella?' she asked.

''Fraid not, Bianca. He's smooth talking in LA as we speak.'

'Tch tch. That Jethro. Always on the go!'

'Yip,' said Dannie with a mirthless smile.

'I've more news!' announced Bianca. 'You'll be glad to know that Deirdre O'Dare intends to grace us with her presence again this summer.'

'That's good to hear! When's she due?' asked Madeleine.

'Some time in June. She phoned to make sure I still had the keys to her house. She's having the place repainted and she needs someone to keep an eye on the decorators.'

'Is Rory coming with her?'

'Alas, no. He will be filming a new epic in Ireland. But I'm sure he'll manage to get over for the occasional weekend. You know how devoted that pair are.'

The church clock struck three. '*Zut!* Is that the time?' Bianca exclaimed, signalling to the waiter. 'I must get back to my Creatives and see how they're settling in. *L'addition, Maurice, s'il vous plaît.* '

'I'll get this, Bianca,' said Dannie. 'I'm always happy to buy Dora Maar a drink.'

'*Que tu es gentille, Madeleine!* I'll see you both later then, shall I? The usual time.' Bianca picked up her basket, hooked it over her arm and strutted off up the main street of the village with an equally strutty Dora Maar hot on her heels.

Madeleine and Dannie shared a smile.

Dannie drained her glass and wiped the foam from her mouth with the back of her hand. 'By the way, I thought you said Daniel had finished his new series,' she said. 'Why did you tell Bianca he was working flat out?'

'It was a diplomatic manoeuvre to get him out of a soirée *chez* Madame Ingram. He needs a breather from being lionised, and I could tell that Bianca's dying to show him off to Colleen.'

'She's hard work, that same Colleen,' remarked Dannie.

'I thought you said she was great gas?'

'Have you ever read any of her books?'

'I've tried to.'

'Then you'll know that humour isn't her strong point. When I said she was great gas, I meant that she's mad as a snake.' Dannie smiled, remembering the figure Colleen used to cut, striding through the village of Kilrowan swathed in her crimson cloak. 'To sum her up in a single word, she's formidable.'

'Yikes,' said Madeleine. '"Formidable" in the French or in the English sense?'

'Scarily enough,' said Dannie after a moment's contemplation, 'I'd say both.'

4

It was the last day of filming on *Child Harry* – for Greta and Simon, anyway. The rest of the cast and crew were relocating to the west coast of Ireland to shoot exteriors. Greta and Simon were in his dressing room, packing up.

'I'm really glad *you've* no exterior shots scheduled, Tum Tugger,' Greta told him. 'The weather forecast is woegeous. Imagine being stuck in a field in Galway with the wind and the rain lashing down. I'm *so* sick of Irish weather. Gimme blue skies and sun and – erm – loads and *loads* of sun! I need a holiday!'

Greta hoped the exclamation mark would register. She had been chittering away non-stop for five minutes as she turned Simon's discarded costume right side out and hung it on the rail. The child was in the doldrums, and she knew it was because he didn't want to say goodbye to her. He had asked the AD to take a photograph of the pair of them earlier on his phone. Greta had positioned herself behind Simon, hunkering down with her arms wrapped around him and her chin on his shoulder, and they'd both been wearing their cheesiest grins. He'd promised to send her a copy.

Turning away from the costume rail, Greta cast around for something else to do to fill in this wretched time between now and the moment when they would have to say goodbye. Now was probably the right moment to give him his present. She reached for the bag that contained the book she'd gift wrapped earlier, but Simon pre-empted her by thrusting a package into her hands.

'What's this?' she asked.

'It's for you,' he told her, keeping his eyes downcast. 'It's a present to say thank you for being such a cool minder.'

'Oh, Simon! You're a complete dote! Here, then – right back at ya.' Greta took Simon's present from her bag and handed it to him.

'You got me one too? Cool. Thanks.'

'Let's unwrap them together, yeah?' suggested Greta in an 'isn't this great *craic*' voice. 'On a count of three. One, two, *three*!' She peeled the sparkly paper back to reveal a small, spotty black and white velour cat. 'Oh – how dotey! It has the cheekiest smile of any cat I've ever seen. It's a real Jellicle cat! And I *love* the little smudge on his nose!'

Simon tore the wrapping away from *Old Possum's Book of Practical Cats* and managed a subdued 'yay'. Then, to Greta's horror, he burst into tears.

Greta knelt down and took hold of his hand. 'What's wrong, Simon? Don't cry, please! Tum Tugger – shh, *shh* – *please* don't cry.'

But Simon just couldn't seem to stop. So Greta took him in her arms and soothed and rocked and soothed and rocked until the small boy finally said, 'Please don't tell anyone I cried.'

'Are you mad? Of course I won't tell anyone.' Sliding a packet of tissues from her pocket, Greta held one to Simon's nose. 'Blow, Tugger,' she said. He blew and she handed him another so that he could mop his eyes.

'What's the big problem?' she asked.

He gave her a watery smile. 'I'm gonna miss you so much. You've been the *wickedest* chaperone.'

'Oh, darlin', I'm gonna miss you too. But hey, we'll keep in touch. And hasn't Anita asked me if I'd be available for babysitting – I know, I *know* you're not a baby' – this at Simon's indignant expression – 'it's a very stupid turn of phrase. We'll make it Tugger-sitting instead, OK? And you'll text me, won't you?'

Greta dropped a kiss on the paw of her Jellicle cat and stowed it safely in her bag. 'I'll treasure this, Tum Tugger,' she said. 'I mean it.'

'And I'll treasure this,' said Simon solemnly, holding *Practical Cats* against his heart. 'Will you sign it for me?'

'It's already signed,' said Greta. She'd written on the flyleaf: '*Chuirfeadh sé cosa faoi chearca duit!* To Tum Tugger with love from Greta. XXX'

Simon opened the book and read the inscription. 'What does it mean?' he asked.

'It means that you'd put legs under a chicken. That you've the gift of the gab,' said Greta. 'You've kept me mightily entertained for the past couple of weeks.'

Simon smiled at her. '*Go raibh míle maith agat,*' he said. 'That's 'thank you' in Irish, isn't it? Did I say it right?'

'You said it pure perfect.'

There came a perfunctory knock and the door to the dressing room opened. An umbrella, a bottle of champagne and an enormous bunch of daffodils came through, followed by Simon's mother, Anita. 'For you,' she said, handing the daffodils and the champagne to Greta. 'For looking after my boy so well.'

'Anita – you shouldn't have.' Greta gave her a hug. 'I've already had the sweetest present from Simon.'

She was feeling emotional now and needed to busy herself in order to ward off imminent tears. Moving to stow the flowers in the wash hand basin, she set the champagne bottle down on the dressing table. Then she took the umbrella from Anita and hooked it onto the mirror above the basin, where it dripped onto the daffodils below. 'What brings you all the way out here to Ardmore?' she asked.

'I thought I'd pick Simon up myself today so that I could say goodbye and thank you to the cast and crew. And to you too, of course.'

'No thanks are necessary. Honest. Your boy was a real pleasure to work with. I just wish all child actors were so easy going. And their mothers,' she added. 'You wouldn't believe some of the harridans I've had dealings with.'

'Stage mothers?'

'Oh, yeah. Some of them would make Joan Crawford look like Mother Theresa. Have you time for a coffee?'

'Thanks, but no. I'll hit major traffic if I don't get going.' Anita looked down at Simon, who was texting morosely. 'Heavens above, Simon! Do you *never* stop texting? C'mon, now – we need to get a move on. Go get your gear.'

Stuffing his phone back into his pocket, Simon trudged across the room to retrieve his backpack.

'Do you want a lift into town, Greta?' asked Anita.

'Yes – come in with us!' piped up Simon. 'We can play I Spy in the car.'

'I can't, *mavourneen*,' Greta told him. 'Mick's already on his way for me.' A chauffeur-driven Merc picked her and Simon up every day and dropped them home. It was one of the perks of the job.

Taking Simon's backpack from him, Anita slung it over her shoulder. 'Have you any work lined up after this?' she asked, unhooking the umbrella from the mirror and shaking it out.

'No,' lied Greta. Her next job was nobody's business but her own. She had heard only yesterday that her application for the job as body double on *Love Lies Bleeding* had been successful and that she was to start work next week. She'd received the news with mixed feelings. Part of her was relieved that she had lucrative new work, while another part of her was aflutter with apprehension. 'I'd love a holiday,' she told Anita. 'But I can't afford one.'

'So would I,' said Anita. 'I was talking to my class about Keats today, and I've never read that line – 'Dance and Provençal song and sunburnt mirth' – with such heartfelt feeling. What wouldn't I give for a blue sky day and some time off.' There was an awkward pause and then Anita said, 'I'd be happy to write you a reference any time. Just give me a call. I'd recommend you to anyone, Greta. That's heartfelt.'

'Thanks, Anita.'

Another awkward pause, then, 'Well. We'd better shift. Goodbye, Greta. Thanks for everything.' Anita kissed her on the cheek and opened the door.

'Goodbye, Tum Tugger,' said Greta.

'Goodbye, Greta.'

'Remember to send me that photograph.'

'Yes.'

The door shut behind them and Greta heard their footsteps receding down the corridor. She moved to the window overlooking the car park so that Simon would see her if he looked back. Her phone was on the window sill, the message icon displayed. Accessing it, she found that the photograph that Simon had had taken was already there. The message that accompanied it read: **Greta and tum tugger frends forever. XXX**

Later, lolling against leather in the powder blue interior of the transport Merc, knackered after her early start, Greta turned her mind to her forthcoming job. She had four days on *Love Lies Bleeding* and the money was sensational. She'd be earning five times as much per day as she was currently earning as a chaperone, and if she was careful, the money would get her through the couple of months until the end of term came and she could find full-time work.

She had asked a few burning questions and had been given some very reassuring answers. All her scenes were to be shot on a closed set, with only those crew members directly involved in the filming process given access to the studio floor. Picture phones and cameras would be banned and there would be a complete embargo on press presence. She had also been warned that she was to ask her 'co-star' no questions of a personal nature. Rory McDonagh was a famously private individual.

Greta slid the complimentary copy of *The Irish Times* from the magazine net on the back of the driver's seat and leafed through it, idly scanning column inches without taking very much in. But a photograph and a feature on page six caught – and held – her attention.

'There's an article about my village in the paper,' she told Mick, the driver.

'Kilrowan?'

'Yeah.'

'What's it doing in the paper?'

'They're bringing in some regulation that means only Irish speakers will be allowed to buy houses in a new housing development there.'

'You'll be all right, so, with your impeccable Erse. Do you miss your village, young Greta?'

She thought about it as she gazed through the window at the sluggishly passing cityscape. Through the smoked-glass rear passenger window of the car she could see rain-spattered commuters waiting for buses and drivers fulminating behind the wheels of their gridlocked cars. 'Yes,' she said. 'I do miss it. I'm not really cut out to be a city girl.'

'Well, when you've finished college you can head back to the wilds of the west and paint pictures for the rest of your life.'

'My idea of heaven,' she said with a smile. Or was it? Greta sometimes wondered how she'd cope when she finally left her college friends behind to set up all on her own. An artist's life was very solitary, after all, and Greta loved being around people.

Shrugging away the thought, she returned her attention to *The Irish Times*. The letters page led her to the cryptic crossword, which she gave up after two minutes. The hours Jared had spent teaching her to do it had been in vain. She managed most of the Simplex, then went to the page that carried the Situations Vacant. *Situations Vacant*. The very words had a depressing ring to them.

She'd been spoiled, she knew, with her chaperoning jobs. The great thing about working on films was that the hours were flexible enough to enable her to continue her studies – she'd only missed two lectures and a single tutorial while she'd been working on *Child Harry*, and the *Love Lies Bleeding* schedule looked workable enough. But it would be fantastic to get a full-time job to keep her going over the summer recess. It was either that or sell her hair for extensions. She'd once threatened to do this, but Jared had told her in no uncertain terms that if she cut off her pre-Raphaelite, strawberry-blonde mane, he'd drop her.

I *can't* go back to being poor! she thought as she scanned the ads to see if there might be something worth following up. Being poor *sucked*. Greta hated not being able to stand a round of drinks in the pub, she hated having to give handmade birthday presents because she couldn't afford to buy gifts and she hated having to ask her parents for hand-outs. Being the eldest of six children meant that she knew how to live on a tight budget: all her siblings still had to be put through school and college, and money was scarce. She didn't want to have to go home for the summer and burden her mother with yet another mouth to feed. She'd *have* to get a job.

'Compassionate, energetic and dependable?' she read in Situations Vacant. Check! 'We need a couple to run a Ballsbridge funeral home.' Bummer. She might be compassionate, energetic and dependable, but she could imagine the look on Jared's face if she suggested that they get a job running a funeral home together. Not to mention the look on the mourners' faces if they rolled up to find a pair of bohos in charge of a D4 coffin shop.

'Needed. A proactive person with very good computer skills and proven experience.' Pah! Strike. 'Receptionist/

secretary required for busy dental surgery – south Dublin.' Hmm. That might be worth investigating – if she could overcome her dentist phobia ... but what was this? 'Are you Nani Nua? Fluent Irish speaker required,' she read, 'to mind three children in the south of France for two months this summer. No housework, some light cooking. References essential. Contact dod@jollyroger-enterprises.com.'

Well – *hello*! Result! Registering the dreary *swish swish swishing* of the windscreen wipers, Greta thought of the Keats poem that Anita had quoted from earlier: *Dance and Provençal song and sunburnt mirth* ... Blue skies! Olive groves! French wine on tap!

She was just about to ask Mick if she could tear the ad out of his paper when another thought struck her. Two months? Two months without her gorgeous, drop-dead-sexy überdude? Two months of celibacy? Two months of worrying about Sirenesque groupies? The four weeks he'd been on the road had been bad enough. She couldn't invite two whole months upon herself ... could she?

Her phone alerted her to a text. '**Baby!**' she read on the display. '**Rock hard jst thinkin bout you. Countin down hours til 2moro.**'

Greta smiled. No, she most certainly could *not* invite two whole months of celibacy upon herself. She texted a minxy reply, pressed send, then slid *The Irish Times* back into the magazine net with its Situations Vacant column intact.

5

At the appointed hour for aperitifs, Madeleine Lennox set off from her home at number one rue des Artistes for Bianca's house, carrying a gift-wrapped bottle. Daniel was routinely sent cases of champagne from people wanting to lionise him, and since neither he nor Madeleine was much in the habit of quaffing bubbly, she was always glad of an opportunity to recycle them. In a corner of the main square, she passed a bunch of local men playing a relaxed game of *boules* on their usual dusty patch. Among them was *her* man.

Daniel cut a strange figure. The local men favoured catalogue casuals and neat hairstyles; Daniel wore loose linen trousers belted with a woven Irish *crois* and the kind of shirt that a seventies hippy might have sported. His hair – more grey than blond now – was worn long. Sometimes – to his daughter Rosa's mortification – he wore it in a ponytail.

'Daniel!' said Madeleine crossly. 'What are you doing ostentatiously playing *boules* when I told Bianca you were holed up in your studio working on your series?'

'I think a man is allowed to play *boules* when the fancy takes him,' remarked Daniel, sliding a Gitane from a pack. 'As for 'ostentatiously', I don't think it's physically possible to play *boules* in an ostentatious fashion. And what on earth made you tell porkie pies to Bianca?'

'She wanted you to come for aperitifs and meet Colleen.'

'Who?'

'Colleen. The writer.'

Daniel flicked his Zippo and looked at Madeleine from under his eyebrows as he drew on his cigarette. 'She's here in Saint-Géyroux?'

'Yes. She's Bianca's first paying guest. I mean Creative-in-Residence.'

'And what made you think I wouldn't want to meet this Colleen?'

'She's very heavyweight. She's not your type.'

'What is my type?'

'Hmm. Might she be moderately good-looking?'

'She might.'

'Might she be thirty-something?'

'Definitely.'

'Might she be a gal who writes indifferent sonnets and is,' Madeleine lowered her voice, 'self-conscious about her cellulite?'

'What cellulite?' Daniel pulled Madeleine closer to him and smiled down at her. 'Does Dannie also have an audience with the mighty Colleen?'

'She does. Her babysitter's minding the girls.'

Daniel slapped her ass. 'Well, you dames have fun.'

'You too. I won't be late. Wait up for me, won't you?'

'Sure.'

Madeleine stood on tiptoe to brush her husband's lips with hers before setting off up the street, oblivious to the fact that her retreating rear was being subjected to much scrutiny by Daniel's fellow *boules* players.

'*Ça suffit, les mecs,*' growled Daniel as he turned back to the game and clocked the expressions on the faces of his team-mates. '*Ç'est ma femme à moi!*'

As she made her way along the thoroughfare that led to Bianca's house, Madeleine exchanged *bonsoirs* with her fellow villagers. She admired Madame Bontemps's new hairdo and paused to swap pleasantries with ancient Monsieur Verdurin, who was sitting as usual outside his front door on a bentwood chair playing chess with Monsieur Venot, the local gardener. She cooed over Françoise Vinteuil's baby, she fended off Raymond Forchville's goofy dog and she waved up at Madame Prévoste, who was watering geraniums on her roof garden, singing something operatic.

'*Bonsoir, Madame Lennox!*' Madame Bouret called to her from the other side of the street. 'Where are you off to on this fine evening, and who is to be the fortunate recipient of a *cadeau*?' Madame Bouret's sharp eyes had clocked the gift-wrapped bottle.

'I'm off to Madame Ingram's.'

'Aha! To meet the famous Irish writer and her, er, '*amie*', hein?'

'*Oui!*'

Sending Madame Bouret a bright smile, Madeleine continued on her way. Word had clearly already got out that Colleen and Margot d'Arcy were 'an item' – gasp! The *tricoteuses* would have a field day, because – to Madeleine's reasonably certain knowledge – the village had never played host to anything quite so exotic as an openly lesbian romance.

Madeleine loved Saint-Géyroux. She loved the ancient, solid houses with their warm sandstone fronts and grilles of intricately wrought iron. She loved the winding, narrow streets and the old-fashioned fascias of shops that hadn't changed for half a century or more. She loved the stately plane trees that shaded the main square where the weekly market took place, and the startling red splashes of poppies that grew around their gnarled roots, and the smell of lavender that perfumed the air in high summer. Any time she strolled through the village, she was filled with a sublime sense of *belonging* – of having found a safe haven in a wicked world.

As she passed the *caveaux* a few doors down from Bianca's house, she heard her name being called. Dannie Palmer swung through the door, a bottle of wine wrapped in brown paper in one hand, a bunch of tulips in the other. She had changed out of her jeans and sweat-shirt and was dressed in a plain shift dress that drew attention to her Nigella-esque curves. A cardigan was draped over her shoulders, she'd swapped her trainers for flip-flops, wound a Provençal scarf around her head and slicked on a little lip gloss. She'd probably put the look together in two minutes flat. What Madeleine wouldn't give to be so laid back about her appearance!

'How's she cuttin', Madeleine?' Dannie asked.

'Up the middle and down the sides,' said Madeleine, linking arms with her friend so that they could be *boulevardières* together. 'Life is good!'

It was true. From the moment Daniel had told her that Dutch Marjan would be leaving Saint-Géyroux, Madeleine had felt a blessed sense of relief. She had told Dannie a fib earlier when Dannie had quizzed her about how it felt to be living under the same roof as a cellulite-free beauty whose job it was to undress for her husband every day. It actually *did* feel a small bit strange. But she never complained to Daniel in case it blocked him creatively. When Daniel was suffering from an artistic block, it was like living with Shrek before he got the princess.

'Your flowers are beautiful, Dannie,' observed Madeleine. 'Are they from your garden?'

'Yes. We got a bumper crop this year. How's your garden growing?'

'Oh, you know what I'm like. I just have to look at a plant and it emits a little shriek and curls up and dies. They positively blush with delight at all the green-fingering Monsieur Venot lavishes on them.'

Dannie looked down at her hands. 'Green fingers is a real misnomer. I tried my damndest to get rid of all the dirt from under my nails after the repotting I did today, but it was impossible. I don't think even Swarfega could shift it.'

'Swarfega?'

'The stuff farmers use to clean their hands. My dad swore by it.'

'Maybe I should get some for Daniel. Oil paint's a bitch to shift too.'

Dannie laughed.

'What are you laughing at?'

'The image of you sashaying into the local hardware store and asking for Swarfega.'

They'd reached Bianca's house. Madeleine pressed the bell and peered though the wrought-iron gate at the front garden. Their hostess was fluttering down the path towards them like a cabbage white. She'd exchanged her palazzo pants for a gown of flowing silk, a camellia was tucked in her hair and a white chiffon scarf streamed in her wake. *'Je vous souhaite le bienvenu!'* she trilled, and for the second time that day, the greeting ritual was observed. 'Mwah mwah!' she went. 'Join us! We're in the garden.'

Along the path the *châtelaine* led them, then up the sandstone steps that led to her beautifully carved front door. Once inside the hall, Bianca turned to them to graciously accept the gifts they were carrying. 'For me? Thank you!' she said, admiring Dannie's tulips, and, 'Thank you, Madeleine! Ooh! Champagne! Claudine!' she said to the maid who had hoved into view from the region of the basement, 'Put these in water and take the bottles to the cellar, please. And you may bring the Pimm's into the garden presently.'

Claudine trailed back downstairs and Bianca turned and preceded her guests onto the balcony that over-looked her magnificent garden. Bianca's landscaped acre boasted a couple of terraces, a meditation pavilion, lux-uriant flower beds, a newly planted arboretum and a tin-kling fountain.

'Your garden's looking fabu—' began Madeleine, but Bianca's theatrically raised hand stopped her in her tracks.

'Behold the Scribe!' she said in a hushed and reverent tone. 'One can only begin to imagine the profundity of the thoughts passing though that beautiful mind.'

There below, a woman was standing on the terrace, gaz-ing towards the horizon with a pensive expression on her face. She was wearing a kaftan in fustian. It was the colour of field mushrooms and it had some kind of runes hand-painted on. Her feet were bare and her splendid red hair was all a-tumble down her back.

Bianca took a step forward and the Scribe turned and looked up. Her beautiful, pensive face took on an expression of uncertainty, as if she had just been awakened from some rapturous dream.

'Forgive me, Colleen,' said Bianca. 'I do not mean to intrude upon you while The Muse is in residence, as – to judge by the faraway look on your face – it so plainly was.'

'Arra, no matter, Bianca,' pronounced Colleen in her rolling brogue. 'Greetings! I see you have brought me a new friend! You must be Madeleine, the Muse of Daniel Lennox. And an old friend, too! Dannie Palmer, it cheers my soul to see you again. Come. Come! Step into the garden.'

Madeleine followed her hostess down the steps feeling weirdly as if she had been invited into Colleen's garden, not Bianca's.

'How's it going, Colleen?' said Dannie, pumping her hand. 'Are you getting much work done in this artists' retreat? I'd say you're finding Bianca's garden inspirational?'

'Inspirational indeed,' said Colleen, reclaiming her hand. 'A word – a single word – eluded me while I sat at my desk today. But the minute I set foot upon Bianca's meditation pavilion, I trapped and captured it on paper for posterity.'

Colleen reached into a pocket and produced a sheet of nubbly hand-made paper. She unfolded it, studied it, then held it out. One word was writ large in a jagged script.

'Piaffe,' read Madeleine.

'Piaffe?' said Dannie. 'What does that mean?'

'It comes from the French, '*piaffer*', suggesting a movement somewhere between a trot and a strut.' For one chillingly horrific moment, Madeleine thought Colleen was going to demonstrate, but she settled herself instead on one of Bianca's white-painted wicker garden loungers and tucked her feet beneath her. 'You might describe a horse as 'piaffing' across a stable yard,' she continued. 'And since my character in gestation is something of a *flâneur*, it is a strikingly apposite verb.'

Before anyone could ask Colleen what a *flâneur* was, they were distracted by the sound of clinking ice. Claudine was trundling down the steps, laden down by a tray on which crystal glinted and ice bobbed around in a big jug of Pimm's.

'Would you care for a glass of Pimm's, Colleen?' asked Bianca.

'Pimm's?' The Scribe pronounced the word as if she had never heard it before. 'Pimm's? No. No Pimm's for me. I shall have a glass of wine, thank you kindly. The red you served at dinner last night was inoffensive.'

'Certainly! Bring a bottle of the Minervois, please, Claudine.'

Setting the tray down on a table, Claudine trudged back towards the house while Bianca busied herself with pouring Pimm's into glasses. Madeleine took the glass she was proffered, and, as she did so, she saw a gate open in the high wall that separated the garden from the outbuildings beyond. A strikingly beautiful woman came through, clad in a gown of semi-transparent pussy-willow-grey cheesecloth. Like Colleen, she was barefoot.

Colleen raised an arm in a gesture of welcome. 'Beloved!' she said. 'Join us.'

The beautiful woman drifted up the garden like a wraith, and when she reached Colleen, she kissed her full on the mouth. 'This is *my* Muse, Margot d'Arcy,' Colleen told Madeleine, and Margot inclined her head and curved her lips in a practiced smile. 'And, of course, you remember Dannie from Kilrowan, Margot?'

'Dannie Palmer – how good to see you again.' Margot moved to Dannie and air-kissed her expertly.

Colleen gestured magisterially at the assembled company. 'Please, sit,' she said.

Madeleine and Dannie sat down obediently at the patio table, Bianca perched on a white peacock chair and Margot sank onto a low wicker pouffe by Colleen's side. 'Tell me, how was your excursion into the realms of poesie this afternoon, love? I trust it was productive?' she asked in a husky drawl.

'I managed a handful of words only. I dedicated most of the day to reading and meditation, in preparation for tomorrow. Tomorrow, I must take up my narrative needle and begin embroidering as adroitly as Arachne.'

'The Nimble-Fingered One,' said Margot, reverently.

'The Nimble-Fingered One?' repeated Dannie.

'Arachne,' said Colleen in the sonorous tones of a *shanachie*, 'was the Greek demigoddess whose skill at embroidery surpassed even that of Athena.'

'Fair play to her,' remarked Dannie.

Colleen ignored her and turned back to Margot. 'I was telling these good people how inspirational I am finding the ambience here in this Sanctuary.'

Bianca looked pleased. 'Thank you, Colleen! That is some compliment.' She turned to Madeleine and Dannie. 'I've furnished the studios with some of the antiques and artefacts I've picked up on my travels,' she told them. 'I like to think there's an eclectic mix.'

'There is, to be sure,' concurred Colleen. 'Bianca has juxtaposed disparate *objets* with wit and a keenly artistic eye. In my studio, a rocking horse sits next to a Biedermeier escritoir, a Sioux eagle-feather headdress is suspended above an amboyna wood chaise longue, a carved Meerschaum is perched upon a satinwood teapoy.' Colleen recited the list as if it were a poem by Yeats.

'What's a teapoy when it's at home?' asked Dannie.

'It's a tea table.'

'Hmm. I must instruct Paloma to set the teapoy in future. And a Meerschaum is …?'

'A type of pipe,' said Bianca.

'But you don't smoke, Colleen,' said Dannie with such disingenuousness that Madeleine suspected she was stirring it.

Colleen raised an autocratic eyebrow. 'No matter. It is the aesthetic that is paramount in a creative retreat.'

A sudden picture of Colleen communing with her inner child, sitting astride a rocking horse with an eagle-feather headdress on her head and a Meerschaum pipe in her mouth, flashed before Madeleine's mind's eye and she gave a little splutter, which she tried to pretend was effected by the fizz of the Pimm's. Colleen immediately fixed her with that same gimlet look she'd bestowed upon Dannie, and Madeleine felt as if she were back at school again.

Thankfully, just then Claudine arrived with a glass of red wine, which she set upon the table in front of Colleen. The Scribe nodded acceptance as though it were a libation.

'I noticed,' she said, 'that you have a most unusual artefact displayed on the console table on your landing,

Bianca. It is, I believe, a Tibetan trumpet.'

'It is!' said Bianca enthusiastically. 'How astute of you to recognise its provenance, Colleen. I picked it up in a souk in Tangier. It's actually fashioned from a human thigh bone.'

'And what is its timbre?'

'I beg your pardon?'

'What sound resonates from it?'

'I, er, I confess that I have never actually played it.'

'Well, that is something we must remedy. I have my bodhrán with me and Margot her tin whistle. We might have a musical evening, experiment with a little improvisation.'

'We … might.' This time Bianca's enthusiasm seemed a tad forced.

'Madeleine, you play the piano, don't you?' said Dannie. 'You might like to join in.'

Madeleine turned alarmed eyes on Dannie, but was spared the necessity of replying by Bianca. 'Alas,' put in their hostess with alacrity, 'my pianoforte needs tuning.'

It was time to change the subject. Dannie was clearly hell bent on monkey business and Madeleine was at serious risk of corpsing. 'Are you working on another novel, Colleen?' she asked, pulling on an expression of intense interest.

'A novel? No, no. Margot and I are collaborating on a play. We hope to finish it before we leave Saint-Géyroux at the end of the summer. Bianca has very kindly invited us to stage it in the pavilion in her garden.'

'For public viewing?'

'For an invited audience, yes,' said Bianca.

A silence fell. Madeleine didn't dare look at Dannie.

'What's it about?' she finally asked.

'It is a celebration of Womanhood. Of the Divine Goddess within.'

'Amen,' said Margot.

'And, er, does it have a name?'

'The working title is *Síle na Gig in the Temple of Hecate.*'

'Who's Sheila Nagig?' asked Bianca.

'Of course – you have no Erse,' said Colleen. '*Síle na Gig* is often translated as 'Sheila squatting'. She is an ancient Irish symbol of fertility.'

'Sheila squatting?' mused Bianca. 'Whatever for?'

'She's showing off her fanny,' said Dannie.

'Excuse me.' Madeleine had choked on her Pimm's. Setting down her glass abruptly, she moved to the steps that would take her back into Bianca's house. 'I've just got to nip to the loo.'

And as she piaffed through the French windows that would take her to Margot's hall and the refuge of the bathroom, Madeleine thanked the good Lord Jesus that her husband wasn't there. Daniel would have creased up crinklier than a Shar Pei.

6

Greta was lying back against pillows, all aglow. Her cousin was off visiting parentals and Greta had had the flat to herself for the entire weekend. She'd spent nearly forty-eight hours in bed with Jared. 'Are all musicians this good in the sack?' she asked him.

'They say that drummers drum with their loins,' he said, slanting her a smile before sliding out from between the sheets. 'I could use a shower before the gig. Are you coming?'

'I think I've come enough for one day, thanks to you,' she said happily.

'I meant to the gig.'

'I can't. I've a babysitting job.'

'Cancel it.'

'I can't, Jared. Anita was in a real bind.'

'You're way too obliging, Greta. If the dame's in a bind, you should at least charge double.'

'It's not the money, honey. It's just that I like Anita, and I don't want to let her down.'

'Is she the woman whose kid you've been minding on the film set?'

'Yes. And I'm really fond of Simon too. He misses me.'

'But he'll be seeing you again on this next film. What's it called again?'

'*Love Lies Bleeding.*'

Greta had decided against telling Jared about the body double thing. Her boyfriend had a mean temper, and because he wasn't comfortable with the fact that she earned money by taking her clothes off for life-drawing classes, it followed that he would be even more uncomfortable with the notion that she would soon be getting naked with a complete stranger. So she'd let on that she was working as a chaperone on *Love Lies Bleeding*. She hated lying to him, but in this instance it made sense to be a little economical with the truth.

'Call this Anita, baby. Tell her you're sick or something.'

'I can't do that! I'd feel like a piece of shit if I backed out at this stage.'

Jared shrugged, then headed for the door. 'You'll be missing an amazing gig,' he told her.

'Maybe I could come along afterwards? Depending on what time Anita's due—'

But she never got to finish the sentence. 'Hey. Don't bother,' Jared said, slamming the bedroom door behind him.

She could tell by the slam that he was in a major strop. There was only one way to mollify him, she knew, and that was to stroke his ego. Slipping out of bed, Greta extracted another condom from the packet and followed her boyfriend into the bathroom.

She was on the bus to Anita's house when the call came through.

'Greta? I'm so, so sorry. I've come down with some kind of dreaded lurgy,' Anita lamented. 'I was all set –

make-up done and everything – but I realised five minutes ago that I won't be going anywhere tonight. I'm going to have to cancel you. I can't tell you how sorry—'

'Anita, no worries. I'm the one who should be feeling sorry for you. Is it the flu?'

'I don't know what it is, but I'll be seeing a doctor tomorrow, that's for sure.'

'It's that bad? Poor you.'

'It's Alan I feel sorry for. I'm a shockingly bad patient.'

'I'm actually not a bad nurse. I looked after all my brothers and sisters any time they got sick, so I did. Do you need me to come round and be Florence Nightingale?'

Oops. She shouldn't have made the offer. She'd just realised that she now had a wide open window of opportunity to make it to Jared's gig – the tail end of it, anyway.

'You're sweet, but no, honestly. Alan's taking good care of me.'

'How's Simon?'

'Simon's fine. He's just pissed off because he won't get to see you.'

'Send him my love, won't you?'

'Will do. Sorry about this, Greta.'

'It's honestly not a problem, Anita. Get well soon.'

'Thanks. I'll be in touch. Bye.'

Greta checked the time, then stuffed her phone back in her bag. Eight forty, and the band were scheduled to be on stage until nine. Yes! She'd make it. If she got off the bus at the next stop and legged it, she'd be pretty sure to catch the encore – and the encore was always the highlight of the show. She just wished she was wearing something a little more rock chick than O'Neill's and trainers.

But the trainers were a good thing after all, she decided,

because just fifteen minutes later she was in the foyer of the theatre. 'I'm with the band,' she told the bouncer.

He curled his lip. 'Isn't everyone? Nice try, but no cigar. You might be surprised to hear this, but a ticket often works. Pay a visit to the box office, babe.'

Greta never paid into Jared's gigs – in fact, she usually watched the band from the wings – but there was no way she was going to get past this bloke without forking out for a ticket. She felt like a tool handing over hard-earned cash to see her own boyfriend perform.

Inside the auditorium, the atmosphere was electric. It was weird to join a crowd that was already so heated up – it made her feel a little like an ice sculpture at a party. Hands were clapping fiercely, fists punched the air – the audience was one massive beast. Bodies swayed to the rhythm of the music, a pungent smell of sweat rose into the atmosphere and the noise was a physical presence. The vibration came in though her feet and coursed through her body – and hey! The band was playing *their* song, the song they always played as their encore, the one she'd told him she loved so much the first time they'd met, the one – he'd told her since – that made him think about her every time he played it live on stage; the one that gave him a hard-on.

On stage, lead guitar was playing his instrument as if he were starring in a skin flick, bass was looking saturnine and Jared was beating the crap out of his kit. And the girl on the violin looked rapturous.

The girl on the violin? What? Where had *she* come from? No fiddle-player had ever appeared with the band before! No *girl* had ever gigged with the band before. But she wasn't just a girl, Greta saw. She was a *beautiful* girl. She was a babe. And she was centre stage.

The band had passed the last bridge and were heading for the finale. This was Jared's cue to unhitch the tom-tom from his kit and strut his stuff. The crowd roared approval as he moved downstage to join the gorgeous violinist, narrow-eyeing her, pulling the strap of the drum around his snake-hips, thrusting the body of the instrument between his thighs. The girl smiled at him – that complicit smile that musicians do so well – and he returned it, running his eyes over her body. Her head was set at a proud angle, challenging him to match her virtuosity. She threw a phrase at him, he hit it right back. She fluttered a swarm of notes at him, he echoed them in drum-skin-tight syncopation. They fairly ricocheted music off each other: it was so fast, so furious and so very, very sexy that you could practically smell the chemistry. Jared had torn off his T-shirt. His torso was slick with sweat as he worked his way up through the crescendo while the fiddle player undulated her hips to the rhythm, a rhapsodic expression on her face. The climax came, the last pulsing blast from the drum, the last shuddering sigh from the violin.

There was an electric moment of silence, and then, like a rampant animal, the crowd roared their appreciation. The noise they made sounded to Greta like the clamouring of Barbary apes; the applause they showered upon the band was like shattering plastic; the blissed-out expressions on their faces made them look like idiot savants. The band took their bows with a piratical swagger, Jared and his inamorata looking glazed around the eyes and muzzy with post-coital euphoria.

The bastard.

Feeling even more like an ice sculpture, Greta made her way past jostling bodies to the ladies' loo, queued, peed, washed her hands, then returned to the auditorium. On stage, roadies were setting up for the next act. She knew one of them, a bloke called Jon.

'Hey, Jon,' she said.

He turned and when he saw Greta, he looked shifty, suddenly. 'Good to see you, Greta,' he said unconvincingly.

'When did the band acquire the fiddle player?' she asked him.

'Oh. She joined us on the road. Did Jared not say?'

'No,' she said with a mirthless smile. 'Why am I not surprised?'

Turning, she made her way backstage to the dressing rooms. The bass guitarist was lurking at the stage door, smoking a joint. 'Is Jared around?' she asked him.

'Er, yeah. But I wouldn't—'

'Maybe *you* wouldn't,' she said, 'but *I* would.'

Greta moved down the corridor and tried a few doors before she hit on the right one. She didn't bother to knock – and unfortunately for them, they hadn't bothered to lock. Inside the room, Jared had the beautiful violinist up against the wall. Her tiny skirt was up around her waist, her legs were locked around his hips and he was banging her as hard as he'd banged his drums earlier.

The girl looked appalled when she caught sight of Greta. 'Jared! Stop, stop!' she babbled, squirming to unhitch herself.

But Jared was too far gone to be able to stop. He carried on, oblivious to anything but the dick that was doing all his thinking for him.

Greta looked the girl in the eye. She had never seen anyone look so utterly mortified.

'Tell him Greta said goodbye,' she said, then strode out of Jared Kelly's life without bothering to shut the door behind her.

'The *bastard*!' Esther said for the hundredth time. 'I can't believe the brazenness of that fucking *bastard*! Picking up a girl on tour and then coming back and spending the weekend in bed with you? The fucking *bastard*!'

Greta was sitting at the kitchen table morosely forking cheesy mash into her mouth and swigging back wine.

'Has he tried to get in touch with you?' Esther asked.

'Don't know, don't care. I'm keeping my phone turned off. And if I get any messages, I'll delete them without checking them. I never want to see him again in my life.' She pushed her plate away. 'Thanks for the mash. It helped.'

'Good.'

There came a sudden blast of music from the flat next door. 'Don't tell me Fuchsia's having *another* party?' asked Greta.

'Yep. Fuchsia's having another party, and we're invited.'

Their neighbour, Fuchsia, was a model, actress, whatever – and a serious party animal. She had recently announced that she was taking time off to travel, and for this relief Greta had given much thanks, because she really didn't relish the idea of back-to-back parties going on in the next-door flat when she had an end of year show looming.

'I'd rather not go, if you don't mind, Esther. I'm not feeling sociable tonight.'

'That's hardly surprising.'

'D'you know what was worse than walking in on them? It was watching them practically make out on stage to "our" song.'

'More anaesthetic called for,' said Esther, sloshing red into their glasses.

'Thanks. You know, that was the biggest bastardy betrayal of all. It was so *public*! Everyone will be talking about how poor Greta O'Flaherty had to stand in a public arena and watch her boyfriend wax orgasmic over another woman on stage. And it's been going on for *weeks* without me knowing.'

There was a silence. 'Fuck him,' said Esther. She hooked an arm over the back of her chair and regarded Greta with a solemn expression. 'Come on. Let's send him to the Bin of Fire.'

'The Bin of Fire! Excellent idea.'

Clinking glasses, they set them down, then moved across the room to where an antediluvian computer was housed in an alcove. Greta accessed the organiser, located Jared's details and said, 'Burn, baby, burn.' Then she clicked on the entry, dragged the contact icon down to the wastepaper bin and dumped Jared into it. 'Yay!' she cried when he burst into flames. 'And there'll be no rising from the ashes for you, you bastarding bastard. Ha. Is there anyone else in here we can send to the Bin?' Greta clicked randomly and the name of an old school friend came up. 'Yeah! She can go too.'

'Why?'

'I put her in touch with a literary agent - the mother of

one of my film kids – so that she could have a look at her novel. She got a sweet book deal and she never said thank you. Burn, bitch, burn!'

'Well hey! This is a Greta O'Flaherty I have never seen before.'

'I don't like bad manners, Esther, and I don't like injustice. I know I'm a walkover usually, but I have a steely side too.'

'A stainless steely side.'

'D'you know what was inscribed over the northern gate to Galway city in medieval times?' said Greta. '"From the ferocious O'Flahertys good Lord deliver us."'

'Hmm. "And though she be but little, she is fierce."'

'What?'

'It's from *A Midsummer Night's Dream*. Burn someone else, you little pyromaniac.'

'Let's see, let's see … yes! You can go in the Bin too, you students' union prick who dissed me at a party. Burn! And you – bad, bad person who never returned my calls. Burn! OK … that's just about satisfied my blood lust.' Greta returned her attention to Esther. 'It's time to move on. Did you happen to get *The Irish Times* on Friday?'

'Yeah. Why?'

'Have you still got it?'

'It's in that pile on the couch.'

Greta crossed the room – veering via the kitchen table so she could grab her glass of wine – and located the paper sandwiched between Esther's rough sketches for *A Midsummer Night's Dream* and that month's *Vanity Fair*. She picked up the paper and went straight to the Situations Vacant column. 'Have a look at this,' she said, folding over the paper and handing it to Esther.

'Situations Vacant?'

'Yep.' Greta pointed to the ad she'd seen last Friday.

'A child-minding job in France? Cool!'

'I'd decided against applying for it because I didn't fancy the idea of being away from Jared for so long, but now he's gone to the Bin of Fire, I can go wherever the hell I like.'

'But the summer's ages away. You're bound to run into him between now and then. Dublin's a small place, Greta.'

'That may be, but I know which areas to avoid. Anyway, I can't afford to socialise. I'm going to be keeping my head down and working flat out for the next couple of months. There's no way I'm going to mess up my end of year show.'

'In that case, let's get your life sorted pronto and send an e-mail to Dod.'

'Dod?'

'That's what's on the e-mail address. See? Dod at jolly-rogerenterprises.com. Maybe we should check them out online.'

'Good idea.' Greta clicked, and while they waited for their sluggish internet connection, Esther reread the small ad. 'Three children, no housework, some light cooking. References essential. You won't have a problem getting references, will you?'

'No. I already have half a dozen. Even the witchiest of the stage mothers supplied me with a good one. And Simon's mammy said she'd recommend me to anyone. She even gave me a bottle of champagne as a thank you present.'

'So there are nice people in the world.'

'Mm. I'd never send Anita to the Bin of Fire.'

'No housework!' said Esther, returning her attention to *The Irish Times*. 'Lucky you. That probably means they have a housekeeper already. Maybe they're really rich.'

'Janey, I hope not. I get uncomfortable around rich people.'

'"Some light cooking." You're well able for that.'

'Sure am,' said Greta as Internet Explorer finally shimmered up on the screen. She'd been helping her mother out in the kitchen since she was six.

'And it'll be Frenchified light cooking – *crêpes* and *ratatouille* and stuff – all washed down with *du bon vin rouge*.'

'I might not get the gig,' Greta pointed out.

'You're in with a bloody good chance, Greta. How many fluent Irish speakers with child-minding experience are going to be available to spend all summer in the south of France?'

'Fingers crossed.'

Sitting back down in front of the computer, Greta flexed her fingers and typed in the e-mail address. 'Um. How do I start? I've no name to go by except Dod, whoever that is. Should I put "To whom it may concern"?'

'No, no! Put *"A chara"*!'

'"*A chara*"! Inspired! *A chara*,' she typed. 'My name is Greta O'Flaherty. I am a twenty-one-year-old fluent Irish speaker who has had considerable experience as a child-minder. I am the oldest of a family of six, so I have been looking after children from as far back as I can remember ...'

Between them Greta and Esther composed a concise yet informative e-mail of some one hundred and fifty words telling Dod just how perfect Greta was for the job.

Then, feeling reckless, they opened another bottle, toasted the e-mail with a rousing *'bonne chance!'* and sent it winging through the ether to dod@jollyrogerenterprises.com.

7

'Good. Slide your left hand a little higher, Rory. Corinna, caress his hair. Good. Very nice.'

Greta's second day as Charlotte Lambert's body double saw her supine on a tiger-skin rug in front of a fireplace. She was glad that the rug was as fake as her orgasm. Rory was between her legs, and what he was meant to be doing to her was not unlike what some dude in a dream had done last night. She felt his hands slide around her thighs, then, 'Cut!' yelled the director and Rory's face emerged from the folds of her petticoats.

'A grasshopper walks into a bar,' he told her.

'And?'

'And the barman says, "Hey! We have a drink named after you." The grasshopper looks bemused and replies, "You have a drink named Steve?"'

'Rory McDonagh! You have the silliest sense of humour of practically anyone I know,' Greta said with a laugh. It was true. Rory's sense of humour was nearly as juvenile as Tum Tugger's. But she loved him for it. None of his jokes was ever even borderline smutty, and she knew it was because anything risqué would be wildly inappropriate in the circumstances.

'Checks!' snapped the director and the crew jumped to it.

'Jesus,' said Rory. 'Marchant's been narky lately. That's not like him. I wonder what's up?'

And then something quite surreal happened. The film's director, David Marchant, went grey in the face and collapsed to the ground in manifest agony just as the camera operator announced, 'There's a hair in the gate.'

'*Au revoir*, Mammy!' called Paloma as she clambered into the back seat of the Lennoxes' jeep and strapped herself in beside her pal Rosa.

'*Au revoir, acushla!*' Dannie waved goodbye to her daughter as the jeep took off down the rue des Artistes with Madeleine at the wheel and her husband Daniel in the passenger seat. The four of them were off to spend the day at the Labadou, down by the River Hérault. The Labadou was a favourite beauty spot with locals because swimming in the creek there was safe and easy – unless you were fool enough to dive from the bridge – and there were minerals and ice cream and *frites* for sale in the shack that operated on the shore. The shack wasn't open yet because it was too early in the season, but this spring the weather had been beautiful in the south of France – balmy and perfect for lazing on beaches; in the summer it was often too hot.

Another splendid day in Saint-Géyroux! Lounging against the doorjamb, Dannie looked up and followed the progress of a vapour trail as it inched its way across the cerulean blue awning of the sky. As the rev of the jeep faded away, she became aware of the low cooing of a dove from a neighbouring garden. Sparrows were quarrelling under the eaves above her head, the tinny ring of the bell chimed eleven from the church on the corner and a glorious smell of baking was wafting forth from Madame Poiret's open front door.

Dannie was tempted to linger and wait for someone to pass with whom she could shoot the breeze, but there were more pressing concerns on her mind. Jethro was back, Dannie was ovulating and a baby was waiting to be made.

Shutting the door, Dannie stepped back into the hall of the *maison de maître* that was home to her and Jethro, loving the familiar feel of the terracotta tiles under her bare feet. She slid her robe from her shoulders and allowed it to drop to the floor. Then she moved down the hallway and out through the French windows that led to the bougainvillea-bright terrace.

Jethro was sitting with his back to her at the table. His feet were up on the garden chair opposite, a basket of croissants and a cafetière were on the table in front of him and a newspaper lay discarded on the sandstone flags. He looked the picture of relaxation, but Dannie's heart sank as she realised that he'd booted up his notebook, and it sank further still as she registered that his cell phone was ringing, its urgent shrill sounding as out of place as small arms fire in a holy place.

'Don't pick up!' she wailed.

Too late. Jethro had already answered.

'Rory!' she heard him say in his deep Southern drawl. 'Where are you, man?'

Drenched in disappointment, Dannie strode past her husband, gave him a basilisk look, then dived into the pool. She swam one energetic lap, then another and another. At the end of each lap, she glanced up to check if Jethro was still on the phone. Yes, yes and yes. Ten laps later, she wanted to scream when she saw that he was now tip-tapping away on the keyboard of his notebook, phone clamped between his collarbone and his ear. Well, feck him! Feck him to hell and back! He was like a feckin' market garden with his BlackBerry and his Apple Mac. He had only arrived in Saint-Géyroux yesterday, and already he was being distracted from his family duties by bloody real-life stuff. If you could call the superficial world of film-making real life.

As she tore through the water, Dannie found herself speculating with bitter resentment about Jethro's other life – the one he lived without her. She had accompanied him to a film première on only one occasion, and had told him in no uncertain terms afterwards that she would never do it again. She had hated the whole red carpet thing: the flash bulbs going off in her face, the journalists hectoring Jethro for quotes, the vacuously smiling starlets competing for attention. She had found herself making small talk with one of the starlets at the post-première party, and she'd felt as if she were talking to a cardboard cut-out. The girl and she had had absolutely nada in common.

What must it be like for a powerful man to be perpetually surrounded by glamorous women, she wondered, not for the first time, and to be married to a woman who never bothered with the external trappings of make-up or hairdos or fancy clothes?

Apart, that is, from lingerie. Dannie was a sucker for the stuff: she owned breathtaking confections of silk and satin and lace; wisps of chiffon trimmed with ribbon and marabou feather and tiny silken rosebuds. As long as Dannie was wearing something fabulous next to her skin, she felt empowered – and she knew that Jethro knew it, too. She knew he loved to sit opposite her at a table in the local café and fantasise about what she might have on under the unprepossessing jeans and T-shirts she favoured. And when he got her home, he invariably took his time finding out in the privacy of their bedroom. Whatever other shortcomings their relationship might have, the sex was unfailingly incendiary.

By the end of lap twenty-six, Jethro was finally off the phone. Hands in the pockets of his robe, he strolled to the edge of the pool and looked down at her. 'Well,' he said. 'How sexy are you? You're like some kind of voluptuous naiad. Fancy trying for another baby?'

But Dannie swam on, pretending not to have heard. She was too angry to leave the pool, she was too angry to make a baby. She crawled another lap, venting energy, seething, but when she made to turn at the shallow end, Jethro was in the water beside her.

'Hey, gorgeous,' he murmured, imprisoning her in his arms and dropping kisses on her shoulder. 'How dare you flaunt your naked golden flesh in front of me while I'm otherwise engaged? All the time I was on the phone I was nursing a rock hard erection, watching you shimmer up and down through the water. By the end of the conversation I was barely making sense, godammit. Come here.' He pulled her closer.

'You never stop, do you, you bastard!' she lamented, pushing her palms hard against his shoulders. 'You never stop your feckin' wheeler-dealing!'

'And you never stop turning me on, you sweet bitch. Look what you've done to me.' Dannie could feel his erection against her tummy. 'God, am I going to enjoy you!

Hell, I'm going to enjoy you at least twice, darling girl.'

Dannie made a more concerted effort to pull away, but the harder she fought, the more forceful was Jethro's riposte, and suddenly his chest was slick against her cheek and his breath was hot in her ear and she found herself faltering. And when he parted her lips with his thumb, she didn't resist. And when he murmured a suggestion, she complied. And when his hand slid between her legs and she felt the surge of lust he conjured in her, Dannie knew that she was lost. As usual.

Daniel and Madeleine Lennox were lying stretched out on the shore at the Labadou, watching Rosa and Paloma, who were drawing with sticks in the wet sand. Pilot – that creature of habit – was snoozing in the shade, his rapid eye movement testimony to the dream rabbits he was chasing.

A gang of young people were lounging nearby, their beauty ostentatiously on display.

'They say you're getting old,' Madeleine said, 'when you look at young people as if they're a species of exotic hot-house blooms. I bet you badly want to paint that orchid you've been eyeing up.'

'On the contrary,' returned Daniel. 'I've been eyeing her up because she's had surgery. She looks as if she's been airbrushed. She'd do well as a photographic model, but she's too damn perfect to be paintable.' He yawned, shot a look at his watch. 'It's nearly close of business. It'll be too late by the time we get home to book that flight to Dublin.'

'You can book a flight on the internet at any hour of

the day or night,' Madeleine told him. 'And you'll be glad to know that I've already done it.'

'Oh? Thanks.'

'And I've spoken to the IMMA people and told them that you want your fee to go to UNICEF.'

Daniel had been asked to give a talk on his work at the Irish Museum of Modern Art in Dublin later in the week, and Madeleine was glad that he had something to distract him: he got so damn moody when he wasn't painting. She hoped inspiration would strike soon.

'When do you think you'll start on a new series?' she asked. 'Have you had any inspired ideas?'

'Gilbert's still harping on about another series of nudes *enceintes*.'

'*Enceintes*,' she repeated. 'It's a much nicer word in French, isn't it? 'Pregnant' sounds so pedestrian.'

The original series of paintings to which Daniel referred – *Madeleine Enceinte* – hung in their bedroom. The final portrait – *Mère et Fille*, depicting Madeleine with a two-week-old Rosa in her arms – was the most beautiful. Daniel had shown his agent, Gilbert Blatin, the paintings, but had emphasised that they were neither for sale, nor for public view. Blatin was gagging for a second series to show in his gallery in Paris and had been encouraging Daniel for the past couple of years to come up with one. But it was proving impossible to find a pregnant girl who was prepared to pose nude: rather, it was proving impossible to find a pregnant 'stunner' to pose nude. 'Stunners', Daniel had once told her, were how the pre-Raphaelites described their tousle-headed muses.

Daniel started toying with a strand of Madeleine's hair

that had come loose from its sleek coil. 'I am – unsurprisingly – beginning to find it all a bit bloody frustrating,' he said morosely.

'Yikes. Does that mean you're going to get stuck into a sculpture?'

Daniel routinely sculpted when he had a creative block because it was a way of venting energy, but he didn't find sculpting anywhere near as satisfying or as joyous as the act of painting.

'Yep. Although I don't know why I bother. I'll never be a Canova.'

'Who was he?'

'He was an early eighteenth-century Neo-classicist. One of his nude sculptures was so touchable that the subject's husband had it locked away where no one but he could look at it. Her arse is nearly as touchable as yours.' He ran a finger along the line of her bikini bottom.

'You smooth talker! I bet *she* didn't suffer from cellulite.' Madeleine lay there in silence for many moments, enjoying the sensation produced by his fingertips, then: 'D'you know something?' she said. 'You have the most skilful fingers of anyone I know.'

'I know I have,' he told her complacently. 'That's why I am an Artist of International Repute.'

'And that's why I love you.'

'For my fingers alone?'

'You have other attributes.' She slid him a smile. 'And they're not just physical.'

It was true. Although Daniel could be irascible and moody sometimes, he could also be tender and affectionate. He'd nursed Madeleine through a wretched cold recently, bringing her hot lemon and Paracetamol and stacks of magazines; he'd held her hand while she'd waited for the all-clear after a hysteroscopy last month; and he always, always woke her in the night when he heard the whimpering noises that told him she was suffering from one of her recurrent nightmares. He'd hold her then, and stroke her, and murmur reassurance until sleep reclaimed her.

Farther along the beach, somebody's mobile phone went off.

'Bloody noise pollution,' grumbled Daniel.

Madeleine smiled. 'You're so irredeemably stuck in the last century, aren't you, Luddy Lennox?'

'Hey! I'm proud to be a Luddite.'

'Maybe you and Colleen *would* get on, come to think of it. She, too, is a self-professed Luddite. If you ever met up you could call yourselves Luddites United.'

'Luddites can't be united on account of the fact that we don't have mobile phones or e-mail addresses. We're an endangered species.'

'But in fact, you *will* be united – at the social event of the year, if not before. Bianca's already talking about her annual *fête champêtre*.'

'Oh, Jesus. The *fête* worse than death, more like. Is it going to be fancy dress again?'

'Kind of. She's going for an all-white theme this year.'

'*Merde.* Do I have to go, Madeleine? I'll feel like an eejit all decked out in white.'

'Yes, you do have to go. I don't want to run the risk of offending Bianca. She's put a lot of work my way.'

'Designed any good websites recently?'

'Sneer at me all you like, arty pants,' said Madeleine with hauteur. 'Branching out into web design was the best thing I ever did. Apart from making Rosa.'

She gazed down the beach towards where her daughter and small playmate were still engrossed in making pictures in the sand. After Rosa had been born, Madeleine had flailed around for a couple of years in career limbo before taking a course in web design. She enjoyed it. It satisfied her creatively, and she was starting to make money from it. But being a technophobe, Daniel didn't understand it. The very idea of web graphics and html was anathema to him, and he had looked at her as if she were as barking as Pilot when she suggested that she design a website for him. 'Images of my paintings on the *internet*?' he'd roared. 'That's a form of artistic necrophilia, Madeleine!' And Madeleine had smoothed his ruffled mane and kissed him and never mentioned it again.

'Rosa's clearly inherited her papa's talent,' Daniel said, regarding his daughter fondly. 'Look at the portrait of Pilot she's made in the sand.'

'How do you know it's Pilot and not some other dog?'

'You can tell by the ears.'

Rosa was utterly absorbed in her artwork. She may have inherited her father's talent, Madeleine thought as she watched her, but she'd inherited her mother's looks. Her friend Paloma had likewise inherited her mother's robust beauty, although there was a look of Jethro about her hazel-flecked eyes, Madeleine saw, as the child looked up from her drawing. She had executed a stick figure of a man in the sand.

'What's the title of your drawing, *ma puce*?' Daniel called over to his daughter.

Rosa looked up, then reflected. 'Its title,' she told him solemnly, 'is *Let Sleeping Dogs Lie* by Rosa Lennox, media: sand and stick.'

'Excellent title, *ma brave*! And what's yours called, Paloma?'

'Mine's called *Welcome Home Daddy*.'

Madeleine smiled at the cherub-faced child, then turned back to Daniel. 'How sweet,' she said. 'He came back just last night.'

'Daddy, Daddy, Daddy! Do it again!'

Paloma and Jethro were playing in the pool. Paloma had come back damp from the Labadou and was now practically waterlogged. The game father and daughter were playing went like this: Paloma would climb up Jethro's back and balance on his shoulders. He would reach up, grab her by the hands and somersault her into the water, whereupon she would dive between his legs, climb back onto his shoulders and the fun would start all over again.

The shrieks were deafening; the poolside was awash, and so many inflatables littered the surface of the water that it resembled a miniature marine park. Tidying the joint was going to be a nightmare. But Dannie's heart swelled big with love as she watched her two most dearly beloveds from the safe haven of her kitchen.

The buzz of the timer told her that the potatoes were done. She drained and rinsed them, then tossed them in some excellent local olive oil and added a dash of red wine vinegar. She was making *salade Niçoise* for supper this evening, with tiny new potatoes and tuna so fresh it still smelled of the sea.

Crossing to the open kitchen window, she called through to Jethro and Paloma. 'Supper will be ready in ten minutes. Paloma, piaffe into the bathroom and rinse out your bathing togs. Jethro, set the teapoy. We'll eat in the garden.'

Dannie took a lemon from the fruit bowl and halved it, and as she squeezed juice over the blanched French beans she cast her mind back to the second time Jethro had made love to her that day. They'd ended up in bed, and that time there had been none of the white-hot urgency that had characterised their earlier coupling. That time Jethro had been infinitely skilful in the way he'd coaxed and teased her to orgasm before allowing himself to come. She loved the authority that her husband brought to bear on their love-making, the way he played her like an instrument – Jethro *owned* her breasts and her ass and her cunt – and when she came with a shudder and an arch of her back, she always felt so vulnerable that she hid her face in the crook of her arm.

Afterwards, they'd lain in silence, hand in hand. She hadn't asked Jethro about the phone call he'd received from Rory earlier, and he hadn't volunteered any information. She'd sensed that if the subject was broached it would lead to a row, and she didn't want the preciousness of their post-coital time marred by bickering. She had resolved not to speak of the matter until Jethro proffered an opening gambit.

A squeal from outside drew Dannie back to the window. 'Get *out* of the pool!' she yelled. 'Paloma – go rinse out your togs at *once*. Jethro, if you don't have that teapoy set in five minutes there'll be hell to pay.'

Jethro hauled first himself, then Paloma out of the pool. The child aimed a kick at his ass, then ran laughing into the house, leaving a trail of glittering droplets on the sandstone flags.

Shaking the wet from his hair, Jethro helped himself to a towel and smiled across at Dannie as she moved onto the terrace and settled herself on a sun lounger. He looked pretty damn hot, she thought as she watched him towel himself dry. Jethro wasn't the handsomest man in the world, but he had an undeniable charisma, and his amber-flecked eyes were extraordinary – they had a quite disarming effect on women who met him for the first time. It made her go all warm inside to think about the first time she had met him. Jethro had been more laid back in those days: he'd worn his hair longer; he'd even been a little overweight. These days he was leaner, rangier, and it wasn't down to exercise or diet, Dannie knew. It was down to stress.

Stepping out of his shorts, Jethro pulled on a robe that he'd left hanging over the back of a garden chair, then reached for his phone.

'Don't,' she begged him. 'Please don't. Can't it wait until after supper, whatever it is?'

'Let me just check this message,' he said. He pressed some digits, then held the phone to his ear as he ambled on bare feet into the kitchen, emerging with table mats and cutlery. Dumping the lot on the table, he listened a little longer, then set the phone down without meeting her eyes.

'Three six nine, the goose drank wine,' sang Paloma, dancing through the double doors. She was carrying Polar, her grubby white teddy bear, and wearing an outsized T-shirt with *Mimi's Remedies* writ large on it. *Mimi's Remedies* was the name of a film that Jethro had directed some years back, in Kilrowan, the little village in Connemara where Dannie hailed from. Every time Jethro worked on a film, he presented Paloma with a souvenir T-shirt, and her wardrobe was now crammed with them.

'Hey sweet pea,' said Jethro. 'Give me a hand setting the teapoy, will you?'

'The monkey chewed tobacco on the streetcar line.' Paloma obligingly followed him into the kitchen, and Dannie heard her gabbling to her dad in her reedy, childish voice. 'Why did the monkey chew tobacco, Dad? Why didn't he smoke it, like Daniel does?'

'Because the monkey was clever. He knew that smoking's bad for you.'

Dannie smiled. She loved to hear Jethro improvise answers to Paloma's queries. No matter how preposterous the question, he always had an answer for her. He was a perfect father, really. Or would be, if he wasn't so feckin' peripatetic.

That was the only fly in the ointment of their relationship. Dannie had spent many sleepless nights wondering what he was up to in LA while she was idling away in this sleepy French backwater, before realising that it actually wasn't worth losing sleep over. Dreamtime was important to Dannie, because she often found that the thorniest problems were resolved in dreams.

Jethro came back onto the terrace bearing plates and the *salade Niçoise*, and Paloma brought up the rear brandishing her favourite salad servers with silly carved cats' heads on. Within minutes the family was sitting round the wooden table and Dannie was dishing out dinner.

'Will you read me my story tonight, Da?' asked Paloma, spearing a cherry tomato. Despite more than three years spent living in France, Paloma's voice still bore strong traces of her Irish accent.

'Of course I will, sweet pea. What's your mom been reading to you while I've been away?'

'She's been making up a story. About Polar.' Polar was sitting beside Paloma, his paws jammed through the wooden slats of the chair to hold him in place.

'Hmm. I don't reckon that I could compete with your mom. I'll tell you a story about Ireland, if you like. About a notorious Irish rake.'

'I don't want a story about a rake,' said Paloma, looking with disdain at a garden rake that had been left leaning against the wall.

'Not that kind of a rake,' said Jethro with a smile. 'A Regency rake. A man called Jack St Ledger. Regency rakes were risk takers and daredevils. And this particular rake was such an über daredevil that he set up a club called the Hellfire Club, where it was rumoured the devil himself appeared—'

'Jethro,' said Dannie, 'how clueless are you? Would the thought not occur to you that this is hardly a fit subject for a bedtime story?'

'I'd like to hear it,' said Paloma, giving her mother a contrary look. 'I like scary stories. And I'd like to know what the devil looked like. Did he have a tail like the one in the cartoon?'

'Yeah. But this particular devil,' said Jethro, 'happened to be a really crap one who was no good at scaring people. In fact, he just made people laugh.'

'Like Casper the Friendly Ghost?'

'Yep.'

'What was his name?'

'Lucy.'

'That's a girl's name!'

'It's short for Lucifer.'

Dannie shot Jethro a look of approval. A crap devil called Lucy would do nicely as the subject of Paloma's bedtime story. But as she raised her glass to take a sip, she found herself wondering how on earth a twenty-first-century Yank like Jethro Palmer was so sussed about something as arcane as the Dublin Hellfire Club.

'Do me a favour, will you, darlin', and refill my glass?' Dannie was sitting cross-legged on the sun lounger, peeling a Satsuma. Judging by the length of time he'd spent in Paloma's bedroom, Jethro had told the child a bedtime story of mythic proportions about Lucy the crap devil.

'With pleasure, ma'am. Shall I fetch us another one?' Jethro upended the bottle into Dannie's wineglass.

'That'd be grand.'

Dannie slid a segment of Satsuma between her lips, relishing the burst of flavour so tangy it almost stung her mouth. Dusk had fallen and the air had grown chilly, but Dannie didn't want to go inside just yet. It was the first time they'd eaten al fresco that year and she wanted to make the most of it, so she'd pulled on a sweater and socks and wrapped herself in a cashmere throw. She loved to spend time in the garden that she worked so hard to maintain. Dannie didn't employ a gardener the way Madeleine did – Dannie loved the sheer physicality of gardening. She loved to get dirt under her nails; loved the smell of fresh earth; loved the satisfying ache of her limbs at the end of a day spent *en pleine air* and loved more than anything the rude exuberance of the plant kingdom. Her garden was presided over by a beneficent, sleepy-eyed Buddha at one end and a smiley Green Tara – Buddha's female counterpart – at the other. Tonight the surface of the pool was smooth as a cabochon sapphire, reflecting the candles that she had lit after dinner.

'How do you know about the Dublin Hellfire Club, by the way?' she asked as she heard him re-emerge from the kitchen.

'They're making a film about it. In Ardmore Studios.'

'Is that the one Rory's working on?' Dannie remembered that Bianca had said something about Rory filming in Ireland.

'The very epic,' said Jethro.

'And it was Rory who rang today?'

'Rory rang, yes.'

From behind her came the soft pop of a cork being drawn, then the sound of wine splashing into Jethro's glass. He moved across the terrace and lowered himself onto the recliner that stood next to hers.

'Why did Rory ring?'

'He rang to ask me a personal favour.'

'And what might that be?'

'The director of *Love Lies Bleeding*—'

'What in God's name is *Love Lies Bleeding*?'

'It's the name of the film Rory's working on.'

'I see. Go on.'

'The director of the film collapsed on set today, with a burst appendix.'

Oh, fuck.

'And they want you to replace him.' She didn't even bother with a question mark.

'Temporarily, yes. Until he's out of hospital. I first

heard about it early this morning, Dannie, via e-mail from the producer. I told them no. Then Rory rang.'

Dannie remained silent.

'I couldn't say no to McDonagh, darlin'. I owe Rory big time. If he hadn't persuaded Neeson and Farrell to get on board, that last film would have sunk without a trace.'

'When might you be flying to Ireland?' she asked in her chilliest voice.

'Day after tomorrow.'

'And when might you be back?'

'Once Marchant's back on his feet. It could take three weeks.'

'So you'll be sleeping in hotel rooms for the foreseeable future?'

'Yes.'

'In that case, Jethro,' said Dannie, setting down her wineglass and rising to her feet with dignity, 'I'm sure you'll not have any objection to sleeping in the spare room tonight.'

Dannie walked through the kitchen and up the stone staircase. She went first to Paloma's room to check that the child was sleeping peacefully before making for the master bedroom. Shutting the door behind her, she stood with her back against it, regarding the portrait that looked back at her from above the bed. Jethro had commissioned a painting from Daniel Lennox not long after they had moved to Saint-Géyroux. He had wanted a likeness of Dannie in the same pose as the one her mother had adopted, many years before, when Daniel had painted her in her house in Connemara. Mother and daughter now hung in the same room, gazing at each other from opposite walls. So similar were they that they could have been mirror images. The only discernible difference between them was that Daniella Senior was rounded with the baby her belly harboured, while Dannie's hands rested against a belly that was flat as an adolescent girl's.

Dannie took a step away from the bedroom door, then turned to face it. In the silence of the cavernous house, the sound of the key turning in the lock sounded like a gun being cocked.

Hostilities had been resumed.

8

'You have new mail,' read the pop-up.

Deirdre ignored it. She was working on her screenplay and it was doing her head in because any time she had to write sex scenes, the only image her mind's eye conjured up was that of Rory and a naked Charlotte Lambert look-alike.

She'd snuck a look at his schedule before he'd taken himself off to Ireland and had discovered that all the scenes with the body double were listed right at the top. It pained her to think of her husband ensconced with some nubile young thing in a bed in Ardmore Studios because a story she'd heard about a very famous actress kept coming into her head. It was said that the actress had once been obliged to shoot a pretty steamy sex scene, one that required full nudity. On viewing the rushes, it was clear to her that penetration had taken place between her co-star and the body double. So when it came to shooting her close-ups, the clever gal had refused to move – with the result that the director hadn't been able to cut in the explicit footage. Deirdre had been appalled to learn that the sex with the stand-in hadn't been simulated, and since then she'd found that any time she watched bed scenes in films, she wondered exactly how far the proceedings had gone. She knew her husband was a rock solid professional and that nothing – nothing, well, *untoward* – would ever occur between him and his on-screen partner, but thinking about it still made her deeply uncomfortable.

Deirdre shook her head and refocused on her screen treatment.

```
'DEE BENEDICT stands looking at a CU photograph
of an ORIENTAL dancer. Her POV turns away to
STEPHEN. STEPHEN autographs an ADMIRER'S cata-
logue, slides a meaningful look back at DEE. We
infer from the look that he is remembering last
night's rampant sex, and as he takes another
glass from the passing waitress's '
```

She deleted 'waitress', then typed 'server's'. Or should it be 'serve-person?'

Oh, *shit!* She couldn't concentrate. She was achieving nothing. Deirdre stood up from her desk and went to the window to distract herself by looking at the view of the ocean. Aoife and Grace were doing callisthenics on the beach, Aoife looking effortlessly graceful, Grace looking as self-important as if she were starring in some Busby Berkeley epic. Deirdre owed it to the girls to spend more time with them: before she knew it, summer would be here and they'd be off at surf camp. Maybe she should leave off writing anything more until she knew for certain that all the body double stuff was in the can? That way she wouldn't be tormenting herself with mental images of skin on skin because all that jazz would be *fait accompli*. And in a couple of months she'd be in France and Rory would fly in to reassure her that he loved her, and her alone. And they'd celebrate by taking a bottle of champagne to bed, and maybe a joint to smoke, and he would make love to her and make her come over and over again, the way only he knew how, and everything would be right with her world once more.

Deirdre stretched and yawned and smiled to herself, remembering, and then decided that yes, the best thing to do would be to put her screenplay on the back burner for a week. She was trying very hard to write something a little darker than the rom com she was so good at, but she wasn't sure that it was working. She was waiting for one of her characters to take her by the hand, as they usually did, and lead her through the tortuous twists and turns of the plot. There was a lot of crap talked about issue-driven or plot-driven scripts, but in Deirdre's experience, screenplays only worked if you engaged with the characters. She refused to write to formula.

Could she afford to take her time? Yes. She had promised her agent that he would have something by the end of the summer, and Deirdre never set herself unrealistic deadlines. Rory being away was a disadvantage – he was such a hands-on dad – but she had Melissa to help her with the kids, and it wasn't as if she had to work nine to five on her screenplay. She could pull out her laptop in the morning after the kids had gone to school, or in the evenings after they'd gone to bed. And once she was in France, she could work in a guilt-free zone. She wouldn't have to worry about not spending enough time with the girls because they'd be in seventh heaven in surf camp, and Bruno would be happy to pootle off to the river every day with whoever she engaged as a nanny.

Wandering back to the computer, she noticed the e-mail icon inviting her to click on it. This latest message had been forwarded from the website for the film production company that she and Rory were thinking about setting up: Jolly Roger Enterprises.

'*A chara,*' she read. *A chara?* Why should somebody writing to Jolly Roger Enterprises want to address her in Irish? And then the penny dropped. When she'd placed the ad for an Irish-speaking nanny in *The Irish Times*, she had inserted the production company's web address in preference to her private e-mail address so that any dodgy mail could be handled by the webmaster constructing the site. Both Rory and Deirdre were extremely circumspect about giving out personal details, for security reasons as much as for reasons of privacy. There had been a rash of kidnap threats to the offspring of Hollywood royalty in recent months, and Deirdre lived in terror of receiving one targeting Bruno or either of the girls.

She returned her attention to the e-mail.

> *A chara*. My name is Greta O'Flaherty. I am a twenty-one-year-old fluent Irish speaker who has had considerable experience as a child-minder. I am the eldest of a family of six, so I have been looking after children from as far back as I can remember, and I am reasonably proficient in the kitchen. Because I am currently studying at the National College of Art and Design in Dublin, I will be available for the entire summer, from mid-June until the end of September, and I can't think of a nicer place to spend the summer months than the south of France! I am genuinely fond of children and can provide excellent references. I also

speak a little French. I would love to be considered for the post as your family's Nani Nua and
very much look forward to hearing from you. *Mise
le meas*, Greta O'Flaherty.'

Deirdre reread the e-mail and smiled. Then she
reached for the phone and speed-dialled a number.

'Rory?' she said when he picked up in Ireland. 'I think
we've found our Nani Nua.'

Greta raised her eyes from her crossword and looked
across the set to where Rory McDonagh was leaning
against a flat, talking on his cell phone. He ran a hand
through his floppy, dirty-blond hair, then switched the
phone off, turned back to his assistant and handed it to
her with a smile. He said something to the girl that made
her laugh, then stretched and yawned before ambling
back towards the vast, rumpled expanse of the four-
poster bed where Greta was sitting demurely with her
legs tucked underneath her.

She'd been sitting there for ages while they lit the
scene, wishing she hadn't left her knitting behind in the
dressing room because she could have finished the
sleeve on the cobalt blue shrug by now. She'd nicked
somebody's *Irish Times* and was desultorily filling in the
Simplex.

Rory flung himself down on the bed beside her.
'How's the crossword going?' he asked.

'It's not,' she told him.

'Give us a go.'

She handed him the pen and the folded newspaper and watched as he started filling in clues on the cryptic crossword. To her amazement, he tore through it in no time at all, leaving hardly any blank spaces. Then he snapped the cap back on the pen, handed it to her and tossed the newspaper casually onto the bed.

'That's amazing!' she said, picking it up. 'It would take me longer than that to do the Simplex!' She looked at the filled-in Crosaire, then looked more closely. 'Arse,' she read. 'Silly billy. Tits. Goody gumdrops. Snot. Quite loud farts.'

Rory gave a debonair shrug. 'Any idiot can fill in a crossword,' he said.

Greta whacked him on the forearm with the paper. 'You had me suckered,' she said with a laugh. 'Janey, my ex-boyfriend would have had conniptions if you'd done that to his crossword. He took it deadly seriously.'

'Silly Billy.'

'Yeah. That's why he's my ex.'

'Not because he was called Janey?'

She shot him a 'you know what I mean' look.

'I know a very famous British actress,' said Rory, lounging back against a bolster, 'who used to spend the entire day doing the *Guardian* crossword. She went to quite extraordinary lengths to complete it – she even rang me in LA once to ask if I knew the answer to a clue.'

'From the UK?'

'Yep.'

'That's extreme.'

Rory raised an eyebrow. 'There was method in her madness. She'd buy a brand new *Guardian* before she got the train to work in the evening – she was appearing in the West End – and she'd sit in First Class surrounded by lofty-looking business chappies who were all labouring over the very same crossword. And then she'd proceed to fill hers in without pausing for thought. And when the train arrived at her station, she'd stand up with panache and drop the paper onto her seat with the filled-in cross-word uppermost. She did this every single evening for the duration of the run. She couldn't get enough of the expressions on the faces of her fellow-commuters. They must have thought she was a member of MENSA.'

'And she really spent the entire day doing the cross-word?'

'Yep.'

'What a weird way to live!'

'Have you not heard the perennial joke about why an actor never looks out of the window in the morning?'

'No.'

'Because an actor needs to have something to do in the afternoon, *mavourneen*.'

This was Greta's third day on *Love Lies Bleeding*, and she and Rory had been getting on fantastically well. She couldn't believe that such a huge star could be so, well, *normal*. No – 'normal' wasn't the right word to describe him – he was *preter*-normal, really. He was laid back, totally without ego, and he had a great sense of humour. He worked hard, was unfailingly polite and had shown Greta astonishing consideration during their nude scenes. On one occasion, when they had been positioned stand-ing by a window, the wardrobe girl had told Rory that he could keep his nether regions covered because they would be obscured by Greta's body. But Rory had just said, 'There's nothing egalitarian about that. If the lady's required to get naked, then it's common courtesy for the gentleman to get naked too.' Rory was an all-round top bloke, and the crew loved him.

Esther had asked her, after her first day on the film, what it had been like to have Rory McDonagh 'make love' to her.

'It's weird,' she told her flatmate. 'I thought I'd be dead morto and self-conscious, but he's a real gent. He makes it easy. We just go for it, then get straight back into our robes and carry on doing the crossword or tell each other silly jokes or flick through mags.'

'You mean he doesn't go off to his star dressing room to spend quality time in splendid isolation?'

'No. He's a sweetheart. He knows that by hanging with me on the set, he'll be putting me at ease. And that makes life tickety-boo for everyone.'

'Does he – well, you know – get *aroused*?'

'No.'

'Do you?'

'Get *real*! No!'

This last denial came a little too pat. While Greta felt no stirrings of arousal while simulating sex with Rory on camera, sometimes at night she would wake from a dream that was highly erotically charged. The faceless protagonist of this recurring dream was almost certainly Rory McDonagh, and Greta knew well that if he wasn't married, she might have harboured, well, *feelings* for him. But she never allowed herself to go there. That particular playground had had an exclusion order slapped on it by her mental Health & Safety professionals. Fire was *so* not a suitable toy.

*

'And – cut!' said Jethro. 'Corinna, you're wrapped. Rory – we'll go for the reverse right away.' The director waited until Greta had pulled her robe on, then he extended a hand and shook hers. 'Thank you kindly, ma'am. Sorry to have to drag you out into the wilds of Wicklow at such an ungodly hour.'

'I don't mind,' Greta told him. 'I'm glad of the extra money, and my body clock loves a challenge.'

It was just six o'clock in the morning of her last day as body double to Charlotte Lambert. It was still dark, and very cold. Barely three days after David Marchant had collapsed with a burst appendix, Jethro Palmer had arrived to assume directorial responsibility over *Love Lies Bleeding*. He was imperturbable, authoritative and incisive, and Rory clearly had a lot of respect for him. On the day that Greta had had to do her most explicit bed scene, Jethro had talked her through it so calmly that her nerves had all but vanished.

Jethro shot a look at his watch, then turned to Rory. 'Give us five to get set up?'

'Sure.'

Rory slid his hands into the pockets of his breeches. His unbuttoned shirt hung loosely around his tanned torso, a strand of hair had escaped from his Regency ponytail and the pupils of his sleepy eyes looked dilated. Greta had seen the glances women crew members snuck at him, and they made her want to laugh. She sometimes wondered how his wife handled the lethal effect he had on the female sex. She probably carried a kosh.

'Jethro! Can you spare a minute?' A deferential PA came scurrying up with paperwork. 'I'm sorry to bother you, but I need authorisation on this ASAP.'

'Excuse me, ma'am,' said Jethro. He gave Greta a courteous smile, then moved away, scanning pages. She could hear him issuing directives in his smooth Southern drawl.

'He is *the* man,' said Rory with manifest admiration. 'Thank Christ he was able to cover for Marchant.' He narrowed his eyes, then looked down at Greta. 'Well. I guess it's *adieu*, little one,' he said.

Greta felt shy suddenly – and not a little sorry to be taking her leave of Rory. 'Goodbye,' she said. 'Thank you for looking after me.'

'Thanks right back at you,' said Rory. He scooped up her hand, then bent his head and kissed the back of her fingers. 'It was my pleasure.'

Feeling even sorrier, Greta disengaged her hand and backed away from him, smiling an awkward smile. Then she heard an 'Ow!' as she turned abruptly and crashed straight into Pete, the gofer who had worked on *Child Harry*. Her elbow knocked into the polystyrene cup he was nursing, sending coffee sluicing everywhere.

'Oh, I'm so *sorry*, Pete!' Pulling a tissue from the pocket of her robe, Greta swiftly set about mopping up the coffee that was soaking into Pete's sleeve. 'What a klutz I am! Oh, shit – you're going to have a big stain on your anorak now!'

'No worries, Greta,' said Pete, shaking drops from his hand and going puce. 'It'll come out in the wash. I, er, I was just on my way to tell you that your driver's been delayed. He had an emergency airport run and he won't be here for another hour.'

'Bummer,' said Greta, continuing her ineffectual mopping. 'Oh well. At least that means I'll get my knitting finished at last.'

'I should be through in fifteen minutes,' came a voice from behind her. 'You can share my car, if you like.'

She turned. Rory was silhouetted against a klieg lamp, his outline dark against the preternaturally white light. *White light! White light!* thought Greta abstractedly. Wasn't that some warning cry in a film she'd seen as a child?

With a relaxed hand, Rory indicated the transport Merc parked on the other side of the field. His driver, Jimmy, was sitting behind the steering wheel, snoozing, a newspaper over his face.

'Are you sure, Rory?' asked Greta, uncertainly. 'I wouldn't want to put you out.'

'Do I look put out?'

She couldn't tell. Because his face was in shadow, his expression was unreadable. 'Well,' she said, 'that's real generous of you. Thanks.'

'You're welcome.'

'Mr McDonagh?' A runner in a puffa jacket approached Rory. 'We're ready for your reverse angle.'

'I'm on my way,' said Rory. It didn't matter that the smile he bestowed on the runner was perfunctory: it still had a visible effect on the girl.

Both women watched as Rory strolled back towards the camera. The band holding his ponytail in place had come loose, and as he reached up to run a hand through his hair, the runner gave a little sigh. 'All men should be made to wear breeches and riding boots,' she said. 'That look is so *hot!*'

'*All* men?' Greta nodded at a sound engineer with builder's bum who was hoisting a boom onto his shoulder.

'OK,' conceded the runner. 'It mightn't sit so well on him. But McDonagh in Regency get-up rocks!'

'If you had an air to that …' remarked Greta with a smile, humming a nondescript little tune as she set off in the direction of the wardrobe truck.

After she'd discarded petticoats and divested herself of her camisole, she sat on the step and watched the sun start to clamber above the dark shoulder of the mountain, sketching a rosy line along the horizon. The last time she'd seen a sunrise had been on a visit to Kilrowan at Christmas, when she'd walked home in the early hours of the morning after a party. Nothing could beat a Connemara sunrise.

Red sky at night – shepherd's delight.
Red sky in the morning – shepherd's warning.

Greta remembered the weather forecast she'd listened to earlier that day, in the Merc on the way out to location. It was weird, she thought as she gazed at the horizon, really pretty damn weird, that such a pretty shade of pink should be the presager of seriously stormy weather.

Some time later, Greta had said goodbye and thank you to the girls in make-up and wardrobe, and she and Rory were moving across the field to where his car was waiting for him.

Jimmy the driver shut the doors behind them, and a moment later they were gliding down a track that led to an open five-bar gate. 'Where to?' asked Jimmy.

Greta assumed that the question was aimed at her, since Rory's driver would surely know that his ride was staying at the Clarence Hotel. 'I'm off the South Circular,' she told him, 'near the canal.'

Rory gave her an interested look. 'The South Circular?

The Meridian Grill was an old haunt of mine, near there. Is it still going?' he asked.

'Yes.'

The Meridian Grill wasn't far from Greta's flat, but she had never eaten there. It was a greasy spoon frequented mainly by insomniac alcoholics and prostitutes on their tea breaks, and it stayed open all night.

'I've just realised I'm ravenous,' said Rory. 'It'll still be open, won't it?'

'It's worth a try,' said Jimmy, shifting down a gear and turning left onto the road that would take them to Dublin. 'And if it ain't, there's a Starbucks just down the road.'

'Not the same thing,' said Rory. 'Dump me at the Meridian, then call it a day, Jimmy. I'll make my own way back to the hotel.'

'I'd be happy to wait for you if you like.'

'Jesus! Get real, man,' said Rory. 'You don't think I'm the kind of jerk who'd keep a driver waiting outside a caff that's only fifteen minutes' walk from where I'm staying?' He leaned back against the smooth leather upholstery, then turned to Greta. 'May I buy you breakfast?' he asked her.

'In the Meridian?'

'Yes.'

'Wouldn't you rather have breakfast in the Clarence?' she asked, puzzled by his choice of eatery.

'I love the Meridian. I love its disreputableness.' Disreputable was the perfect word to describe the Meridian, Greta thought. 'The last time I ended up there was with David Lawless, after we'd gone on a bender.'

'Well, sure. I'd love to join you! Thanks a million.'

She was on the verge of asking him about the bender – she couldn't imagine theatre royalty such as the renowned director David Lawless sitting hung over in the Meridian – then reminded herself just in time that personal questions were off the agenda. The embargo she'd been issued with when she accepted the job had remained firmly in place. The only thing Rory had let slip about his family life was that his wife wrote screenplays and that one of his daughters had been named Aoife, after the film star Eva Lavery.

Jimmy had switched the radio on. MOR music faded out and then the voice of the early morning DJ jangled in her ears. 'It's time for all the showbiz gossip!' he announced cheerfully. 'In LA last night the red carpet was unrolled for a star-studded cast. Attending the première of—'

'Find something else, Jimmy, would ya?' said Rory. 'That wank-speak does my head in.'

'Sure,' said the driver equably, aiming the remote. 'What do you want?'

'Something that's right for this hour of the morning. Spillane.'

'Coming up.'

'D'you know any of Davy Spillane's stuff?' asked Rory, turning to Greta.

She shook her head; she'd never heard of Davy Spillane.

'Before your time,' said Rory with a smile. 'You're in for a treat.'

Conjecturing, Greta decided that jazz would be Rory's thing. But she'd got it wrong. When the beat of a bodhrán and the plaintive sound of uilleann pipes slid over the speakers, Greta found herself thinking that Rory McDonagh was full of surprises.

Half an hour later, Jimmy let them off outside the Meridian. The lights were on inside the café, but the sign on the door read 'Closed'.

'Bummer,' said Rory, peering through the glass panel on the door. 'We must just have missed her.'

'Missed who?'

'Maureen Reilly. She runs the joint. There she is now.'

Rory tapped on the glass, and Greta saw the shadowy figure of a woman move to the door.

'We're closed,' the woman mouthed through the glass panel, and then a big smile spread across her face and the door swung open. 'Well, if it isn't Rory McDonagh!' said Maureen Reilly, standing centre stage in the doorway with her arms akimbo. She reminded Greta of an older, heavier version of Rizzo in *Grease*. 'Howrya, love? It's been a long time since I last seen you! Funny, I was just talking about you the other day. My granddaughter tells me you're Torso of the Year in *Heat* magazine. How's it feel to be a Hollywood hotshot?'

'Disadvantaged. You can't get decent bacon butties in Hollywood for love nor money,' Rory told her, depositing a big kiss on her cheek. 'If I rolled up outside the poshest hotel in Tinseltown at an ungodly hour of the morning looking for a bacon butty, they wouldn't be able to rustle one up. Not even if I offered them an obscene amount of money.'

Maureen narrowed her eyes at him and raised a painted brow. 'I know you, you chancer,' she said. 'And you don't

113

need to offer me an obscene amount of money. All I want is another one of those.' She pointed to her other cheek, and Rory obliged with an even bigger smacker. 'I'm closed,' she told him, 'so I can't let yiz in. But I'll see what I can do fer yiz.'

Maureen shut the door and Greta saw her waddle off in the direction of what was presumably the kitchen.

'She hasn't changed at all,' Rory said. 'Stuck in a time warp. Even the lipstick's the same.'

'Did you use to come here a lot?' asked Greta.

'Yeah. We'd come here after a session, have a big fry-up, then meander on down to the quays to an early house for a hair of the dog. Jesus! I can't believe I'm waxing nostalgic! I must sound like a veritable old.' He smiled down at her. 'What age are you, Corinna?'

'Twenty-one.'

'Same age as my inamorata when I first met her,' he observed as he fished a ringing mobile from his pocket and inspected the screen. 'Hey, Francine,' he said into the mouthpiece. He listened for several moments, then said, 'No, that's cool. I'll do it as a favour to you.' A smile. 'E-mail it to me and I'll get it off to you this afternoon.' Rory slid the phone back in his pocket, then turned to Greta. 'Have you ever heard of something called the Proust Questionnaire?' he asked. 'My PR person just asked me to fill it in.'

'The Proust Questionnaire? Not the one that appears on the back page of *Vanity Fair*?'

'Yeah. That's the one.'

'Wow! I *love* the Proust Questionnaire. It's the first thing I turn to!' Greta started rummaging in her tote bag, then with a flourish, she pulled out a dog-eared copy of

Vanity Fair. 'Look! I have it here.'

'Give us a go,' said Rory, reaching for the magazine. 'Who's answered the questions for them this month?'

'Colleen, the writer.'

'Colleen?' A smile started to play around Rory's mouth. 'No shit! Let's see what she has to say.' Leaning against the doorjamb, he opened the magazine at the last page. 'Great pic,' he observed.

The photograph on the top left-hand corner showed Colleen in a characteristic pose. The author was gazing out to sea with a melancholy smile playing around her beautiful, bee-stung mouth, strands of wild red hair whipping around her face.

Rory cleared his throat and adopted a bogus brogue. '"Colleen and her partner Margot d'Arcy live cut off from the rest of the world on an island off the west coast of Connemara, Ireland"', he read. '"Colleen has been described as the female sex's answer to James Joyce. Her lyrical, uninhibited style" – blah blah blah. Christ. I wonder what myth I should dream up for myself.' He looked pensive. 'How about: "Rory McDonagh loves to dance in the free-form style of Isadora Duncan. Every morning he dons a robe of diaphanous silk and joins in singing with the dawn chorus as he trips the light fantastic along the sand in front of his LA beach house."'

Greta dimpled up at him. 'I get the feeling that you're not going to take the Proust Questionnaire as seriously as the man himself intended.'

'Damn right. Proust was a right solipsistic little fucker.'

'What's solipsistic mean?'

'When you believe yourself to be the centre of the universe. Like Colleen. Let's see ... random sample question.

"What do you regard as the lowest depth of misery?" '

Greta thought about it. 'Being made to read the complete works of Colleen,' she said.

'Right answer. "Who is your favourite hero in real life?" '

'That's easy. Daniel Lennox, the artist. I am a complete and utter fan. He was giving a talk here in Dublin last week, and—'

'Is that a fact? Daniel's—'

But Rory never got to tell her that Daniel Lennox was his neighbour in a small village in the south of France, because the door to the Meridian Grill opened abruptly and Maureen was revealed in all her bouffant-haired glory. Greta could have sworn that she'd reapplied her lipstick in the brief space of time she'd been gone.

'Look at you, sex pot!' said Rory admiringly. 'Not a grey hair to be seen. What's kept you so young-looking, Maureen Reilly?'

She hit him a dig on his forearm. 'Don't think I'm going to fall for your smooth talk, Mister McDonagh. Now,' she said, handing over a tin foil package. 'Here's two bacon butties for the pair of yiz.'

'You're a star turn,' said Rory. 'How much do I owe you?'

'You owe me a signed photograph for me granddaughter,' said Maureen.

'I'll put one in the post with pleasure. What's her name?'

'Cristal. Me daughter named her after the champagne.'

'I'll send her a bottle along with the photo.'

'Don't be wasting your good money. And next time, don't be calling into me and annoying me way after

116

closing time.' But Maureen looked anything but annoyed as Rory scooped up her hand and kissed the back of it, just as he'd kissed Greta's hand earlier. 'Get away out of that,' she said, 'up to your old tricks.'

'Hell, I'm an old dog, *mavourneen*. I haven't been taught any new ones.' Rory gave Maureen a roguish look as she turned away with a switch of her hip and a smile and shut the café door behind her.

Rory looked down at Greta. 'Let's go sit by the canal,' he said. 'And you can advise me on how to fill in that poxy questionnaire.'

They strolled along the tow path, unwrapping their butties and making small-talk. It felt good to take their ease on the bank of the canal, watching commuters caught up in snarled traffic, pedestrians power walking their way to work and fitness freaks early-morning jogging under the dusty sycamores. Choosing a bench adjacent to where a flotilla of swans had moored themselves, they polished off their breakfast. The sun was squinting through cloud now, and Greta felt the urge to greet it by shrugging off her jacket. She regretted it the moment she'd slung the garment over the back of the bench. Underneath she was wearing a thin cotton T-shirt and for some reason she felt more naked than she had done last week, when she'd peeled off a nightdress on the bedroom set in Ardmore Studios.

'Bloody good, aren't they?' said Rory, wiping his mouth with the back of his hand. 'I love big butties.'

Greta laughed and bit into hers, wondering what Esther would say if she could see her now, sitting alongside one of the biggest stars in the Hollywood firmament, shooting the breeze and eating bacon butties.

A girl in vest and white shorts gave Rory a curious look as she jogged past them, as if she might have met him somewhere before and couldn't remember where. Rory winked at her and the girl jogged on, looking even more uncertain.

'What if someone recognises you?' Greta asked him. 'Paparazzi, or a crazed fan or someone?'

'Nobody will recognise me,' he said. 'No one is going to look at a bloke eating a butty on a public bench and think: Oh look – there's that film star what's-his-name. Anyway, they're all too caught up in their own business. Just look around you.' He nodded at a girl who was sitting in the passenger seat of a Volvo stuck in gridlock on the other side of the canal. The girl was wearing a school uniform and gazing dreamily through the window at the swans. 'What d'you imagine she's thinking?' Rory asked.

Greta took a closer look. On the rear shelf of the Volvo was a schoolbag with a pair of ballet shoes hanging from the strap by their ribbons. 'She's thinking,' said Greta, 'that one day she will dance in a production of *Swan Lake* and be the most fêted ballerina in the world. And she's picturing herself at the curtain call, taking curtsey after curtsey with a massive bouquet of white roses in her arms, and she's being showered with white rose petals, and there's a gorgeous man in black tie and DJ waiting for her in the wings with more roses.'

Rory looked at her and smiled. 'That's *exactly* what she's thinking,' he said.

Greta smiled back at him, then looked back across the canal to where a bloke in a suit was sitting listlessly behind the wheel of his Ford Mondeo. A gleaming motorbike had just pulled up alongside the Mondeo and was revving its engine ostentatiously, as if to attract attention. It worked. The listless bloke turned to stare at the leather-clad biker. 'What's *he* thinking?' Greta asked Rory.

'He's thinking,' he said, 'that he should trade in his Mondeo for a Harley and ditch the suit for a set of leathers. Then he'll get a rude tattoo, tell his boss to stick his job up his arse and set off round the world with a girl on his pillion.'

'That's *exactly* what he's thinking,' said Greta. 'Aren't you clever?'

'What about her?' The woman Rory pointed at was waiting by a bus stop, engrossed in Colleen's latest tome.

'She's really reading chick lit,' said Greta, 'but because she doesn't want anyone to know, she's taken the dust jacket off Colleen's book and wrapped it round her girly novel. And she doesn't really need those glasses – she's just wearing them because she thinks they make her look intellectual.'

'Talking of things intellectual …' Rory reached for the magazine that lay on the bench between them, flicked it open at the picture of Colleen and looked at Greta gravely. 'You're in for a Proustian grilling,' he said. 'First question: "What is your principal defect?" Colleen says hers is her capacity for suffering.'

'Mine is my capacity for crying at sentimental movies,' said Greta.

'So you're a sentimentalist? Did you ever see a movie called *Mimi's Remedies*?'

'Yes.'

'Did it make you cry?'

'Yes.'

'Me too,' said Rory.

'It was the last movie Eva Lavery made before she died, wasn't it?'

'Yes. It was.'

'She was a brilliant actress. I read somewhere that you were a good friend of hers.'

'I was a very good friend of hers.'

'Did you see the big feature about her in last Saturday's *Irish Times*?'

'No.'

'I have it at home. You can have it, if you like.'

'Thanks. I'd really appreciate that.' He looked thoughtful for a moment, shook his head as if setting a memory adrift, then returned his attention to the Proust Questionnaire. '"Who are your favourite prose writers?" Hmm. Mine has to be Pixie Pirelli.'

'Pixie Pirelli?' said Greta. 'But she's a chick lit writer!'

'I know,' said Rory. 'She's also a mate of mine, so that makes her my favourite writer.'

'Really? She's *my* favourite of all time, too! What's she like?'

Rory shrugged. 'She lives up to her name.'

'What do you mean?'

'She's away with the fairies. Which brings us neatly to our next question. "Who is your favourite hero of fiction?" Mine's Dennis the Menace. Who's yours?'

'Um. I know I should say Mr Rochester or Heathcliff or some such, but I'm gonna go for the lowbrow option and say Alex in Pixie Pirelli's *Hard to Choos.*'

'Interesting choice. Why him?'

'He's just so drop-dead sexy.'

'I'm very glad to hear it,' said Rory, with a bland smile. 'I'm all set to play him in the film version.'

'Oh! You'd be *perfect* casting!' said Greta, then felt herself blush scarlet as she realised the implication of what she'd just said. 'What's the next question?'

'"What's your most marked characteristic?"' he asked.

Greta thought about it. 'I'm too gullible,' she said.

'How so?'

'I tend to think the best of everyone. I always assume that people are trustworthy and, well, *nice*. You could introduce me to my worst feckin' enemy and I'd shake hands and smile and be like, "Please *do* borrow all my money with pleasure, chicken!"'

'I think,' said Rory, 'that that is a rather endearing character trait.'

'It's kinda dangerous. My mam loves to tell me a story about it.' Greta copped herself on. The last thing a megastar like Rory McDonagh would want to listen to were her childhood reminiscences. 'But I won't bore you with it.'

'You're not boring me. I'd like to hear it.'

'Really?'

'Really.'

'Well, she told me that when I first saw an open fire — when I was just a toddler — I went teetering towards it with my arms outstretched and a big welcoming smile on my face. Mam scooped me out of harm's way at the last moment.'

'You were going to embrace it?'

'Yes, I was.' There was something disconcerting about Rory's expression. Greta dropped her eyes. 'Any more questions?' she asked with an attempt at nonchalance.

Rory resumed his scrutiny of the questionnaire. '"How would you like to die?"' he read. 'How would *I* like to die?'

He shut the magazine and leaned against the back of the bench, stretching an arm along its length. 'How about while sitting on a canal bank eating bacon butties in the company of a pretty girl?'

Greta laughed. 'Your wish could very well be my command,' she said. 'I just happen to have a luger handy. Get ready to meet your maker, buster.'

Rory laughed right back at her.

'What are you laughing at?'

'I love the idea of a girly girl like you packing a pistol!'

'Hey!' she said indignantly. 'I could be a member of the SAS for all you know. Like her.' Greta indicated a cross-faced little old lady who was dragging her pug dog along the tow-path. 'Yo, sister!' she called after her, but there was no reaction from the superannuated dog-walker. 'She heard that, you know,' Greta told Rory. 'But she knows better than to acknowledge our sisterhood in public. She's just pretending to be deaf.'

Rory raised an eyebrow at her. 'You've got nearly as active an imagination as Pixie Pirelli, Greta, haven't you?'

He'd called her Greta, not Corinna. 'Hey!' she said. 'How did you find out my name?'

'I heard Pete call you that earlier, and it rang a bell. Someone mentioned the name Greta to me recently, but I can't remember who or in what context. Funny, isn't it, when an unusual name crops up twice in the same week?'

'It's not that unusual,' said Greta. 'The girl in the flat next door to me's called Fuchsia – I think that's a much more unusual name than – oh, *shit*.'

'What's up?'

'I've just remembered I've no key – I left a message on my flatmate's phone asking her to be there to let me

in, but she's probably left for work by now. Shit shit *shit*.'
Greta fished in her bag for her phone. The message icon
was displayed and she guessed Esther had been trying in
vain to reach her. 'Excuse me,' she told Rory as her thumbs
twinkled over the keypad. 'I just hope she's still – Esther!
Hi! Are you still at home?'

Esther's voice on the phone sounded pissed off. 'Yeah.
And I should be out of here by now. Why aren't you picking up messages?'

'Sorry,' said Greta. 'I didn't hear my phone go off.'

'I can't hang about here any longer, Greta. I'm gonna
have to leave the key in Brannigan's.'

Brannigan's was the newsagents down the road from
their flat. Greta and Esther had never had any scruples
about leaving their spare key with old Mr Brannigan, but
since his son had taken over the business, they rarely re-
sorted to doing that. Brannigan Junior was a narky fecker.

Greta shot a look at her watch. 'OK. I'll be home in
five minutes. See you!'

'I'll be gone. Will you cook something tonight, Greta?
I've yoga after work.'

'Sure.'

'You're gonna have to do a shop. There's nothing in the
fridge except blue-mouldy cheese and the champagne that
kid's mother gave you.'

'All right. Um, Esther?'

'*What?*'

Greta had wanted to ask her cousin if she'd recorded
the arts programme she was anxious not to miss – the
one that was broadcast at an ungodly hour of the morning – but Esther's tone made her change her mind.
'Nothing,' she said.

'Oh, fuck fuck *fuck*,' said a stressed-out Esther. 'There's the eight o'clock news. I'm outta here. See you later.'

The line went dead and Greta put the phone back in her bag. Rory was lobbing bits of bread into the canal for the swans. The rhythmic gesture reminded her of the way the first boy she'd idolised had skimmed pebbles on a far-away beach, in a faraway time. There were pale gold hairs on Rory's forearm and there was a white band on the third finger of his left hand, where his wedding ring had been. The continuity girl was always running after him on set, reminding him to take it off. On one occasion the camera had panned in on his hand as it had travelled along her thigh, and she remembered how—

'I'd better make tracks!' she said, jumping up as the last crust of bread hit the surface of the water.

Rory looked up at her. His eyes were greener than she'd ever seen them. 'I'll come with you since it's on my way – pick up that *Irish Times* piece on Eva Lavery.'

He got to his feet and took her jacket from where she'd hung it over the back of the bench. As he helped her into it, a finger brushed the side of her neck, the palm of his hand made fleeting contact with the small of her back. He reached for his own coat and slung it over his shoulder, then paused, looked around. Something had clearly caught his attention.

'What is it?' Greta asked him, following the direction of his gaze.

A tramp was lying slumped in a sleeping bag on a bench a little farther down the tow-path. A dog sat on the ground beside him and, as Rory approached, the mongrel's tail moved against the ground. Greta watched as Rory slid a hundred euro note from his jeans pocket and tucked it into the greasy sleeping bag. He said something in a low voice, then scratched the dog's ear before moving back to where Greta was standing with one leg wound a little defensively around the other.

'What a Good Samaritan thing to do,' she said.

He shrugged. 'It's called spreading a little happiness.'

The first drops of rain began to plop out of the sky as they left the tow-path, and as the rain got heavier, they started to run. Rory spread his coat above their heads and Greta clutched his arm as they pelted towards the South Circular, finally making it to Brannigan's. They tumbled in through the door of the shop, dripping wet and laughing.

Brannigan Junior eyed them suspiciously as he reached under the counter and produced her key ring. He wore the kind of expression that told you he hated seeing other people having fun. 'Your flatmate left this for you,' he said.

'Thanks so much.' Greta took it from him and hooked it onto her finger. 'I promise it won't happen again.'

'It's a big responsibility,' grumbled Brannigan. 'What if—'

But Greta didn't wait to hear 'what if'. She turned and made for the door. As they passed the magazine stand, something caught her eye. 'Oh look, Rory,' she said excitedly, 'there you are, on the cover of *Heat*! 'Torso of the Year So Far'!'

'Arse of the year so far, more like,' said Rory, taking her hand and pulling her out of the shop. As the door shut behind Greta, she saw Brannigan Junior lumber towards the magazine stand and she knew that it would soon be all over the neighbourhood that Rory McDonagh had bestowed the honour of his presence on Brannigan's newsagents off the South Circular Road in Dublin's pre-mière flatland district.

Next door to Brannigan's was a flower shop, Eros. Greta twinkled her fingers at Laura, the proprietor, then made a swoony face as she got a load of the display in the window. 'Oh! Aren't they just gorgeous!' she said. 'Laura does the most amazing—' but her song of praise to Laura was interrupted by the sound of a phone going off.

'Excuse me,' said Rory, checking out the display. 'I'd better take this. It's Jethro.'

'No worries. I'll go on up and stick the kettle on.' She pointed. 'That's my door,' she told him. 'I'll leave it on the latch. I'm on the second floor, first on the right.'

Greta opened her front door, snibbed the lock, then took the stairs two at a time and let herself into the flat. She washed the bacon butty smell off her hands in the bathroom, then stuck her head around the sitting room door to check that the joint was tidy. Janey! Just as well she had – a load of Esther's underwear was heaped on a radiator. She scooped up the offending items, swung into her cousin's bedroom and stuffed them in a drawer. Her image in the mirror over the chest of drawers looked back at her and she leaned in to fluff her hair a bit and check for mascara smudges.

In the kitchen, she filled the kettle, fetched mugs from the press, then moved to the fridge to get milk. Uh oh. She'd forgotten Esther's adjuration to stock up. The fridge was barer than Mother Hubbard's cupboard. But there, on the bottom shelf, was the bottle of champagne that Anita had given her on her last day of filming on *Child Harry*. Feck it, Greta thought recklessly. They'd drunk enough tea on location this morning. They deserved a treat.

As she peeled away the foil from the neck of the bottle, she heard the familiar creak of the front door. There came a footfall in the corridor, a knock to the door of the kitchen, and then Rory was in the room, a bouquet of creamy roses in his arms.

'These are for you,' he said, handing her the flowers.

They were Vendellas, she knew, probably the most expensive blooms in the shop. There must have been two dozen of them.

'Oh!' she said. 'Thank you!' And then, because she couldn't think of anything else to say, she added, stupidly, 'There's a card, too!'

There was no way she could access the card with a bottle of champagne in one hand and a massive bouquet in the other. 'Um – will you do this?' she asked Rory. 'There's no milk for the tea, so I thought we might as well crack open a bottle instead.' She handed him the bottle and started to pick at the knot on the ribbon attaching the card to the cellophane. Having finally succeeded in detaching the little envelope, she pulled it open and extracted a rectangle of cream vellum. It bore the legend:

'To 'Corinna'. Thanks for some of the best vicarious sex I've ever had. XXX'

A small smile curved her mouth.

Rory was dexterously loosening the wire cage that held the cork in place. His eyes met hers as he discarded it. Then he wound his fingers around the neck of the bottle.

A plume of vapour escaped as the cork came away with a sound like a sigh.

9

'Deirdre?'

It was her agent, Blake Parker, on the phone.

'What's up, Blake?'

'The shit has hit the proverbial. Mira Grant has broken her leg.'

'Oh, no. Oh, *no!*'

''Fraid so. Ironic, isn't it? Being the first day of shooting, "break a leg" was probably the last adjuration she heard before she went on set.' Blake paused, presumably to allow Deirdre an opportunity to laugh at his little joke. She didn't oblige. 'You know what this means?' he asked.

Of course Deirdre knew what this meant. It meant more rewrites on *Gold Diggers*. Mira Grant played Audrey Caswell, one of the most popular characters in the series, and Deirdre had been responsible for writing six of the episodes in which the actress featured heavily.

'How did it happen?'

'She tripped over a cable. Some luckless spark will lose his job over it.'

Deirdre slumped. 'Do they want to write her out?'

'No. She's to be confined to a wheelchair. Get your laptop out, baby. You're going to have to make those fingers bleed.'

'You're telling me that all her scenes will have to be

rewritten? Made wheelchair friendly?'

'Got it in one.'

'No can do, Blake.'

'Sorry, babe. Must can do. I have your contract here in front of me.'

'I'm contractually obligated?'

'Yup.'

'Hell and *death*!' Deirdre felt like banging her head off her desk. '*Why* did this have to happen to me now, with Rory away?'

'You have a nanny, don't you?'

'Yes, but I have *three kids*, Blake. Three kids plus deadline equals nightmare. My nanny isn't Wonder Woman.'

'Hire a second nanny.'

'Ha! If only it was that easy.'

'I'm sorry, babe,' said Blake before adroitly changing the subject. 'You'd better think about hiring a wheelchair, too.'

'A wheelchair? Why?'

'You're going to need to do some research – find out how it feels to be wheelchair bound. As we speak, the stage carpenters are constructing ramps all over the back lot, and Mira's practising whizzing up and down them. She's determined that she's going to be the most famous actress confined to a wheelchair since Joan Crawford in *Whatever Happened to Baby Jane*? Wanna know her latest diva demand?'

'Oh, God. What is it?'

'You're gonna have to make the wheelchair a baby blue one.'

'Baby blue? Why?'

'She wants it to match her eyes,' said Blake. 'Bye, babe.'

Deirdre put the phone down, wanting to cry. She had been so *glad* to see the back of *Gold* fucking *Diggers*, and now it had been returned to her like something clambering out of the cellar in a horror film. How Sod's bloody Law was it that this should happen when Rory wasn't around? As a lone parent she'd have to work flat out, and so would poor Melissa. But Deirdre couldn't expect her nanny to be in three places at once – she'd have to organise interviews to get someone else on board, and she *hated* interviewing staff. Hell's teeth, there was nothing else for it. She'd phone the agency that – wait! No. She'd phone Nani Nua in Ireland, see if she could take time off college to fly out to LA. Accessing the organiser facility on her laptop, Deirdre picked up the phone and punched in the number that Greta O'Flaherty had sent in her e-mail.

'*Slán.*'

'Um, hello – is that Greta?'

'It is. Who's this?'

'Greta – hello. It's Deirdre O'Dare here.'

'Deirdre O' – oh! *Deirdre!* Hello! How lovely to actually talk to you at last!'

Deirdre could hear the smile in the girl's voice. She smiled back: she hadn't heard a Connemara brogue in yonks. 'I'm really sorry I haven't phoned before,' she said. 'I tend to do everything via e-mail these days, but you're absolutely right – it *is* good to talk. Oh, jeepers – I sound like an ad for that telephone company.'

'No, you don't sound like an ad at all. You sound as if you really mean it, and most ads don't.'

Deirdre laughed. 'Thanks!'

'So what can I do for you, Deirdre?'

'I was wondering if there was any way you could help me out. Something's come up, and I could do with an extra pair of hands here in LA.'

'When?'

'Now.'

'Oh, Deirdre, I'm so sorry. I can't. I just can't. I've my end of year show coming up, you see, and—'

'No worries, no worries! I thought it would be worth a try, that's all. I'll be able to find someone here, no problem. There are masses of agencies – that's how I got my current girl, Melissa.'

'The one I'll be replacing?'

'Yes. I was lucky. I've heard some horror stories recently about kidnap gangs infiltrating agencies.'

'Oh. Listen, Deirdre – I hope you don't think I'm being forward, but … can I make a suggestion?' asked Greta.

'Please do.'

'Um, are your parents still alive?'

'Yes. They live in Wicklow.'

'And might either of them be able to fly over for a time to help you out? I hope I'm not interfering – please tell me to get off your case if I am – but there's often nobody better than a doting grandma when you're stuck for someone to care for your wains.'

Deirdre thought for a moment. This solution was so blindingly obvious that she wondered how she hadn't worked it out for herself. 'Greta, that's an inspired idea. Just inspired! I'll put a call in to my mother right away. She'd be thrilled to have the chance to spend quality time with the kids, I know she would. She hasn't seen them for nearly a year.'

'And she'll be glad of the chance to help you out, I'm sure. The best mammies always are. I'm just sorry that I can't be of more help to you.'

'You *have* been of help. That's the soundest advice I could have got. Thanks so much, Greta.'

'You're welcome.'

There was a pause. Deirdre would have loved to have stayed longer on the phone, shooting the breeze with her Nani Nua, finding out all about her, but there were other phone calls to be made – urgent ones. 'I'll be in touch before we head for France, Greta. I'm really looking forward to meeting you.'

'Likewise. Good luck, Deirdre.'

'Goodbye, Greta.'

Deirdre put the phone down and thought for a moment. Today, Monday, was the day her mother worked in a charity shop: she'd leave it until later to phone her. But there was another phone call she had to make. She needed to make contact with a wheelchair supplier so that she could research just how difficult it was going to be getting Mira up and down that cantilevered staircase in her plywood mansion on the back lot. As she punched in the number for Directory Enquiries, Deirdre gave a mirthless smile. She'd have them send her a chestnut coloured wheelchair, to match *her* eyes.

Deirdre's mother did fly over from Ireland to help out, and as Greta had predicted, she was glad to. But even with three pairs of hands on board, keeping the McDonagh-O'Dare household shipshape was tough going. Deirdre was stressed, she was knackered, she missed Rory and she hated *Gold Diggers* worse than ever. But finally, finally, the six episodes were ready. Blake was happy, Mira Grant was happy and the money men were happy. It was just as well. Those rewrites took her nearly three months.

*

From: Sam Newman
Date: 18 June 2006 15:37
To: Madeleine Lennox
Subject: French leave

Hey, beloved Auntie –

Hope all's well with you and good ol' Uncle Dan? Thanks for the invite. I'd be glad to spend summer in Saint-Géyroux, licking my wounds and taking photographs. Yes, I know you loved Perdita and, yes, I know it's sad it's all over, but when irreconcilable differences and all that crap crops up, what's a man to do?

Arriving tomorrow: it would be jolly sporting of Uncle Dan if he could pick me up from Gignac on the Harley. Cannot wait to feel the wind on my face. Dublin sucks.

Your affectionate nephew,
Sam

'Yo, beautiful!' Sam Newman strolled through the door of the kitchen in number 1 rue des Artistes and hooked his camera case over the back of a chair before taking

Madeleine in his arms and bear hugging her.

'Sam!' exclaimed Madeleine. 'Oh, it's so lovely to see you! Big hugs!'

'How goes it, Auntie?' he said, plonking a kiss on her cheek.

She gave him a dig. 'Don't *call* me that! You know I hate it.'

Sam set her down and regarded her through narrow blue eyes. 'You look gorgeous,' he said. 'You look Frencher than ever.'

'And you look more like Brad Pitt than ever.'

'Brad Pitt is *ancient*!'

'I mean a younger version, of course,' she amended. 'How was your flight?'

'Dublin to London was crap. London to Montpellier was just peachy.'

'How so?'

'I flirted with the flight attendant. She was a Sienna Miller look-alike.'

'So you're as incorrigible as ever.'

'I'm a little out of practice, but I guess it's like riding a bicycle. I'll segue back into things.'

'What are you segueing back into?' Daniel walked into the kitchen, unzipping his leather jacket. He shrugged it off, slung it over a chair and set a carrier bag on the table.

'I'm segueing back into flirt mode, now that I'm a free man again.'

'Well you can lay off flirting with my missus,' said Daniel, taking a couple of bottles of red wine from the bag and examining the labels.

'How can I lay off flirting with Madeleine? I've

always flirted with my auntie, and she'll be perfect material to practise on.'

'Practise away,' Madeleine told him with a provocative smile.

'Thanks for the wine,' said Daniel.

'I know it's a bit coals to Newcastle, but there was an in-flight promotion on, and that girl was very persuasive.' Sam broke a chunk off the baguette that was lying on the table and bit into it. 'What's for dinner?' he asked. 'I'm starving.'

'Daniel's going to do omelettes.'

'*Daniel's* cooking?'

'I'll have you know I do a pretty mean omelette,' said Daniel, sliding the bottles into the wine rack. 'The secret is to add a little cold butter and a teaspoon of water to the eggs.'

Sam raised an amused eyebrow. 'Well, well. You've brought him to heel beautifully, Madeleine.'

'I can still bite,' Daniel warned his nephew.

'Sit down,' Madeleine told Sam, helping herself to an apple from the fruit bowl, 'and tell us all. How long are you staying, for starters?'

'That depends on you two, really. How long are you prepared to have me?'

'You know you can stay for as long as you like,' Madeleine told him, '*mi casa es su casa* and all that jazz.'

'In that case, I might take you up on your very generous offer and stay for some time. Is the old airing cupboard still a dark room, or has it been changed back into an airing cupboard since I was last here?'

'It's still a dark room,' said Madeleine.

'Cracking.'

'I'd the feeling you'd do a Terminator on us and be back,' she added.

'I'll get started tomorrow,' said Sam. 'I've some stock to develop.'

'So you're not here just for the holiday?' asked Madeleine.

'Damn right I'm not. I couldn't come to the Languedoc and *not* take photographs.'

'The first thing he did when he got off the bus in Gignac was take out his camera,' said Daniel. 'And he made me stop at the Pont du Diable so that he could get a shot of cloud formation.'

'It was knock-out. You just don't get the same quality of light anywhere else in France. No wonder all those froggy painters migrated south, fleeing from cities.'

'How is Dublin these days?'

Sam shrugged. 'Poxy. That city has disappeared up its own ass.' He looked down at his fingers, picked at a cuticle. 'Of course, another reason I don't want to have to go back there any time soon is that I run the risk of bumping into Perdie.'

Madeleine sat up on the long refectory table that ran most of the length of the big kitchen and bit into her apple. 'What happened, Sam? I always thought the two of you were so good together.'

'It was the thorny issue that's responsible for a lot of good relationships crashing and burning,' he told her.

'And that is?'

'She thought it was time for us to have a baby, and I didn't.'

'I see,' said Madeleine. 'That's sad.'

'Yes,' said Sam. 'It is.'

'Is it because you're not ready to settle down yet?'

'No. It's more to do with the fact that I don't want to be responsible for bringing a child into this messed up world. I think it's a morally reprehensible thing to do.'

'Oh, Sam!' said Madeleine. 'Did you really think this through?'

'Yes, I did – and so did Perdita. The decision to call it off was mutual.'

'But when you—'

'Auntiekins, Auntiekins. Please let's change the subject.'

There was a beat or two, then Madeline said, 'OK. Well, all I can say is those Labadou chicks had better watch out.'

'What do you mean?'

'Sam Newman is available and, presumably, willing.'

He smiled. 'Maybe I'll go down there tomorrow. Take Rosa with me. Where is she?'

'She's in her room making a plasticine zoo,' said Madeleine.

'Maybe I'd be better off working in plasticine,' said Daniel. 'More malleable than fucking fibreglass.'

'Oo-er,' said Sam. 'I take it you're working on a sculpture right now?'

'You take it right.'

'Why do you do it to yourself, Daniel?' Sam asked. 'You know you hate it. Have you ever even *finished* a sculpture?'

'Not one. Mostly I think I do it to piss off my agent. His voice goes all panicky on the phone when I tell him I'm sculpting.'

'Sam! Sam!' There was a pattering of bare feet across the hall, then Rosa came careering into the kitchen, arms outspread for a hug. Sam obliged her by doing the picking up and swinging round thing. 'Yay! You're here!' she sang.

'My best girl!' said Sam, nuzzling her neck. 'My coolest cousin!'

'Come, come,' gabbled Rosa, taking his hand and dragging him across the floor. 'Come with me up to my room and let me show you the zoo I made. You can take a picture! There's an elephant and a monkey and an arf—'

'What's an arf?'

'You know – *you* know! With the long necks and spots?'

'Oh, right. Now I have you. A giraffe.'

'And there's penguins and a lion with a real fluffy mane – I cut some fur off Madame Verdurin's cat and stuck it on.'

'Coolaboola! That's a genius idea!'

'And there's a pig and a unicorn and a …'

Rosa's voice faded away as the cousins crossed the hall and climbed the stairs together.

'It's a shame,' said Madeleine, watching them go. 'About him and Perdita. He'd make a fantastic father.'

'Merci, Mademoiselle!' Madeleine dropped a handful of change into the pocket of her beach bag, took a bite of choc ice, then turned and wandered back down the shore to where Rosa and Paloma were paddling in the river. The sand was hot under her feet: a heatwave had been forecast. Summer had officially started. It was the day after Sam's arrival and he had caused a stir by arriving at the Labadou on Daniel's Harley, wearing cut-off denims and a sleeveless vest under his motorbike leathers.

'Come and get 'em!' called Madeleine, and the two little

girls came sprinting towards her, followed by a lumbering Pilot. 'I wanted a *glace pralinée*,' protested Rosa as her mother handed her a choc ice.

'They were clean out of *glaces pralinées*,' said Madeleine. 'So eat up or shut up – and scoot!' She sat down on her beach towel and Pilot came and licked her bare knee before romping off after his charges. Madeleine sometimes felt that she didn't need a childminder when she had Pilot. He was easily as solicitous as the nanny St Bernard in *Peter Pan*. 'Are you sure you don't want an ice cream?' she asked Dannie, who was lying next to her.

'No, thanks. I'm feeling lumpy and premenstrual. I'll hate myself even more if I pig out on ice cream. I ate nearly an entire box of chocolate-covered amaretti last night watching *Mimi's Remedies* for about the tenth time.'

'Doesn't it make you homesick for Kilrowan, watching that film?'

'Not really, now that I've no family there. I'm grand and settled here. I'd like to go back for a visit some time, though. Give Paloma a taste of her heritage. She's becoming too Frenchified altogether.'

'You should get Deirdre's new nanny to talk Irish to her.'

Dannie looked flummoxed. 'What on earth are you talking about?'

'I ran into Deirdre O'Dare in the village this morning, and—'

'Deirdre's in town? Since when?'

'She got in late last night, *sans* the girls. They've gone off to some summer camp in Malibu. Anyway, apparently Rory hit on the idea of hiring an Irish-speaking nanny for the summer because he's worried that the kids are becoming too Americanised. Deirdre was on her way to pick the girl up from the airport when I ran into her.'

'Cool. Had she any other news?'

'No. She was in a tearing hurry. I told her to drop by later for aperitifs – you'll come too, Dannie, won't you?'

'I'd love to. Otherwise I'll end up eating too many amaretti and crying over *Mimi's Remedies* again. I can be a real sad bitch when I'm living on my own.'

'What's the story with Jethro?'

'The fecker's at the film festival in Sydney. He'll be there for at least another week.'

'How are things between the pair of you these days? OK?'

'Things are always dodgy between me and Jethro. I think we row more than any couple I know.' Dannie's eyes searched the strand for her daughter. She and Rosa were tormenting a stoical-looking Pilot. 'But we always call a truce. For Paloma's sake as much as for anything else. The reason I married Jethro was because I wanted some kind of stability in her life.'

'So you didn't marry him because he's a sexy son of a bitch *and* great company *and* the pair of you happen to be cracked about each other?'

'That too.' Dannie smiled at Madeleine, then rolled over onto her tummy. 'Oh look,' she said. 'There's Margot d'Arcy, parking her bike.'

Farther up the beach, Margot was bending over, padlocking a bicycle to a post. Her *derrière* in a batik sarong looked gift-wrapped, and a gaggle of local boys were ogling the vision like kids at Christmas.

'Did you get your invitation yet?' Dannie asked Madeleine. 'To Bianca's all-white *fête champêtre*?'

'Yeah. Have you looked out your party gear yet?'

'I'm sure I'll find something suitably pristine. I'm kinda pissed off that Jethro's not going to be here for it. He has a gorgeous cream linen suit that he wears with a Panama. I'm a pushover for that colonial look. Don't ask me what it says about my psyche.'

'Maybe you could lend it to Daniel. He's threatening to wear Y-fronts and a vest to wind Bianca up.'

A ribald laugh from farther up the beach made them look up. Margot was moving along the shore towards them. Her sarong had come adrift and the boys were clearly thrilled to see her attributes displayed to advantage in a teeny tiny thong.

'She's in bloody good nick, I'll say that for her,' said Madeleine, taking in the long, toned legs and taut tummy as Margot spread the length of batik cotton out on the sand and settled herself down on it. From her pretty raffia basket, she produced sunglasses, a fountain pen and a notebook, then she gazed towards the middle distance for several moments before opening the notebook and penning a few words. 'Her missus asked Daniel if he'd paint her.'

'Paint Margot?'

'No. Colleen.'

'Janey! What did he say to that?'

'He very diplomatically told her that he was taking a breather from work for a while. Oops!' Madeleine nodded towards Margot. 'Looks like she's got herself an admirer.' Farther down the beach, a man had dropped to his hunkers beside a rattled-looking Ms d'Arcy. She had pushed her sunglasses up onto her head and was clearly casting around for an escape route.

'We'd better come to her rescue,' said Dannie, raising an arm. 'Margot! Hey! Why not come and join us?'

Margot sent them a look of relief before unfurling herself and picking up her sarong with a flourish. Then she strolled across to where Dannie and Madeleine were lounging, tossing her hair and looking like something out of an upmarket holiday brochure.

'Thanks,' she said, spreading her sarong again. Dannie noticed that the batik design on the swathe of cotton was a pattern of rather graphically executed *síle na gigs*. No wonder the bloke had come on to her! 'Every time I come down here for some quality writing time, I get set upon by great hairy men,' said Margot with a shudder. 'It's meant that I haven't been able to sunbathe topless – I'm going to have tide marks if I'm not careful.' She reached up and undid the halter neck on her bikini with a practised hand, and the eyes of all the men on the beach swivelled in her direction. You could practically hear the unvoiced groan of lust and the groan intensified when Margot produced a tube of sun cream from her bag and proceeded to squirt the stuff onto her breasts before massaging it into her skin.

'How are you getting on,' Madeleine asked politely, trying not to look, 'in Bianca's Sanctuary?'

'I beg your pardon? Forgive me – I am a trifle deaf today. I don't think those Hopi ear candles had the required effect.'

'I asked you how you're getting on in Bianca's Sanctuary. We haven't seen you in weeks.'

'It's very pleasant,' said Margot in the manner of a restaurant reviewer bestowing one – no, on second thoughts, two! – Michelin stars. 'We're finding the ambience most conducive to work. We have immersed ourselves in it, which is why we've been so very anti-social.'

'So the writing's going well?' asked Dannie.

'It is,' said Margot. 'We are now fairly advanced in our negotiations with the dead.'

'What?'

'"Negotiating with the dead" is how Margaret Atwood describes the author's mystique, in her book of the same name. As the Sibyl says in the *Aeneid*, "The gates to death's dark kingdom stand open day and night. The arduous task, the most difficult thing, is to find your way back to the light." That is what Colleen and I are seeking. Our way back to the light.'

'Good on yiz,' said Dannie.

'Are you going to Bianca's *fête champêtre* on Saturday?' asked Madeleine, keen to change the subject.

'Yes. I am very much looking forward to it,' said Margot. 'I understand it's one of the social highlights in Saint-Géyroux.'

'It is,' said Madeleine. 'Bianca's a brilliant hostess.'

The shrill warning cry of some bird made Madeleine look up. Sam was sitting up high on the Pont du Diable – the bridge that spanned the creek – swinging a leg over the edge, laughing with some of the Labadou gang. In spite of the fact that there was a fatality every other year or so, the local boys still dived from the parapet. Machismo demanded it.

Margot followed the direction of Madeleine's gaze. 'Who's that divine blond boy?' she asked. 'He's like an Adonis.'

'That,' Madeleine told Margot, 'is Sam Newman, Daniel's nephew. He arrived from Dublin yesterday.'

'What does he do?'

Margot was still looking skyward at the vision that was Sam, and Madeleine remembered that she'd read somewhere that Margot and Colleen were bisexual. She rather feared for Sam. 'He's a freelance photographer,' she said.

'Is he staying here long?' asked Margot.

'Well, he has no plans to go back to Ireland in the near future. He's going to bum around the Languedoc for a while.'

The predatory gleam in Margot's eyes intensified. 'Will he be a guest at Bianca's *fête champêtre*?'

'I'm sure he will,' said Madeleine, feeling even more fearful for her nephew. But then, she reminded herself, Sam was perfectly capable of looking after himself.

Margot put the top back on her sun cream and took her notebook out of her bag. The notebook, Madeleine noticed, was constructed from the same nubbly hand-made paper that Colleen used. 'I wonder would he be interested in a part in *Síle na Gig in the Temple of Hecate*?' she asked. 'I could write something specially for him.'

'I'm not sure that he's the theatrical type,' said Madeleine diplomatically. 'What part had you in mind?'

'Adonis.'

'Where does Adonis come into the story?' asked Madeleine.

'Aphrodite lent him to the goddess Persephone, who was one of Hecate's holy trinity—'

'Stupid cow,' said Dannie, adding hastily, 'I meant Aphrodite, of course, not you.'

'And Persephone was so taken by his beauty that she refused to give him back. The row between the two goddesses was finally settled by Zeus, who decreed that

Adonis should spend four months of the year with Aphrodite, four months with Persephone and four months of the years with whichever goddess he chose.'

'Lucky boy,' remarked Dannie.

'Speaking of Adonis,' said Madeleine, looking over to where Sam, golden of hair and torso, was strolling barefoot across the sand. 'Here he comes now.'

'Hello there, Auntie,' said Sam, flopping down onto the sand beside Madeleine and dropping a kiss on her shoulder. He was dripping with water and two drops hung from his earlobes like diamonds.

'You dived!' said Madeleine, genuinely cross with him. 'You *promised* me you wouldn't dive from the bridge. You know how much it freaks me out, Sam.'

Sam gave her a guilty look. 'I'm sorry,' he said. 'I forgot.' Turning to Dannie, he said 'hi' before focusing the beam of his attention on Margot. 'Introduce me,' he said.

'This is Sam Newman,' said Madeleine, pretending she hadn't seen the appreciative look the bold boy bestowed upon Margot's breasts.

Margot ran the tip of her tongue over her top lip, then showed her little feral teeth in a catlike smile. 'How very nice to meet you, Sam,' she said. 'Did you *really* dive from the bridge? I must say, I'm impressed.'

'No prizes for guessing who are going to be playing the parts of the goddesses,' said Dannie later as she and Madeleine packed up their stuff and prepared to head for home. 'I'd say the fur will fairly fly between the pair of them. Do you think he'd be up for it?'

'Nah. Somehow I can't see Sam dolled up in an Attic

tunic and Grecian sandals, disporting himself around Bianca's pavilion.'

'He'd be a real crowd puller, that's for sure.'

Madeleine hefted her beach bag onto her shoulder. 'Who's going to be the messenger who delivers the bad news?'

Dannie looked perplexed. 'D'you mean in Margot's play?'

'No. In real life.' She turned and indicated their two girls, who were playing some game with pebbles on squares they'd drawn in the sand. 'Rosa! Paloma! It's time to go home!' she called.

Wails of protest came from the pair of them.

'Ignore them,' said Dannie, turning away. 'They'll come to heel sooner or later.'

Margot was pushing her bicycle up the track that led up to the road, provoking further remarks from the youths who had admired her so fulsomely earlier in the afternoon. The subject under discussion was how fine a thing it would be to die and be reincarnated as the saddle on her bike, and either Margot's French wasn't up to scratch or she was still aurally challenged after her Hopi ear candle experience.

'Don't forget aperitifs tonight *chez nous*,' Madeleine reminded Dannie.

'I'll look forward to that. I've a gorgeous gooey Brie that needs to be eaten, I'll bring it with me. *If* I can get a sitter for Paloma. Did you know that Jeanne-Marie's moved to Montpellier?'

'No, I didn't. Bummer. It's Sod's Law, isn't it? No sooner have you found a reliable babysitter than something comes up and whisks them away elsewhere.'

Madeleine looked over her shoulder to make sure the kids were following. They were trailing behind, giving out yards to Pilot, who was shaking out his wet fur and sending drops of water flying all over them. 'Listen – you really don't need to worry about finding a babysitter tonight,' she told Dannie. 'You're more than welcome to bring Paloma with you.'

'You're very kind, thanks. But sometimes it's nice to relax over a couple of glasses of wine in the knowledge that someone else has the job of putting the wain to bed.'

'I know what you mean. I don't seem to have very much time to myself these days. I felt a pang of envy when I got a load of all the words in Margot's note-book.'

'Envy?'

'Yeah. I still haven't written that sonnet.'

At that moment, Paloma and Rosa came tearing up, giggling like loons.

'What are you pair of minxes up to?' asked Dannie.

'Look at Pilot!' laughed Rosa. 'We've turned his ears inside out!'

Madeleine turned to look at the big dog, who was panting along behind his tormentors. They had indeed turned his floppy ears inside out and secured them on the top of his head with a be-pompomed bungee. The poor animal looked utterly mortified.

'Oh, poor Pilot!' said Madeleine, hunkering down to perform remedial work. She removed the bungee and rubbed Pilot's silky ears. And then she found herself smiling as the first lines of a brand new sonnet came creeping into her head.

My friend brought me a gift of runny Brie,
My nephew brought a gift of vintage wine.
How glad I am the pair of them combine
To bring the gift of happiness to me ...

She *was* happy, she thought now. She was happy to have the company of Sam, she was happy to have friends like Dannie and Deirdre, she was happy to have a beautiful, healthy daughter and she was happy to be married to a shit-hot artist who loved her unconditionally. How many people could put their hands on their heart and profess to be truly happy?

As she reached the top of the hill, some superstitious impulse made her diverge from the pathway and reach for the bole of a tree.

'What are you doing?' asked Dannie.

'I'm touching wood,' said Madeleine.

10

Deirdre swung through the doors of the airport, clutching
Bruno by the hand. She was running late – she'd been
delayed by a *flic* checking tax discs and Bruno had needed
a loo stop. The gleaming airport concourse was empty
apart from a man wielding a mop and a straggle of
passengers – Dubliners, to judge by their accents.

Deirdre glanced around for someone who would fit the
description that Greta had sent her by e-mail. The girl had
offered to jpeg her a picture, but Deirdre had been having
hellish problems with attachments and she didn't want her
computer lying down and dying on her again. Her greatest
fear was that she'd contract a virus while she was in Saint-
Géyroux, because the nearest computer hospital was miles
away in Montpellier. Now that she was finally in her
French haven and soon to be untrammelled by child care
concerns, she wanted to get some serious work done on
her screenplay. She hadn't had a chance to do anything
with it while she'd been working on the *Gold Diggers*
rewrites, and she'd heard an industry rumour recently that
film noir was set to make a comeback. If that was the case,
she wanted her screenplay to be first off the blocks.

'Five foot four, curly reddish hair, blue eyes', Greta's
description had read. Deirdre had pictured a strapping
Connemara lass. She knew the type: pale skin prone to

freckles, ginger hair, a sturdy farm worker's build. But there was no one on the concourse who answered that description.

She accessed her phone, then remembered that she hadn't had the nous to key Greta's number into the memory. She'd have to have her paged. Deirdre was just about to move in the direction of the information counter when a girl who'd been standing gazing through a plate glass window turned suddenly and looked straight at her. Her hair, loosely pinned back behind delicate ears, was a tumbling mass of strawberry blonde curls. Her face was a perfect heart shape, her mouth a smiling cupid's bow, her nose a tip-tilted retroussé. Her eyes slanted upward a little at the outer corners and were of an astonishing China blue. She wore no jewellery apart from a Claddagh ring and no make-up, and she was dressed very simply in sandals and a cotton frock that matched her eyes. She was, quite simply, exquisite.

'Deirdre?' said the girl, moving towards them. 'Bruno? Oh – how lovely to meet you at last! I'm Greta.'

Greta elected to travel in the back of the car beside Bruno. She had brought him a present, a little cat in black and white velour that she told him she had made herself. She had embroidered a face on the cat and had given it a most mischievous smile and a kooky little smudge on its nose. 'It's a Jellicle cat,' she'd told him and had recited the chorus of the poem over and over again in her lilting Connemara accent until Bruno nearly had it by heart. She was utterly unselfconscious, utterly delightful, and utterly – to use the French word – *ravissante*.

As she drove, Deirdre shot looks at the rear-view mirror from time to time to gauge how the pair of them were getting on. It was clearly love at first sight – and it was clearly reciprocal. The expression on Bruno's face as he looked up at this *goddess* who had descended from the skies above the Aéroport Montpellier Méditerranée verged on the worshipful. By the time they'd negotiated the city and the northbound motorway and finally reached the winding road that led to Saint-Géyroux, Bruno was lolling in Greta's arms, toying with strands of her hair.

'Would you like to meet Pluto?' Deirdre heard him ask.

'Who's Pluto?'

'He's my best friend. He's waiting for me in the garden at home.'

'Well, if he's your best friend, of course I'd like to meet him.'

'Talk Irish to me.'

'*Is maith liom caca milis.*'

'What does that mean?'

'It means "I like sweet cake."'

'Cool! Tell me that rhyme again.'

'Say 'please'.'

'Please.'

'OK. Say it with me.'

The pair of them launched into the refrain about Jellicle cats dancing under a Jellicle moon, and they were still chanting it as the car pulled up outside the house in the rue Lamballe. Deirdre killed the engine, got out of the driver's seat and went round to the boot to retrieve Greta's luggage. 'Welcome to Saint-Géyroux, Greta,' she said as the pair of them piled out of the back of the car.

'Thank you!' said Greta. 'Hey, let me take that.'

'It's fine – you travel light,' said Deirdre, shouldering Greta's backpack. 'Go on through.' She held the front door open and Greta passed into the house, Bruno clinging to her hand. 'The cloakroom's through there if you need the loo.'

'I'm fine, thanks.'

'I'm afraid the place is looking a bit basic.' Deirdre dumped the backpack on a trunk in the hall and led the way into the sitting room. 'The decorators have been in and I haven't had time to put things to sorts yet.'

Greta sniffed the air. 'Mm. I love the smell of fresh paint,' she said.

'You still get a whiff of it? I must be inured by now. I've been burning scented candles to get rid of it.'

'Where did you find your gorgeous angel?' Greta asked, looking up at the gold-painted caryatid hanging above the doors that led out to the patio.

'I got it in the *marché aux puces* in Gignac.'

'*Marché aux puces?*'

'Flea market.'

'So 'puce' is the French word for flea?'

'Yeah. It's also a term of endearment.'

'In that case,' Greta said, smiling down at Bruno, 'maybe you should call your Jellicle cat 'Puce'?'

Bruno gave a delighted gurgle. 'Legend!' he said.

'Pucey cat, pucey cat, where have you been!' quipped Deirdre.

But Bruno ignored Deirdre's little joke. 'Come and meet Pluto,' he said, dragging Greta across the room and out into the garden. Deirdre followed them as far as the double doors, where she remained leaning against the jamb, observing. 'There he is!' Bruno told Greta.

'Where?'

'There! Hiding under that bush. Pluto, come and meet Greta.'

Deirdre watched as Greta hunkered down, holding out a hand, as one would to a puppy or a cat that you want to caress. 'I think he might be a bit shy,' she heard herself say in a low voice to Bruno.

'He is,' Bruno whispered back. 'But he likes you. I can tell.'

'Hi, Pluto!' Greta was still holding out a hand to Bruno's imaginary friend. 'Won't you come and shake hands with me?'

'There!' said Bruno. 'He's coming. See? I told you he'd like you!'

'Well, it's a real pleasure to meet you, Pluto. I think the three of us might have a lot of fun together!'

Deirdre had to hand it to Greta. She'd greeted Pluto just as warmly as she'd greeted Bruno earlier, as if he was someone she'd wanted to meet for ages.

Bruno punched the air. 'Yay! We'll be like the Three Mouseketeers! D'you want to come and see my room?'

'I'd love to.'

Bruno led Greta back into the sitting room. 'I know! I'll get us Oranginas first,' he said.

He scooted off in the direction of the kitchen and Deirdre turned to Greta and smiled.

'Flying colours,' she said.

'Sure, he's a charmer,' said Greta. 'What a sweet kid! And isn't your house just gorgeous, Deirdre,' she added, looking around her. 'I love my job already, so I do.'

'You haven't met the girls yet.' Deirdre raised an ominous eyebrow.

'I'm sure I'll – oh!'

Greta froze suddenly, her hands covering her mouth. Her Siamese cat eyes had gone wide with incredulity, and – since she was gazing at the portrait of Deirdre that hung over the fireplace – Deirdre felt a flash of embarrassment. Maybe this girl was a good Irish Catholic who would find it shocking to find a nude portrait of her employer on such flagrant display?

But she couldn't have got it more wrong. 'Oh!' Greta said again. 'It's beautiful! It's a Daniel Lennox, isn't it? It has to be!'

'Yes,' said Deirdre. 'Daniel painted it about ten years ago. It doesn't usually hang there – since the kids got self-conscious about that kind of thing it's been living in my bedroom – but the painters must have decided to put it up for a lark.'

'So you actually sat for Daniel Lennox?'

'Yes. He's a good friend. He lives here in the village.'

Greta turned even wider eyes on her. 'No *shit*! Oh – I'm sorry – it's just that – you mean he actually *lives* here in Saint-Géyroux?'

'Yes. In fact, we've been invited to his house tonight, for aperitifs.'

Deirdre thought that Greta might faint. Her translucent skin went paler still and her hands remained clamped against her mouth. 'But – oh, God! That means I'm going to meet him? *God!* I'm going to meet Daniel *Lennox*!'

Deirdre smiled. 'I take it you're a fan?'

'I wrote a paper on him last term. My bedroom wall at home in Connemara is wallpapered with prints of his

154

work. I've been to all his retrospectives – I even made my flatmate record the radio broadcast of a talk he gave at IMMA recently. I've worshipped him for years.'

Deirdre laughed. 'You'll be happy to meet him, then?'

'Happy?' The smile Greta sent Deirdre was radiant. 'I'll be pure *thrilled* to meet him!'

'What's so special about Daniel?' Bruno was standing in the doorway with a bottle of Orangina in each hand and Deirdre could tell by the stains around his mouth that he'd been at the Nutella. Pucey the cat was sticking out of his pocket and there were Nutella stains on his mouth, too.

'I think that Daniel Lennox is the greatest painter that ever lived,' said Greta reverently.

'Even better than Courbet?' asked Bruno.

Greta's reverent expression turned into one of astonishment. 'What are you, an infant prodigy? How come you know about Courbet?' she asked.

'There's a painting by him in the gallery in Montpellier, of a lady with the biggest butt you've ever seen.'

'It's true,' said Deirdre. 'It's Bruno's favourite painting. I like to think that he has a precocious talent for art appreciation, but really I think it's just a boy thing.'

'Will you take me there some day?' Greta asked Bruno. 'I'd love to see if the lady's butt is bigger than mine.'

'It's *miles* bigger! You wouldn't believe how big it is. It's bigger than … than King Kong's butt.'

'It has been the butt of many jokes,' said Deirdre wearily. 'I daresay Greta would like to see some of the *other* paintings in the Musée, Bruno.'

'Hmm. The rest of the stuff's kinda borin',' said Bruno, considering. 'But there's quite a good statue of a man sticking a sword through a bull's head. And after we look at him we could go to the cinema in Montpellier and you could buy me popcorn.' And Bruno promptly launched into the donkey's song from *Shrek*, the one about loving big butts.

'Sorry about this,' Deirdre said to Greta with a rueful smile. 'I hope you're not regretting having taken the job.'

'No fear.' Greta turned to Bruno. 'It's a deal,' she told him.

'Come on up to my room!' Bruno moved into the hall and started doing a kind of break dance.

'I'm very glad we had the decorators in,' said Deirdre. 'His room's normally a tip, but even he hasn't had time to trash it in the short space of time since we've arrived. Your room's on the top floor. I hope you'll like it – I'll come up and show you round in a minute. I just want to make a quick phone call first, if you don't mind.'

'No problem.'

'Come *on*, Greta,' said Bruno from the hall.

'Come on, Greta, *please*,' Greta corrected him.

'Come on, Greta, *please*! And then when I've finished showing you my room, I'll show you round the village, and then maybe we could go down to the Labadou and—'

'There won't be time for the Labadou today,' Deirdre told him. 'We're due at the Lennoxes' at seven o'clock.'

'Bummer bummer bummer bummer *Batman*!' Bruno raced up the stairs, followed by a visibly glowing Greta.

Deirdre stood looking after them indulgently, then reached for the phone.

'Hi, darling,' she said when Rory picked up. 'Well. She's arrived.'

'Who's arrived?'

'Nani Nua.'

'Oh, yeah? What's she like?'

'Well, Bruno's smitten. And I imagine that every other red-blooded male in the village will be too. It's time for the good burgher-women of Saint-Géyroux to lock up their husbands.'

'Uh oh. She's hot?'

'It's not just that she's hot. She's *gorgeous*. She's got a great smile and she's got a great personality, and she didn't bat an eyelid when Bruno introduced her to Pluto or when he confessed his penchant for big butts. And – most amazing of all – I think she's even going to be able to put manners on him!'

'No shit!'

'She's also completely star struck.'

'Don't tell me Depp's in town again?'

'No. The beauty of it is that it's not some stellar actor or musician she's star struck by. It's Daniel Lennox.'

'That old fart? Why?'

'She's like, I dunno, a *disciple* or something. She literally nearly fainted when I told her we'd be going to his gaff for aperitifs this evening.'

'And you reckon Bruno's genuinely taken with her?'

'Absolutely. And you'll be glad to know that she's already taught him some Irish.'

'What words of wisdom has she imparted?'

'*Is maith liom caca milis.*'

Rory laughed. 'She obviously figured him out pretty smartish. So you're a happy bunny?'

'I'm a *deliriously* happy bunny.'

'That's all that matters. I'll look forward to meeting her.'

'What time does your flight get in on Saturday?'

'Midday.'

'Good. That means you'll be back in time for Bianca's *fête champêtre*.'

'Fuck Bianca's *fête champêtre*.'

'Why?'

'Because, my darling, I have no intention of spending the afternoon poncing around Bianca's garden.'

'What do you intend doing, then?'

'I'm going to send Bruno off to the Labadou with Nani Nua and I'm going to spend the afternoon in bed, riding the arse off my trouble and strife.'

Deirdre smiled. 'I can't wait,' she said.

Upstairs, Bruno was making his tidy room very untidy indeed by pulling stuff out of toy boxes and off shelves and emptying cupboards. He had introduced Greta to his two favourite teddies and shown off his collection of Kelly Osbourne dolls, and he was now proudly displaying an electronic Etch-a-Sketch.

'Look at this!' he pronounced, demonstrating. 'And this!' A box of Lego Wild Hunters was upended on the floor. 'And this!' He lifted down a model of Hogwarts that took pride of place on top of a bookcase. 'It's got a clock tower that ticks and loads of spooky stuff.'

'Cool!'

'And just wait till you see this!'

While Bruno busied himself with setting up some game on his Xbox, Greta crouched down and inspected his bookcase. It was crammed with hardbacks and soft-backs and big glossy picture books, all with multiple cracks

158

on their spines, all clearly well-thumbed and loved.

'You must be a great one for the books,' she told him.

'I am.'

'Good. In that case you'll be glad to know that I have a book for you, in my backpack.'

'What's it called?'

'It's called *The Turf-Cutter's Donkey* and I thought you might like it because it's set in Ireland. My mammy used to read it to me when I was a little girl, and her mammy before her read it to her.'

'Will you read it to me?'

'Sure. It can be your bedtime story, if you like.'

'What's it about?'

'It's about two children, Eileen and Seamus, who run away from home and have loads of adventures with the gypsies and the Danaans.'

'Who are the Danaans?'

'The Danaans are a tribe of brave Irish warriors who can do magic and who wage war against the Firbolgs.'

'Who are the Firbolgs?'

'They're a crowd of dirty thickos.'

'What about the donkey? Is he like the one in *Shrek*? Pluto's mad about the donkey in *Shrek*.'

Greta smiled. 'No. The turf-cutter's donkey can't talk, for starters. But he has magical powers too. The book's full of magic.' She pulled a picture book from the shelf and started to leaf through it. It was a Kelly Osbourne paper doll book with loads of different threads to dress Kelly up in. 'You're a big fan of Kelly, so,' she observed.

'Yep. I had loads of posters of her up on my wall before my room got decorated.'

'What about Pluto?' she asked. 'Is he a fan of hers too?'

'Nah. He's more into Pink. We have rows about it sometimes.'

Greta put the Kelly Osbourne book back and selected an illustrated volume of large-print Hans Christian Andersen fairy tales. '*The Little Mermaid*!' she said. 'I loved that story when I was little. It always made me cry.'

'I prefer *The Marsh King's Daughter*. It's scarier.'

'Does Pluto like to read too?'

Bruno turned and put a finger to his lips. Then he made an elaborate show of looking round the room before saying, 'It's OK. He's not here. I didn't want to hurt his feelings if he was. The fact is, Pluto finds reading real difficult. I'm trying to teach him. That's why I've hung on to some of my old babyish books, like those fairy tales.'

'I'll teach him to read the Jellicle poem if you like,' said Greta. 'We could order the book from Amazon. And there are loads of other poems in it that we could teach him.'

'Cool!' said Bruno. 'Are all the poems about Jellicle cats?'

'No, there are poems about all kinds of different cats. There's Rum Tum Tugger and there's Old Deuteronomy and Mungojerrie and Rumpelteazer and Magical Mr Mistoffelees—'

'Magical Mr Mistoffelees? I like the sound of him. I'm going to learn magic. I'd love to be like Harry Potter.' He returned his attention to his Xbox. 'Now, wait till you see—'

'Holy shmoly!' Deirdre was standing in the doorway. 'What exploded in here?'

Greta looked up at her from her crouched position on

the floor. 'Oops,' she said with an apologetic moue. 'Sorry. He's after showing me all his stuff.'

'I knew it couldn't last,' said Deirdre with a sigh. 'You'll be glad to know that Aoife and Grace are quite tidy by comparison. Come, Greta, and let me show you your room.'

'Thank you.' Greta turned to Bruno. 'Hey, you! If you want to be a magician, you'd better start practising your magical powers.'

'What do you mean?'

Greta looked at her watch. 'I'm gonna be back here in five minutes. And if you're as magical as Mistoffelees, this room will have been magicked back to the way it was when I first saw it.'

She could see him thinking hard. 'Just how magical is Mistoffelees?'

'The poem says he's *singularly* magical. But you, Bruno, have an advantage over him.'

'Oh? What's that?'

'Sure, haven't you Pluto to help you?' Greta raised an eyebrow at him, then turned and left the room.

She followed Deirdre along the corridor and Deirdre threw a smile over her shoulder at her. 'Nice try,' she said, ascending a staircase and turning right at the top. 'I wonder will it work? Oh, by the way – the decorators didn't make it as far as the top floor, but don't worry – your room's in good nick. It's rarely been used. Here we are.'

Deirdre opened a wooden door that led into a sizable room with white plaster walls. The floorboards had been lime-washed and light spilled in from a tall window beyond which Greta could see a balcony bright with geraniums in pots. There was a scrubbed pine table to the left of the window and a raffia-bottomed chair. On the right was a comfortable-looking armchair with loose white linen covers, and beyond that an alcove had been curtained off as a storage space with a rail for clothes. The bed had been made up with blue and white striped linen and the iron frame had been painted a matching shade of blue. Rag rugs lay on either side of the bed and on one of the bedside lockers an enamel jug containing marguerites had been placed.

'Oh! It's beautiful!' said Greta, moving into the room. 'Flowers by the bed and all! How thoughtful of you.'

'It's not too, well, Spartan?' There was an anxious note in Deirdre's voice.

'No. It's perfect. Yay! I have a balcony! Amn't I steeped! I can sit here of an evening after Bruno's gone to bed and have a glass of wine and listen to cicadas.' She moved across the room, opened the French window and stepped out. The balcony was just wide enough to accommodate a slatted wooden table and a matching folding chair. Beyond the balcony stretched a vista of terracotta rooftops, with pigeons perched on chimney pots and a cloudless sky above.

I'm going to paint that roofscape, thought Greta. And I'm going to paint a still life of the inside of my room. And any time I go off on jaunts with Bruno I'm going to take my sketchbook with me and paint and paint and paint. I'm going to love it here!

'I'm going to love it here!' she told Deirdre as she turned back into the room. 'Hey! What a great photograph!' she remarked.

Above the bed hung a black-and-white photographic print framed in bleached wood. It was a riverscape and had clearly been taken in fading light. A kind of phosphorescence rose from the water and an ancient-looking bridge was silhouetted against a pearly grey sky.

'That was taken by Sam Newman. He's a photographer,' said Deirdre. 'He also happens to be Daniel Lennox's nephew. His wife – Daniel's wife, that is – her name's Madeleine – told me he's in town, so you may get to meet him tonight.'

'Where was the photograph taken?'

'Not far from here, down by the Labadou. The river is the Hérault, the bridge is the Pont du Diable.'

'The Pont du Diable. The Devil's Bridge?'

'Yup. You'll be seeing a lot of it.'

'What do you mean?'

'It's where the local kids go to hang out. My crowd spend practically all day, every day there in the summer.'

'Is it far?'

'About ten minutes in the car.'

'You know I don't drive.'

'I know. But I'm happy to leave you off there and come back for you later. If you're feeling energetic, there are bikes – although it's a bit far for Bruno to cycle. And there are always lifts to be had with other mothers. I'm sure you noticed that there are a fair few people-carriers trundling around the village. I know, I *know* how ecologically unsound they are, but they make up for that particular vice by cutting down on the number of trips people make.'

Greta turned back to the photograph. 'It must run in the family,' she said. 'He has a real eye for composition.'

'Sam? He certainly has. I'm sure he'd be *more* than happy to ferry you to and from the Labadou, Greta.'

'That'd be grand, so it would.' Greta looked around at her *chambre meublée*, then smiled at Deirdre. 'D'you know something? From the minute I first heard your voice on the phone, I knew I was going to like you. You sounded like a *friend*, not a boss.'

'And I hope that's what we'll be. Friends. I'm crap at being a boss. I feel like an impostor when I issue orders.' Deirdre glanced at her watch. 'Bruno's five minutes are up. Shall we go see if he's worked any magic on his room? Knowing him, it'll be even more trashed.'

But when they reached Bruno's bedroom, the child was sitting cross-legged in the middle of the floor, wearing an inordinately smug expression. And the room was as ship-shape as a Sunday supplement stylist's dream.

'Well,' said Greta. 'This is sure proof of your magical powers, Bruno.'

'Call me Mistoffelees.'

'Call me Mistoffelees, *please*.'

'Please.'

They shared a smile.

'Pluto helped,' said Bruno.

'Of course he did,' said Greta.

11

Madeleine looked at the sonnet she'd just penned. It was crap. She tore the page out of her notebook, screwed it up and tossed it into the bin. 'Crap, crap, crappety crap,' she sang as she set about getting glasses down from the shelf. It was ten to seven and Deirdre and Dannie would be arriving soon for aperitifs.

'What's crap?' asked Sam, strolling into the kitchen.

'I just tried to write a sonnet. It was a complete waste of time.'

'What was it about?'

'I thought it might be nice to write something for Daniel's birthday.'

'When *is* his birthday?'

'You mean you don't know the date of your own uncle's birthday?'

'Can't say I do.'

'It's not until August, but I felt a kind of creative vibe come on me today, and I thought it might be worth having a go.'

'I don't imagine there are very many words in the dictionary that rhyme with Daniel.'

'You're right. There's only one.'

'And that is?'

'Spaniel.'

Sam laughed. 'Not the most apposite animal to compare to our towering Artist of International Repute. Why don't you write a sonnet about me instead? I bet loads of words rhyme with Sam.'

'Three spring instantly to mind.'

'Let me guess. 'Wham', 'bam' and 'ma'am'?'

'Correct. But I'm not sure they would sit very elegantly in a sonnet. Here. Open this for me, will you?' She handed him a bottle of red and set about peeling garlic cloves to add to the hummus she'd just made.

'Sam, Sam, Sam ...' he mused as he peeled away the foil. 'How about this?' He cleared his throat, then pronounced in declamatory fashion:

> *There once was a young man named Sam,*
> *Who found himself in a bit of a jam.*
> *Through a faulty French letter*
> *He became a begetter*
> *And ended up pushing a pram.*

Madeleine gave him a look of admiration as the cork came away from the bottle with a soft *plop*! 'Well!' she said. 'That's some bravura improvisation, Sam Newman. Maybe you and Margot d'Arcy should work on a collaboration.'

'No thanks. She's scary, that same Margot d'Arcy. She looks as if she could eat a man for breakfast.'

'Wait until you meet Colleen.'

'Don't tell me she's even scarier?'

'I'd say she could manage a man *and* a woman for breakfast.'

'Wow. This dozy little ville is becoming a veritable

hotbed of vice,' said Sam with a laugh. 'Maybe I'm in with a chance of getting laid this summer. I'm convinced those Labadou gals have got even hotter since the last time I was here.'

Madeleine gave him a thoughtful look. 'Sam? You know you said you didn't want to be a father for ethical reasons?'

'Yeah?'

'What if you become one by default?'

'What do you mean?'

'Well, as you put it yourself in that wonderful work of poesie, "through a faulty French letter" …'

'That's not going to happen.'

'You can't say that for certain.'

'I can. I'm investigating a vasectomy.'

Madeleine set down her knife and turned concerned eyes on him. 'Oh, Sam! Are you sure that's a wise thing to do?'

'Absolutely.'

'But what if you change your mind?'

He shrugged. 'If I ever feel an overwhelming urge to become a father, I'll go down the adoption route. At least that way I'll be doing something altruistic rather than adding to the population of a stinking planet that's already overburdened with stinking humanity.'

'You really *are* a misanthropist, aren't you?'

'Dyed in the wool,' said Sam cheerfully.

'Hi!' A knock came to the sliding door that led to the garden. Through the glass panel, Madeleine could see the smiling faces of Dannie and Paloma. 'I let myself in through the side gate,' Dannie said, putting her head around the door. 'I hope you don't mind?'

'Of course not. Come in, come in!' said Madeleine. 'Paloma, dotey, Rosa's up in her room. D'you want to go on up to her?'

'Yip.' Paloma scampered across the kitchen and out into the hall. They could hear her reedy voice calling out to her friend as she ran up the stairs.

Madeleine greeted Dannie with a kiss on the cheek. 'Red or white?' she asked.

'White, please.'

'Will you do the needful, Sam?' she asked. 'There's a bottle open in the fridge.'

'Sure.' Sam scooped a glass from a shelf, tossed it into the air and caught it with an adroit hand.

'Where did you learn to do that?' asked Dannie admiringly.

'I worked as a bartender in the States for a year. I've found that that little trick never fails to impress the ladies.' He poured a generous measure of white wine into a glass with the aplomb of a showman, then handed it to Dannie with a bow.

'Well, Tom Cruise, eat your heart out!'

'What's Tom Cruise got to do with it?'

'He played a bartender who pulled stunts like that once, in a crap film called *Cocktail*.'

'Never heard of it.'

'That's because it was made way before your time, young man. *Sláinte*!'

'*Sláinte* back at ya!'

'Where's Daniel?' Dannie asked, taking a sip of wine. 'God, that's good.'

'Daniel is upstairs in his studio working on a sculpture,' Madeleine told her.

'A sculpture? That's a bit un-Daniel, isn't it?'

'Yes, it is. He only sculpts when he's creatively stymied. I wish he wouldn't. He always abandons the work half-finished and that puts him in a bad mood. Oops. Here he comes now.'

Daniel sloped into the kitchen wearing the paint-stained overalls he wore to work and a disconsolate expression. His expression mellowed when he saw wine and company.

'Hey, namesake,' he said, dropping a kiss on Dannie's cheek. 'Good to see you.'

'I suppose you'd forgotten I'd invited Dannie and Deirdre for aperitifs?' said Madeleine.

'I had forgotten, yes. Where's Jethro, Dannie?'

'He's at the Sydney Film Festival.'

'D'you know, I was thinking about branching out into film,' remarked Sam, 'until I realised that that would make me the puppet of the money-men.'

'Jethro's no puppet!' protested Dannie.

'Jeez, I know he's not, Dannie. But Jethro's one of the lucky ones – he's established enough to pick and choose what films he makes.'

'Stick with still photography,' said Daniel. 'It's what you know best.'

'Ah, but I'm a young dog still,' Sam said with a big smile, 'and I can learn new tricks.'

Daniel yawned and rubbed an eye with a grimy finger. 'You're a young dog barking up the wrong tree. You don't want to get into the movie business. No disrespect to Jethro,' he added, turning to Dannie.

'Sure, there's none taken,' she replied.

Madeleine handed Daniel a glass of wine. 'Take that

upstairs,' she told him, 'and have a shower – wash the dust away.'

Daniel shambled towards the kitchen door. 'That fucking sculpture's doing my head in,' he said to no one in particular as he went through.

Madeleine turned back to Dannie and Sam. 'Take your drinks though to the garden and admire the new jasmine that Monsieur Venot planted. It's growing like the clappers.'

'I can smell it from here,' said Dannie. 'What kind is it?'

'You'd need to ask Monsieur Venot that, my dear,' said Madeleine, throwing Dannie a smile as she moved through to the pantry that adjoined the kitchen.

The pantry was really the domain of Mme Thibault. Madeleine sometimes felt like a trespasser when she crossed the threshold because Mme Thibault had been housekeeper to the Lennoxes for years. In fact, she was more than housekeeper. She was major domo, retainer and wise woman all wrapped into one, and she cooked better than Elizabeth David. Her pantry was as well stocked as the food department in Harrod's and her freezer was something a desert island castaway might fantasise about.

Madeleine took a jar of olives and one of quails' eggs from the cupboard. Macadamia nuts, Bombay mix and Daniel's favourite Twiglets – which he got a pal in Britland to ship to him on a regular basis – were slung into bowls. She had just set a dish of celery salt on the tray for dipping the eggs into when the front doorbell rang. Madeleine moved through to the hall, where Daniel was leaning up against the console table, reading the mail that had arrived for him that morning.

'Anything of interest?' she asked as she passed him by.

'Nah. Blatin's making mewling noises about a new series, but he can go fuck himself. I'm not painting to order.'

'Be off with you,' Madeleine told him now. 'You'll feel better after a shower.'

Obediently, Daniel made for the stairs and Madeleine passed on through the hall into the courtyard that fronted the house. She reached for the big, elaborate wrought iron key that hung by the gate, inserted it into the lock and pulled at the handle. Deirdre O'Dare was standing outside on the street with an oleander flower stuck in her hair.

'Hi! Daniel will be glad to see you,' said Madeleine. 'You always cheer him up.'

'What's wrong with him?' Deirdre asked as she stepped through.

'The muse has been avoiding him and he's pretty pissed off with her.' Madeleine shut the heavy oak gate behind them before leading the way back through the courtyard. 'Why don't you come in through the side entrance, the way most people do?' she asked.

'Because I love this courtyard. It's one of the most magical places I know.'

It was true. When Madeleine had first entered Daniel Lennox's courtyard several years ago, she had felt as if she were stepping into a sanctuary. The place was a bitch to maintain because there was so much exotica growing there, but it was well worth the gardener's overtime. Bianca Ingram had tried to persuade Daniel to allow an editor friend of hers to do a feature on the courtyard for a glossy French *Homes & Gardens*-type magazine, but Daniel had laughed at her and told her it would be akin to allowing an infidel into a temple. He'd been quite chuffed with his analogy and had told Madeleine she could use it in a sonnet. She told him right back that there was no rhyme for the word 'temple'.

'I *also* choose to come in this way,' Deirdre continued, 'because I once happened upon Sam sunbathing starkers when I came in by the side entrance.'

'I would have thought that might have been an experience well worth running the risk of repeating,' replied Madeleine with a laugh.

'Definitely not when you're a happily married woman.' They passed into the kitchen. 'Mmm, what's that gorgeous smell?' asked Deirdre. 'Have you been burning candles?'

'No. It's jasmine. Go and join Dannie and Sam on the terrace,' said Madeleine, 'and I'll fetch us some nibbly bits.'

In the pantry, Madeleine grabbed another bottle of wine and tucked it under her arm before hefting the tray and carrying it through to the garden. Dannie and Sam were taking their ease on wicker chairs and Deirdre was sniffing a strand of jasmine.

'Where's your new nanny?' Madeleine asked her, setting the tray down on the table. 'I thought you were going to bring her and Bruno with you?'

'I was,' said Deirdre. 'I didn't think that Bruno would want to stay at home on his own with a girl who's, well, who's still a virtual stranger, really. But they were getting along so well playing Tomb Raider that I decided to leave them to it. Anyway, she was tired after all the travelling and I think she might have been a bit intimidated by the prospect of meeting Daniel.'

'What?' said Madeleine. 'Why?'

'She's a big fan of his. She's an art student and she says Daniel's her greatest influence.'

Madeleine set the tray down on the table and sent Deirdre a look of bemusement. 'Well, whaddayaknow! What's she like?'

Deirdre gave a beatific smile. 'She has me lost for words,' she said. 'She's, well – she's pretty damn perfect! She can cook, which is a lifesaver for me. She has a sense of humour, which is always a bonus. And most importantly of all, Bruno loves her. I called Rory as soon as I got back from picking her up at the airport and sang her praises down the phone. We couldn't have prayed for a better girl.'

'Janey! Will you lend her out?' asked Dannie. 'Now that Jeanne-Marie's gone, there's a serious shortage of child minders in the village.'

'Only if you ask *very* nicely!'

'What's her name?'

'Greta O'Flaherty.'

Sam drained his glass. 'What age is she?' he asked, sounding interested.

'Twenty-one.'

'What's she look like?' This time he sounded even more interested.

Deirdre shrugged. 'Well, she described herself in an e-mail to me as being five foot four with curly reddish hair and blue eyes. She's from the Connemara Gaeltacht.'

'So she's a grown-up version of the ginger nut on the John Hinde postcard.' Sam set his glass down and got to his feet.

Deirdre shrugged again. 'You said it,' she told him. But

Madeleine could see a flicker of private amusement in her eyes.

'So how does a bogger from Connemara feel about joining the jet set?'

'We're not the jet set!'

'Hello? You're only married to one of the most famous film stars on the face of the planet,' Sam pointed out.

'She doesn't know that.'

'What? How come?'

'I haven't told her. All I said was that we both work in the film industry.'

'Why weren't you more specific?' asked Dannie.

'I don't know, really. I always feel a bit like I'm bragging when I tell people I'm married to Rory. It changes the way they look at me, and I hate that.'

'Well, your little Irish colleen's in for a big surprise when she gets a load of her new employer,' observed Sam. 'When's he due?'

'He'll be here on Saturday.'

'Thank fuck for that,' said Daniel. 'I can drag him along to Bianca's poncy party for company.'

'If he gets here on time,' said Deirdre, quickly inventing an excuse. She hadn't forgotten that Rory had promised her an afternoon in the sack. 'He's not sure he'll make his flight.'

Pilot suddenly loped onto the terrace. 'Yo, Pilot!' said Sam. 'Fancy a pint?'

Pilot wagged his tail.

'I'll take that for a yes. Come on then.'

'You can't take him with you,' said Madeleine.

'Why not?'

'That poodle of Mme Poiret's is in heat again. Half

the dogs in the neighbourhood are in pursuit of her, and I don't want her coming to me blaming Pilot for her next litter, the way she did last time.'

'You mean Pilot can still get it up? Whoa. Respect, Pilot, man.' Sam rubbed the dog's ears, then reached for his phone. 'So long, ladies,' he said. 'I'm gonna stroll down to the centre of this buzzy ville for a *demi* or two. Then it's off to a club. And then I think I'll round off the evening by treating myself to a private dancer in one of the many de luxe venues available to me.'

'Don't forget your cocaine,' Madeleine said to his retreating back. 'And your Viagra.'

'I don't need Viagra, Auntie,' said Sam, and he shot her a wicked smile before disappearing through the garden gate.

'Is the girl really a ginger minger?' Dannie asked Deirdre.

'She is anything *but*,' Deirdre told her. Then she turned to Madeleine. 'I understand Perdita and Sam are no longer an item?'

'Sadly, yes.'

'In that case, it's probably just as well that Sam is currently wearing sandals.'

'What on earth are you talking about?'

'Because if he sported socks,' said Deirdre with a smile, 'that girl would knock 'em right off.'

'She's a looker?'

'Yes. And it's just as well, because Bruno is politically incorrect enough to take against anyone who is – how might I say it? – *challenged* in the looks department. And he's so *chuffed* to have her all to himself! Once Aoife and Grace arrive, his nose is going to be seriously out of joint.'

'Why?' asked Dannie.

'Grace is inclined to be a manipulative little minx and she'll be bound to try and lure Greta away from Bruno. Poor Aoife will have her work cut out trying to keep the peace.'

'Kids. Who'd hav 'em?' said Madeleine, noticing abstractedly that Dannie flinched at the glib adage.

'Mammy?' Paloma's voice came floating down from an upstairs window. 'Can I stay the night with Rosa?'

'I'm not the person to ask,' Dannie told her.

'Madeleine? Can—'

But before Paloma could even voice the question, Madeleine called back, 'Of course you can, sweet pea.'

'Yay!'

'"*Thank you kindly*, Madeleine" is the correct response!' Dannie called after her, but the prompt came too late. Paloma was gone.

'My Nani Nua's putting manners on Bruno, believe it or not,' said Deirdre. 'She makes sure he says 'please' and 'thank you'. *And* she's going to cook supper for him. Caspo Tatties, whatever they are.'

'Well, aren't you the smug bitch,' said Dannie.

'I've an idea,' said Madeleine. 'Why not stay here for supper, the pair of you? I've a really splendid cassoulet in the freezer – one of Mme Thibault's specialties.'

'Well, sure! I'd love that.' Deirdre checked her watch. 'But I'd better phone home and just make sure it's OK with Greta.' She fished her mobile out of her bag and dialled. 'Bruno? Put Greta on to me, will you? Sorry – oh sor-*ree* for interrupting your fun!' She covered the mouthpiece with her hand. 'Je*sus* – what a palaver! He's pissed off with me for interrupting their game, dontchaknow. Oh

– hi, Greta. Listen, I've been asked to stay to dinner at Madeleine and Daniel's, is that all right with you? Great. Great! Great! I'll be home around ten o'clock, OK? Thanks, Greta, you're a star. And help yourself to wine, if you like. There's white in the fridge and red on the rack.'

Madeleine got up and reached for the bottle. 'Looks like you've really landed on your feet with her,' she said, refilling their glasses.

'Looks like it,' said Deirdre happily. 'She says Bruno's even promised to have a bath before bedtime.'

'Wow,' said Dannie. 'Greta the Great – hey, that's an anagram. Maybe she has a clone somewhere?' she added hopefully.

Deirdre looked smugger than ever. 'I'm reasonably certain she's one of a kind.'

A sound from behind made the women look round. Daniel had strolled onto the terrace. He'd changed into loose cotton trousers and a baggy T-shirt. His hair was damp and his feet were bare and he smelled of soap, and Madeleine felt herself fall head over heels in love with him all over again, as she did most days.

'*Bonsoir, Monsieur Lennox*!' said Deirdre.

'Deirdre O'Dare!' he replied, greeting her with a kiss. 'A pleasure to see you, as ever.'

'Deirdre has news for you, Daniel,' said Madeleine. 'Allow her to fill you in on your new fan.'

'New fan?' Daniel lowered himself onto a recliner.

'Well,' said Deirdre. 'She's …' The three of them listened as Deirdre waxed eulogistic about Greta again.

And when Deirdre mentioned Greta's mass of strawberry blonde curls and her heart-shaped face and her China blue eyes, Madeleine found herself thinking that she personally would not like to have quite so perfect a nanny as all that.

'"So they built another cottage with big windows and a fine thatched roof, with a grand stable for the little grey donkey. And when the holidays came, they all went up to Dublin on the turf barge and came back by the bus." And that, sleepyhead, is the end of the chapter.'

Greta shut the book and looked down at Bruno.

'Can I have another chapter?' he said drowsily.

'No. Tomorrow.'

'I'd like to go to Dublin on a turf barge.'

'Maybe one day you will. Now, Mistoffelees, it's time for you to go to sleep. Am I allowed to kiss you good-night?'

'Yes.'

'Yes …?'

'Um. Please.'

Greta dropped a kiss on Bruno's forehead and smoothed his hair. He had his two favourite teddies and his Kelly Osbourne doll tucked in beside him, and Pucey the cat was clutched in his fist. 'Night night, *mavourneen*,' she said.

'*Mavourneen*?' said Bruno sleepily. 'That's what my pop calls my momma.'

'I'm going to meet your pop soon. Your mam told me he's coming for the weekend. Will I like him, d'you think?'

'Everybody likes my pop.'

'Oh? Why's that?'

'Pluto?' said Bruno, turning his face on the pillow. 'Am I allowed to talk about my pop?' There was a pause, then

Bruno turned back to Greta and looked at her solemnly. 'Pluto says I'm not allowed to talk about him when he's not here.'

'That's fair enough.' Greta turned on the night light and turned off the reading lamp before moving quietly towards the door. On the threshold she turned to him. 'Sleep tight, sweetheart,' she said.

'Night night, Greta. I'll see you in the morning.'

'Bright and early.'

'Not too early.'

'All right, Mistoffelees. Not too early.' She blew him a kiss and stepped out into the corridor, leaving the door a little ajar so that she could hear him if he called to her.

Downstairs, she loaded the dishwasher, then poured herself a glass of wine. She moved into the study beyond the kitchen, hoping to find a magazine to read, but there was only a *Figaro* in the magazine rack and an issue of *Vanity Fair* she'd already read. The bookshelves were empty: Deirdre hadn't got round to putting books back since they'd been painted, she'd told her. But Greta remembered that she'd seen a copy of American *Vogue* in the sitting room. She strolled into the room and picked it up from the coffee table. The model on the front had the look of a younger-looking Deirdre, she thought, looking up at the portrait that the decorators had hung over the fireplace.

Daniel Lennox's painting depicted a nude Deirdre luminescent on a chaise longue draped in blue velvet. She was lying on her stomach, but her head was turned so that whoever viewed the painting locked eyes with her immediately before letting their gaze travel over the geography of her body. One arm hung languidly over the edge of the chaise longue, the other supported her chin. She wore a distinctly come-hither expression.

Greta moved into the hall, turning off lights as she went. The walls of the downstairs cloakroom were covered in paintings that had to be the work of Bruno and his siblings. Another portrait of Deirdre looked down at her, but this portrait had a pink face and orange hair and a big, beaming smile instead of a come-hither expression.

What must it be like to sit for Daniel Lennox? Greta wondered as she hit the dimmer switch by the front door and climbed the stairs to her room. Might he and Deirdre have talked together? And if they had, what might they have talked about? Might they have joked and laughed? Might they have listened to music? Or would Daniel insist on silence during a sitting? She remembered a biography she'd read of the artist Gwen John, and how humbled she'd been when Rodin had chosen her to be his muse and model. She'd been happy to hold the most demanding poses for hours on end. She'd considered it an honour.

Greta hadn't been too sorry when Bruno had opted out of aperitifs at *chez* Lennox earlier. She was knackered after her day spent travelling, and she knew that her social skills would have been non-existent and she would have run the risk of coming across as a brain-dead bimbo. But she didn't see it as a missed opportunity. She was certain to run into the great man some time during the two months she was scheduled to spend in the village, especially since he and the O'Dares were friends.

Opening the door to her room, Greta kicked off her sandals, then moved across to the French windows. The moment she stepped out onto the balcony, she felt as if someone had draped an invisible pashmina over her shoulders. She looked up. The sky was indigo overhead, a glimmering shade of amethyst on the horizon. A golden moon smiled down on her, the peppery scent of geraniums rose from the window box, a cicada whispered somewhere below. Setting the wineglass on the table, Greta wound her hair into a loose knot, then leaned her elbows on the balustrade and rested her chin on her hands. The wine had brought a flush to her cheeks. She touched a finger to her face, felt the strap of her dress slide down her arm, heard the tinny sound of a church bell strike seven, eight, nine …

"'But soft! What light from yonder window breaks?"' A man's voice rose from the street below.

Greta straightened up so abruptly that her tawny hair came tumbling down over her shoulders.

"'It is the East, and Juliet is the sun!"'

Greta took a step backward, and pulled her strap back up onto her shoulder.

"'Arise, fair sun, and kill the envious moon, who is already sick and pale with grief, that thou her maid art far more fair than she."'

Craning her head a little, Greta could just make out the silhouette of a man standing in a doorway on the other side of the street. 'Are you talking to me?' she asked.

The man stepped out of the shadow and moved into the centre of the narrow street. 'I am,' he said. 'Is your name Greta O'Flaherty, by any chance?'

Greta was astonished. 'How do you know that?'

'I'm a mind reader.'

'Oh yeah? So what am I thinking?'

'You're thinking that this is the most preposterously romantic thing that's ever happened to you, and you're hoping that maybe I'll turn out to be the kind of man you want to marry and live happily ever after with.'

'Ha! You're very sure of yourself!'

'I'm not. I'm a feckin' chancer.'

'You're Irish?'

'*Tá gaeilge orm.* But that's about the extent of my Erse. My report always read "Could do better. Must try harder."'

Greta smiled and moved back to the balustrade. She leaned her elbows on it again, taking care this time that the strap of her dress stayed put.

'Who are you?'

'My name is Sam Newman.'

'You're the photographer!'

'How did you know that?'

'There's a photograph by you hanging on my bedroom wall.'

'Is it any good?'

'I like it.'

'In that case, I'll let you have one of you, if you like.'

'What do you mean?'

'I took one, just now.'

'You took a photograph of me? When I wasn't looking?'

'I did. I hope you don't mind. It would have been criminal not to record that image of you as Juliet for posterity.'

'Juliet?'

'That's what I was quoting from, earlier. Romeo's speech from the balcony scene in *Romeo and Juliet*.'

'I'm impressed. You may have got "could try harder" in Irish, but I'd say your English teacher gave you full marks.'

'Do you want to know how the rest of the speech goes?'

'Give it a lash.'

'It goes: "See! How she leans her cheek upon her hand: Oh! That I were a glove upon that hand, that I might touch that cheek."'

'Shut up!' To cover her confusion, Greta reached for her wineglass and took a sip.

'Oh! That I were that goblet!' said Sam Newman. 'That I might touch that pretty, pouting mouth.'

Greta tried hard to look cross, but couldn't manage it. 'You're a very bold boy, do you know that?' she told him.

'Might I be so bold as to ask a favour?'

'What favour?'

'Might I join you for a glass of wine?'

'*No!*' said Greta, instantly regretting her firmness of tone. 'I mean – well, no, it wouldn't be fitting, under the circumstances.'

'Why not?'

'I am employed as nanny to Bruno O'Dare and I don't want to get the boot on my very first day for entertaining strange men in my employer's house.'

'I'm not a strange man. Deirdre's known me for yonks.'

'Maybe. But I haven't.'

'You will if we live happily ever after. When's your day off?'

'I don't know. I haven't sorted that with Deirdre yet.'

'Can I take you swimming on your day off?'

'Swimming?'

'Yes.'

'To that place – the Laba-something – that Deirdre told me about? The Laba – Lab a…' Greta was covered in confusion again. She wondered if he remembered that 'laba' was the Irish word for 'bed'.

'The Labadabadoo?'

She laughed. 'You really are silly, Sam Newman.'

'The best way to a woman's heart is to make her laugh.'

'Who said that?'

'I did.' The way he cocked his head on one side and the roguish smile he sent her reminded her of someone. 'Well. Will you come swimming with me? I'll pack a picnic. What do you like to eat?'

'I like bacon butties,' she said, remembering now who he reminded her of.

'It's a deal. I make great bacon butties. What's your phone number? I'll text you.'

She told him and watched as he entered it into his phone. Then, taking a step backwards, he kissed both hands and sent the kiss soaring upwards. '"O blessed blessed night! I am afeared, being in night, all this is but a dream, too flattering-sweet to be substantial."'

'Get away out of that!'

Sam Newman unleashed a lethal smile upon her, then turned and strolled away up the deserted village street.

Greta gazed after him, pensively.

12

Deirdre switched on her laptop, then watched through the window as Greta and Bruno mounted bicycles and set off together down the rue Lamballe. The new nanny had suggested that Bruno spend the day showing her around the neighbourhood and she'd packed a picnic to take with them.

Deirdre was glad of an opportunity to start work. She should really have been getting the house back to sorts, but she decided she'd wait until the weekend, when Rory would be around to give her a hand hanging pictures and un-bubble wrapping all the stuff that had been stowed away in boxes.

She'd got home from the Lennoxes' last night to find a note from Greta that read: *V tired. Gone to bed. Bruno sleeping tight. Hope you had a fun evening* ☺

She *had* had a fun evening, but now it was time to knuckle under and get some work done. She'd need to work at full throttle if she wanted to spend quality time with Rory when he came home on furlough. But her computer was taking for*ever* to boot up. What was wrong with the dozy thing? She'd had it serviced before she left LA and it had functioned smartly enough when she'd sent e-mails yesterday.

At last! She opened the file containing her screenplay and scrolled down to where she'd left off.

185

DEE BENEDICT stands looking at a CU photograph
of an ORIENTAL dancer. Her POV turns away to
STEPHEN. STEPHEN autographs an ADMIRER'S catalogue, slides a meaningful look back at DEE. We
infer from the look that he is remembering last
night's rampant sex, and as he takes another
glass from the passing serve-perso—

Well, bugger political correctness, for a start! She'd make
the serve person a waiter, plain and simple. She deleted
'perso' and typed 'waiterrrrrrrrrrrrrrrrrrrrrrrrrrrrrrrr' –
whoa! What was happening? Deirdre jabbed at the space
bar and the runaway *rrr*s stopped. But the minute she
hit the key again, the same thing happened. There must
be something jamming it. Trusting there was nothing more
serious wrong, she tapped a few other keys at random. Uh
oh. Something was up. The *f* key didn't respond at all, and
neither did the *s*, the *d* or the *g*. She tried *y* and instantly regretted it, because *y* became 'yyyyyyyyyyyyyyyyyyyyyy'.
When she pressed *u*, all she got was a dull clunking sound.

A virus! *How* could her computer have become in-
fected with a virus? She was religious about keeping her
firewalls and anti-virus programs and spyware up to date
and she never, ever opened attachments without checking them out first. Oh, *fuck*. What godawful timing.
What was she going to do?

In a panic, she tried to access her organiser to locate
the number of the computer hospital in Montpellier.
The programme didn't respond. Reaching for the
telephone directory, she consulted it with frantic fingers,
then dialled a number.

''Allo?'

Oh, God. She was going to have to try and make herself understood. Deirdre's French was woeful at the best of times, but to have to try and explain a technical problem to a computer boffin was going to be a nightmare. Luckily, the receptionist sussed instantly that she was both a Luddite and a French-language mangler and she switched at once to heavily accented English.

'Madame, I suggest you bring ze laptop in to us. We cannot 'elp you over ze telephone.'

'Can it be fixed today?'

She could almost hear the Gallic shrug over the line. 'Zat ees not for me to say.'

'I can't do without it!'

'Zat ees what everybody says. You want your computer fixed, we 'ave to see it first.'

'OK,' said Deirdre, shooting a look at her watch. 'I'm on my way.'

Ripping the plug out of the socket, Deirdre tucked the laptop under her arm, fished keys off a hook, then realised that – hell's teeth! – if she was delayed in Montpellier, Bruno and Greta would be locked out of the house. She'd have to find them and give Greta a spare key. But Greta's number was in her organiser on the laptop – she still hadn't had the cop-on to key it into her phone, and Bruno didn't have a cell phone. Why why *why* was she so fucking scatty? Rory had said something about getting Bruno sorted with a phone ages ago, and she hadn't got round to it. Where might the pair of them have gone? She was going to have to try and find them and she hadn't a clue where to look – unless she could prevail upon someone to do her a favour?

She keyed in Dannie's number but was diverted to voice-mail. She tried Madeleine next, remembering even as she dialled the number that Madeleine had said something last night about meeting a client today. But someone picked up.

'Lennox,' came the laconic greeting. It was Sam's voice.

'Sam! It's Deirdre here – I wonder can you help me?'

'What's up, Deirdre?'

'I have to get my ass into Montpellier – my computer needs emergency surgery – and Bruno and the new nanny have gone off cycling. I've no way of contacting them, and they won't be able to get into the house if I'm stuck in town. Could you be a star and come and wait for them here until they get back? I need someone to let them in.'

'Sure. You've to leave right away?'

'Yes.'

'I'll be over in five.'

'Thank you!'

Deirdre took advantage of the five minutes' grace to make herself a little more presentable. She had no desire to expose herself to the sartorial snootiness of the beautifully coiffed and shod demoiselles of downtown Montpellier. By the time Sam arrived, she was looking a little less frayed around the edges.

'You're a star!' she told him. 'I've no idea how long they'll be gone, but they took a picnic, so I don't imagine they'll be back until after lunchtime. Help yourself to any-thing you want. There's the makings of lunch in the fridge and feel free to raid Rory's wine rack.'

'Stop fussing, and just go go go!' said Sam, shooing her through the door.

She gave him a quick kiss on the cheek and was gone.

*

The computer hospital wasn't far from the Place de la Comédie. Deirdre parked the car badly and legged it, the offending laptop clamped between ribcage and elbow.

When she got there, a queue of long-faced people sitting in a line greeted her. It was like a scene from a veterinary hospital and she had an image of loads of laptops undergoing brain surgery in the rooms beyond. She approached the receptionist.

'We spoke earlier,' she said breathlessly. 'I have a sick laptop.'

'As do all zeese people.' With a languid hand, the receptionist indicated the queue of bereaved laptop owners.

'I'm prepared to pay extra,' said Deirdre, 'if you can get me to the top of the queue.'

The receptionist made a moue and turned her attention to her computer screen. 'You are the fourth person so far today to 'ave made that request,' she said. 'I can offer you a VIP diagnostic, but even so eet eeze unlikely that a technician will be available to look at your machine until later this afternoon.'

'Fuck it!' Deirdre nearly said – but luckily didn't. She didn't want to botch her chances of getting VIP treatment.

'I suggest you leave your machine with me and call back later. At, say …' the receptionist looked down her patrician nose at her screen again 'half past four o'clock?'

'Half past four?' said Deirdre meekly. 'That's brilliant. *Merci beaucoup, Madame.*'

Fuck fuck fuck it, she thought again as she signed a chit. Should she go home and phone the joint later to see if her computer had been sorted? But if it *was* ready for her at half past four o'clock, she'd never make it back to town before close of business. Bummer. She'd just have to write off the day.

'*Merci*,' she said again, pushing the chit across the counter towards the receptionist. '*Vous êtes très gentille.*' And then she handed over her computer and left the shop.

What was she going to do in Montpellier for four hours? She'd have lunch, that's what she'd do. But she'd make it a late lunch. First she'd go shopping and buy herself something lovely in white to wear to Bianca's forthcoming *fête champêtre*.

Madeleine Lennox had introduced her to a shop that stocked the most exquisite stuff in town. Deirdre usually tried to avoid shopping anywhere in France because the saleswomen were all so alarmingly snooty, but the *vendeuses* in this exclusive little boutique had perfected the knack of making you feel like a princess. They routinely extracted thousands of euros from the women who patronised them.

It wasn't far. It was in a fashionable enclave on one of the narrow lanes off the Place de la Comédie. The moment she walked through the door, the salesgirls were vociferous in their delight at seeing Deirdre again. What had she in mind? Something in white? Hmm? White was not really Madame's colour – how about this pricey little wisp of chartreuse chiffon? Ah, the dress code happens to be strictly white? *Ne vous inquiètez pas* – we will find something perfect for Madame … something elegant? Or something pretty? Something perhaps a little … sexy?

Something pretty would be good for a garden party, Deirdre thought. Some type of a tea dress. But hang on

– Saturday would be the first time Rory was going to see her again in weeks. It might be good to combine sexy with pretty.

Mais bien sûr! The *vendeuses* knew exactly what she needed. They embarked on a flurry of gesticulation, to-ing and fro-ing across the shop floor. Underwear, of course, was the first consideration. An exquisite little Twenties-looking bra in ivory silk; French knickers to match; an outrageously overpriced pair of stay-ups with ribbons. A shoestring strapped slip dress in featherweight silk, to be worn under a confection of cream lace so fragile it looked as if it would melt if you eyed it too hard. A pair of pearl drop earrings. Dainty T-strap shoes in ivory kid, the kind that a Busby Berkeley dancer might have worn. A small purse embroidered with seed pearls.

She came, she saw, she conquered – but Deirdre nearly hyperventilated when she handed over her credit card. She had never overcome the middle-class guilt associated with excess. She fled the shop with the *vendeuses* cooing appreciative *au revoirs* at her retreating back.

Lunch next. *Croque Monsieur* and a glass of red wine – *no! Salade* and Evian. She wanted to look svelte on Saturday. She sat on the terrace of a busy café on the Place de la Comédie and idly leafed through *Elle* magazine as she toyed with her salad. Oh! Bliss! There on the centrefold was her new frock! She felt a frisson of pleasure. How gratifying for her fashion sense to be endorsed by *Elle*! But then, as she studied the photograph, she wasn't so sure …

The model was an old-fashioned beauty of the forties film star variety. She had been styled as such, reclining on a chaise longue in a boudoir setting, surrounded by lots of satin cushions and wielding an ostrich feather fan. She was dewy of skin and glossy of hair, she was coy yet provocative, and she was very, very young.

Oh, God. Had the *vendeuses* bumsteered her? Was she, Deirdre, too old for this look? Were these the kind of clothes that a wealthy man might buy for his very much younger mistress? Deirdre had a sudden vision of herself rolling up at Bianca's *fête champêtre* looking like mutton dressed as lamb. Bianca got away with wearing white because – like Elizabeth Hurley – she had claimed it long ago as her signature colour, but white was so *virginal* – and it had been a long time since Deirdre had been a virgin: cue hollow laugh. Maybe she should have played safe and gone for something a little plainer, a little more elegant, a little less, well, *girlish*?

Shucks. It was too late now, she decided, summoning the waiter. The damage was done. Maybe if she stuck to salad and Evian water for the rest of the week some miracle would happen and she'd shed half a stone and carry the look off somehow? But her period was due, and even if she lost half a stone, she'd still look bloated. Feeling completely pissed off, Deirdre paid her bill, hefted her glossy carrier bags and headed for the computer store.

The boffin who came out of surgery to consult with her had good news and bad news. The good news was that her computer did not have a virus. The bad news was that there had been a spillage. A spillage? It looked like orange juice, he told her. *Orange juice?* How had orange juice got into her computer?

Bruno. Of course.

'So what can I do?' Deirdre asked, wishing her French was better.

The boffin evidently wished so too because after some futile French techno-talk, he asked the receptionist to act as interpreter. The hard drive was intact, said the receptionist, but the computer itself was destroyed. Was there anything that could be done? *Mais bien sûr!* There was an option open to her, but it was an expensive one. The boffin could download all Deirdre's programs from her intact hard drive and load them onto a brand new computer. How long would that take? A day.

'So if I come back here this time tomorrow, will I have a brand new computer ready to go, with all my stuff on it?' asked Deirdre.

'You will, Madame,' the receptionist assured her.

'Done deal.' And Deirdre left the computer store and marched back towards the Place de la Comédie thinking that Bruno's spilled glass of orange juice had probably been the dearest drink in the history of the universe. But there was absolutely no use in crying over spilled juice.

'How did it happen?' she asked Bruno on her return. He was bouncing on the trampoline in the garden, and Greta and Sam were reclining alongside on sun loungers. Well, Sam was reclining, bare chested. Greta was rather more decorously perched.

'I'm sorry, Momma. It happened yesterday. I was looking for a book on Amazon and I knocked over my juice. Only a small bit splashed on and I didn't think it was important because it had happened once before at home, and Dad just put the keyboard in the washing machine.'

'You can put a *keyboard* in the washing machine, Bruno, but you most certainly cannot put a *laptop* in the washing machine. Anyway, I thought we had a rule about not drinking anything when we're working on computers?'

'But that's a stupid rule. You break it all the time. You always have coffee in front of the computer, and wine.'

'It's my computer,' said Deirdre, huffily, 'ergo I make the rules. And you'd better bloody stick to them in future. You have caused me no end of grief, my boy.'

Bruno stopped bouncing and looked chastened. 'Sorry, Momma,' he said.

'You'd better mean it.' Deirdre turned to Sam. 'Thanks so much for holding the fort, young Newman. I hope you didn't have to hang around here *all* day?'

'I did. Greta and Bruno didn't get back until an hour ago. But it was no hardship. I just soaked up a few rays and read my book.'

'Did you get an awful fright when you got back to find a strange man in the house?' Deirdre asked Greta.

'No. I already knew who Sam was. I met him by chance last night.'

Deirdre was flummoxed. 'You *met* Sam? What do you mean?'

'Oh, don't get me wrong,' said Greta, sounding very flustered. 'I wasn't out or anything like that, I, er—'

Sam intervened like the gallant he was. 'I happened upon Greta sitting on the balcony of her bedroom,' he said, 'when I was on my way home from roistering. And very fetching she looked too.' He sent Greta a smile, then rose to his feet and pulled on his T-shirt.

There was an unmistakable vibe there, Deirdre thought. Maybe she ought to help it along a little? 'Won't you stay for a drink, Sam?' she asked. 'Or for supper?'

'Thanks very much for the offer, but I can't. I promised

Daniel and Madeleine I'd cook for them tonight. Goodbye, Deirdre. See you, Bruno. *Au revoir*, Greta.' And Sam disappeared through the French windows, into the shade of the house.

Deirdre slid a look at Greta, who was still perched on the edge of the sun lounger. She was looking a little pink around the cheeks, but it might just have been from the sun.

'You're very fair-skinned, Greta,' she observed. 'You must take the greatest care while you're here. I hope you're slapping on masses of factor 50.'

'Oh, to be sure I am.'

'And you must remember to carry water with you – *everywhere*. It's incredibly easy to get dehydrated in this heat.'

'Yes.' Greta looked up at her with her astonishingly blue eyes and an expression of such candour that Deirdre felt a rush of something strangely akin to love for the girl. 'Deirdre?' she said. 'Sam asked me, if I was free, could I go with him to some kind of party on Saturday afternoon?'

'That'd be Bianca's *fête champêtre*.'

'Oh, yeah – *that's* what he called it! I hadn't a clue what it meant.'

'Well, if you don't mind dragging Bruno along with you, feel free to go,' Deirdre told her. 'I can't let you off Bruno detail on Saturday, I'm afraid, because I'm going to have to work. There'll be no partying for me.'

'Oh, what a shame!'

'Yes, it is,' said Deirdre grimly, thinking about the lacy ensemble that had cost her the earth. 'I'll simply have to catch up big time this weekend.'

'Well, I'll be more than happy to take Bruno along,' said Greta.

'Yay!' Bruno started bouncing again, this time to the rhythm of his favourite song. 'I *love* big butts …'

'The only thing is,' Greta went on, 'Sam says this party is an all-white affair, and I don't have anything that fits the bill. I thought I might be able to borrow something from you – a T-shirt and shorts or something, or an old frock. Whatever you might be able to spare.'

And Deirdre looked down at the sweet, wholesome, old-fashioned beauty of Greta's heart-shaped face framed by those tumbling strawberry blonde curls and said, 'I've got a better idea.'

'Oh?'

She picked up the glossy carrier bag that contained the dress she'd bought that day, the dress that she wouldn't be wearing on Saturday after all, and handed it to Greta. 'Have a look in there,' she said.

Greta peered into the carrier bag and Deirdre saw her face go pinker still. 'Oh, no, Deirdre,' she said, shaking her head. 'This is the kind of bag that even *smells* dear. I can't be wearing your new designer frock.'

'The frock's not new,' said Deirdre, switching effortlessly into improvisational mode. She knew that if Greta guessed the dress was brand new, she would back away from it like a startled fawn. 'I bought some underwear and accessories in an obscenely overpriced shop that happened to be next door to the menders. I've had that dress for yonks - it's the only white thing I possess, and it needed a new zip. You're welcome to it – it's way too young for me anyway.'

Greta looked doubtful as she drew the gossamer creation out of the carrier bag. 'It's beautiful,' she said. 'Are you sure, Deirdre? I'd hate for anything to happen to it.'

'I'm absolutely sure,' said Deirdre. 'It'll look far better on you than on me. You're welcome to it.'

Greta looked from Deirdre to the dress and back again, and Deirdre was touched to see that the girl was blinking back tears. 'Thank you so much,' she said. 'Thanks a million, Deirdre. That's the nicest thing that anyone's done for me in ages.'

'I'll draw the line at the shoes and the accessories, though,' said Deirdre, snatching back the bag in mock proprietorial fashion. 'I'll be returning them to the shop.'

Well ... maybe *not* the underwear, she thought with a smile, remembering the darling little ribbons on the stay-ups. The underwear could be Rory's welcome home present.

13

INT. GEORGIA'S APARTMENT — typed Deirdre.
FADE IN

We are CLOSE on Georgia's face. Despite her
sunglasses, it is clear she has been crying.
She is still wearing the earrings that Stephen
gave her —

A tentative knock came to the study door.

'Yeah?' Deirdre said abstractedly, all her attention on
her computer screen.

'I'm sorry to disturb you, Deirdre. I just wanted to ask
what you thought. Is it – does the dress look all right on
me?'

Deirdre pressed save, then turned.

Greta was standing framed in the study door, a vision
in fragile white lace. Her legs were bare, her hair was
loose and her eyes were shining.

'You look absolutely breathtaking,' said Deirdre.
'You'll take the sight from Sam's eyes.'

Greta bit her lip and looked away in embarrassment.
'Arra, away out of that!' she said.

Deirdre cocked her head on one side, assessing. 'Tell me
this. Did you ever think about becoming a model, Greta?'

'Yes. I've worked in the past as a model in life-drawing classes.'

'No, I meant as a *model* model. Fashion, beauty products – that kind of thing.'

Greta shook her head. 'I'm not really into fashion. Anyway, I'm not tall enough to be a model.' She looked down at her feet. 'Do the gutties work?' she asked.

'Gutties?'

'The shoes. That's what my grandpa always used to call canvas shoes. Gutties. I bought them in the market the other day.'

Greta was wearing a pair of plain white, rope-soled espadrilles. 'Yes, they work,' said Deirdre. Actually, she thought, they worked better than the shoes and expensive stockings she had bought. There was something ingenuous about Greta's pared-down simplicity.

'Yo!' Bruno came hurtling into the room, but was brought up short by the vision that was his Nani Nua. '*Yo!* You look all – all white and pretty!'

'*Go raibh míle maith agat!*' said Greta, ruffling his hair. 'Are you ready to go to this shindig?'

'Yeah, yeah, yeah!' Bruno was wearing white shorts and a T-shirt and he was carrying Pucey cat.

'Do you know the way to Bianca's house?' Greta asked him.

'Yeah, yeah, yeah! I love big butts …' sang Bruno, tossing Pucey cat and failing to catch him.

'But me no buts,' Greta told him. 'And pick up Pucey.' She turned back to Deirdre. 'Are you sure you won't be able to make it along? Not even for a drink later?'

'No. I'm under serious pressure now. I should have done more work on this screenplay while I was in LA, but I was sidetracked by something that's far too boring to go into.'

'We'll go so, and not be distracting you any more. Goodbye, Deirdre. And thank you, *thank* you again for the frock. I've never worn such a gorgeous frock ever in my life before.'

'Enjoy the party,' Deirdre told her with a smile, adding an automatic, 'be good, Bruno.'

Returning her attention to her computer with a sigh, listening to the sound of Bruno's receding chatter, Deirdre leaned her chin on cupped hands, and re-read the following:

```
We are CLOSE on Georgia's face. Despite her
sunglasses, it is clear she has been crying.
She is still wearing the earrings that Stephen
gave her.
```

Hang on, Deirdre said to herself. When exactly *did* Stephen give her the earrings? That was an important new plot point. Should it have been at the gallery? Or at the dinner to celebrate the exhibition opening? Shit, shit, shit. She found the gallery scene and scanned it, searching for a good place for Stephen to hand over the gift. There wasn't one. It would have to be at the dinner, so. She clicked, double clicked and started scrolling down the dialogue.

The character of Georgia had come to her a couple of days ago and had taken Deirdre quite by surprise. Georgia hadn't featured in her original treatment, and while she was a wonderfully enigmatic character, Deirdre wasn't quite sure how she was going to contribute to the narrative. She was going to complicate things, that was for sure. Deirdre had found herself going off on a plot-line she hadn't anticipated, and it meant that progress on her screenplay was slower than ever.

A laugh from the street made her look up. Through the window she could see Greta and Bruno walking along the rue Lamballe. Bruno was swinging Greta's hand and chattering away like a monkey on speed. Greta was smiling down at him and Deirdre could tell by her expression that she was really listening to him and genuinely interested in what he had to say. Not many adults ever really listened to the chitterings of children, she knew. She really had struck lucky the day she'd opened her mailbox and read the message that began 'A chara ...'

As Greta and Bruno rounded the corner, Deirdre saw a taxi roll down the street from the other direction. It drew up outside the house, but before Rory could emerge, Deirdre was on her feet and running out to greet him.

'Oh, oh, oh!' she cried, flinging her arms around his neck and covering his face with kisses. 'I've missed you so much! I've missed you *oh* so much! Come in, come in – come in at once!'

She practically hauled Rory across the threshold. Once inside, he dumped his bag on the floor of the sitting room and pulled her down onto the couch.

'No,' she said, resisting. She squirmed away and got to her feet, backing off with a smile. 'No – not yet. Let's wait until this evening. I have the most beautiful new lingerie for you to take off.'

'Lingerie? Hmm. I had a dream last night, about you doing the hoovering wearing a French maid's outfit. How about it?'

'Well, you know how much I love hoovering,' said Deirdre. 'But I wouldn't want to shock the new nanny.'

'Oh, yeah. Nani Nua. How are you getting on with her?'

'She's a treasure. I'd be lost without her, Rory. Childminders in this village are as rare as hen's teeth these days, according to Madeleine and Dannie.'

'What about Jeanne-Marie? She was always game.'

'She's gone to live in Montpellier.'

'So, introduce me to this treasure.'

'You'll have to introduce yourself. She's gone to Bianca's *fête champêtre* with Bruno. You just missed them.'

Rory struck his forehead with the heel of his hand. '*Shit!* I'd forgotten about Bianca's fucking *fête champêtre*. Do I have to go?'

'Yes, you do. Daniel's banking on you being there. He phoned earlier and said he'd call in on his way.'

'What time?'

'Some time after three.'

'How is the auld bollix?'

'He's sculpting.' Deirdre's tone was borderline ominous.

'OK, enough said. He needs cheering up, in other words.'

'Yep.'

There was a beat, then Rory said, smiling at her, 'You look great.'

'So do you.' She returned the smile and they remained like that for several moments, just looking at each other and smiling, each enjoying the sight of the other after so many weeks spent apart.

The clock on the church tower chimed three and Rory got to his feet and stretched. 'I'd better grab a shower,' he said. 'But I could use a cup of coffee first. Is there any made?'

'*Bien sûr.*' Deirdre always had coffee on the go when she was working. 'I'll get you a mug.' She went into the kitchen and filled the mug that had 'Papa' writ large on it. It had been a present from Bruno on Rory's last birthday.

When she went back into the sitting room, Rory had pulled an *Irish Times* from his flight bag. 'Thought you'd be interested to know what's going on in your native land,' he told her. 'Take a look at this article.'

'What's it about?'

'It's about the revival of interest in the Irish language.'

Deirdre took the paper from him and studied the column he'd indicated. '"It is well known,"' she read, '"that if you are bilingual as a child it is much easier to learn a third or fourth language later in life. Instead of being perceived as a dead language, perhaps Irish should be promoted to parents of school children as a useful second language to have as well as one that preserves our own heritage."'

'So how's Bruno's Irish coming along?' Rory asked now.

Deirdre looked guilty. 'D'you know – I haven't asked.'

'Has he learned any at all?'

'Does it really matter, Rory? He's so besotted with that girl that even if he only learned a smattering of Erse it would be worth having hired her. And actually, I did hear him say "*Go raibh míle maith agat*" this morning at breakfast.'

'Jesus – the child can say thank you in Irish when he hardly even bothers to say it in English! Nani Nua must be doing him good if she's putting manners on him. How are the girls getting on?'

'Great. They sent e-mail earlier – come and have a look, it's rather sweet.'

Deirdre led the way into her study, sat down in front of her computer and clicked on her inbox. The following materialised.

> Dear Mom & Pop,
>
> Surf camp is cool. We are gonna be real surfer dudes when we finish. Bad luck that we are not a bit nearer the sea in France. When can we go to Ireland to show off our skill to grandpa?
>
> Love Aoife.
>
> PS: Grace says she has a boyfriend, but I don't think he is really.
>
> PPS: Surf camp may be cool, but we kinda miss you guys. See you in two weeks. Melissa says she will definitely be able to take us to the airport by the way, and Grace is real pissed because she wanted Natasha Richardson to do it.

'I'd say Natasha's glad to be let off the hook,' remarked Rory. 'Grace would have single-handedly alerted every gossip mag in LA to the fact that she was going to be seen onto a plane by Natasha Richardson.'

'Talking of gossip mags, somebody told me you were Torso of the Year in *Heat* magazine a while back. Did you get a copy?'

'Are you mad? Why would I want to look at a pic of my torso?'

'You might not want to, but I'd like to have it. I could stick it on the bedroom wall while you're off filming, to remind me of what I'm missing.'

'You're not missing much,' he said.

Deirdre stood up and ran her hands over his shoulders. 'On the contrary. You look super fit. Have you been working out?'

'Me? Work out?' He laughed hollowly, then bent his head to kiss her. Deirdre felt his hands slide under the back of her T-shirt.

She was just about to change her mind about postponing the pleasure of his company until later – how many opportunities for love-making came their way, after all? – when the doorbell rang.

'That'll be Daniel,' she said. 'Run up and have your shower, Rory – and be quick. I can't afford to be lolling around shooting the breeze with Monsieur Lennox. I'm *so* behind with this screenplay. I went through living hell when I thought I'd lost my hard drive.'

'No worries, *mavourneen*,' said Rory, stripping off his T-shirt as they moved into the hall. 'Just remember what Winston Churchill said.'

'What did he say?'

'He said that the only thing to do if you're going through hell is to keep going.'

'Ta muchly for those reassuring words. Now – shoo!'

Rory headed for the stairs and his shower and Deirdre opened the door to Daniel, who was wearing flowing white robes and a white headdress à la Lawrence of Arabia.

'Hello, gorgeous!' she said, standing on tiptoe and kissing him on the cheek. 'Don't you look splendid! Where did you get the *gúna*?'

'Madeleine got it for me in a fancy dress hire shop in Montpellier.'

'You look very dashing.'

'Thanks. I feel like a fucking tool.'

'Come in,' said Deirdre, stepping aside to allow Daniel to pass through into the house. 'Where's Madeleine?'

'She's gone on ahead to Bianca's.'

'So, d'you fancy a beer while you're waiting for Rory? He's having a quick shower.'

'A beer would be good.'

Daniel followed Deirdre into the sitting room, and as she passed through to the kitchen she heard him remark, 'I thought you'd hung that portrait in your bedroom?'

'It *was* in the bedroom,' she called back to him. 'The painters who were redecorating the joint obviously thought it was a jolly jape to hang it there. I've been waiting for Rory to arrive and help me rehang it. Do you want a glass for your beer?'

'Nah. I'll have it straight from the can.'

Deirdre slid a can of Amstel from the fridge shelf, then returned to the sitting room. Daniel was sitting on the couch, gazing at the portrait he'd made of her.

'Thanks,' he said, keeping his eyes on the painting as she handed him the can. 'Hell. I'd forgotten how good I was.'

'*Was?*'

'I haven't painted anything since my last muse left town.'

'But you're sculpting?'

'Yeah.'

'Why do you do it, Daniel, when you dislike it so much?'

'I do it,' said Daniel, snapping the tab on his beer, 'because it helps vent all that pent-up energy. Pah! I'm

206

not sure it's working this time round. Maybe I should take up something else. What would be good?'

'Knitting?' suggested Deirdre flippantly. 'I used to knit in the days when I was an actress, but I was crap at it. Greta knits. She says she finds it therapeutic.'

'Who's Greta?'

'The new nanny I told you about. The one who's a big fan of your work. You will be nice to her if you run into her at Bianca's, won't you? She was hoping to pluck up the nerve to ask for your autograph.'

'What do you mean, "pluck up the nerve"?'

'You have a reputation for being scary, Daniel.'

'I do? But I'm a pussycat.'

'*I* know that.'

'Actually, I'm rather looking forward to meeting your new nanny. Sam hasn't shut up about her.'

'Hasn't he really?'

'No. She was practically the sole topic of conversation at the dinner table the other night. He says he's dying to photograph her.' Daniel looked round the room. 'Where are all your photographs and stuff, by the way? Have you gone all Zen and got rid of them?'

'No. I asked Bianca's girl to come round and tidy them all away while the painters were in. I haven't got round to unpacking them yet. That's Rory's chore for the weekend.'

Rory's voice came from the doorway. 'What's this about a chore for the weekend?' he said. He had slung a white towel around his waist and his hair was damp from the shower. Even at a distance, Deirdre could get the gorgeous, soapy smell of him. God, how she'd missed that! 'Hey, Lennox, ya bollix,' he added.

'Bollix right back at ya,' said Daniel, getting up from the couch. The two men met in the centre of the room and observed the matey male greeting ritual of hugs and manly back-slapping.

The ritual complete, Rory turned back to his wife. 'Is a man not allowed to take time out to relax after weeks spent slaving on a hot film set? What chores have you lined up for me?'

'It's no big deal, darling,' she told him. 'It's just that all those boxes stacked in the dining room need to be unpacked. They're full of books and photographs and crap that Claudine cleared away for the painters.'

'Crap being the operative word. How come you accumulate so much *stuff*, Deirdre? I can't believe that we have two houses crammed full of useless artefacts and books that have never been read.'

'I'd read them if I had time to read them,' Deirdre told him. 'Now, listen up. Don't you think that you should go and get dressed and not keep Daniel hanging around?' She was becoming more and more anxious to get back to her screenplay. She badly wanted to get that business with the earrings sorted.

'I am dressed,' said Rory. 'Since I don't possess a single item of white clothing, I thought I could go to Bianca's sporting a white towel.'

'Nice try, but no cigar,' said Deirdre. 'I bought you some white stuff to wear when I was shopping in Gignac the other day.'

'Crap,' said Rory. 'I might have known I wouldn't get away with it. That's the one bummish thing about being married to a screenplay writer,' he told Daniel. 'They look to the future in terms of plot and anticipate all the developments.'

'Be off with you,' said Deirdre. 'You'll find the clothes in a Bon Marché bag in the wardrobe.' She turned to Daniel as Rory left the room. 'Do you mind if I leave you to your beer?' she asked him. 'I really do have to get back to work.'

'No worries.' Daniel lounged back against the armrest of the couch and returned to his scrutiny of Deirdre's portrait.

'Enjoy the *fête champêtre*,' she told him.

'Yeah,' said Daniel without enthusiasm.

'Send Colleen my love.'

'Jesus, she will be there, won't she? I'm gonna avoid her. She wrote me a letter outlining all the reasons why I ought to paint her.'

'What was the chief one?'

'She said that I was the only person in the world who would be able to capture her tormented soul on canvas.'

'What does a tormented soul look like?'

'Well, I've always been a subscriber to Philip Pullman's theory of daemons.'

'And that is?'

'That souls take the form of certain animals.'

'And what might Colleen's be?'

'A monitor lizard.'

Deirdre slanted him a smile, then left the room to readdress the problem of Georgia's earrings. As she sat down in front of her computer screen, Rory's words about screenplay writers echoed in her mind. *They look to the future in terms of plot and anticipate all the developments …*

Well, not this time, she thought. She really, really hadn't anticipated the arrival of Georgia and just how the newcomer was going to affect her plotline. Georgia had simply marched straight into her screenplay without knocking – demanding to be written – and Deirdre hadn't a clue in what direction she was heading.

Dannie and Madeleine were sitting on Bianca's terrace, nursing glasses of white wine. Dannie was wearing white jeans and a T-shirt and Madeleine was sporting white linen Capri pants and a matching vest.

'You look cool as a cucumber,' Dannie told her. 'Those Capri pants are very elegant.'

'These old things?' Madeleine was genuinely astonished. 'I've had them for years. I dragged them out of the back of the wardrobe expecting to find moth holes in them.'

Bianca's party was buzzing. Everybody had made an effort and decked themselves out in white. Even Colleen had doffed her usual mushroom-coloured fustian and was wearing a kaftan of white lawn, subtly embroidered with pale gold Celtic symbols. She was holding court like a *shanachie* in Bianca's pavilion, talking to members of the village readers' group. Madame Verdurin had dozed off and her head was lolling on her chest, while Madame Prévoste was nodding politely. The pregnant Poiret girl was reclining on a sun lounger on the terrace with her swain, Joel Renard, dancing attendance on her. The mayor was talking politics with the local radio presenter whose dazzling white suit matched his Colgate smile. Several ladies who lunch were sporting meringue-like mother-of-the-bride hats. Further down the garden, Margot had bagged Sam and was sitting on a swing in the shade of a pear tree, swaying to and fro and looking up at him from under her eyelashes. She was dressed in a diaphanous white cheesecloth shift and it was pretty clear that she was naked underneath. Daniel's fellow *boules* players were chatting together in the shade of a cypress tree, looking self-conscious in white overalls, Dora Maar was resplendent in a white sequined velvet collar and Bianca was fluttering around like a fairy in chiffon, greeting guests and effecting introductions and twinkling like the white-hot star of the show she was. A string quartet was playing 'A Whiter Shade of Pale'.

Claudine was keeping an eye on the catering staff, clearly relieved not to have to be obliged to stagger around with a tray herself on this occasion. A long trestle table had been set up on the terrace and it was just as well that French women never got fat, because simply looking at the food on display would turn any other woman into Madame Blobby. The table had been spread with white linen and sprinkled with daisies. White Parian china dishes were heaped with food – which was, thankfully, *not* white, apart from the meringue roulade. There was spinach, pecan and blue cheese tart, there was broccoli and cherry tomato salad, there was Tuscan pizza strewn with red and yellow peppers. There was pink Normandy pork, Mediterranean ratatouille and Moroccan couscous. Transparent slices of smoked salmon lay atop nutty brown bread, miniature crab cakes were heaped on a bed of sliced lemon, blinis were speckled with caviar. A cocktail waiter was serving margueritas and bottles of champagne were nestling in a trough full of ice.

'She'd put you to shame,' said Dannie, watching Bianca greet yet another guest. 'She's a feckin' fantastic hostess. Jethro and I really ought to have a party some time soon.'

'We're way overdue too. I did think about doing something for Daniel's birthday in August, but he hates a fuss being made of him. Oh, look! Isn't it lovely how Joel's so solicitous? He's fetched a cushion for Valérie.'

At the other end of the terrace, Joel Renard was tucking a cushion under the small of Valérie Poiret's back.

Dannie looked morosely over at the happy couple. 'I'd love a bump like that,' she said.

'Really, Dannie? You want another baby?'

'More than anything,' Dannie confessed.

'Are you trying?'

'Oh, yes. But Jethro's away so much, sometimes he misses my most fertile time. I've started to keep a record of when I'm ovulating.'

'Well, don't get too fixated, Dannie. They say there's no greater barrier to conception than being stressed.' Madeleine went to take a sip of her wine, but the glass never made it as far as her mouth. 'Wow. Who's that?' she said.

A girl was coming down the steps that led to Bianca's garden. She looked as if she should be in a Merchant Ivory film or a BBC period drama.

'That,' said Dannie, 'has got to be Deirdre's new nanny. She's got Bruno by the hand. Janey mackers, but she's gorgeous! What's her name again?'

'Greta.'

Keeping her eyes downcast and looking a little uncertain, the girl called Greta made her way across Bianca's beautifully manicured lawn and sat herself down on the sandstone rim of the fountain. Bruno clambered up to sit beside her and started trying to dam the flow of water by putting his hands over the jets. He was obviously enjoying the feeling of the pressure against his palms, because he dissolved into a fit of the giggles. Greta was trying to shut him up, but his giggles were clearly so infectious that she couldn't maintain her façade of propriety. She was laughing openly as she batted at his hands.

'Well! No wonder Sam's smitten,' said Madeleine.

'He's not the only one.' The *boules* players were casting covert glances in the direction of the fountain.

On the other side of the garden, Sam, who had started to push Margot on the swing, suddenly spotted Greta. He looked up at Margot, who was like the girl in the Fragonard painting, suspended somewhere between heaven and earth, said something to her, then quite summarily abandoned her. The momentum of the swing was such that there was no way of slowing things down. Margot had to swing on and she looked extremely cross about it.

'Aha! Look – Sam's sniffed her out,' observed Dannie.

'Oops,' said Madeleine. 'Margot doesn't look too pleased.'

'But the nanny does,' said Dannie. 'Hey – this is great fun! It's like some kind of new spectator sport.'

'Or that computer game that Rosa and Paloma love to play. What's it called?'

'The Sims.'

Greta had greeted Sam with a shy smile. Her porcelain pallor was suffused now with a little pink as Sam sat down beside her. Having got bored with the fountain, Bruno was looking around for something else to amuse him. Seeing Dora Maar strutting her stuff along the path that led to the pavilion, he got up and ran after her, but was waylaid by Rosa and Paloma. The three of them sat down on the grass and started repeatedly rolling down one of Bianca's green baize banks.

'How sweet!' said Madeleine.

'What?'

'Sam and Greta. Look! They've taken their shoes off. They say that's an expression of mutual trust.'

'If you take off your shoes in front of someone?'

'Mm hmm. As long as it's spontaneous. And that pair are positively sparking with spontaneity. Look at the body language!'

'Let's hope,' said Dannie, 'that they don't spontaneously combust.'

Sam and Greta were cooling their heels in the fountain, deep in conversation. From time to time, Greta would raise her eyes to where Bruno and his small *copines* were playing, making sure all was well in his world.

'She's doing her job, I'll say that for her,' said Dannie. 'She's keeping an eye on Bruno. Most girls would be completely distracted by that ride Sam.'

'But hey – Margot's not giving up that easily. Look, there she goes!'

Having finally managed to stop swinging, Margot was now wafting past the *boules* players, distracting them momentarily from their tales of Olympian bowling. When she reached the fountain, she greeted Greta warmly.

'I wonder how they know each other?' speculated Madeleine.

'*I* know how they know each other,' said Dannie. 'I've just recognised her. That's little Greta O'Flaherty from Kilrowan. I haven't seen her in years.'

'You mean you know her?'

'Not really, but I knew her mother. She's the daughter of the local art teacher in the village school. How well she's come on!'

'Greta O'Flaherty! What brings you to Saint-Géyroux?' Margot was forcing air-kisses on Greta.

'Oh!' said Greta. 'It's Miss d'Arcy, isn't it?' It felt weird being air-kissed by someone you barely knew, but she supposed that's how they did things here in France.

'Yes. How funny! The last time I spoke to your mother, she didn't mention that you were going to be in the Languedoc.'

'I only just got here a week ago,' explained Greta. 'I have a job, child-minding.'

'Really? Well, I imagine that's more fun than sitting around starkers in draughty studios.'

'Sorry?' For one horrific moment Greta thought that Margot was referring to her brief stint as a body double, but Margot added with a practised smile, 'A painter friend of mine told me that you were modelling for life-drawing sessions.'

'Oh. Yes. That's true,' said Greta, wondering if this was too much information for Sam. Being a life model was hardly an orthodox job – but then, there was nothing very orthodox about Sam either.

She was right, the news didn't seem to faze him at all.

'In that case,' he said, 'maybe you'd be interested in sitting for Daniel?'

'Daniel *Lennox*? Are you having me on? You *really* think your uncle would be interested in painting me, Sam?'

'I'm reasonably sure he would. He's looking for a new model.'

'Wow!' Greta bit her lip in an attempt to curb the big smile she knew was spreading across her face. 'I'd give anything to sit for him.'

'*You* won't have to give a thing. He'll pay you the going rate. More, probably. He's fairly *flaithiúlacht* when it comes to paying his models.'

Margot looked a bit miffed. 'I understand that impoverished students have to make money somehow,' she said, bestowing a patronising look on Greta. 'I, too, modelled while I was at university, but it was a very different kind of modelling.'

Picking up his cue like a trouper, Sam said. 'What kind of modelling did you do, then?'

'I was a fashion model,' Margot told him, swishing her hair, 'before I got married.'

'You were married?'

'Yes. Everyone assumes I'm a dedicated lesbian because of my relationship with Colleen, but it may interest you to know that I swing both ways.'

'You certainly do,' observed Sam with a nod at the garden swing, adding, 'Sorry. Bad joke.'

Margot looked at Sam over the rim of her champagne flute, then drained it. 'May I ask you to do me a favour, darling, and refill my glass?'

'Er, sure.'

'Thanks. On second thoughs, I'd love a glass of red. I'm sick to death of champagne.' She raised a provocative eyebrow. 'If we're allowed to drink red wine, that is?'

'I don't think the dress code extends to the beverages. Greta, can I get you something to drink?' asked Sam.

'Um, just water, thanks.'

'Can't I tempt you to a glass of champagne?'

'No, thanks. I'm on Bruno duty, remember?'

'And what a lucky boy he is, to be the focus of your attention.' Sam sent a smile over his shoulder at her as he headed towards the drinks table on the terrace.

'So.' Margot sat down beside Greta on the edge of the fountain and gave her an appraising look. 'You're here as an au pair?'

'Yes.'

'How long have you been in Saint-Géyroux?'

'Nearly a week.'

'How are you settling in?'

'Really well. I love it here.'

It was true. Greta loved everything about Saint-Géyroux. She loved the village, she loved the house in the rue Lamballe, she loved Bruno. She had the kindest, most generous employer in the world, she was living a stone's throw from the painter she admired more than any other in the world – and who actually might be interested in painting her! – and she had a gorgeous, ridey bloke coming on to her. Life couldn't get any better – well, apart from the news she'd had that morning. And while that wasn't exactly *bad* news, it was going to take a bit of getting used to …

'Whose children are you looking after?' asked Margot.

'Sorry? Sorry – I was miles away.'

'I asked whose children you're looking after?'

'The O'Dares'.'

'The O'Dares'?' Bianca looked baffled. 'Oh – you mean the *McDonagh*-O'Dares?'

'Do I?'

'Yes. Deirdre kept her own name when she married.'

'Oh? Who's she married to?'

'You mean you don't *know*?'

'No.'

Margot tinkled her trademark crystalline laugh. 'In that case, you're in for a rather divine surprise, darling.'

'Am I?'

'You most certainly are. Deirdre's married to Rory Mc Donagh.'

'Sorry, what did you say?'

'Deirdre O'Dare is married to the actor Rory McDonagh.'

'No ...'

'Yes.' Margot raised a cynical eyebrow. 'You honestly expect me to believe that you didn't know that?'

Greta was lost for words. Her world had just crashed and burned around her. This couldn't be happening. Please, God, please. Make this a dream, she prayed. Make this a nightmare that I'm just about to wake up from.

'No wonder you're looking so shaken,' continued Margot. 'Imagine finding out that your employer just happens to be one of the sexiest film stars on the planet! And there he is now.'

Like an automaton, Greta turned and followed the direction of Margot's smoky gaze. There, standing on the balcony, talking to Bianca, was Rory.

He was leaning against the balustrade, wearing a white shirt open at the neck. His hair was longer than the last time she'd seen him and his cheekbones seemed more prominent. He laughed at some remark of Bianca's and as he raised his wineglass in a toast to his hostess the gold ring on his wedding finger glinted in the light. Bianca smiled at him, then leaned in to give him a peck on the cheek before shimmering off through the French windows. Rory look a sip from his wineglass, yawned, then looked down at the garden. His eyes wandered over the assembled crowd of chattering guests and came to rest on Greta's face. They had never looked greener.

Greta gazed back at him, transfixed.

14

'Well,' said Dannie. 'It looks like the new nanny's just found out the identity of the McDonagh-O'Dare pater-familias.'

'What do you mean?' asked Madeleine.

'Take a look at the expression on her face.'

Madeleine glanced towards the fountain. Greta had risen and was standing barefoot on the grass, looking towards where Rory was descending the steps of the balcony. Her face had gone nearly as white as her dress, her China-blue eyes were huge and her lips were parted in astonishment.

'It's not surprising that Rory's such a mega-star if that's the effect he has on women. She's looks as if she's been turned to marble,' added Dannie.

'She's exquisite.' It was Daniel's voice, and it came from behind Madeleine's chair.

She looked up. Her husband was leaning against the chair back, looking at Greta through very narrow eyes. Madeleine knew that look. She had seen it in his eyes when he had first approached her, years ago in the Demeter Gallery in Dublin. It was the all-seeing, analytical look of a seasoned painter – but it was also the look of a hunter whose quarry has just strayed into his sights.

'You've found your stunner?' she asked him.

'I think so,' said Daniel slowly, not taking his eyes off the girl.

Madeleine felt a mixture of emotions. She felt a rush of pure venom that another woman could provoke such a reaction in her husband and she felt a rush of relief that his muse had arrived at last. She disguised both emotions with a show of flippancy. 'Well,' she said, 'at least you can stop working on that bloody sculpture. It was doing my head in, as well as yours.'

Over by the fountain, Rory had now joined the two women and Sam had arrived with their drinks. It looked as if Sam was effecting introductions, because Greta had recovered some of her mobility and she and Rory were shaking hands rather stiffly. It seemed small-talk was the order of the day.

Madeleine had to admire the skill with which Margot annexed Sam, laying a hand on his arm and positioning herself so that he had perforce to turn his back to Greta. She had also positioned herself against the light, which meant that her cheesecloth skirts were more transparent than ever. Madeleine took a look at Daniel to see if he'd noticed, but it seemed that nothing could distract him from the vision that was Greta O'Flaherty.

Madeleine had never raised objections to Daniel painting other women. It was his job, after all, and to object to it would be as counterproductive as a woman objecting to her husband earning a living as a gynaecologist or an obstetrician. Naked women were an occupational hazard. But Madeleine couldn't help feeling an inchoate fluttering of fear.

Greta turned suddenly and looked across at the terrace, and the eyes of the two women met. Madeleine wasn't the only one who was scared, she realised now. Daniel's stunner was terrified too. Why? What had she to be fearful of? What secrets was she keeping?

The only thing Madeleine was certain of was this: there was something about the arrival of this girl in Saint-Géyroux that meant mischief.

'Rory McDonagh, this is Greta O'Flaherty,' said Sam. 'Greta, this is Rory. Greta's your new nanny,' he told Rory. 'Um. Let me rephrase that. Greta's your *sprogs'* new nanny.'

'I – I'm pleased to meet you.' Greta took Rory's hand, and as she did so, Margot laid a proprietorial hand on Sam's arm and drew him aside.

Greta's eyes roamed the garden, casting around desperately for some escape route. A group of people on the terrace were watching her intently and she felt panic rise. Act normal, she told herself. Just act normal.

'I know this is a frightful cliché,' murmured Rory, 'but it would appear that we need to talk. Let's take a stroll.'

Together they moved across the lawn towards the swing. Greta felt like a marionette in motion as she put one foot in front of the other.

'Sit down,' said Rory when they reached the swing.

She sat, face averted, hands in her lap.

'How did this happen?' he asked.

'I answered an ad in *The Irish Times*,' she told him, 'for an Irish-speaking nanny. Deirdre – your ... your wife – e-mailed me and checked out my references. I had no idea that you were married to her. Please believe me. I'm not some kind of deranged stalker.' Greta started to cry.

'Shh. Shh.' Rory looked around a little uneasily. 'Swivel around on the swing so you're facing away from the house. You don't want anyone to see you crying.'

Again, she did as he told her. 'I'm sorry,' she said in a small voice. 'I'll go – right away. I'll pack up and go back to Ireland.'

'What reason will you give?'

'I'll make some excuse. I'll pretend I got a phone call from my mam to say that something's happened and they need me to come home.'

And then she thought: *what* excuse? Would she have to pretend that one of her siblings had had an accident or that something awful had happened to her mam or her dad? Oh, no, no – she would hate to tell a lie like that – it would be sure to rebound and bring bad cess on her, and worse – on her family. But *what* was she going to tell Deirdre? What other reason could she possibly give for hot-tailing it out of Saint-Géyroux after professing to be so happy here? And she'd be leaving Deirdre in the lurch, and she liked her *so* much! Oh – this was tragic.

'Please stop crying,' said Rory. 'Jesus, Greta, please stop.'

The terseness in his voice told her that, like most men, he was deeply uncomfortable around weeping women. Greta tried to pull herself together, but she couldn't help herself. The tears were coming faster than ever now, turning the fabric of her dress transparent where they landed.

'Listen to me,' said Rory urgently. 'Just calm down and listen to me. Does Deirdre know that you worked on *Love Lies Bleeding*?'

'No. Nobody knows about that. Except my cousin. And you.'

'And Jethro Palmer. He just happens to have a house here. Fuck. This is grim.'

Grim was the word. Five minutes ago, Greta had felt as happy as she'd ever felt in her life, and now she'd been pitched down to a level of wretchedness so *crippling* it was unbearable. She didn't want to have to leave Saint-Géyroux! She didn't want to go back to Dublin, back to that horrible, overcrowded city, back to the place where that bastard Jared Kelly was probably strutting his stuff all over Temple Bar, boasting about the groupies he'd scored and the stupidest one of all who'd gone blubbing off to France. And she didn't want to go back home to Connemara. Not just yet. The tears kept coming.

'Dad!' Bruno had jumped up from the place on the lawn where he'd been sitting with Rosa and Paloma. 'Dad!' he shouted again, racing across to Rory and flinging his arms around his waist. '*Conas atá tú?*'

'Hey! You've got some Irish!' said Rory.

'Yeah. Greta's been teaching me. Greta's legend. She's the best *best* nanny in the history of the universe. She'd gonna take me into Montpellier and – hey, Greta? Why are you crying?' Bruno detached himself from Rory and went over to where Greta was sitting on the swing. 'What's wrong?' He peered into her face with such a concerned expression that it just made her cry harder. 'Please don't cry, Greta.'

'I'm sorry, sweetheart,' she said, scooping him up onto her lap and putting her arms around him. 'But even grown-ups have to cry sometimes.'

'But what are you crying about?'

'I'm crying,' she told him, 'because I have to go away from here.'

'That's OK, I'll come with you. It ain't that bangin' a party, anyway.'

'No, sweetheart. I don't mean the party. I mean Saint-Géyroux.'

'You mean you have to go back to Ireland?' Bruno's voice went up a pitch.

'Yes.'

'What? No – *no!* You can't leave! You're my Nani Nua! Please don't go, Greta. Oh, please don't! Dad – make her stay! You've got to make her stay!' And Bruno started crying too.

'Oh, Jesus,' said Rory, running a hand through his hair.

'Please don't go! You can't go, Greta!' Bruno was boo-hooing now, tears spurting out of him like a cartoon character.

'Hush, hush, sweetheart,' said Greta. She mopped up her own tears with the hem of her skirt, then set about mopping up Bruno's. People nearby were giving them curious looks and Rory was looking increasingly uncomfortable.

'Jesus,' he said again, shaking his head distractedly. He shoved his hands in his pockets then shifted from one foot to the other and back again. Finally, as the level of Bruno's bawling rose, he said in a rush, 'Look, Bruno, it's OK. Greta made a mistake, all right? She thought she was going to have to go back to Ireland, but she doesn't have to. It was just a mistake. She's not going anywhere.'

The words worked like magic. Bruno stopped crying as abruptly as he'd started and Greta looked up at Rory, eyes wide with apprehension. 'What?' she said. 'I can't—'

'You can. Deirdre needs you, and it's plain to see that Bruno does too.'

'I do! I do!'

'Rory, you know as well as I do that we're—' Greta wanted to say 'asking for trouble if I stay on', but she didn't want to give out too many distress signals in front of Bruno. Instead, she finished the sentence in Irish, hoping that Rory would understand. But his response wasn't the one she was looking for.

'We'll get through this somehow,' he said. 'We'll just have to manage.'

Greta gave him a doubtful look. 'You're *sure* about this?'

'Yes! Yes! Of course he's sure! You *have* to stay.' The small boy hugged her tighter, then said in a shuddery voice, 'It was awful. Pluto nearly got sick when he thought you might go.'

'Oh! Poor Pluto.' Greta brushed Bruno's hair back from his forehead. 'Is he OK now?'

'Yes. But it gave him an awful fright. Promise you won't go. Promise me and promise Pluto.'

Greta gave Rory a questioning look. He regarded her gravely, then inclined his head.

'I promise,' she said.

'You have to say "solemnly".'

'I solemnly promise,' said Greta.

'"I solemnly promise I will not leave you and Pluto,"' Bruno prompted.

'I solemnly promise,' repeated Greta, 'that I will not leave you and Pluto.'

'Amen.'

'Amen.' Oh, God. There was no going back now.

'If you do, we'll run away and join the Danaans, like Seamus does in the book.'

'And wasn't the same Seamus an awful eejit?' she told him, taking his face between the palms of her hands and planting a kiss on his forehead. 'Now. Run back and carry on the game you were playing with your gal pals. Look, over there – they're waving at you.'

Bruno clambered down from Greta's lap, then reached into the pocket of his shorts and produced Pucey. 'Will you look after Pucey? I'm scared he might fall out of my pocket when I'm rolling down the hill.'

'Of course I'll look after him. Bye, you two.' And Bruno and his imaginary friend went galloping away.

There was silence for a couple of moments, and then Greta said, 'I'm not a hundred per cent comfortable with the idea of staying on, Rory. I really do think it would be better if I—'

'Look. The decision's made, OK? Believe me, I'm not a hundred per cent comfortable with the idea either, but the alternative's equally unattractive. Deirdre can't do without you, Bruno's besotted with you and you can't break a solemn promise to a child.' He drew his breath in, then let it out in a sigh. 'Anyway, what in hell's name is a bloke meant to do when faced with two blubbing babies?'

'I'm not a baby.'

'I'm perfectly aware of that. I meant Bruno and Pluto.'

Another silence fell, then Greta said, 'Does Jethro Palmer really have a house here?'

'Yes. He does.'

'Is he due any time soon?'

'I'll ask Dannie. I think he's in Australia right now.'

'What will you tell him?'

'I won't tell him anything. I'll ask him to be very, very discreet. And it goes without saying that you will have to be very, very discreet also, Corinna.' Rory struck his forehead with the heel of his hand. 'I mean, Greta.'

They looked at each other and Greta knew they were both thinking the same thought.

Rory voiced it. 'It's just as well you changed your name.'

Greta nodded. A frisson went though her when she thought of the consequences of anyone finding out that the Corinna Connelly credited on the cast list of *Love Lies Bleeding* was actually nanny to the children of its leading actor. She looked down at the little stuffed cat that Bruno had asked her to mind for him – the one modelled on the Jellicle cat that Simon had given her. She'd made one for Esther and another as a birthday present for her youngest sister, fashioning tail and whiskers from wool and working the animal's features in black embroidery silk. She'd tried to reproduce the cheeky expression of the original, but for some reason its smile now struck her as malicious rather than cute.

'Time to change the subject,' said Rory. 'It's too dangerous a topic to discuss, and we'll not bring it up again. My final word on it is this: you and I never got up close and personal. We've never met before. OK?'

'We've never met,' repeated Greta.

There was a pause. 'What was that Bruno said?' Rory asked, his tone exaggeratedly jocular. 'About running away and joining the Danaans?'

'The Danaans are in his bedtime story,' she told him.

'What are you reading him?'

'*The Turf-Cutter's Donkey*.'

'I remember it.'

There was a smile in his voice, but Greta couldn't bring

herself to look up at him. Winding Pucey's tail around her finger, she made a mental note to add a bigger smudge to his furry face. That might make him look less spiteful.

'I remember how it ends,' continued Rory. '"There was the turf pile, and there the road to home. They could see the whitewashed cabin at the edge of the bog and the blue turf-smoke rising from the chimney. In all the wonderful past—"'

'"They had not seen anything more lovely,"' murmured Greta.

'Introduce me.'

It wasn't Rory's voice that made her look up. It was a new, unfamiliar one.

The man standing looking down at her was instantly recognisable. He was tall, with leonine features and a mane of silver-streaked dark blond hair that skimmed powerful shoulders. Furrows were etched around his mouth and on his high forehead. He wasn't remotely handsome, but he exuded charisma. It was Daniel Lennox.

Rory obliged with perfunctory introductions. 'Daniel Lennox, this is Corinna ... I mean, this is Greta. And I'm afraid I don't remember your surname, Greta.'

'O'Flaherty,' Greta told him.

'Where on earth did 'Corinna' come from?' Daniel asked him.

Greta shot Rory a look of alarm, but his demeanour remained unruffled. 'Isn't there a famous poem about a barefoot girl called Corinna?'

'You're right. You're a ringer for her, Greta O'Flaherty.'

'Sorry?'

'The girl in the Robert Herrick poem. The one where he tells her she's so beautiful, adornment is unnecessary. You really have astonishing hair, you know. A pre-Raphaelite might envy you it. Sam tells me you've worked as an artist's model?'

'Yes.' Daniel Lennox's artist's eyes were deceptively lazy. She knew full well that he was busy making mental pictures of her.

'Might I paint you?'

She was still feeling unsettled, but she managed a smile. 'I really would like that,' she said. 'But I may not be able to spare the time. I'm working as a nanny to Rory's kids.'

'I'm sure we can come to some arrangement,' said Daniel. 'You have days off, don't you?'

'Yes.'

Daniel took a card from his jeans pocket and a pen from the breast pocket of his black T-shirt.

'What happened to your Arab threads?' Rory asked.

'Bianca asked me to take them off. I kept knocking things over in them. I nearly smashed her Biedermeier spinning frame.' He scrawled something on the back of his card before handing it to Greta. 'That's my private number. Call me any time.'

'Thank you,' she said, looking down at the number and feeling a bit unreal. She – a puny, unworthy student of art – had the private number of one of the finest painters of the twenty-first century and an invitation to call him any time …

A surge of pure gratitude rushed through her – gratitude to whoever was up there looking after her, masterminding her fate. If she had followed her earlier instinct to high-tail it out of Saint-Géyroux, she would have missed this opportunity of a lifetime. She would simply *have* to stay on here now. She couldn't turn down an opportunity to sit for the man she admired most in the world, any more than she could break her solemn promise to Bruno.

It goes without saying that you will have to be very, very discreet …

Oh, she would be more than discreet! She would she be the very *soul* of discretion. Not only that, she would be the best Nani Nua in the world to Bruno and his siblings. She would be the best nanny since Mary Poppins. She would do everything in her power to be of help to Deirdre: she would cook and clean and be her laundry maid; she would bring her mugs of coffee in the morning and glasses of wine in the evening; she would put vases of fresh flowers on the window sill in her study and give her neck rubs at the end of each desk-bound day, and she would scatter rose petals on Jo Malone-scented baths for her, the way she'd read that butlers do in posh resorts. Deirdre O'Dare would *never* have any cause to regret that she'd hired Greta O'Flaherty as her Nani Nua.

'Thank you very much,' Greta told Daniel again, and her thanks came from the very bottom of her heart.

'Read that Herrick poem,' said Daniel in his master-and-commander growl. 'I want to paint you as Corinna.'

That girl again … 'OK,' said Greta meekly. 'Where'll I find the book?'

'There's no need for the book,' Rory told her. 'You'll find it on the internet.'

'Are you serious?' said Daniel. 'You can read *poetry* on the internet?'

'Yep. You can do just about anything on the internet. I'd forgotten that you were stuck in the last century, Lennox.' Rory gave a brief smile, then stretched and yawned. He gave the impression of being perfectly un-ruffled, but Greta knew that inside, he must still be stewing.

A brittle laugh made them turn. Margot was talking to the white-toothed radio presenter.

'Who's that woman?' asked Daniel. 'Wasn't Sam talking to her earlier?'

'She's the partner of Colleen, the writer,' Greta told him.

'Colleen's a lesbian?'

'They swing both ways.' Sam had joined them. He had nicked a bloom from Bianca's magnolia tree and was twirling it between his fingers. 'Margot was most anxious to make that clear, for some reason.'

Daniel raised an eyebrow. 'Don't you think you're being a little disingenuous? She quite clearly fancies you.'

'She's not my type.' Sam looked down at Greta. So did Daniel.

Rory gave her a meaningful look. 'I hope you've no regrets about coming to live here,' he said.

'None, Rory. I have none.' She was glad to realise that her voice was level.

'Me neither. No worries.' Raising his wineglass to her, he drained it, then said, 'Can I get anyone a drink?'

'Red please.' Daniel handed him his glass.

'Same for me.' Sam did likewise.

'I'd love a refill of water,' said Greta.

'Coming up.' Rory turned and strolled away.

'"Put on your foliage, and be seen to come forth, like the spring-time, fresh and green, and sweet as Flora,"' said Daniel.

'What the fuck are you on about?' asked Sam.

'It's from the Herrick poem. 'Corinna Goes a-Maying'.'

'What's a-Maying?' asked Sam.

'It was once traditional for young people to go gathering blossom in the month of May,' said Daniel. 'You can probably do it on the internet now.'

'What a gay thing to do,' remarked Sam. He looked at Greta and handed her the magnolia flower. 'That would look better in you hair than mine, I fancy.'

'"Take no care for jewels for your gown or hair…"' said Daniel.

Sam shot him a look. 'What are you *on*, Daniel? All this spouting of poetry is making me nervous. And you turned up in a frock today. I think your mid-life crisis must be imminent.'

'I've already been through it,' said Daniel. 'I'm an old pantaloon now.'

'OK. Strike mid-life crisis. *Dementia* is imminent,' announced Sam. 'If you're comparing yourself to a pair of pants.'

'Consult your dictionary,' Daniel told him. 'That is, if you own such a thing.'

'I don't need one. I'll go Googling on the spooooky iiiinnterneeeet.'

'Googling?'

'Forget it, Grandpa. I'd better give Rory a hand. He won't manage to juggle four glasses on his own.' Sam headed off towards the terrace and Greta could see the eyes of the behatted ladies who lunch following his progress all the way.

There was a pause. 'Why were you crying?' Daniel asked.

'What?' The question took Greta quite by surprise.

'You've been crying.'

'Did you see me crying?' asked Greta uneasily.

'No.'

'Then how can you tell?'

'I'm an artist. Artists see things that other people can't.'

Greta knew he was right. There was no keeping secrets from artists: they could read your soul in your eyes. And then she thought that the truth would probably come out while she was sitting for him, so she might as well be up-front with him now. She looked down at the magnolia flower that Sam had given her and rubbed one of its waxy petals. 'I was crying,' she said, 'because I thought I might have to go back to Ireland.'

'Why don't you want to go back to Ireland?' asked Daniel.

'It's not the right time for me to go back there.'

'Why not?'

She looked up at him with pleading eyes. 'I learned something new about myself today. I – please don't tell anyone. I don't want anyone to know just yet.'

'I'm a reliable keeper of secrets,' said Daniel.

'I'm pregnant,' said Greta.

15

EXT. STEPHEN'S HOUSE
BY THE RIVER. Running WATER. A PLANE overhead.

We are CLOSE on GEORGIA. She is talking on her
phone, wearing the earrings Stephen bought her.
She looks up at the sky, shades her eyes with a
hand.

GEORGIA: I can't. Someone told me that women in
their first trimester shouldn't fly unless they
really have to.

Georgia smiles, listens.

GEORGIA: Didn't Stephen tell you, Dee? I'm
pregnant.

CUT TO:

Deirdre took off her glasses, set them on the desk
beside her laptop, then slumped back in her chair. God,
she was knackered! A click on today's word count had
told her she'd notched up around 2,000 – bloody good
going for a glorious summer afternoon when she should
have been floating around Bianca Ingram's garden
dolled up in her new frock, instead of stuck in front of

the computer screen in the study wearing scruffy sweat-pants and a T-shirt.

She stood up, stretched, then glanced at her watch. Twenty to seven. Padding into the kitchen on bare feet, she opened the fridge door and reached for the bottle of white wine … that wasn't there. Shit! She'd forgotten she'd told Sam to help himself yesterday. There'd only been a glass and a half left in the bottle and Sam had polished it off.

Damn, damn and blast. There was red wine and white aplenty on the rack, but she wanted something cool. Beer? Nah. Orangina? Ick. Deirdre usually rewarded herself at the end of a working day by lounging on her terrace with a glass of crisp, dry, very cold white wine, listening to Bruno's tales of the adventures he'd been on with Pluto. Today she had neither white wine nor Bruno.

The house felt very empty without her baby boy's babble. Wandering across to the open French window, Deirdre leaned against the jamb and watched a sparrow cooling off in the bird bath. She'd love a swim, but there was no pool in their house in Saint-Géyroux. The Labadou was an option, but the thought of the drive there and back put her off. Dannie had a pool in her garden and there was one in the basement of the Lennox house, but those gals would be at Bianca's *fête champêtre*. Bummer! How she *wished* she'd thought to stick a bottle of white in the fridge …

There'd be white wine by the gallon at Bianca's. And champagne. Maybe she should mosey down there? The sound of laughter from the next-door garden made Deirdre realise that she craved company as much as alcohol. Moving back into the kitchen, she forced her addled brain cells to think. Had she anything to wear to this white-fest? Nope. Only a white swimsuit, and she could scarcely show up wearing that. Oh, hell's teeth! It wouldn't matter a toss if she didn't observe the dress code at this late stage of the day – the party would be winding down around now, anyway.

However, she could hardly roll up in her shabby work clothes. Deirdre ran upstairs, dived into her walk-in wardrobe and slung on a colourful cotton sundress. She wound her hair into a chignon, slicked on a little lip gloss and hid her mascara-free eyes behind sunglasses. There was no time to apply *maquillage*, and Rory hated the stuff anyway. Back downstairs, she grabbed her bag from the hook by the front door and hit the street.

The tinny church bell was striking seven as she walked past. Through the open door of the building, she could see Madame Bouret lighting a candle by the altar rail. Since first coming to Saint-Géyroux, Deirdre had been inside the church once only – and that visit had been motivated more by curiosity about its old world interior than any inclination to worship. Deirdre O'Dare had given up believing in God years ago.

Seven o'clock on a fine summer evening! Her spirits lifted as she rounded a corner onto the main square of the village and saw how pretty it looked, with its bunting and its bougainvillea and its troughs of bright begonias.

'*Bonsoir, Madame O'Dare*,' said the local *curé* as he passed by on the other side of the street.

'*Bonsoir, Père Boucher*,' said Deirdre with a bright smile.

Bonsoir! chirped the budgerigar swinging in his cage on the window sill of Madame Roche's house. *Bonsoir!* chorused several *boules* players from their pitch under the plane tree. *Bonsoir!* fluted Madame Prévoste, perched aloft in her roof garden.

Bonsoir! Bonsoir! Bonsoir! The word floated down from balconies and drifted out through open windows and fluttered through screen doors, punctuating Deirdre's progress as she made her way across the square, past the *caveaux* and down the road that led to Bianca's house.

The gate and the door to Bianca's des res stood open in invitation, and as she climbed the front steps, Deirdre thought what a lovely thing it was to live in a village where you could trust everyone implicitly and where the crime rate was so low that the local *gendarme* was practically redundant. If Bianca lived in Paris or Dublin or in LA, her valuable collection of artefacts would have been well and truly depleted by now.

Through the hall Deirdre went, out onto the balcony, where she accepted a glass of champagne from a flunkey in a white waiter's jacket, whom she recognised as Madame Verdurin's grandson. '*Bonsoir!* Welcome back to Saint-Géyroux, Madame O'Dare!' he said with a smile, and Deirdre rewarded him with a '*Merci beaucoup!*', thinking how good looking the boy had grown since she'd last visited the village.

Below, in Bianca's garden, more good-looking people drifted around, all dressed in white, all talking and laughing and sipping from champagne flutes and wine goblets and beer glasses.

There were Madeleine and Dannie engrossed in conversation on Bianca's terrace; there were Colleen and Margot strolling along the pathway that led to the meditation pavilion; there was Bianca laughing flirtatiously with the local radio presenter; there was Bruno rolling on the grass with Paloma and Rosa – and there was Greta, sitting on a swing, surrounded by a trio of male admirers which comprised Daniel and Sam Newman and Rory.

Suddenly, Deirdre wished she hadn't come.

Down on the terrace, Madeleine and Dannie were finding it pretty tough to be thirty-something.

'Look at her! She has *three* of them dancing attendance on her! She's like the feckin' hot nanny from *Friends*,' laughed Dannie.

'What hot nanny?'

'Did you never see the episode of *Friends* where Ross and Rachel hired a nanny? She was so incredibly stunning that every single guy in the series fell for her.'

Madeleine raised an eyebrow. '*Just* the guys? Then that nanny had nothing on this one. Take a look at the way Colleen's watching her.'

Colleen was standing in the yoga pavilion, hands resting upon the trellised railing, looking as regal as Eva Perón urging the Argentineans not to cry for her. She was regarding Greta with interested eyes.

'Hmm. Maybe I should drop Greta's mother in Connemara a line,' reflected Dannie, 'and warn her that her daughter's attracting a lot of attention in this little *ville*. Not all of it welcome.'

'I'd say she's happy enough with the attention she's receiving from my nephew,' said Madeleine. 'Wouldn't it be a fine thing if she and Sam hooked up together? They'd make a stunning couple.'

'They would,' agreed Dannie. 'They're a pair of rides.'

'While we're just a pair of *rides*,' mourned Madeleine, pronouncing the word French-fashion. 'Doesn't it feel awful to be a wrinkly?'

'Give us a break! You're not a bona fide wrinkly until you try to straighten out the creases in your socks and realise that actually you haven't any on.'

'That's the best incentive I've ever heard to do my ankle-toning exercises.'

On the other side of the garden, Sam had started to push Greta on the swing. Greta was laughing infectiously, the way a child might – no posey Margot-type swinging for her! Rory and Daniel, meanwhile, had left love's young dream to it and were moving purposefully in the direction of the drinks table.

'How weird!' said Dannie.

'What's weird? That Daniel has finally managed to tear himself away from Mademoiselle *Jeunesse Dorée*?'

There was something about Madeleine's tone that made Dannie shoot her friend a look, but her expression was well hidden behind the oversized sunglasses she was wearing. 'No, no. Not at all,' said Dannie equably. 'It's just struck me that that girl – what's her name again?'

'Greta.'

'That Greta has a real look of Charlotte.'

'Charlotte?'

'Charlotte Lambert, the actress Jethro worked with in Ireland a couple of months ago.'

Madeleine took a moment to study the vision that was Greta, then shrugged. 'She's very Lizzie Siddal. Come to think of it, Charlotte Lambert played Lizzie Siddal in that truly dreadful biopic of Rossetti, didn't she?'

'Who's Lizzie Siddal?'

'She was the most famous pre-Raphaelite muse of them all. You'd know her from that Millais portrait of the drowned Ophelia.'

'The one with her hair all floating round her?'

'Yep.'

'I'm a sucker for that painting! I stuck a poster of it on my bedroom wall when I was a kid. It's real romantic.'

'The reality wasn't remotely romantic. Siddal was so desperate for money that she held that pose in a bathtub full of water and very nearly died of pneumonia.'

'So all that guff about suffering for your art is based on truth?' Dannie reached for the bottle to refill their glasses. 'Shock, horror!' she said. 'Someone's had the nerve to breach Bianca's dress code. Look – here comes Deirdre O'Dare dressed in a riot of colour.' A festive-looking Deirdre was stepping onto the terrace. 'Hey, Deirdre! Good to see you. Come and join us.'

'I can't.' Deirdre stooped to kiss her friends. 'I want to locate my husband and pick what brains he has left after an afternoon spent drinking with Jethro. I need to find out how he rates the new nanny.'

'We were just talking about her,' Madeleine told her. 'You should have seen the expression on her face when she made the connection that she was working for Rory. It was priceless.'

'You'll find your man over by the drinks table.' Dannie nodded towards where Rory and Daniel were standing at the other end of the terrace. 'And I think you'll find that he's given the seal of approval to your Nani Nua. We watched him giving her a grilling earlier.'

On cue, Rory looked up. He smiled when he saw Deirdre and said something to Daniel, and then the pair of them were moving across the terrace to join their womenfolk. It was funny, thought Dannie, that two men so famous in their respective fields could go virtually unrecognised here in this little French backwater. Well, not unrecognised, precisely, since everyone in the village knew who they were: *unremarked* was probably a better word. No one in Saint-Géyroux was remotely impressed by their fame or fazed by their presence. Apart from Deirdre's Nani Nua …

On reaching his wife, Rory laid a hand on her shoulder and dropped a kiss on her lips, and Dannie was glad to see that Deirdre, who'd been looking a bit droopy, brightened.

'Sit down with your gal pals, why don't you, and shoot some breeze,' said Rory. 'Philippe?' he said to a passing waiter, 'Could you bring more champagne for the ladies, please?'

'*Tout de suite, Monsieur McDonagh!*' Philippe saluted him and scuttled off, looking only too happy to be of service.

'You certainly made an impression on your new nanny, McDonagh!' Dannie told him as he drew up two more chairs for himself and Daniel.

Rory's face was expressionless. 'I did?'

'Oh, yes, indeedy! I suppose you're inured to the reaction you get when fans recognise you, but I swear I thought that poor girl was going to faint when she set eyes on you.'

'I suppose she nearly fainted when you rolled up, too, Daniel,' remarked Madeleine, 'since she's your biggest fan. Did you ask her to sit for you?'

'I did.'

'And has she agreed?'

'She has.'

'Well, thanks be to God for that,' said Madeleine. 'I'll be glad to see the back of Mr Grumpy Sculptor-Man and his endless requests for Band-Aids. Look at the cut – literally – of his fingers.' Daniel was sporting a rash of Simba Band-Aids on his big hands, presumably to conceal all the cuts that had been inflicted by his chisel. 'He was going through sticking plasters at such a rate,' continued Madeleine, 'that I ran out of grown-ups' Band-Aids and had to steal Paloma's Lion King ones.' Her tone was light and bantering, but Madeleine's face behind the sunglasses was nearly as devoid of expression as Rory's.

'Lion King Band-Aids sit well on Daniel,' remarked Dannie with a smile.

'I'm going to need to invest in a box of them if I carry on working at the rate I did today.' Deirdre was studying a broken nail morosely. 'I'm surprised my fingers aren't bleeding. Ah! Champagne! Thank you, Philippe.' She held out her glass so that the waiter could refill it. 'What'll we toast to?' she asked.

A sudden burst of childish laughter from the other side of the garden made them turn as one. Greta was clinging onto the swing with Bruno on her lap. Sam had wound the ropes tight as a tourniquet and, letting go and stepping back, he was now watching in amusement as the pair spun crazily round and round.

'How about a toast to our Nani Nua?' suggested Deirdre.

'If you had an air to that …' said Dannie.

'You're right,' said Daniel. 'It sounds like something out of Old Moore's Melodies.'

'Or a poem by Yeats,' said Deirdre, adopting a Colleen-esque accent.

'Jesus,' said Rory, 'don't get Daniel started on poetry. He's been quoting Herrick all afternoon. More poetry's been spouted in this garden today than in Plato's bloody Symposium.'

'Nani Nua!' said Deirdre, and 'Nani Nua!' chorused Dannie and Madeleine and Rory and Daniel, all raising their glasses.

But while the toast sounded heartfelt, Dannie wasn't convinced that every single member of the company shared the sentiment.

On the other side of the garden, Sam was holding his phone at arm's length, taking a picture of the laughing face of his uncle's new muse.

And Dannie remembered what Madeleine had said one day, about the ultimate muse being money. If that was indeed the case, she calculated, doing some desultory mental arithmetic, then little Greta O'Flaherty's face was worth a fortune.

'No more spinning round!' commanded Greta. 'Or you'll laugh yourself sick, Bruno, and throw up all over my dress.'

'And that would be criminal,' said Sam, sliding his phone into the hip pocket of his baggy linen trousers. 'It's a beautiful dress.'

'It's not mine,' confessed Greta. 'It's Deirdre's. She lent it to me because I had nothing white to wear here today.'

Bruno was lolling in Greta's lap, gazing up at her. 'Pluto had nothing white to wear either,' he told her. 'But he likes to be different.'

'Where is he now?'

'He got bored of this party. He's gone off to our secret place. He's decided he's going to live there with the Danaans.'

'Down by the—'

'Shh! Don't tell Sam. It's *our* secret place, remember?'

'OK, Mistoffelees. And you're sure Pluto's happy there all by himself?'

'He's not by himself. He has the Danaans. But he wants us to come and visit sometimes. Hey, look! Paloma and Rosa have ice creams.' Paloma and Rosa were tightrope walking along the rim of the fountain, flaunting vanilla ice creams at Bruno and rubbing their tummies. 'Where did they get them?'

'I guess Bianca has ice cream in her freezer. Why don't you go and ask them?'

'I will ask them,' said Bruno, clambering off Greta's lap. 'What's ice cream in Irish?'

'*Reoiteog.*'

'*Is maith liom reoiteog!*' yelled Bruno, taking off in the direction of the fountain.

'Don't fall in!' Greta called at his retreating back. She turned back to Sam with a smile. 'He's a clever wee dote! His Irish is coming on nicely, so it is.'

'What did he just say?' asked Sam.

'He said, "I like ice cream."'

Sam gave her an interested look. 'The pair of you get on really well, don't you?'

'Yeah. He's a great kid.'

'What's this secret place he was on about?'

Greta tucked a bare foot up under her and swivelled a little on the swing. 'It's a place we found by accident one day, halfway between here and the Labadou. We were exploring on our bikes and Bruno wanted a pee, so he took himself off into this great big giant oleander bush and came back all excited, saying it was like the wardrobe in *The Lion, the Witch and the Wardrobe*, but with no snow.'

'And was it?' asked Sam.

'It's a lovely place, yes. It's a stretch of the riverbank that you can't get to any other way than by going through this bush.'

'So the bush is a kind of portal to a secret garden?'

Greta smiled. 'You could say that. There's a flat rock for swimming off, and a cave. That's where Pluto's gone to live, with his magical warrior pals.'

'Who's Pluto when he's at home?'

'Pluto is Bruno's imaginary friend. Hmm. I wonder …'

'What are you looking so thoughtful about, suddenly?'

'I wonder if it isn't a good thing that Pluto's gone to live there. It means that Bruno's letting go a little.'

'What do you mean?'

'Well, it's like anything in life, isn't it? Children reach a stage when it's time to let go of, say, a security blanket, or a favourite teddy, or an imaginary friend. It's all part and parcel of growing up. I can remember quite clearly the night I made the decision to stop sucking my thumb. It was the night before my fourth birthday.'

A sudden yell from Bruno made Greta nearly fall off the swing. As she hauled herself to her feet, she heard the soft bleep of Sam's phone. She swung back to him. 'You never took a picture of me looking like an eejit!' she said.

'I did,' said Sam with maddening equanimity. 'You looked so very silly that the moment deserved to be captured for posterity. If you were a celebrity, I'd send it to

Heat magazine and make a fortune.'

'You bastard! You complete *bastard*. Give me that phone!' Greta slid off the swing and tried to grab it from him, but Sam held his phone aloft, laughing at the ineffectual hopping movements she made in her attempts to recover it. It was useless. Giving up, Greta huffed back to the swing.

'*Bastún salach!*' she muttered under her breath. '*Bhreast thú!*'

'You're beautiful when you're angry, Ms O'Flaherty.'

'*Amadán! Slíbhín!*'

Laughing, Sam moved towards her and took hold of her hand. 'Let me make amends for my unchivalrous paparazzi behaviour,' he said, 'by cooking dinner for you tonight. I'm an excellent cook, and I'll make you whatever you want.'

'No.' Mutinously, Greta cast her eyes downward.

'Come on,' cajoled Sam. 'What culinary delicacy might I set before you that might dissipate your anger, oh lovely girl? What mouth-watering morsel might tempt you? Thai chicken salad? Panzanella? Four and twenty blackbirds baked in a pie?'

A smile moved the corners of Greta's mouth. When she looked up again, Sam's face was just inches from hers.

'I would like you to cook me,' she told him, 'my favourite food of all.'

'Bacon butties?' said Sam.

'Bacon butties,' said Greta.

16

'"Now start to work!" the Wise Woman told him. "Sweep the ashes, fetch the water, cut heather, and make me a fine soft bed."' And that,' Greta told Bruno, 'is the end of the chapter.'

'No! How does the next one start?'

'It starts: "In the little whitewashed cabin on the edge of the bog, they were all very sad without Seamus."' Greta shut the book.

'Won't you read it to me now?'

'No. That's tomorrow night's chapter.'

'But I want to know what happens to Seamus! Does he find the four-leafed shamrock with the dew-drop in the heart of it? Does he get to go home?'

'That, Mistoffelees, would be telling.' Greta kissed a forefinger, then planted the kiss on the tip of Bruno's nose.

'Can you really make a bed out of heather?'

'Heather,' Greta told him, 'makes the finest beds in the world.'

'Does everyone in Ireland sleep on heather beds?'

'Yes,' said Greta with a smile. 'And we keep pigs in the kitchen too.'

'Cool! I'd love a pet pig. Hey! We could make a heather bed in the cave for Pluto.'

'No heather grows around here, I don't think. But we

could make a bed out of lavender for him. That would smell even sweeter than heather.' Greta leaned down to tuck Bruno in. 'But not quite as sweet as you do, *mavourneen*, after your bath.'

'You smell lovely too. Different. What is that smell?'

'It's my perfume. It's called Mitsouko, and I wear it because my mam wears it and it reminds me of her.'

'Are you wearing it today because you're missing your mom?'

'Yes,' said Greta.

She *was* missing her mother. She longed so to tell her about the baby, but she didn't want to worry her with the news just yet. Greta's mother had enough on her plate without having to fret about the fact that there'd soon be another mouth to feed in the O'Flaherty clan. She did not, however, tell Bruno that there was another reason she was wearing Mitsouko. She was wearing it for Sam.

'Why did you change out of that white dress you wore to Bianca's party?' asked Bruno.

'Because it was a party dress, and the party's over.'

'It was a lovely dress. For a dress,' said Bruno, putting suitably scathing emphasis on the word 'dress'. 'You looked like someone out of *Final Fantasy*.'

'What's *Final Fantasy*?'

'It's a computer game. My sister Aoife loves it.'

'I'm dying to meet her.'

'Why?'

Greta sensed diplomacy was called for: Bruno sounded testy, and Greta knew all about sibling rivalry. 'Because,' she said, 'Aoife might teach me how to play *Final Fantasy*.'

'I don't want you to meet her. I want to keep you all to myself.'

'Well, that won't be possible, Mistoffelees.'

'Why not?'

'It's called 'being exclusive', and being exclusive isn't allowed when you've brothers and sisters. I should know.'

'But I met you first! You and me are special!'

'I know that. And we'll always have something special that nobody else will have.'

'What's that?'

'You and me are the only people in the world who know where Pluto's gone to live.' She dropped another kiss on the tip of his nose. 'Now, Mister Mistoffelees with the most kissable nose in the world, I'm going to say night night, sleep tight and don't let the bedbugs bite.'

'There'd be bugs in heather beds.'

'To be sure there would. Heather bed bugs.'

'Are beds in Ireland full of bugs?'

'They're pure swarming with them.'

'Cool,' yawned Bruno. 'I love bugs. *Bug's Life* was my favourite movie after *Shrek*.'

'We'll get it out on DVD some evening, will we? And watch it together, just the two of us?'

'Yes. I mean, yes, please.'

'Good boy! It looks like I might be putting manners on you after all.' Greta moved to the door and turned down the dimmer switch. 'G'night, Mistoffelees!' she said.

'G'night, Greta. I love you.'

'I love you, too.'

Stepping out onto the landing, Greta paused at the top of the stairs, bracing herself to go down. From below she could hear the murmur of voices: Deirdre's bright and animated, Rory's rather more subdued. She was glad that Sam had offered to cook for her that evening. She didn't think she could face the prospect of sitting down to dinner with the happily married McDonagh-O'Dares. Greta took a deep breath, smoothed the blue cotton of her dress and descended the stairs.

In the kitchen, Deirdre was slinging leaves into a dish and Rory was making French dressing.

'Supper's a bit late this evening,' said Deirdre, 'due to Bianca's fête. We really should have taken Madeleine and Daniel up on their offer, Rory, and gone to eat with them in Gignac. There's bugger all to eat in this house apart from store cupboard staples.' She turned back to Greta. 'Thanks for feeding Bruno, by the way.'

'No problem.' Greta had left the party a little earlier than the others in order to get Bruno fed and bathed and put to bed at a reasonable hour.

'You don't have a wheat allergy, I hope?' said Deirdre. 'I'm going to do something with pasta.'

'I've no problem with wheat,' said Greta, 'but I should have mentioned to you earlier that I'm having dinner with Sam tonight.'

'Oh?' Deirdre instantly stopped shredding lettuce and gave Greta an interested look. 'In Gignac?' Since there was no restaurant in Saint-Géyroux apart from the small café, locals tended to drive to the nearby town of Gignac if they wanted to eat out.

'No. He's cooking for me.'

'Then you're in for a treat,' observed Rory. 'He's an excellent cook.'

'What's he cooking for you?' asked Deirdre.

'I know you'll think this is a bit bog-trotter of me, but I put in a special request for – um. For …'

'For?' Deirdre prompted her.

'For … bacon butties.'

Greta couldn't meet Rory's eyes. She knew that he too would be thinking about the last time he'd eaten bacon butties. The words of his answer to the question in the *Vanity Fair* Proust Questionnaire came back to her – the question that read: 'How would you like to die?' *While sitting on a canal bank eating bacon butties in the company of a pretty girl …*

Greta picked up her bag and moved towards the door, glancing at the display on her phone in order to cover her confusion. 'I'd better go,' she said.

'We won't wait up,' said Deirdre with a smile.

When the kitchen door shut behind Greta, Deirdre turned to Rory.

'Can you get over how *sweet* that was?' she said. 'She was *so* mortified by the fact that she has a penchant for bacon butties! What a totally adorable, unsophisticated little thing she is!'

Rory was pouring olive oil into a bowl.

'Rory? Isn't she adorable?'

'Yes,' said Rory, dipping a finger into the French dressing and tasting it. 'She's totally adorable.'

'Hey, beautiful.' Sam answered the door with a dish towel slung over his shoulder. 'Come on in.'

As she stepped over the threshold into Daniel Lennox's courtyard, Greta felt as if she was stepping into a painting by the man himself. This was a sacred space she was entering! This was hallowed ground. This space

– this *sanctuary* – smelled of fertile damp earth, the air that caressed her was a warm embrace, the plash of running water, a lullaby.

And the colour: what astonishing jewel-like colours! Jungle green predominated, with here and there splotches of startling cinnabar and shocking pink. Topaz and amber gleamed from hiding places like the eyes of prowling tigers, and passion flowers – their lash-like petals looking as if they'd been coated with purple mascara – glared down with surprised indignation, as if questioning Greta's right to be there. I am indeed unworthy, Greta thought as she gazed around. I am *so* unworthy to be here.

'It's magic!' she said to Sam.

'Yeah. I guess it is.' Sam stooped to turn off the tap feeding the hosepipe that trickled water at his feet. 'But it's a bitch to take care of. I was on watering detail this evening. Come on through.'

He indicated a flight of stone steps that led up to yet another massive carved oak door. They climbed, then, holding the door open for her, Sam gestured to Greta to precede him through. She found herself in a vast white-washed hall with a vaulted ceiling and a staircase that branched halfway up. Hanging in the stairwell was a river-scape in oils, which Greta recognised instantly.

'*Nocturne Number Three!*' she said in an awed whisper. 'I have a print of it on my bedroom wall at home!'

Sam gave the painting a cursory glance as he crossed the flag-stoned hall. 'The canvas needs to be restretched,' he observed. 'Come along, kitten. The kitchen's this way.'

Greta followed him, trying hard not to look as nosy parker-ish as she felt. She registered a massive fireplace, several solid oak doors, elaborate plasterwork on the walls. In a prominent position, high above the stairs, a plaster representation of a man's face grinned down at her. He'd been given a makeover: pink rouged his cheeks, and carmen glossed his mouth.

'Fun!' said Greta.

'That's the work of Molly,' Sam told her, following the direction of her gaze. 'Daniel's daughter by his first wife.'

'Does she live here?'

'No. She lives mostly with her mother in Paris. Rosa – her half-sister – lives here.'

'Rosa's his daughter by his current wife? One of the little girls I saw playing with Bruno today?'

'That's right,' said Sam, opening the kitchen door. 'You'll meet her tonight: I'm babysitting.'

The kitchen smelled of freshly baked bread and a strong scent of jasmine wafted in from the garden through the open glass doors. Cooking implements littered the surface of the long refectory table, which also boasted a big bowl of oranges, a big bowl of eggs, a big bowl of dried lavender and a small bowl of olives.

'Make yourself right at home,' Sam told her, handing her the olives. 'And I'll bring drinks out onto the terrace.'

Make yourself right at home! Greta smiled as she wandered across the terracotta-tiled kitchen floor and out through the sliding doors. Oh, she couldn't *wait* to fire an e-mail off to Esther to tell her that she'd been instructed to 'make herself right at home' in the house of the most famous Irish painter of them all!

Like the courtyard, the terrace was littered with pots and troughs in which more lush, jungly plants grew. Setting her bag and the bowl of olives down on a slatted wooden table, Greta moved from pot to pot, examining the assorted flora. Pausing by a plant dripping with blood-red blossoms, she toyed with one of its tassel-like flowers.

The sound of a footstep made her turn. Sam had followed her onto the terrace. She saw that he had a bottle of wine in one hand and two long-stemmed goblets in the other. She'd have to dream up some plausible excuse for not joining him in a glass.

'Do you know much about gardening?' she asked him.

'Love Lies Bleeding.'

Her eyes widened in shock. 'I – I – what do you mean?' she said.

'Love Lies Bleeding. To answer your question fully, I don't know much about gardening, but I do know that Love Lies Bleeding is the name of the plant you were looking at. It's also the name of a song by Elton John, as well as being the title of the movie Rory McDonagh's just finished working on in Ireland.'

Change the subject, change the subject, change the subject …

'When are you going back? To Ireland,' Greta asked him.

'I've no plan to go back any time soon. I've plenty of inspiration here.'

'For photographs?'

'Yep.' Sam set to work with a corkscrew. 'Speaking of which, have you checked your phone recently?'

'No. Why?'

'Take a look.'

Greta moved to the table and took her phone from her bag. The message icon was displayed, and when she clicked on it, an image shimmered onto the screen. It was the photo Sam had taken of her on the balcony of her room, on the evening of the day she'd arrived in Saint-Géyroux. She remembered the indigo sky, the golden moon. She remembered how she'd twisted her hair into a loose knot, how the strap of her dress had slid down her arm; she remembered the velvet breath of the evening air, the smell of geraniums, the sound of cicadas. Sam had captured the moment for her and preserved it for eternity.

'Thank you,' she said. 'It's a lovely photograph. I've hardly any nice photos of me. I always end up looking like an eejit.'

'You don't look like an eejit in this.'

'For once. I'm just thinking that it's a real pity my mam doesn't have a mobile phone. She's the only person I know who loves me enough to want a picture of me.'

'Forward it to Bruno.'

'He doesn't have a phone either.'

'Poor deprived little sod. He must be the only kid in the Western world who doesn't have a cell phone.'

'But he will have tomorrow. I'm taking him into Montpellier to buy one.'

'You might save yourself the trouble of a trip into Montpellier. There's a phone shop in Gignac.'

'I know, but he wants me to take him to the multiplex.'

'What's showing?'

'Some animated film about insects.'

'Can I come?'

'As if! You don't want to see an animated film about insects!'

'How do you know?'

The illuminated display on her phone had shut down. Greta could feel Sam's breath on her shoulder and the cotton of her dress suddenly felt very insubstantial. Before she could decide whether or not she wanted him to touch her, he'd moved away.

'Glass of wine?' he asked, picking up the bottle.

'No, thanks. I'm on antibiotics.'

'Never stopped me.'

'I get sick if I drink on antibiotics.'

'You had a glass of wine on your balcony the other night.'

'I wasn't on antibiotics then,' she said.

She hadn't tested positive then, either. It had taken some nerve to go into the local pharmacy and ask for a pregnancy testing kit. She wondered why 'May I have a pregnancy testing kit, please?' wasn't standard issue under 'useful phrases' in her Rough Guide. It had taken her at least three long minutes to make herself understood to the girl behind the counter.

'In that case, what can I fetch you? Water?'

'Yes, please.'

Sam sloped off into the kitchen and Greta sat down at the table and studied the rear view of the house. The sliding glass doors at ground level were the only concession to modernity. Otherwise, the building was as stolid as its eighteenth-century neighbours, the wrought iron deceptively delicate looking, the massive sandstone blocks gleaming gold in the fading rays of the low-slung sun. A balcony ran the length of the first floor, tall windows ranked at intervals, each with its blue painted shutters open, a tangerine sunset reflected in the panes.

'Where is Daniel's studio?' she asked Sam on his return.

'At the top of the house. It has the most amazing light. The roof is half Velux.'

'I'd love to see it.'

'And so you shall, poppet.'

'You'll show it to me?'

Sam gave her a 'doh!' look as he poured Evian into a tumbler. 'Without the great man's imprimatur? Are you mad? I'd rather stick my head in a lion's maw than stick it round the door of Daniel's studio without asking his permission. Even Madeleine isn't allowed to enter his lair without knocking.'

'So what did you mean just now when you said that I'd see it?'

'You'll see it when you sit for him.'

'Oh, of course!' Greta gave herself a mental hug. She found the notion of stepping across the threshold of Daniel's studio so thrilling that she laughed out loud. 'I can't *believe* I'll be sitting for him,' she said. 'Esther will be *so* jealous!'

'Who's Esther?'

'My cousin. She's a fan too.'

Sam handed her the tumbler. 'What do you paint, Greta?' he asked.

'Landscapes, mostly. It's what I love best. Especially Connemara. It's so wild – I just feel really at home there.'

'Is your stuff abstract or representational?'

'Representational.'

'Daniel will be glad to know that. Somebody once said that abstract art is a product of the untalented, sold by the unprincipled to the utterly bewildered.'

'Hello? I wouldn't call Matisse and Picasso untalented.'

'Touché.'

A silence fell and Greta couldn't decide whether it was an awkward silence or a comfortable one. She decided to rekindle the conversational spark, but could think of nothing more scintillating to say than, 'What does Daniel make of Britart, Sam?'

'He despises it. The only conceptual Brit artist he has any truck with is Banksy.'

'Banksy? Yay! Anyone else?'

'No. He went ballistic when he heard that Charles Saatchi had bought one of his paintings. He issued his agent with a directive to buy it back, regardless of the cost.'

'Did he get it?'

'Sadly, no.'

Greta frowned. 'It's weird, but there's something not quite right about the idea of a Daniel Lennox canvas displayed in the same room as Damien Hirst and the Chapman brothers and all them yokes.'

Sam smiled. 'I know what you mean.'

'What about Tracey Emin? What does Daniel make of her?'

'When he heard that her famous tent was destroyed in the Momart fire, he opened a bottle of champagne and proposed a toast to the conflagration that consumed it.' Sam sat down beside her, cocked his head on one side and looked hard at her. 'Speaking of toasts,' he said, reaching for his glass, 'what'll we toast to on this fine evening? The start of a beautiful friendship?'

'Sounds good,' said Greta, mirroring his gesture. She was feeling shy, suddenly. 'Here's to the start of a beautiful friendship.' She took a gulp of sparkling water – wishing it could be wine – then set down her glass. When she raised her eyes to Sam's again, she saw that he was looking at her mouth.

'You have a little trace of something,' he said, 'just there, on your bottom lip.'

'Here?' Greta rubbed with a finger.

'No. Allow me.'

Sam reached out a hand and ran his thumb along Greta's lower lip. When he withdrew it, she wished – on reflection – that she'd obeyed the overwhelming impulse she'd felt to draw his face down to hers and kiss him. But it was just as well she had resisted temptation, because the next thing she heard was a child's voice calling from the balcony above.

'Hello!' said Rosa Lennox. 'You're Bruno's nanny, aren't you?'

Greta looked up. 'That's right. You must be Rosa.'

'I am. And your ears must feel like they're on fire.'

'What?' said Greta with a laugh. 'What on earth do you mean?'

'Bruno wouldn't shut up talking about you all afternoon,' said Rosa.

At around midnight, Madeleine pulled up outside the side gate of number one rue des Artistes. Daniel was asleep beside her, but he woke when she killed the engine.

'Too much red wine,' he grumbled, swinging his legs out of the passenger seat.

'You should have paced yourself a bit better.'

'I tried. But that waiter at the fête worse than death kept refilling my glass.'

'You can't blame him for the fact that you consumed an entire bottle of Leflaive at dinner,' Madeleine told him waspishly, opening the gate.

'It would have been rude not to, seeing as how it came compliments of the chef.' Daniel followed her through the gate, then stopped short. 'Hey. Sam must still be up. What on earth made him decide to light so many candles?'

There were candles everywhere on the terrace – in jam jars, on saucers and in ashtrays. The garden looked magical, as if aglow with fireflies, and the scent of jasmine was so intense it was almost overwhelming.

As Madeleine moved down the path towards the terrace, she saw that Sam was sitting on the swing seat: but he wasn't alone. Greta O'Flaherty was sitting beside him and Rosa was lying curled up between them, her head on Greta's lap. The couple looked so beautiful together that Madeleine stopped in her tracks. 'Wow,' she said. 'If they ever got it together, imagine what stunning babies they'd produce. If Sam hadn't decided that he's getting the snip, that is.'

Daniel winced. 'I dunno where he's going to get the bottle to do that. Hell – you're right,' he added, pausing to admire the pair. 'They make a great couple.'

Sam looked up. 'Hello, Auntie,' he said, getting to his feet and stretching. 'How was dinner?'

'Dinner was fine. How was your evening?'

'Very pleasant indeed, thank you. May I introduce you to Greta O'Flaherty?'

Greta made to rise, but Madeleine said, 'Don't bother getting up. You'll disturb Rosa. Here – let me take her from you and I'll carry her up to bed.'

Madeleine gathered up her sleeping daughter gently. The child stirred, half-opened her eyes and smiled when she saw her mother. 'Shh. Go back to sleep, sweetheart,' said Madeleine, smoothing her hair.

Crossing the terrace with Rosa in her arms, Madeleine passed through into the kitchen. She traversed the hall and climbed the stairs clumsily, Daniel's voice resounding in her ears. 'Welcome to my house, Greta O'Flaherty,' she'd heard him say as she'd left the garden. 'Maybe you'd like to have a look around my studio, since you're going to be spending so much time there?'

And Greta had sounded faint with excitement as she'd stammered her response: 'Yes – oh, yes, thank you! I'd be downright honoured, Daniel, so I would.'

17

'*Bonjour, Madame Bouret!*'

'*Bonjour, Madame O'Dare!*'

Deirdre's cleaning lady was polishing the mirror in the hall. Yikes! thought Deirdre, catching a glimpse of herself in the gleaming glass. Her hair was all over the place and she was still wearing a post-coital flush. She and Rory had miraculously found time for a little hanky-panky that morning after Bruno had left their bed.

'I see you have not yet opened the boxes,' said Madame Bouret.

'The boxes?'

'The boxes in which you packed away all your things.'

'Oh, yeah. I was going to get Rory to do that.'

'I will do it for you if you like.'

'No, thanks, Madame Bouret. Rory knows where everything goes.'

'Very well.' The woman looked a tad stung by the implication that she, Madame Bouret, didn't know every bit as well as Monsieur McDonagh where everything should go in the house. 'We need more Cif,' she said, sounding petulant.

'I'll put it on the list,' said Deirdre.

'And bin bags.'

'Those too.' Deirdre shambled into the kitchen. The

aroma of melting charentes butter had the immediate effect of banishing all thoughts of Cif and bin bags from her mind. Greta was standing by the stove, cooking pancakes.

'Morning, Deirdre,' she said.

'Good morning, Greta. Pancakes for breakfast? What a lucky boy you are, Bruno.' She ruffled the top of Bruno's head, and he went 'tch!' He was busy eating a pancake with one hand and colouring in a picture of a donkey that Greta had drawn for him with the other.

'Do you want a pancake?' Greta asked her.

'No, thanks.' Deirdre flicked the switch on the kettle. 'Coffee is what I want. Strong and black, to get the brain cells going.' She yawned, then sat down at the table beside her cherub. 'Is that the donkey in *Shrek*?' she asked him, studying the animal, which had legs striped in yellow and green.

Bruno gave her a 'doh!' look. 'No. It's Long Ears.'

'Who's Long Ears?'

'He's the turf-cutter's donkey. From the story Greta's reading me.'

'Is it a good story?'

'It's brilliant. It's an Irish story of *mystery* and *adventure*. That's what it says in the book, Greta, isn't it?'

'That's what it says in the book,' agreed Greta.

'And it happens in the Gaeltacht – where Greta's from. Can we go there some time soon?'

'You want to go to the Gaeltacht?'

It was Rory's voice. Deirdre turned and smiled at her husband. Standing framed in the kitchen door, he looked nearly as shagged as she felt.

'The Gaeltacht isn't far from where your grandpa lives,'

Rory told Bruno as he moved to the fridge and took out a carton of tomato juice. 'We could kill two birds with one stone and take in a visit to *dadóg* as well.'

'Kill two birds with one stone,' repeated Bruno. 'That's stupid. Why would anybody want to go around throwing stones at birds?'

'It's an expression,' said Rory. 'It means to do two things at once.'

'Why not just say that then?'

'Because sometimes it's more fun to play with words, darling,' said Deirdre, glancing at her watch. 'Which is exactly what I should be doing now.'

'Playing with words?'

'It's how I earn my living.'

Bruno stuck a forkful of pancake into his mouth. 'What's pancake in Irish, Greta?' he asked.

'It's *pancóg*,' she said. 'And it's rude to talk with your mouth full.'

Deirdre watched as Greta slid another pancake onto Bruno's plate and sprinkled it with a little sugar. 'What are you up to today, Greta?' she asked her.

'I'm going into Montpellier to get Bruno sorted with a phone.'

'Oh, yes. I'd forgotten about that. Rory can give you a lift, can't you, Rory? He's going in to pick up some new software I ordered.'

'No, it's OK,' said Greta. 'I—'

'Rory? You can give Greta a lift into Montpellier, can't you?'

Rory hesitated, then Greta said, 'It's no bother, honestly. Sam said he'd drive me in. I'll text him and remind him.'

Well! thought Deirdre. Good for Greta O'Flaherty! It

looked as if things were motoring along nicely between her and Monsieur Newman. 'Did you have fun last night?'

'Yes,' said Greta. 'I met Rosa – she's a sweetie pie – and Daniel showed me around his studio.'

'Daniel allowed you into his studio?' said Deirdre, astonished. 'Wow. That's some privilege. He hardly allows anyone in there.'

'So Sam told me. But he's going to be painting me soon, so I suppose he wanted me to see where I'd be sitting for him.'

'Is he going to be painting you in your nude?' asked Bruno.

'Oh, I don't think so,' white-lied Greta.

'If he does paint you in your nude,' said Bruno matter of factly, 'don't let him give you a butt the size of the Courbet woman's butt.'

Greta laughed. 'You're incorrigible, Bruno.'

'What's that mean?'

'Um. I don't know the exact meaning. It's a big word my cousin uses.'

'It means,' said Rory, 'that you are a little tyke.'

'I'm incorrigible,' sang Bruno, giving his donkey a purple tail. 'I'm a little tyke!'

'By the way, Deirdre,' said Greta, throwing another knob of butter into the pan. 'Daniel asked me when I might be free to sit for him. I said I'd have to talk to you about it, since you call the shots.'

'Um,' Deirdre considered. 'It could be problematic, since my work load's so ridiculous right now. I can't really spare you except in the evening, and that's obviously not going to be a good time for Daniel.'

'Why is the evening not a good time for Daniel?' demanded Bruno. 'Greta could go there after she finishes reading me my story.'

'Because the evening light's no good for painting,' Deirdre told him.

'I suggested that maybe first thing in the morning might be good, before Bruno gets up,' said Greta.

'First thing in the morning? Like – at *dawn*?'

Greta nodded. 'The light will be fantastic then.'

'But – *dawn*!' Deirdre was impressed. 'You're really prepared to get up at that ungodly hour to sit for Daniel?'

'I'd be more than happy to. Honestly. And I don't mind going to bed early of an evening, so you needn't worry that I'd get too knackered to look after Bruno.'

'It really means that much to you to sit for Daniel?' asked Rory, sitting down at the table.

'Yes. It does.'

'Well, I don't see any reason to object,' said Deirdre, 'as long as you're around once Bruno's awake. Could you get yourself back here by nine o'clock to take care of breakfast?'

'Nine o'clock? That would be perfect – thanks so much, Deirdre! That'll mean four hours in the studio.'

'Is four hours long enough for Daniel?'

'Yes. He says that the expression goes dead after a while and you can't see the soul behind the eyes any more.'

Greta's soul was shining out from behind her eyes now, Deirdre realised. She glanced at Rory to see if he'd noticed how fired up Nani Nua was at the prospect of sitting for Daniel, but he was looking at some article in a back issue of *The Irish Times*. Funny – she thought she'd seen him reading that one yesterday.

The strains of her ringtone came from Greta's bag. She excused herself and pulled out her phone. 'Hi, Sam,' she said into the receiver. 'Is that offer still on of a lift into Montpellier? Fantastic. I checked out that film, by the way. There's a showing at four forty at the Gaumont Multiplex. Do you know where that is? Great! See you in an hour's time, so.' She dropped her phone back into her bag and turned back to Deirdre with a smile. 'I'm sorted.'

'You're going to a movie?'

'Yes. The new Disney.'

'Hey, Rory – why don't you—' Deirdre began, then trailed off. She had just been about to suggest to Rory that he share a ride into town with Sam and Greta before realising that that would be doing a courting couple no favours. 'Why don't you stop off in Gignac and pick up the makings of a barbeque?' she improvised instead. 'We could ask the Lennoxes over this evening, and Dannie and Jethro.'

Rory looked up from *The Irish Times*. There was something rather guarded about his expression. 'Jethro? Isn't he still in Australia?'

'No. Dannie told me yesterday that he's due back today. Hey! A barbeque might be fun. I'll invite them for seven.'

'Yay!' said Bruno, giving the donkey blue ears. 'A baarbie. Will you get spare ribs, Dad?'

'Yes.'

'Why are they called *spare* ribs?'

'Haven't a clue.'

'Wasn't it something to do with Eve?' said Deirdre.

'Wasn't the original woman meant to have been created from a spare rib of Adam's?'

'That's stupid,' said Bruno. 'How could you make a person from a rib?'

'You couldn't,' said Deirdre. 'But God could.'

'But you don't believe in God, Momma!' Red hooves, next. 'Do you believe in God, Greta?'

'I'm not sure,' said Greta slowly, pouring more pancake batter into the pan. 'I'm more a believer in Kismet.'

'What's Kismet?'

'Fate.'

'The fête worse than death,' said Deirdre. 'That's how Daniel described Bianca's garden party. But it wasn't, was it? I thought it was a lovely party.' There was a pause, then, 'Wasn't it?' she said again.

'Yes,' said Rory and Greta simultaneously. But Deirdre saw that they didn't look at each other.

'Madame O'Dare?' Madame Bouret put her head around the door. 'There is a man at the door who wishes to speak to the householder. I think perhaps he is a Jehovah's Witness.'

'Yikes. Can you get rid of him, Madame Bouret?'

'*Bien sûr.*'

'By the way, Madame, did you meet Greta? She's our new nanny.'

'Yes. We met earlier.' Madame Bouret gave Greta a perfunctory smile and her head disappeared back round the kitchen door.

'I introduced myself,' said Greta. 'She looked at me as if I was speaking ancient Egyptian when I told her my surname.'

'Madame Bouret is what they call a treasure,' said

Deirdre. 'But she's a shocking gossip. Don't tell her anything you don't want the rest of the village to know.'

'OK. Thanks for the warning.'

'What's 'gossip' in Irish, Greta?' asked Bruno.

'*Cúlchainteoir.*'

'Cool! Madame Bouret's a *cúlchainteoir.*'

'Don't let her hear you call her that,' said Deirdre.

'It doesn't matter,' said Bruno happily. 'She won't understand. Irish is the *coolest* language ever invented. I could go round calling everybody rude names and they'd never even know.'

'Aha,' said Greta, 'in that case I will take great care not to teach you any rude names.'

'Spoilsport.' Bruno set down his magic marker. 'There. It's finished.'

'It's lovely, darling,' said Deirdre automatically. 'We'll put it on the wall in the cloakroom along with all the others.'

'No,' said Bruno. 'It's for Greta. I made it specially for her.'

'Well, thank you, Bruno,' said Greta. 'I'll put it up on the wall of my room.'

Deirdre got to her feet with a sigh. 'Time to make like a wage slave,' she said, 'and write a few thousand more words.' She took the cafetière out of the cupboard, rinsed it with hot water, then started to spoon Illy into it.

'How's progress?' asked Rory.

'Slow. Things were motoring along quite nicely until a new girl walked into my head and jammed a spanner in the works.'

'A new girl?' asked Rory. 'You've dreamed up a new character?'

'Yeah. Her name's Georgia.'

'And what kind of spanner did she jam in the works?'

'It's a new twist to the plot,' Deirdre told him. 'She's pregnant.'

'Oh!' The pancake that Greta had been flipping missed its mark and fell, hissing, onto the stove.

'My *pancóg*!' said Bruno.

'No worries,' said Deirdre, 'there's plenty of batter left. Greta can make you another one.'

And as she sloshed hot water onto the grains in her cafetière, the left side of Deirdre's brain went to work, trying to calculate the exact time and date when Georgia had conceived her baby.

'Bruno, *acushla*. Don't you think you should change out of your pyjamas?' suggested Greta as she cleared away his plate. 'Sam'll be here soon, and you don't want to keep him hanging around.'

'Why can't I go into Montpellier in my pyjamas?'

'Because you'll look like an *amadán*.'

'*Amadán amadán amadán*.' Bruno slid off his chair and padded across the kitchen floor. Pucey was poking out of his pyjama pocket. 'Did you see my new cat, Dad?'

'Cool,' said Rory. 'Where did you get it?'

'Greta gave it to me. She made it herself. What do you think I should have as the ring tone on my new phone, Greta?'

'We'll work that out when we get it. Now go, Mistoffelees!'

'Bar-bie. Barbeque barbeque barbeque. We're gonna be having a baar-bie.'

Greta waited until the door had shut behind Bruno before turning apprehensive eyes on Rory.

'I'll phone Jethro,' he said, 'and clue him in. Give me your phone number so I can let you know what's happening.' Greta dictated it and he entered it into his phone. 'What time does your film finish?' he asked.

'I suppose around half six.'

'So you'll be back in Saint-Géyroux by half past seven?'

'I guess so.'

'In that case,' Rory said, 'I should have time to talk to Jethro and alert him to the fact that there's something akin to a Feydeau farce being staged in the village.'

'I'm sorry,' said Greta. She bit her lip and looked down at a cuticle she'd taken to worrying. 'I wish I'd never seen that ad in the paper.'

Rory shrugged and ran a hand through his hair. 'I wish we'd never placed it. But there's not a lot to be gained from wishful thinking.'

She raised her eyes to his. 'We'll just have to muddle through somehow, won't we?'

'Yeah. No worries,' said Rory. But his body language told her otherwise.

Having notched up a further thousand words on her screenplay, Deirdre decided to have a late lunch on the balcony off her bedroom and watch the world go by for twenty minutes. She fixed herself a baguette stuffed with smoked chicken and salad and moseyed out onto her wrought-iron eyrie. On the street below, Madame Mercier was scrubbing her doorstep, Madame Verdurin's cat was snoozing in the shade and Daniel Lennox's dog Pilot was ambling homeward.

A sleek black limousine glided down the street, looking utterly incongruous, flanked as it was by doughty eighteenth-century residences. Deirdre knew that the incumbent of the limo could only be Jethro Palmer, on his way back from the airport. She'd texted both Dannie and Madeleine to ask if they fancied coming to a barbecue *chez* McDonagh-O'Dare that night and both had texted back in the affirmative.

Settling back in her chair, Deirdre tucked into her lunch.

'*Bonjour, Madame Mercier!*' she heard from below.

'*Bonjour, Madame Bouret!*'

Deirdre got to her feet again and peered over the balustrade to see Madame Bouret bearing down upon Madame Mercier. The latter stood up and peeled off her rubber gloves. They wore the air of adversaries squaring up for a sparring match.

'*Quoi de neuf?*' Madame Mercier was, as always, on the trail of gossip, looking for news.

'*Ah … vous savez que Madame O'Dare a employé une jeune fille irlandaise?*'

Hmm. Deirdre's ears pricked up. Madame Bouret was talking about Greta.

'*Oui, je le sais,*' came the reply from Madame Mercier.

'*Eh bien, en vidant la poubelle de sa chambre ce matin j'ai trouvé un test de grossesse …*'

Something about the waste-paper basket in Greta's bedroom? Had Madame Bouret been rooting through the waste paper baskets? What a consummate nosy parker her cleaning lady was!

Madame Bouret paused dramatically. *Et la ligne était bleu!*

What? What line was blue?

'*Ce qui veut dire?*

'*Ce qui veut dire qu'elle est enceinte!*

'*Non! Vraiment?*

Enceinte? Deirdre wondered what that meant. Her French dictionary was downstairs in the study. She'd look it up after lunch.

'*Maman!* Madame Mercier's daughter emerged onto the front step of the house opposite. '*Viens vite! Il y a un souris dans la cuisine!*

So there was a mouse – *un souris* – in Madame Mercier's kitchen? Aha! La belle Mercier wouldn't like Madame Bouret being in the know about that. It would soon be all over the village that Madame Mercier's house was infested with rodents.

Deirdre watched in amusement as Madame Mercier bustled back in through her front door and Madame Bouret continued on her way, armed with powerful new knowledge. She supposed that old adage about knowledge being power was what made people gossip. Deirdre had never been much of a gossip herself: she didn't like the way she felt when she was made privy to information that she had no business knowing, and she hated it when people started a conversation with the words 'Did you hear about so-and-so?' Schadenfreude was an emotion that was – for the most part – alien to her.

Deirdre finished her baguette, then scattered the crumbs on the table top for the sparrows to bicker over. On the street below, Daniel Lennox was strolling in the direction of the village square, presumably to join his mates in a game of *boules*. How privileged he was to take life easy like that! How Deirdre would have loved to cycle down to the Labadou for a swim and a *glace* and a natter with Madeleine and Dannie. It would even be a grand thing to idle on here, taking her ease on the balcony, but sadly, there was work to be done.

Downstairs, she dumped her plate in the dishwasher in the utility room, made fresh coffee, then went back into the study.

Before returning her attention to her screenplay, however, she ran a finger along the spines of the reference books aligned haphazardly on the shelf to the right of her desk and located her French–English dictionary. Leafing through to *E*, she read down the list the following: *enceignais … enceindre … enceinte.*

'Enceinte, *a.f.* With child, pregnant.'

18

Spoke 2 Jethro. Rest assured. He's never met u.

Thank God, thought Greta. It was clear from Rory's text message that he'd managed to get hold of Jethro before that evening's barbecue. What had Rory called it? This 'Feydeau farce'.

Greta pressed reply, and sent the following: Ty. Sory 4 all da lies & sory 4 landing u in it. Wil prtend ive nevr met hm 2.

In the back seat of the car, Bruno was trying out ring tones on his new phone. 'These ring tones are all crap,' he said.

'Well, stop playing them, then, and allow us to listen to Bob Marley in peace.' Sam reached out a hand and turned up the volume on 'Stir it Up'.

'I'm going to download 'I Love Big Butts' from the internet onto my phone when I get home,' said Bruno. 'This phone is brilliant. It can do anything. I bet it could even fly to Mars if it wanted. Send me a picture, Greta.'

'Send me a picture, Greta, *please,*' said Greta automatically.

'Pleeeeeeeze.'

'Send him the one I took of you on the balcony,' suggested Sam.

'OK.'

Greta found the photo in multimedia messages and was just about to press send when she was distracted by the *beep beep!* of an incoming message. She accessed it to see '**Ur 4given**' from Rory, then sent the picture flying off to 'Recently Used'. Klutz! *Klutz!* She'd just sent her photo winging its way to Rory's phone.

Oh! What was he going to *think* of her? Should she send him a text to explain? No, no – that would just make things worse. What a *complete* klutz she was! What an *amadán*. The situation would be funny if it wasn't so acutely mortifying. '*Shit!*' she said, with feeling.

'What's wrong?' asked Sam.

'I'm after sending that picture off to the wrong phone.'

'Oh? Whose phone did you send it to?'

'An ex-boyfriend,' she improvised.

'Ow. That could have some kick-ass consequences.'

'It could.'

'Send it to me!' demanded Bruno from the back.

'OK,' said Greta. 'But hang on. I want to be sure I've got it right this time … there!'

The image sent, Greta stuck her phone back in her bag and looked out of the passenger seat window. They'd left Montpellier far behind and had just negotiated the final roundabout onto the road that would take them to Saint-Géyroux. Olive groves and vineyards embraced terracotta-tiled farmhouses and cypress trees punctuated the landscape like dark green exclamation marks. Greta hadn't done any painting yet: she hadn't been able to find the time. And once she started sitting for Daniel, there'd be even fewer hours in the day in which to paint. But that was a minor sacrifice.

'Who else is coming to this barbecue tonight?' Sam asked her.

'As well as your lot? Um, Dannie Palmer and her husband.'

'Jethro's back? Cool. He's one shit-hot film director. He's worked with some amazing stars. Penélope Cruz, Johnny Depp, Charlotte Lambert. Did you know that?'

'No,' said Greta, hating herself for the lie. She could feel Sam's eyes on her now and the left side of her face felt hot.

'You're very alike, you know,' he remarked.

'Who?'

'You and Charlotte Lambert.'

'Get away!'

'No, you are,' he persisted. 'Although you are much more beautiful, Greta O'Flaherty.'

'Get away out of that!' she told him again. 'And keep your eyes on the road.'

'Oh, look!' piped up Bruno's voice from the back. 'There's that lezzer.'

'What?'

'That lezzer. She's hitching a ride.'

By the side of the road, Margot d'Arcy was standing next to a bicycle, holding out her thumb. She was wearing the sarong she favoured – the one with the *síle na gig* pattern – and a skimpy bikini top.

'Bruno!' said Greta. 'Where did you learn that word?'

'Lezzer?'

'Yes.'

'Paloma Palmer told me it. She says that that woman and the other one who goes around in a billowy dress are lezzers.'

'Well, you mustn't call them that!' Greta told him, trying not to laugh. 'It's not very politically correct.'

'My dad says that political correctness spells the death of civilisation,' parroted Bruno.

'He could be right,' said Sam, indicating and pulling over. 'I'd better give her a lift.'

'And don't you *dare* call her a lezzer, Bruno,' said Greta.

'Hi!' said Margot as Sam lowered the passenger window. 'My knight in shining armour!'

'What's the problem?' Sam asked her.

'I have a *pneu crevé*,' she said, leaning forward and swishing back her hair. 'And nothing to pump it with.'

'A what?' said Sam, aghast, and Greta turned and looked intently at the walnut veneer of the dashboard.

'I have a flat tyre.'

'Ah. In that case, in you hop,' said Sam gallantly. 'And I'll stick your bike in the boot.'

He tugged at the lever that released the lock on the boot, swung his legs out of the driver seat and opened a door for his damsel in distress. Margot slid into the back beside Bruno, who gazed at her with manifest fascination. Margot gave him the kind of smile that people who don't really like children give, then settled back against the upholstery and strapped herself in. The seat belt had the effect of emphasising her cleavage and Bruno looked even more fascinated.

'Thanks so much,' said Margot. 'I had run out of water and I was afraid I might get dehydrated.'

'That's easily done in weather like this,' said Sam, wrestling with Margot's bicycle. 'There's a bottle of water on the back shelf. Help yourself.'

'What are those things on your skirt?' asked Bruno.

'They're traditional Celtic symbols,' said Margot, reaching behind her for the water bottle. 'They're associated with fertility and they were also believed to ward off evil in pagan times.'

'They look like ladies doing a wee,' said Bruno.

Leaning forward, Greta turned the volume on the CD player even higher.

Rory came to the door wearing cut-off denims and a T-shirt with *Love Lies Bleeding* emblazoned on the front.

'Snap!' said Dannie, indicating Jethro's identical T-shirt. 'Coincidentally enough, my husband's been there, done that too.'

'Hey, McDonagh,' said Jethro, slapping Rory on the back. 'The last time I saw you was on celluloid.'

'Oh yeah? How green grow the rushes?'

'They're looking good,' said Jethro.

Rory stepped back and held the door open. 'Come on through,' he said. 'Where's Paloma?'

'She's coming with the Lennoxes,' Dannie told him.

Dannie had packed Paloma off to play with Rosa after lunch because she wanted to have a serious talk with Jethro. They'd gone over the same old ground, with her trying to elicit promises from him to cut back on his workload and him agreeing to everything she said while fielding calls. Dannie had got stroppier with every call he took and had finally huffed off to take a shower. But of course, Jethro had joined her in the shower, and inevitably, sure as eggs was eggs and Madonna was bendy, they'd ended up having white-hot sex.

Out by the barbecue, Deirdre was sprawled on a

recliner, marking pages with a red pen. 'Hi,' she said when she saw Dannie and Jethro. 'Glad you could make it.' She set down her printout, then rose to greet her guests.

'We're the first?' asked Dannie.

'Yeah. The Lennoxes should be here soon, and Sam's on his way back from Montpellier with Bruno and Greta.'

'They seem to be getting on like a house on fire, that same Sam and Greta.'

'They do, don't they?' said Deirdre.

'Mmm. Do you think they might …'

'The answer to that is I haven't a clue!' Deirdre moved briskly in the direction of the drinks table. 'Have some wine at once!'

Dannie thought there was something a bit forced about the brightness of Deirdre's demeanour. Maybe she'd been having a tough day in the office? 'How's the screenplay coming along?' she asked.

Deirdre furrowed her brow. 'It's a little *comme çi, comme ça*,' she said. 'Two paces forward, one back, I guess – my manuscript's covered in red pen. I'm bloody glad to have an excuse to chuck it aside – this barbecue was a brainwave. If I hadn't invited you shower around, I'd still be stuck at my desk. Here,' she thrust a glass of white wine at Dannie and grabbed a glass for herself. 'Let's get sloshed.'

'Is your Nani Nua teetotal, by the way?' asked Dannie. 'I noticed that she stuck to water at Bianca's the other day.'

'I don't think she's teetotal,' Deirdre said with that same little furrow of her brow. 'Maybe she just doesn't like to drink when she's on Bruno duty. Aha! Speaking of devils …'

Bruno bounced into the garden, waving his mobile phone. 'Can I go on the internet, Momma, and download a ring tone?'

'Not without someone to supervise you,' Deirdre told him. 'And don't you dare go asking Greta. She's done enough for you for one day and she's probably knackered after the trip into Montpellier in this heat.'

'Bummer,' said Bruno.

'Let's see your new phone,' said Rory. Bruno handed it over, looking as proud as if he'd invented the phone himself. 'Wow. It's pretty high spec. And you've got pictures on already!'

'Show me,' said Deirdre. 'Oh. A picture of Greta. Will you take one of me, Bruno?'

'Yep.' Bruno took back his phone and aimed it at his mother. 'There!' he said, then took a look at it. 'Ha! You look like Yoda.'

'Thanks a bunch,' said Deirdre, taking the phone. She studied it, then showed the image to Rory. 'Do I really look like Yoda?' she asked.

'Well,' he said, with a shrug. 'You do have your hamster face on.'

'Bastard!' she told him, hitting him a dig.

'Hi!' Bruno's new nanny wandered onto the terrace. She was wearing a pretty sundress patterned with peonies, and – to judge by her apprehensive expression – Dannie figured that she still hadn't got used to the fact that she was working for Hollywood royalty.

'Hi, Greta,' said Deirdre. 'I don't think you've met Dannie Palmer, have you?'

'Our paths crossed years ago, in Kilrowan,' said Dannie, shaking Greta's hand. 'But you probably don't remember me. I knew your mam to say hello to.'

'Oh! I'm very glad to meet you,' said Greta.

'And that's Dannie's husband, Jethro Palmer. Jethro!' Deirdre called over to where Rory and Jethro were confabbing by the barbecue, trying to work out the best way to light it. 'Come here and meet my new nanny. Oops! I mean *Bruno's* new nanny, of course.'

Dannie watched as Jethro strolled across the terrace, preparing herself for the tiny stab of jealousy she always felt when she witnessed her husband turn on his Southern charm. But although he performed the meet-and-greet ritual with his usual panache, scooping up Greta's hand and kissing the back of her fingers, he didn't smile that smile that made women melt or murmur his usual compliments. In fact, there was something a little steely about his expression when introductions were effected.

'Jethro Palmer, this is Greta O'Flaherty,' said Deirdre.

'Pleased to meet you, Jethro,' said Greta in a small voice.

'Likewise,' pronounced Jethro before turning brusquely and moving back to the barbecue. But, Dannie thought, strangely enough, Jethro didn't look pleased at all. How rude! The poor child was clearly in awe of him and he hadn't even bothered to switch on his famous charm to put her at ease.

'Hey, Deirdre!' A voice from behind made Dannie turn. Sam Newman was standing just inside the French windows that opened onto the terrace, with Margot d'Arcy by his side. 'Greta says you have a puncture mending kit I might borrow,' said Sam. 'We have an emergency. Margot has a *pneu crevé.*'

'A *pneu crevé?*'

'A flat tyre,' said Margot with a smile. 'Sam very kindly came to my assistance.'

'And I shall do so again,' Sam told her, performing a bow worthy of Jack Sparrow. 'Where'll I find the kit, Deirdre? I'll fix Margot's flat for her.'

'It's in the kitchen.' Deirdre moved towards the French windows. 'Why don't you help yourself to a drink, Margot, while Sam's mending your tyre?'

'Well, thanks, I'd love one.' Margot stepped onto the terrace and Sam followed Deirdre into the house.

'Yo! You ants – *duff!* – doing a dance – *duff!* – please don't end up in my pants,' sang Bruno, hunkering down to investigate a trail of ants that were meandering across the terracotta slabs.

Margot bestowed a saccharine smile on him before moving to the drinks table and pouring herself a glass of red. 'How are you today, Dannie?' she asked.

'Great form.' Dannie took in the sarong, the bikini top and the film-star sunglasses worn as a hair-band and said. 'And it's grand you're looking yourself, Margot.'

'Thank you! I've been working on my tan as well as working on my playscript. I'm lucky to have a job that allows me to work out of doors.' Margot's predatory eyes slid in the direction of the barbecue, where Rory and Jethro were still shooting the breeze. Jethro was lobbing a tennis ball from one hand to the other, laughing at something Rory had said.

Dannie dutifully picked up on her cue. 'I don't think you've met my husband, have you?' she said, raising a hand and beckoning him over. Jethro chucked the ball at Rory, who caught it adroitly, then moved across the terrace towards them, stapling on a smile. 'This is Jethro

Palmer,' said Dannie when he drew abreast of them. 'Jethro, this is Margot d'Arcy.'

'A pleasure to meet you, ma'am!' growled Jethro, sweeping up Margot's hand and depositing a kiss on the back.

'Ah, but we have met before,' said Margot, and the look she gave Jethro was flirtatious.

'We have?'

'Yes. In Kilrowan, when you were making *Mimi's Remedies*. I was an extra in the film.'

'Forgive me,' said Jethro. 'Of course I remember. How could I forget a face as lovely as yours?'

Margot simpered a bit, but Jethro was *plámásing*, Dannie knew. He wouldn't have a clue who Margot was: he'd dealt with hundreds upon thousands of extras in his time.

'Bianca tells me that you worked on a film about the Irish Hellfire Club?' Margot said.

'That's right,' said Jethro.

'And you're starring as Jack St Ledger?' Margot aimed her practised smile at Rory.

'You've been boning up on your *Heat* magazine,' said Rory.

'Hardly.' Margot's laugh was scathing. 'It may interest you to know that I'm a descendant of his. One of my great aunts going way back was a mistress of St Ledger.'

'Really?' said Rory. 'He was quite a womaniser.'

Margot raised a flirtatious eyebrow. 'Typecasting?'

'Not at all. I'm a happily married man.'

Rory's smile was urbane, but there was a flinty look in his eye. Oh, poor him! thought Dannie. And poor Deirdre. How *awful* it must be to have women coming on to her man all the time. Would Margot have had the nerve to flirt like that if Deirdre hadn't taken herself off to the kitchen, she wondered. Or indeed, if Colleen had been there to cast a cold eye on her?

'You're co-starring with Charlotte Lambert, I believe?' Margot persisted. 'Charlotte's a wonderful actress.'

Bruno, who was still monitoring the ant migration, looked up at this. 'Sam thinks Greta looks like Charlotte Lambert,' he announced. 'He says she's the spit of her. Doesn't he, Greta?'

All eyes turned towards Greta, who was sitting on a garden chair with her hands in her lap. Her usually porcelain face had flushed pink as the peonies on her dress and her expression was one of agonised embarrassment. Dannie felt sorry for the girl: she clearly hated being the centre of attention.

'It's true – there is a resemblance,' remarked Margot, sounding a tad reluctant to endorse Greta's beauty.

Others must have been equally reluctant, thought Dannie, since Margot's observation was met by a resounding silence.

'Did you hear the one about the cowboy who wears a hat, waistcoat and chaps all made of paper?' The chirrup of Bruno's voice broke the silence. 'He's wanted for rustling.'

Margot looked at the child with a blank expression. 'I don't get it,' she said.

'Rustling! *Rustling!* Paper *rustles*!' said Bruno. 'And so do cowboys when they steal cattle!'

Margot gave a little laugh. 'It's a very silly joke,' she said.

'My dad says that the silliest jokes are always the best,' Bruno told her. 'Don't you, Dad?'

'Yep,' said Rory. And as he returned his attention to the barbecue, Dannie saw him shoot a look at Greta. But Greta wasn't laughing.

19

At precisely five o'clock the next morning, Greta rang the Lennoxes' door bell. She had set her alarm for half past four and had had a quick shower and a cup of coffee to wake herself up before hitting the street with an apple to go. As she stood waiting for someone to come to the gate, Greta looked up. The sky was pale, opalescent blue, the sun a coppery glimmer on the horizon. There was no one to be seen, no sound to be heard: the village was still fast asleep.

Daniel opened the gate to her, looking shambolic in paint-spattered overalls and yawning like a lion.

'Hello, lovely girl. Come on in.'

Greta stepped into the courtyard of number one rue des Artistes as if she'd been doing it all her life. She had expected to be crawling with nerves, but in fact she had woken that morning feeling preternaturally calm. It was as if this was meant to be, she thought – this union between her and Daniel Lennox was fated, somehow. Kismet.

Daniel led the way through the courtyard, into the hall. 'Do you need anything? Coffee, juice, something to eat?' he asked her.

'No thanks. Just water, please.'

'There's water in the fridge in the studio. Follow me.'

Daniel led the way up the stairs, turning right where the staircase branched. Through an archway they went, then down a long passage, flanked by several doors, that led to another, spiral staircase. They climbed, then Daniel threw open the door to the studio.

The last time she'd visited it had been at night, when the space had been artificially lit. Now the sun glimmering in through the massive skylights made the big room look as if it had been given the Midas touch: every object contained within the four walls appeared gilded. Motes floated in the air like gold dust and the fabric draped over the daybed that stood on a platform in the centre of the room could have been woven by the captive princess in *Rumplestiltskin*.

Greta breathed in the familiar, heady smell of linseed oil, then turned to Daniel with a smile. 'It feels like coming home,' she said.

'In that case, *céad míle fáilte*,' said Daniel, returning the smile. He cocked his head to one side and gave her a look of enquiry. 'Have you read that poem yet?'

'What poem?'

'The Herrick one I bored you to tears with at Bianca's party. Forgive me. I was a bit pissed.'

'You mean the one about Corinna? Um, no. I did mean to, but Bruno has been hogging the internet, looking for ring tones.'

'No worries. I have it here somewhere. Sit down.'

Greta sat down on the edge of the wooden platform and watched as Daniel crossed the floor and rummaged on a shelf so laden with books it looked on the verge of collapse. At the other end of the room, an easel stood next to a long trestle table that bore all the tools of his trade: bottles, palettes, knives, sponges, tubes, tins, spray cans of fixative and paper bags of pigment. Pencils and paint brushes and sticks of charcoal bristled in jam jars, paint-smeared rags drooped from overflowing carrier bags and a cardboard box under the table housed a glass pyramid of empty wine bottles. Daniel checked out a couple of volumes before hitting on the right one, then leafed through until he found the page he was looking for and handed the book to Greta. She read:

> *Get up, get up for shame!*
> *See how Aurora throws her fair*
> *Fresh-quilted colours through the air.*
> *Get up, sweet slug-a-bed, and see*
> *The dew bespangling herb and tree!*

'Hence the daybed,' said Daniel. 'Everybody assumes from the title that Corinna's tripping daintily around a maypole festooned with ribbons, but, in reality, she's a lazy minx.' He glanced up, then back at her. 'And Aurora is most obligingly throwing her "fair fresh-quilted colours" through the glass ceiling.'

They regarded each other in silence for several moments. 'Are you ready to go to work?' he said. She nodded. Daniel gestured towards a screen that stood in a corner. 'There's a screen, if you want it.'

'There's no need.' Greta rose to her feet and slid her feet out of her sandals. Reaching down, she took hold of the hem of her blue cotton frock, gathered up the fabric and pulled it over her head. Underneath, she was naked.

Daniel moved towards her and reached out a hand to

take the dress from her. He threw it over the back of a bentwood chair, then circled her, assessing.

'Beautiful,' he said. 'Perfect.'

Later that morning, Greta pulled the blue cotton dress back on.

'You'll be stiff tomorrow,' Daniel warned her. 'Better take a bath tonight. Or better still, have a swim.'

'I'm not sure I'd fancy cycling down to the Labadou in the dark.'

'There's a pool in my basement. You're more than welcome to use it.'

'You're very kind.'

Daniel opened a drawer and took out a pack of Gitanes and a handful of euro. 'Shall I pay you now, or would you prefer a cheque at the end of the month?'

'I don't think you should pay me at all, Daniel. I've told you – it's a privilege and an honour to sit for you. I'm the one who should be paying *you* – for the master classes.'

Greta had learned more in one morning than she could have done in a whole term of tutorials. Daniel didn't utter a word while he was painting, but when he mixed pigments, or during her well-earned break from holding the pose, he'd talk about the painting process: about the tricks he used to obtain certain textural effects, about the painters who had influenced his own idiosyncratic Expressionistic style, about the similarities between portraiture and landscapes and about the dynamic between figures and textures. He told her to study the masters: Da Vinci for shade, Rembrandt for expression, Chagall for composition and Picasso for line. He spoke of the sensuality of painting, the wet drags and rubs and smudges, and of how, when he painted, it was with such white-hot energy that he became oblivious to anything but his subject matter. It was true, for as Greta had reclined on the daybed with one arm pillowing her head, the other hanging slackly over the side of the mattress, the intensity of his expression had made her wonder if he could read her thoughts.

'Of course I must pay you,' said Daniel in a tone that told her refusal would be futile. 'Cash or cheque?'

'A cheque at the end of the month will be fine.'

'I'll write six and post-date them.' He drew a cigarette from the pack, and lit it with paint-stained fingers.

'Why six?'

'One for each remaining month of your pregnancy. Actually, make that seven. I'm going to want you for a month after your baby is born.'

'Why?'

'For the final portrait in the series. Mother and child.'

Greta touched wood.

'I'm sorry to be pre-emptive. But you're safely through the first trimester, you're young, healthy and you don't smoke.' He looked ruefully at his cigarette, then stubbed it out. 'And nor should I be smoking around you. Forgive me. Have you told anyone else yet that you're pregnant?'

'Just my cousin. I share a flat with her in Dublin and I thought it only fair to let her know, since she may want to let out my room. She was going to keep it for me until I came back in the autumn, but I won't be needing it now.'

'Have you let NCAD know you won't be back?'

'Yes. I sent them an e-mail.' She scuffed the floor with a toe. 'Um, there is one thing you should know, Daniel.'

'What's that?'

'I'd like to have my baby in Ireland. I'd like to be with my mother when the time comes.'

'That's perfectly understandable. But I'll want a portrait of you full term, and that means you won't be able to fly home.'

'Oh. Oh, dear. Well, I suppose boat and train would—'

'Boat and train? When you're that advanced? Are you mad?'

'But how else could I travel?'

'S-class Merc. With a driver. I want to be certain, Greta O'Flaherty,' Daniel told her, 'that you and your baby are transported home as carefully as one would transport a tray of rare phoenix eggs.'

'An S-class Merc!' Greta clapped her hands. 'Oh, how lovely! I'll be going home in the lab of luxury, so!'

'The lab? You mean the lap.'

'No, I don't. As a child, I always called it 'the lab'. It's been "the lab of luxury" in our family ever since. Oh, I can't wait for my ma to see me roll up at the garden gate in an S-class Merc!'

Daniel gave her an indulgent smile. 'What colour would you like?'

Greta remembered the transport Merc that had taken her to and from Ardmore Studios every day when she'd been working first as a chaperone, then as a body double. 'I'd love a powder blue one,' she said. 'If that's all right?'

'And would you like your driver to be the strong and silent type, or cheerful and chatty?'

'Oh, cheerful and chatty, please.'

Daniel gave her an appraising look from under his eyebrows. 'You will promise to come back to me, Greta, after the baby is born?'

She nodded. 'I solemnly promise. How soon d'you think you'll need me?'

'As soon as it's safe for you and the baby to travel.' He reached for a rag and started to clean the brush he was still holding.

'It'll be a couple of weeks, then, I suppose. New babies are really portable – unless they're colicky. Then they scream blue murder for hours on end. Oh, please God don't let my baby be colicky,' she added fervently.

'What makes you so knowledgeable about babies?'

'I'm the oldest of a family of six.'

'Presumably this is your parents' first grandchild?'

'Yes.'

'How do you think they'll take the news?' he asked.

'Arra, they'll be happy once they know I'm happy.'

'And are you?'

Greta didn't even need to think about it. 'Yes, I am. I'm very, very happy.'

'You're very young to be having a baby.'

'I was born to have babies. It's what I've always wanted. I know it's a dead old-fashioned thing to say, but I'm not cut out to be a career girl. I just want to be able to paint and have babies and live in the country. And sure, haven't I loads of other reasons to be happy?'

'Enumerate them.'

'What?'

'Tell me all your reasons to be happy.'

'I'm healthy, I love my family and friends, I'm working in a dream job and you have given me the opportunity of a lifetime.'

'I have?'

'Yes. Every art student I know would kill to be in my shoes right now.' She gave him a big smile.

'Except I've noticed that you don't often wear shoes.'

'I hate wearing them. It's probably a throwback to my childhood. I never bothered with shoes at home during the summer holidays when I was growing up.'

'Elemental.'

'My dear Watson,' she quipped.

Daniel threw back his head and laughed. 'No. That's *elementary*.'

'What's the difference?'

'Elemental has to do with the four elements. Elemental sums you up for me. You're like something half-tamed: a child of nature, a little *fauve*.'

'And what does elementary mean?'

'Elementary means easy.'

'Arra, the English language is a queer auld yoke.'

'And Irish isn't?' Daniel raised an amused eyebrow. 'By the way, have you given any thought to where you might live once the McDonaghs have gone back to the States at the end of the summer?'

'No. I'm sure I'll find a room somewhere in the village.'

'I wouldn't dream of expecting you to find a room. You'll stay here. We have masses of space.'

Greta looked doubtful. 'Are you sure?'

'Absolutely. All of my long-term models have stayed here.'

'In that case, I'd love that! As long as Madeleine doesn't mind.'

'She won't mind.' Daniel narrowed his eyes at her and smiled. 'You make me feel very … avuncular,' he said.

295

'Thank you,' Greta replied, even though she hadn't a clue what 'avuncular' meant.

Daniel reached for a palette knife. 'Off you go then, Corinna. You can find your own way out?'

'I can.'

'In that case, *au revoir* until the same time tomorrow.'

'*Au revoir*, Daniel!'

Greta slipped her sandals back on, crossed the uneven wooden floor to the door and turned the handle. She noticed that the smell of linseed oil in the room had intensified as the sun had risen higher in the sky and she wondered if Daniel had noticed it too. But a glance over her shoulder told her that there was no point in saying anything to him. Daniel had reverted to work mode and was gazing at the canvas on his easel with the fierce, rapt expression of a shaman. Noiselessly, reverently, Greta closed the door to the master's studio behind her.

In the corridor below, a stained-glass window threw a kaleidoscopic pattern onto the stone-flagged floor. She paused to examine it, trying to identify the jewel-coloured glass fragments in painterly terms: French ultramarine, yellow ochre, rose madder, vermilion, cerulean blue, Hooker's Green No. 1 …

'What are you doing?'

She turned to find Sam standing in the corridor, wearing nothing but pyjama bottoms.

'Oh – hi! I'm trying to work out the names of the colours on the window.'

'You funny girl.' Sam yawned and stretched. 'I suppose you've been up for hours?'

'Yep. I've been up since Aurora's been throwing her fair fresh-quilted colours through the air.'

'You've clearly been spending too much time sequestered with Daniel. Translate, if you would be so kind.'

'I've been up since the crack of dawn,' said Greta. 'There was a cock crowing in a garden two doors down from me as I was having my shower.'

'That's Monsieur Verdurin's cock. It's a bloody nuisance. He should be served with an ASBO or put in a pot.' Sam rubbed his eyes, then said, 'Tell me this. Why can't a rooster ever get rich?'

'Hmm. Why *can't* a rooster ever get rich?'

'Because he works for chicken feed.'

Greta smiled. 'Your jokes are nearly as bad as—'

'As whose?'

'As … Bruno's.'

Sam took a step closer to her. 'You smell nice,' he said. 'What perfume is that?'

'Mitsouko.'

'Mit-what-o?'

'Mitsouko. It's the Japanese word for 'mystery'. It's a dead old-fashioned perfume – my mam and my granny both wear it.'

Sam breathed her in again. 'You smell peachy.' Reaching for her hand, he started to lead her down the corridor. 'Come and have breakfast with me,' he said.

'I can't. I've got to get back to mind Bruno. I told Deirdre I wouldn't be any later than nine o'clock.'

'Bummer. I forgot you had a real-life job.'

Emerging from the corridor, Greta paused to look up at *Nocturne Number Three*, the painting in oils that hung over the stairwell. Daniel had captured the turbulence of the river at night in bold strokes of murky blues and greens so dark they looked almost black.

'I still can't believe that I'm looking at the real thing,' said Greta. 'Can I touch it?'

'Be my guest.'

Greta reached out her free hand and caressed the canvas with her fingertips. A little dust rose, and Sam said, 'Madame Thibault had better get her feather duster out.'

'Who's Madame Thibault?'

'She's our housekeeper. She's thick as thieves with Madame Bouret, who does for Deirdre. The cleaning ladies in this village are a kind of mafia, so don't say anything in front of them that you don't want repeated.'

'Mmm – Deirdre mentioned that to me already,' said Greta abstractedly. 'Does Daniel never frame any of his paintings?' She ran her palm over the brush strokes, feeling as if she was stroking the hide of some fabulous beast.

'No. He paints them to be touched as well as looked at. I can't wait for the paint to dry on the portrait he's doing of you.'

Sam slanted her a wicked look and Greta felt herself blush. 'You're such a bold boy, Sam Newman,' she said, reclaiming her other hand and moving towards the stairs.

'Well, you know what ye olde proverb says. Faint heart never won the babe.'

'Daniel says there's a swimming pool in the basement,' remarked Greta, just to change the subject.

'There is.' He indicated a low door tucked away at the foot of the staircase. 'Come and see.'

'I don't have time now. But he told me I could come for a swim later, when I'm off duty.'

'Do. When will you be free?'

'Around nine o'clock.'

'I'll see you then.' Sam opened the front door for her with a theatrical flourish. On the other side of the door stood a woman with a cloth in her raised hand.

'I am polishing ze knockair,' she said.

'Madame Thibault!' said Sam. 'How's it going? Allow me to introduce Greta O'Flaherty.'

'*Bonjour, Madame,*' said Greta.

'*Bonjour, Mademoiselle,*' said Madame Thibault in return. 'I am 'appy to make your acquaintance.'

The response was cordial, but Greta noticed a curious flicker in the woman's eye. She guessed that maybe Madame thought she and Sam had been up to no good – which was a reasonable assumption, since Sam was only half-dressed.

Together they strolled across the courtyard. Sam plucked a passion flower from a trailing vine and handed it to her before opening the gate to let her out. '*Au revoir, petite,*' he said as she passed through. '*A neuf heures!*'

'Nine o'clock?' she said, tucking the flower behind her ear. 'What's happening at nine o'clock?'

'We're going swimming, poppet.'

'Oh. OK.'

Acquiescing with a smile, Greta set off down the street. It was a very different street to the deserted one she'd walked down earlier. A postman was delivering mail, a young mother was pushing a buggy, an elderly man was shaking a rug from a window and two women were standing on a doorstep engaged in gossip.

They looked around as Greta passed by. '*Bonjour, Mademoiselle!*' they said.

'*Bonjour, Mesdames!*' she said brightly. '*Quel beau temps!*'

'*Oui, oui!*' they chorused in return.

Hearing the church bell chime nine, Greta quickened her step. But before she reached the turn-off that led to the rue Lamballe, she looked back over her shoulder. Sam was still lounging in the gateway to the Lennox house, watching her, and the two gossips were standing in their doorway, nodding meaningfully at one another.

'"Here we made the path through the forest. I can't see it now for the darkness, but I know it's there." Bending low, he ran along the track and disappeared. Eileen did not watch his going. She was too interested in the other people in her storybook who were coming to life and greeting each other." And that's the end of the chapter.' Greta shut the book.

'No!' protested Bruno, as he did every night when Greta finished reading to him.

'People coming to life and greeting each other?' remarked Deirdre, who had just come into the bedroom with a basket of laundry. 'That sounds like what's going on in my screenplay.'

Greta looked around with a smile. 'It must be fun when that happens,' she said. 'When characters come to life.'

'It can be,' acknowledged Deirdre. 'But sometimes the more mutinous characters don't behave the way you want them to.'

'It must be a bit like playing the Sims.'

'I guess it is.' Deirdre started folding a pair of Bruno's dungarees. 'But between the jigs and the reels, you get there in the end.'

'Between the jigs and the reels!' Greta rose to her feet. 'My grandpa always used to say that. Let me put away the laundry,' she said, indicating the basket.

'No. You are now officially off duty.' Deirdre glanced at her watch. 'And I'd get a move on if I were you. Aren't you meant to be meeting up with Sam at nine o'clock?'

'Yes.'

'Well, it's five past now. Shoosh!'

'Kiss! Kiss!' Bruno stretched up his arms and Greta leaned down to kiss him before leaving the room with a cheerful 'Goodnight!'

'Goodnight! Have fun!'

'Thanks!'

Taking the stairs two at a time, Greta swung into her room, grabbed her swimsuit from where she'd left it hanging over the chair on the balcony, then legged it back downstairs and made for the kitchen. From inside she could hear the sound of the dishwasher being stacked: Rory was clearing away supper. Greta hesitated, then backed away on silent feet and left the house by the front door.

How blissful it was not to bother with a jacket! She'd had an e-mail from Esther that day in which she'd moaned on about the fact that it was pelting rain in Dublin. Greta knew that thunderstorms had been forecast, but so far her stay in Saint-Géyroux had been rain free. Humming a little tune, she ran down the rue Lamballe, navigated the twists of the rue du Jujubier, then turned onto the rue des Artistes. Sam was lounging in the gateway of number one, wearing exactly the same demeanour as the last time she'd seen him. The only thing different about him now was that he had on denim cut-offs and a T-shirt.

'Hello, corner boy!' she said, standing on tiptoe to kiss his cheek.

'*Ciao, Bella!* Looking forward to your swim?'

'Too right! What did you get up to today?' she asked as she stepped into the courtyard.

'I was kept very busy shopping.'

'Shopping for what?'

'You'll find out soon enough.'

In the courtyard, a bird started to sing. Sam turned to Greta, caught her hand in his and put a finger to his lips. A series of pure, melodic notes sounded, then a liquid trill was followed by a lush aria.

'A nightingale?' she mouthed and he nodded.

The most virtuoso birdsong Greta had ever heard had been that of the blackbird who returned every spring to nest in the garden of the house in Connemara where she'd grown up – but that was Ha'penny Place stuff compared to this avian opera star, this Kiri Te Kanawa of birds. The Keats poem that had been drummed into her at school came back to her, the one about the nightingale, the one that Anita had quoted from all that time ago in grey, rainy Dublin: *Dance, and Provençal song and sunburnt mirth* …

I love it here, thought Greta. I love living in France, I love my work, I love my surrogate family, I love my unborn baby. She looked at Sam, who was gazing upward toward the purple sky. And I love the idea of falling in love …

There came a pause in the nightingale's song. Greta and Sam stood still for several more moments, waiting for the concert to start again, but the diva didn't oblige.

Sam shrugged. 'Let's go,' he said.

In the hall, he moved to the door that he'd told her led to the swimming pool and held it open for her. Passing through, Greta found herself at the top of a stone staircase. The pool was lit from above by small spotlights set into the vaulted brick ceiling and from below by spotlights in its mosaic floor. The mosaic depicted Aphrodite rising from the waves, and the face of the goddess was that of Madeleine Lennox.

'Oh! It's pure lovely!' said Greta.

'Isn't it?' said Sam, pulling the door shut behind him. 'My auntie made only one stipulation when she agreed to marry Daniel, and that was that he get Aphrodite's face remodelled.'

'Why?'

'The original face belonged to Daniel's ex-wife. I'm not surprised Madeleine wanted it replaced. Imagine skinny dipping in a pool with the first Madame Lennox peering up at you.'

Greta shot him an indignant look. 'I hope you're not expecting me to skinny dip, Sam Newman?'

'No, darling. You may preserve your modesty. There's a changing room over there.'

Sam gestured to a door that was half concealed by a luxuriant palm in a pot. At the foot of the palm, a raffia mat was spread. The mat had been scattered with blue and white hydrangea petals, a picnic basket stood open beside it and two champagne flutes stood sentinel beside an ice bucket containing a bottle.

'You've organised a picnic!' said Greta. 'What a sweet thing to do!'

'My sweet nature has often been remarked upon,' said Sam. 'Careful on the steps, darling. They're very steep.'

Greta removed her sandals and trod carefully down steps that had been well worn by the passage of centuries of feet. At the bottom of the staircase, she turned in the direction of the changing room while Sam stripped off his T-shirt.

The changing room had mosaic walls too, with prancing nude gods and goddesses up to no good. Greta changed into her plain black high-necked Speedo and hung her dress on a peg. Her reflection in the full-length mirror looked back at her. How bonkers life was! Here she was wearing a swimsuit that could have been designed by a nun, while earlier that day she'd been lying starkers in front of Sam Newman's uncle without batting an eyelid.

When she emerged from the changing room, she kept her eyes averted. She did this quite deliberately to enable Sam time to give her the once-over. Greta knew from experience that men's eyes couldn't help but automatically check out women's bodies in bathing suits, and she didn't feel it was fair to engage them in eye contact until they'd done so – unless you wanted to look like a tease.

When she finally looked at Sam, he was smiling.

'What are you smiling at?' she asked.

'I'm smiling,' he said, 'because you look about twelve years old. Come on. Let's get in.'

Sam flung himself into the pool while Greta followed him into the water a little more cautiously. They lapped and larked for forty minutes or so, and after a Guess the Song Underwater competition, Sam announced that it was time for their picnic. Sliding himself up onto the poolside, he held out a hand to help Greta. Then he reached for a towelling robe and wrapped it around her before shrugging into one himself.

'What have we got?' said Greta, peering into the basket. 'Yum! Cheese, baguette, baby tomatoes, figs, cherries. Oh! Chocolate-coated strawberries! My favourite!'

'I told you I was kept busy shopping today,' said Sam, stripping foil from the neck of the champagne bottle. 'I pootled around the market with my gingham-covered shopping basket and my ears out on stalks, eavesdropping on the tittle-tattling Saint-Géyroux mafia.'

'What were they tittle-tattling about?'

'Well, everyone seemed very curious about you, poppet.'

'Oh? Who was doing the nosy parkering?'

'The usual suspects. Madame Bouret, Madame Thibault, Madame Mercier and Madame Ingram.'

'Bianca's a gossip?'

'Bianca is a top-notch gossip,' said Sam, popping the cork and reaching for a champagne flute.

'No champagne for me, thanks,' said Greta.

'Still on those antibiotics?' Sam poured a glass for himself and took a gulp.

'Yes.'

'What are they for?'

'Um, I had a virus.'

'That's funny. Why would a doctor prescribe antibiotics for a virus?'

Greta was unsure of herself. Being robustly healthy meant that she had never taken antibiotics in her life. 'Don't ask me,' she said, fiddling with a cuticle.

'Antibiotics only work for bacterial infections,' said Sam. 'They don't work for infections caused by viruses. I don't think you *are* on antibiotics, Greta O'Flaherty.'

'What? What makes you say that?'

'I think you're not drinking for a very different reason.'

Greta stiffened. 'What reason?'

'I think – from something Bianca let drop – that you are expecting a baby. Is it true?'

Greta bit her lip, then looked down at the petal-littered mat. 'Yes,' she said.

Some time after ten o'clock, Madeleine decided to go for a swim. She wrapped herself in a sarong and headed for the pool. But as she stepped through the door, the sound of a girl's voice made her stop in her tracks.

'I never knew he'd be here. I promise you. If I'd known, I never, *never* would have come to Saint-Géyroux.'

Sam and Greta O'Flaherty were sitting side by side on a raffia mat at the pool's edge, wrapped in towelling robes, their feet in the water. Sam said something to his companion in a low voice: Madeleine couldn't make it out, but it was clear that he was reassuring the girl. He smiled at her and dropped a kiss on the top of her head. Greta looked up at him and Madeleine saw her eyes entreat his. Then Sam leaned into her, took her beautiful face between the palms of his hands and kissed her on the mouth. Greta froze: her body stiff and unyielding in Sam's embrace. After several moments, Sam released her and gave her a look of enquiry.

'I feel like Georgy Porgy,' he said, 'who kissed the girls and made them cry. What's the matter, sweetheart? Don't you want to?'

'I'm sorry,' said Greta. 'I'm not ready yet.'

'Once bitten?'

'I … suppose.'

'It won't stop me from trying.'

'"Could do better. Must try harder."'

'Come again?'

'That's what your Irish teacher wrote in your school reports. Remember?'

'How do you say 'must try harder' in Irish?'

'*Caithfidh sé iarracht níos mó a dhéanamh.*'

'You make it sound like a poem, Greta O'Flaherty,' said Sam, putting a brotherly arm around her. 'I'll just have to try again, tomorrow.'

And as Greta laid her head upon his shoulder, Madeleine backed through the door and shut it quietly behind her.

20

In the *maison de maître*, Dannie shut the bedroom door on a sleepy Paloma. She was sleepy too, she realised. She usually treated herself to a siesta in hot weather, but Jethro hadn't allowed her a siesta today …

From the top floor of the house came the murmur of voices on a soundtrack. That entire storey had been converted into a work space for Jethro when they'd moved in, with edit facilities and an office and a screening room. Jethro had taken himself off up there after supper to look at rushes, telling her that he wouldn't be more than a couple of hours.

Dannie could manage to stay awake for an hour or so. She'd head to bed and read until he came down, she decided. Changing into a nightgown of thin indigo-coloured silk, she plumped up her pillows and settled back against them with a glossy new gardening book. But the book did not prove riveting enough to keep Dannie Palmer awake.

She woke some hours later, the sole occupant of the bed, with the book still open on her pillow. Checking the clock, Dannie saw that it was four a.m. Four o'clock in the morning, and Jethro still hadn't come to bed! Well, feck him, stuck in his edit suite, poring over rushes! Dannie rarely intruded on her husband when he was working, but this was *insane*. She'd feckin well *make* him come to bed – unless perhaps poor workaholic Jethro had fallen asleep over his console?

Not bothering with slippers, Dannie moved out onto the landing and up the staircase that led to the edit suite. As she climbed the stairs, the soundtrack became more audible. Except, Dannie realised, it wasn't a soundtrack: that was no actor's voice she could hear, it was Jethro's voice, and he was issuing directive in his wonderfully persuasive Southern drawl.

'Beautiful,' he was saying. 'That's just beautiful. Now, angle your leg for me a little … a little more. That's terrific. And arch your back for me, please … yes. Yes! Beautiful. Run your hands over your breasts … good girl. Good girl … orgasm is imminent, so perhaps you could throw back your head – careful! We're in danger of seeing too much of your face here. Hide it in the crook of your arm. Beautiful. Beautiful. Your body is beautiful.'

Beautiful. Beautiful. Your body is beautiful. He'd murmured those very words to her yesterday, as she'd climaxed in the shower, hiding her expression in the crook of her arm the way she always did when she came.

Emerging at the top of the stairwell, Dannie's eyes registered the image that shimmered on the screen. It was the flawless body of a young woman. She was lissom and golden and silken of skin – luminescent, as if lit up from inside.

'Rory?' she heard Jethro's voice again. 'Let's see you kiss her breasts, suck on the nipples. First left. And now the right … that's beautiful. Beautiful … and cut.'

But the camera rolled on. Dannie watched as Rory McDonagh raised himself on his elbows and said something to the girl on the bed. She lowered the arm that had been shielding her face and said something in return, pushing a strand of strawberry blonde hair back from a smiling face that was as flawless as her body.

It was Greta O'Flaherty.

Dannie turned and left the edit suite on soundless feet.

In the house on the rue Lamballe, Deirdre woke up knowing that something was very wrong. What was it? She turned to Rory, but Rory wasn't there. So that was why she'd had bad thoughts! Her subconscious had alerted her to the fact that her husband had gone AWOL. She sat up in the bed and listened to the silence in the house for several moments before sliding out from between the sheets and crossing to the door. Unhooking her robe, she slid it on, knotted the sash and moved onto the landing.

There was no sign of Rory in either the upstairs or the downstairs sitting rooms. Moving to the kitchen door, Deirdre pushed it open. Greta was standing by the window, nursing a mug of coffee, gazing dreamily at a silvery sky. Her halo of hair was silhouetted against the dawn glow, a glow that made the thin cotton of the kimono she was wearing semi-transparent.

'Greta?'

The girl turned so abruptly that coffee swilled over the rim of the mug. Her hands flew to her face in alarm as it went crashing to the floor.

'Oh, God, Greta – are you all right?' Deirdre moved swiftly to the sink and turned on the tap. 'Quickly, quickly, put your hand under the cold tap.' Wordlessly, Greta followed her across the room and stuck her hand under the flowing water. Deirdre saw that her hand was trembling. 'Is it a bad burn?' she asked.

'No, no – the coffee was only lukewarm. It's just that you gave me such a – such a turn.'

'I'm sorry. Are you sure you're OK?'

'Yes, honestly. I'm fine.'

Greta turned the tap off and reached for a cloth. Then she moved back to the window and started mopping up the spilled coffee. 'What has you up so early, Deirdre?' she asked.

'I woke up to find Rory gone.'

'Oh. He – he said he couldn't sleep.'

'You've spoken to him?'

'Yes.'

'Where is he?'

'He's gone for a cycle. There's a note.' Greta indicated a Post-It attached to the sugar bowl on the table.

Deirdre picked it up and read in Rory's angular handwriting: 'Gone for a marathon cycle. Badly need fresh air. Will bring back *pains-au-chocolat* for breakfast.'

'I'm not surprised he's antsy for exercise,' conjectured Deirdre. 'Hanging round on film sets sends you into a kind of torpor.'

'I know.' Moving to a cupboard, Greta helped herself to a dustpan and brush.

'You know?'

'Yes. I, um, did some child-minding work on a film recently.'

'Really? Where?'

'Ardmore Studios.'

'That's where Rory was filming!'

311

'Yes, I know.' Greta busied herself with brushing up the shards of pottery. Then she got to her feet and toppled the remains of the coffee mug into the bin. 'I'm sorry about the mug, Deirdre. I'll replace it.'

'No worries. It's only a mug. I'm sorry I gave you such a fright. Look at you! You're still shaking.'

'I must have taken too strong a hit of caffeine.'

'I'll take a hit myself. I might as well get to work, now that I'm awake.'

'Why don't you give Rory a call?' suggested Greta. 'Join him for a cycle?'

'No. I get the impression he needs some head space. He's been a bit irritable recently, and that's not like him. He really needs a break. He's working himself into the ground.'

'Can't he take time off?'

'No. He has films lined up back to back for the rest of the year.'

'Why doesn't he just say no?'

'It's not in an actor's nature to turn down work. You never know when the viewing public's going to go off you. Look at what happened to Tom Cruise.'

'The only really big mistake poor Tom Cruise made,' Greta said, looking thoughtful, 'was to fall in love and shout it from the rooftops.'

'Shouting it from the rooftops isn't public enough for anyone any more. You have to shout it from Oprah's couch.'

Greta gave a wan smile, then made for the kitchen door. 'I'd better make tracks. I don't want to be late for Daniel.' On the threshold, she paused, pulled the folds of her kimono tighter around her, then turned back to Deirdre.

'Sorry again, for the mess,' she said.

Deirdre shrugged. 'There's no use crying over spilled coffee,' she said. 'In fact, I'm rather glad you did spill it.'

'Oh? Why?'

'You've given me an inspired idea for a plot point in my screenplay. I'll have to put you in the acknowledgements.'

'Fun! What's the idea?'

'Georgia's going to accidentally spill coffee on a very important document.'

'What kind of document?'

'Stephen's divorce papers,' said Deirdre with a smile.

After Greta had finished her morning session with Daniel, she descended the staircase in number one rue des Artistes to find Sam waiting for her at the bottom.

'"Could do better,"' he said. '"Must try harder."'

'What?'

She was totally unprepared for what happened next. Sam grabbed her hand, pulled her unceremoniously into his arms and kissed her so long, so languorously and so very, very masterfully that Greta found herself melting into him, snaking her arms around his neck and wishing that the kiss might last for ever.

'Oh!' she said when Sam finally broke away, leaving her limp with lust. 'That wasn't fair! You took me completely by surprise.'

'I've been planning strategy since I woke up,' he said. 'And I decided that a pre-emptive strike was the best way to manoeuvre you into my bed.'

'You're very full of yourself,' she told him crossly.

'What makes you think I want to go to bed with you?'

'Hmm,' he said, toying with a strand of her hair. 'There's something about the expression in your eyes that tells me you want to go to bed with me. They say that the eyes are the window of the soul.'

'So what's my soul saying to yours?' she asked, trying to look challenging.

'Your soul is saying,' said Sam, caressing the thin cotton covering her breasts, 'that you like what I'm doing to you. Your soul is telling me that you would like me to touch more of you. Where exactly would you like me to touch you, Greta O'Flaherty? Here?' He slid his hand down her spine and cupped her ass. 'Here?' he pulled her into him and she could feel his erection hard against her tummy. 'Here?' He lowered his mouth to hers and ran his tongue along her lower lip.

'Get a room!' It was Rosa's voice.

Greta disengaged herself immediately and examined her hair for split ends.

'You were snogging!' Rosa said. 'You – were – snog-ging, you – were – snog-ging!'

'And what's wrong with that?' Sam asked. 'It means we like each other.'

'Does that mean you're boyfriend and girlfriend?'

Greta and Sam exchanged looks. 'Well, Greta O'Flaherty? What do you say? Would you like to be my girlfriend? Or are you still not ready?'

Greta hesitated.

'Say yes!' commanded Rosa.

Greta smiled at him. 'Yes,' she said. 'I think I might be ready now.'

'You're blushing, Greta!' said Rosa. 'You're in luuuurve!'

Madeleine came out of the kitchen, drying her hands on a tea towel. 'Paloma's on the phone, Rosa. She wants to borrow some PlayStation game.'

'Mama! Mama! They're in luuuurve!'

'Stop tormenting them,' said Madeleine, 'and go and talk to Paloma.'

Rosa skipped into the kitchen singing, 'Sam's in luuuurve! Sam's in luuuurve!'

Madeleine made to follow Rosa, then paused. 'You might like to know that we're taking Paloma to a show in Montpellier this evening,' she said, looking back at them.

'Oh?' said Sam. 'What's on?'

'*Cats*.'

'Poor you.'

'We're going to head in around midday and do some shopping first.'

'What time'll you be back?'

Madeleine smiled. 'We won't. We've booked into the Sofitel. You'll have the house to yourself tonight, Sam Newman.' The kitchen door shut behind her.

Sam looked down at Greta and raised an eyebrow. 'Well? How would you like to stay over tonight?'

She smiled back at him. 'Why don't you try asking my soul? See what she has to say?'

Sam took a step towards her, gathered her in his arms again and looked directly into her eyes. 'Your soul is *extremely* happy. It's saying: "Oh, yes, please, Sam's soul – what a good idea! I knew from the first minute I saw you, when you quoted *Romeo and Juliet* to me on the balcony of my bedroom, that we were destined to be together."'

'Kismet,' she said.

'What?'

'It means destiny.'

'Kismet? Kiss *me*, more like,' said Sam, reaching out a hand and trailing a finger down the side of her neck.

Greta took a step backwards. 'Appealing as the invitation is,' she said, 'I'll have to turn it down. I've a job to go to, so I have.'

She moved across the hall and out into the courtyard, followed by Sam.

'Make sure Bruno's tucked in nice and early this evening. Speed read him his bedtime story.'

'I will not! That's not fair.'

Sam rolled his eyes. 'I might have known you'd subscribe to that 'death before dishonour' credo. What would you like for supper? And don't say bacon butties.'

'But I love bacon butties!'

'They're not appropriate for the occasion.'

'What is appropriate?'

'I thought oysters, with asparagus. Followed by fresh peaches. And chocolate.'

She widened her eyes disingenuously. 'Aren't they all meant to be aphro – aphro – oh, I give up. What's their names?'

'Aphrodisiacs.' Sam plucked a passion flower for her as he had done yesterday, tucked it behind her ear, then held the gate open. 'I'm going to need them,' he said, 'if I'm going to stay up all night.'

'You rude boy!' said Greta, raising her face for a goodbye kiss before turning and walking away up the street.

When she reached the corner, she didn't need to look back this time to know that Sam was still watching her.

*

Dannie Palmer watched from a landing window of the *maison de maître* as pretty little Greta O'Flaherty walked along the rue des Artistes. She was wearing a demure blue cotton dress, she was barefoot and she had a passion flower tucked behind her ear.

How very appropriate, thought Dannie, drooping a little. She was exhausted. Jethro had come to bed at around five o'clock and tried to instigate sex, but Dannie had pretended to be asleep. Her mind had gone into meltdown. She had wanted badly – *so* badly – to confront him, but had resisted the temptation, knowing that she should sleep on it. But she hadn't slept. She'd had no quality dreamtime last night to help her sort out the real-life nightmare that confronted her.

She'd had a phone call from Deirdre earlier that morning inviting Paloma to come round and watch an advance DVD of the new *Narnia* movie that Rory had got hold of. Deirdre had been in high spirits, babbling away about Bruno and Nani Nua, and every time she mentioned Greta's name the vision rose before Dannie's mind's eye of the girl lying recumbent under Deirdre's husband, his mouth feasting on her golden flesh. She remembered the caress in Jethro's voice when he'd told her how beautiful she was, how he'd coaxed her to arch her back, to run her hands over her breasts, to hide her face in the crook of her arm … *ugh!*

When Deirdre had confided in her the shocking news that the girl was pregnant, Dannie could take no more. She'd made an excuse about someone being at the door and put the phone down.

From the street, she could hear the sound of villagers greeting each other as they set about their daily routine;

from Paloma's room she could hear the PlayStation; from her own bedroom came the sound of Jethro's phone. Dannie turned away from the window, moved swiftly across the landing and opened the door. Jethro was reaching out a hand for the phone that pulsated on the bedside table.

'Don't you *dare* pick up!'

Jethro took one look at Dannie's expression and put the phone down.

'What's the problem?' he asked, sitting up in bed.

'You're asking *me* that?' Dannie closed the door and leaned up against it. '*You're* the one with the problem, pal!'

'I am?'

'You most *certainly* are. What the fuck made you pretend not to know Greta O'Flaherty when in fact you know her pretty damn intimately?'

Jethro looked guarded. 'What are you talking about?' he asked.

'Did it turn you on when you watched Rory sucking her nipples? Did you get off on telling her to "angle her legs"? Did you have an erection when you told her just how beautiful her naked body was?'

'Oh, Christ,' said Jethro, putting his head in his big hands. 'I warned Rory that this was so not a good idea.'

'You've got a lot of explaining to do, Mister Palmer.'

He raised his head, looked at her and sighed. 'Actually, I don't. It's a very short story.'

'You'd better tell it fast.'

'Greta O'Flaherty was body double for Charlotte Lambert.'

'So I gathered from the steamy footage on the rushes you were editing last night. Why did you pretend not to know her?'

'Rory persuaded me to – against my better judgement. He said that Greta would lose her job if Deirdre found out.'

'Has Rory fucked her?'

'I don't know the answer to that, Dannie. He was the one who suggested her as body double for Charlotte. He saw her hanging out in the studio – she had a job as a chaperone, apparently – and he spotted the resemblance.'

'So he got her the job. And presumably that's how she got the childminding job, too. Talk about nepotism!'

'He claims he didn't know that she was the new nanny until he got here.'

'Spare me!' Dannie gave a cynical laugh. Then she crossed her arms and cleared her throat. A question was still burning to be asked. 'Did *you* fuck her, Jethro?'

'No.'

'Did you masturbate when you watched her on the rushes?'

'*No!* I was working! It's my *job*, Dannie!'

'But you clearly found it something of a turn-on. You came to bed with an erection last night.'

'That's because I found the idea of making love to *you* something of a turn-on. Jesus, Dannie! When are you going to get wise to the fact that you are all the woman I need?'

There was a silence.

'Are you telling me the truth?'

'The fact that you feel the need to ask that question is a little disappointing. You should know that I'm telling you the truth, Dannie. It may be old fashioned to bandy about words like 'honour' and 'principle', but that's what I am. I'm a man of my word. I'm a gentleman. I thought you knew that.' Swinging his legs out of bed, Jethro headed for the bathroom.

I'm a gentleman. I thought you knew that. There had been something chilly in his tone. Dannie knew she was being unreasonable, knew that she should accept her husband's word, but something in her soul blazed white hot still when she thought of that golden girl responding to Jethro's blandishments. She pictured again that gesture Greta had made when Jethro had instructed her to hide her face in the crook of her arm, and she heard again the intimate timbre of his voice, and it felt like a betrayal.

Moving to the window, she looked down at the swimming pool and the warm terracotta tiles and the bright proliferous bougainvillea on the terrace, and she cast her mind back to the day they'd made love in the pool, and again later in the big bed behind her, trying to make a baby. And she thought of how Greta O'Flaherty, golden of limb and soon to be big with child, had strolled casually into this idyll that was Saint-Géyroux and was now wreaking havoc.

Dannie turned back to face the room. Jethro had come back from the bathroom and was shrugging into his robe.

'Did you know that she was pregnant?' she asked, moving across the room to where the phone rested on its charger.

'Who's pregnant?'

'Greta O'Flaherty. Deirdre told me.'

'No. I did not know that.'

Dannie picked up the phone and crossed to the door.

'You're going to call Deirdre, aren't you?' Jethro said. He sounded uneasy.

'Yes. I am.'

'Chrissake! Leave well enough alone, Dannie, can't you? Just forget about it.'

'What? Forget about the fact that one of my best friends is being cuckolded under her own roof by her nanny and her husband? That that same nanny is carrying a baby that may be the half-brother or sister of the child she's been hired to mind? Get real, Jethro. That girl has got to go.'

Jethro sagged visibly and sat down on the bed, putting his head in his hands again. 'Dannie—'

'She's *got to go*!'

Punching in Deirdre's number with a trembling thumb, Dannie turned on her heel, slammed the bedroom door behind her and moved towards the stairs.

Deirdre's phone went straight to voice mail. Dannie hesitated, then decided to go for it before second thought syndrome had a chance to kick in.

'Hi, Deirdre,' she said into the receiver, 'It's Dannie. Can you phone me please? It's urgent.'

'She's pregnant.'

'What? Who's pregnant?'

Rory and Deirdre were in the kitchen, sitting over the remains of a late breakfast of croissants and cherries. Starving after his cycle, Rory had wolfed down two *pains-au-chocolat*. Deirdre was dabbing at her plate with an index finger, determined to finish every last flake of the crumbly pastry.

'Greta is.'

Rory set down the script he was studying and picked up one of Bruno's magic markers. 'How do you know?'

he asked, clicking the lid of the marker off, then on again.

'I heard Madame Bouret tell Madame Mercier that she'd found a pregnancy testing kit in the wastepaper basket in Greta's room. It was positive.'

'How could she tell?'

'The blue line was showing. That means a positive result.'

Rory frowned. 'Surely those kits aren't that reliable?'

'Oh yes, they are,' Deirdre said with authority. 'I tested positive every time I used one – and they'd be even more reliable now, seeing's as it's more than seven years since I last needed to test. It's a bummer.'

'What is?'

'Greta being pregnant. I was going to ask her if she'd take a sabbatical from college so that she could come back to LA with us at the end of the summer. But if she's pregnant, she's going to want to go home to Ireland.'

'You seriously thought about asking her to take a sabbatical?'

'Yes. Bruno's really going to miss her and it won't be easy finding a replacement.'

'Why not?'

'Well, there's the Irish thing for a start.'

'Don't worry about that,' said Rory.

'What? But you were so keen on the idea!'

Rory shrugged and continued to click the cap of the marker off and on, off and on. 'Yeah, well, it's too late for Aoife and Grace, anyway.'

'What do you mean?'

'I've decided that I can't wait for them to learn Irish before they see their *dadóg*. I'm going to book flights for them to Galway from LA—'

'But I've already booked their flights to Montpellier!'

Rory ran a hand through his hair and Deirdre noticed the furrow between his eyebrows. He looked tired. 'I really want to get them to Ireland sooner rather than later, Deirdre, and they may as well do it while I'm working there. I can join them in Galway when I have time off.'

From his expression, Deirdre knew that he was thinking about the state of his father's health. 'Oh. Maybe you have a point,' she conceded. 'When did you last speak to your dad?'

'About a week ago. He's lonely, Deirdre, and he's sounding very frail.'

Deirdre contemplated. She was longing to see her girls, but she couldn't afford to take time out in Ireland. She had her deadline to think about. 'What about Bruno? Do you want to take him with you?'

'No. That's too much like a travelling circus.'

'And then there's Greta. Daniel would throw a flying fit if he was deprived of his new muse just as he's started painting again.'

'Is Greta at Daniel's now?'

'Yeah,' Deirdre checked her watch. 'She's due back soon. I'd better clear away the breakfast things.' She got to her feet and started to scrape cherry stones into the bin.

'Can't she clear away?' said Rory.

'It's not fair to overload her. I did say in the ad that there was to be no housework. And being in her first trimester, she'll be tired. I remember how knackering I found the first few months.'

'Then she shouldn't be working for Daniel as well. Those early starts can't be good for her.'

'Darling, you couldn't keep her away from that studio if you tried.'

'You have a point. And I guess it's not that arduous a job.'

'I'll have you know,' said Deirdre with a degree of hauteur, 'that holding a pose is *bloody* hard work. I had to soak in the bath for an hour after a session *chez* Monsieur Lennox, remember? Well done for putting that portrait back, by the way.'

Deirdre's nude portrait had been reinstated in their bedroom and Rory had unpacked the artefacts that had been boxed away while the painters had been in: books and ornaments and family photographs were now all back where they belonged. Deirdre had been particularly pleased to see the big framed collage of photographs that Aoife had made for her last birthday back in its prominent position on the kitchen wall. It showed Aoife and Grace and Bruno at various stages of their lives from babyhood to the present day, and there were pictures of Rory and Deirdre taken on significant events: at the *Vanity Fair* Oscar party, at Deirdre's thirtieth birthday celebrations and on their wedding day.

Deirdre paused in her scraping of the plates. 'Oopsie!' she said.

'What's up?'

'It just struck me that Sam Newman might not be so pleased to find out that our Nani Nua's pregnant.'

'What makes you say that?'

'He says it's morally reprehensible to bring a child into this world. Apparently he feels really strongly about it. And in the light of what we're doing to planet earth, he could be right. Life's becoming scarier and scarier.'

Rory did that thing with the marker again. 'And why might he not be pleased to hear that Greta's pregnant?'

Deirdre turned to her husband with a smile. 'Haven't you seen the body language between those two? They're quite clearly smitten with each other.'

'What's smitten mean?' Bruno walked in through the kitchen door. He was still wearing his pyjamas, clutching Pucey in one fist and rubbing his eyes with the other.

'Smitten,' said Deirdre, 'means when you're cracked about somebody.'

'You mean like the way you and Dad are cracked about each other?'

'That's exactly what I mean,' said Deirdre, sending her husband a radiant smile. But Rory was concentrating on Bruno's marker, still clicking the cap off and on, off and on.

Bruno trundled to the fridge and took out a carton of grape juice.

'What do you want for breakfast, baby?' asked Deirdre. 'Dad picked up *pains-au-chocolat*.'

'Can't I have *pancógs?*' said Bruno.

'Well, you know I'm not very good at pancakes. You'd better wait until Greta gets back.'

'When will she get back?' asked Bruno, clambering onto a chair and pouring juice into a tumbler.

'Five minutes or so. Darling, will you stop fiddling with that marker? The clicking's getting on my nerves.'

'Sorry.' Rory set the marker down on top of his script.

'D'you want to run lines some time later?' Deirdre asked him, slanting him a smile. 'Running lines' had become their secret code for 'having sex'.

Rory smiled back at her. 'That might be nice,' he said,

getting to his feet and dropping a kiss on her shoulder. 'I'm off to have a shower. I must reek after that virtual *tour de France*.'

'I used the last of the shower gel this morning,' Deirdre called after him. 'You'll find more in the shower room cupboard.' She resumed clearing the table, wiping placemats and stacking plates in the dishwasher.

'Pop's phone is crap compared to mine,' said Bruno, picking up Rory's mobile. 'He should get a new one. His phone couldn't fly to the moon, let alone Mars. Oh. Why has he got a picture of Greta on it?'

Deirdre turned. 'What did you say?' she asked.

'Pop has a picture of Greta on his phone.'

Deirdre reached out a hand. 'Show me?' she said.

She clicked to reilluminate. The image on the display was of Greta on the balcony of her bedroom, leaning her elbows on the balustrade. The strap of her dress had slid down over her shoulder; her beautiful face was framed by tendrils escaping frond-like from her piled-up hair and she was wearing a faraway expression. She looked like a fairy tale princess. A very sexy fairy tale princess.

'Maybe she sent it to him by mistake,' said Deirdre slowly.

'Greta's real scatty,' Bruno told her. 'She did that in the car yesterday.'

'What did she do?'

'She sent her picture to someone by mistake,' said Bruno. 'But it wasn't to Pop. She said the shit word when she sent it, because she said she'd sent it to an old boyfriend.'

'I see.'

'Your phone is crap compared to mine too.' Bruno had

picked up Deirdre's phone and was examining it. 'I have the best phone in the family. I have the best phone in the *family*. Yay! Yay! Yay! You have a message, Mom. Shall I check it for you?'

'Mmm,' said Deirdre abstractedly. She stared at Rory's phone for a moment or two and then she did something she'd never, ever done before. She clicked on the message menu and went to the sent items. Scrolling down, she found the following: Spoke 2 Jethro. Rest assured. He's never met u.

'The message is from Dannie,' announced Bruno. 'She says it's urgent. What's urgent mean?'

But Deirdre wasn't listening. Accessing Rory's inbox, she scrolled down again until she saw the name Greta displayed.

And this is what she read: Ty. Sory 4 all da lies & sory 4 landing u in it. Wil prtend ive nevr met hm 2.

The land line rang. Bruno picked up. 'Momma?' he said. 'It's for you.'

'Who is it?'

'It's Dannie,' said Bruno, handing over the phone just as Greta burst breathlessly through the kitchen door.

'Sorry I'm a bit late,' she said, sending a big smile to Deirdre before moving to the table and hunkering down beside Bruno. '*Pancóg?*'

'*Pancóg!*' said Bruno, wrapping his arms around Greta's neck. '*Sa, agus go raibh maith agat!*'

Deirdre automatically put the phone to her ear. 'Yes?' she said.

'Deirdre?' Dannie's voice sounded shaky. 'I left a message on your mobile, but you mustn't have got it. Can you come over here right away? There's something you need to know.'

327

21

'Momma's in a weird mood,' said Bruno. 'She didn't even say goodbye. What does 'urgent' mean, Greta?'

'Why do you ask, *mavourneen*?'

'Dannie said it. She left a message on Momma's phone and said it was *urgent*.'

Greta got up from her hunkers and moved to the fridge. 'That was Dannie on the phone?'

'Yep.'

''Urgent' means 'very important',' she said, helping herself to eggs and milk.

'Dannie must really really need to talk to Momma then,' said Bruno, picking up Pucey and making him dance on the table. 'Why do cats hate flying saucers?' he asked.

'I don't know. Why do cats hate flying saucers?'

'Because they can't reach the milk.' The land line rang again and Bruno picked up. 'Hello? Yes. Yes. I'll go get him.'

Sliding off his chair, Bruno skidded over to the kitchen door. 'Pops!' he hollered 'Phone!'

'Coming.' Rory's voice came from the direction of the downstairs shower room.

Pulling on an apron, Greta started sifting flour into a bowl. 'Did you know that there's a musical on in Montpellier about cats?' she asked Bruno. 'Rosa's going with her mam and dad this evening. Will we ask your dad to book tickets?'

'Cool! Yeah! We could all go.'

Greta cracked an egg, dropped it into the bowl, then reached for a spoon.

'Oh – sorry, Greta,' Rory said as he rounded the kitchen door. He was damp of hair, he smelled of soap and he was wearing nothing but a towel wound round his hips. 'I didn't know you were here.'

'I just got back from Daniel's,' she said, trying not to look.

Crossing to the table, Rory picked up the phone. 'Yeah?' he said. 'No. I'm not due back until the day after tomorrow. *Shit*. How did that happen? OK. Book me on a flight right away, will you? I'll organise a cab myself. No – it's simpler if I use the local firm.'

Rory put down the phone and ran a hand through his hair.

'What's up?' asked Greta.

'I've to go back to Ireland. The schedule's been re-jigged and they need me ASAP.'

'No, Dad!' wailed Bruno. 'We wanted us all to go to a show about cats in Montpellier!'

'It'll have to wait until next time I'm back. Is Momma in her study?' he asked Bruno.

'No. She went out.'

'She went out?'

'Yes. Dannie rang and asked to speak to her. She said it was *urgent*.' From the way he stressed the adjective, it was clear that Bruno relished using his new grown-up word.

'Urgent?' Rory reached for his cell phone. Greta saw his expression stiffen. 'Was Momma checking out my phone?' he asked.

'Yep,' said Bruno, making Pucey do the splits. 'She was admiring the picture of Greta.'

Greta sloshed too much milk into the pancake batter.

'What's a cat's favourite song?' asked Bruno.

But nobody answered.

'It's 'Three Blind Mice',' said Bruno.

'I know it's only half past nine in the morning,' said Dannie, setting a bottle of Remy Martin on her kitchen table. 'But we're both going to need a drink.'

'What's going on?' Deirdre asked, looking unsettled.

Dannie poured brandy into two glasses and slid one across the table to Deirdre before sitting down opposite her. She steadied herself, hating herself for being the harbinger of fresh hell. 'I'm sorry. I am *beyond* sorry to have to tell you this, Deirdre,' she said. 'It looks as though Rory has been having an affair with your nanny.'

Deirdre looked blank. She opened her mouth as if to say something, then shook her head.

'I'm sorry,' Dannie said again, and then she told Deirdre the story. She told her about Greta being hired as a body double for Charlotte Lambert on Rory's recommendation and about the film footage that Jethro had been viewing last night, and about the duplicity that had been going on between Jethro and Rory and Greta. And Deirdre sat there stiff and uncomprehending as she listened, and then something finally happened behind her eyes.

'The text messages,' she said.

'Text messages?'

'I found text messages on Rory's phone. From Greta.

And there was a photograph ... and he was the one – he was the one who suggested hiring an Irish-speaking nanny. Oh – oh, God. It all makes sense. Oh, God.'

'I'm sorry, Deirdre. I'm really, really sorry.'

But nothing in the world could have prepared Dannie for Deirdre's reaction. Her friend's face drained of all colour, her eyes clamped shut and an awful keening sound emerged from her mouth.

'Deirdre? I'm sorry. I'm so, so sorry to be the one to have to tell you.'

Dannie put out a hand to touch her friend on the arm, but Deirdre stood up and lashed it away. Dropping to her knees, she curled in upon herself and the inhuman sound that came from her was that of an animal in a snare.

'Deirdre! Deirdre, please ... oh, sweet Jesus!' Hunkering down, Dannie put a hand on Deirdre's hunched shoulder, but Deirdre shook it off. Clamping her hands over her head, she started rocking from side to side and the keening sound became shriller and shriller. Oh, God. This was awful, *awful*. Jethro had been right. She should never have opened her mouth. Stumbling to her feet, Dannie ran to the door of the kitchen and out into the hall. 'Jethro!' she yelled, but he was already on the stairs.

He pushed past her into the kitchen, took one look at Deirdre and turned to Dannie. 'Call the doctor,' he commanded. 'Right away.'

Dannie grabbed the phone and scrolled down for the doctor's number, but her fingers were so clumsy that it took her two goes before she found the right one. In French, she asked the doctor's receptionist if he could come straight away. '*Trente minutes, Madame Palmer*,' came the reassuring response.

It was the longest half hour of Dannie's life. Jethro was kneeling beside Deirdre, trying to take her in his arms, but she fought him off convulsively, banging her fists against his chest. Her face was contorted; her keening was alternating with rapid, shallow breaths: she was literally gulping for air. Oh, fuck. What had Dannie *done*? What demons had she unleashed? For Deirdre really did look as if she were possessed by a demon.

'What's wrong with Deirdre?' Paloma's voice made Dannie turn. Her daughter was standing in the doorway, a bemused expression on her face. 'Is she sick?'

'Yes,' said Dannie, ushering Paloma back out into the hall and shutting the kitchen door. 'But don't worry. The doctor's on his way.'

'What made her sick?' asked Paloma. 'Was it something she ate?'

'Maybe,' said Dannie. She couldn't let Paloma know the truth. The real answer to the question she had just asked was: 'Your mam did. Your stupid, interfering mam made Deirdre sick.'

On the table in the hall, the phone started to ring.

'I'll get it!' said Paloma, making a dash, but Dannie stopped her with a brusque 'No!'

'But it might be Rosa! She's coming to play PlayStation.'

'Let the machine pick up, sweetheart.' Paloma looked mutinous, but she did as her mother asked.

Dannie heard her own voice instructing the caller to leave a message and then the beep sounded. 'Dannie?' It was Rory. 'Hi – I understand Deirdre's with you. She left her phone behind, so that's why I'm calling your land line. Could you pass on a message to her? I just got a call to say that I'm needed for work a day early – I'm leaving on the next flight out. Tell her I'll try her again from the airport. Thanks.' The beep sounded its long tone and then the line went dead.

The sound of the doorbell made Dannie jump: the doctor was early. But it wasn't the doctor on the doorstep; it was Madeleine Lennox and Rosa.

'I'm just dropping Rosa off for her PlayStation session,' said Madeleine. 'She can only stay for a couple of hours because we're off into Montpellier to go—' she hesitated, registering the sounds coming from behind the kitchen door, then shot Dannie a look of enquiry. 'What's up?'

'Rosa, Paloma! Off you go upstairs,' said Dannie and the two girls moved towards the staircase, casting curious looks in the direction of the closed kitchen door.

Dannie put a finger to her lips, then shut the hall door behind Madeleine and led her into the sitting room. 'It's Deirdre. She's in the kitchen with Jethro, and the doctor's on his way. I – I stupidly told her some bad news. Oh, *Jesus!* How stupid was I! I've gone and opened a Pandora's box, Madeleine.' And Dannie started to cry.

'Shh, shh,' said Madeleine, putting her arms around Dannie and drawing her down onto the sofa. 'Tell me about it.'

Dannie did. For the second time that day she recounted the story of Greta O'Flaherty, wishing that she could rewind her life and erase the events of the past twenty-four hours.

'I shouldn't have told her,' she said when she finished. 'I should have left well enough alone.'

'How could you not have told her?' said Madeleine, shaking her head. 'It would have been a shameful thing not to have told her. You couldn't allow Deirdre to live under the same roof as that girl!'

'Maybe I didn't go about it the right way.' Dannie sagged back against the cushions. 'Maybe I wasn't thinking straight. I had hardly any sleep last night and I was – I guess I was incensed. I was angry with Jethro too for not coming clean, and I was … I was …' Dannie couldn't say it. She could hardly bear to admit, even to herself, that part of her had been motivated by jealousy: she was jealous of the fact that Greta O'Flaherty, the golden girl who had responded so compliantly to Jethro's honeyed directive on celluloid, was pregnant, and she, Dannie Palmer, was not. She wanted to burst Greta's bubble of happiness, she wanted to trample on it, she wanted to see the girl walk down the rue des Artistes looking shame-faced instead of smug.

'She's pregnant, you know,' she told Madeleine.

'Greta's pregnant?' Madeleine looked astonished. 'How do you know?'

'Deirdre told me.'

They looked at each other in silence, neither of them voicing the question that was crying out to be asked.

Suddenly Madeleine's eyes went even wider and she clamped her hands over her mouth. 'Now I know – *now* I know what she meant when I came across her and Sam in the swimming pool that night!'

'What are you talking about?'

'I walked in on them when they were having a private chat, and I heard Greta say something like "If I'd known he was here, I never would have come."'

'Oh, shit. Oh, *shit*.' Dannie put her head in her hands and silence descended again, broken by the ringing of the doorbell. 'The doctor,' said Dannie, getting to her feet. 'Thanks be to God.'

'Will he sedate her?' asked Madeleine.

'I hope so.'

But Dannie knew that no drug could ease the pain Deirdre was suffering. No drug had yet been invented, no miracle cure concocted, no magic potion dreamed up that could assuage the pain of a broken heart.

Greta and Bruno were standing outside the house on the rue Lamballe, watching Rory sling his bag into the boot of the taxi. He turned and looked back at them, then moved to Bruno, swung him up into his arms and kissed him robustly on both cheeks. 'Goodbye, you little tyke,' he said, setting him down. 'Be good for Momma, and Greta.'

'Kiss Greta goodbye too,' commanded Bruno.

Rory hesitated, then leaned in towards Greta and aimed a kiss at her cheek. Unfortunately, Greta moved to her left when she should have moved to her right and the kiss ended up plonked awkwardly in the wrong place, somewhere a little too close to her mouth.

Across the road, a lace curtain twitched.

'Goodbye, Greta,' said Rory. 'Take care.' The look he gave her before turning and getting into the taxi was borderline meaningful.

Greta and her charge watched the taxi disappear down the rue Lamballe, waving until it rounded the corner.

'Pop always goes away,' Bruno grumbled as they went back into the house. 'He's really only a part-time pop.'

'He works very hard.'

'So does my momma. But she can stay at home. Does your momma work, Greta?'

'Yes. She's a teacher.'

'What does she teach?'

'Art.'

'And is that why you want to be an artist?'

'I suppose that had something to do with it.'

'What does your pop do?'

'He's a potter.'

'Does that mean he goes down potholes? My pop had to do that in a film once. It was really exciting.'

'No. It means he makes pots.'

Greta was answering on automatic pilot. She was feeling a little uneasy. Had Deirdre seen her picture on Rory's phone? And if she had, what must she have thought? Greta supposed she could explain if Deirdre asked about it, tell her it was just a stupid mistake – which it *was*, of course. Still …

'Can we go to Pluto's cave today?' asked Bruno.

'No, *mavourneen*. I don't think that's a good idea.'

'Why not?'

'I think we should wait here until your mam gets back.'

'But she might be ages!' complained Bruno. 'She and Dannie always 'shoot the breeze' and that takes forever and forever and forever and forever and forever and—'

'OK, Bruno. Cut it out.'

Bruno looked up at her, open-mouthed. 'That's the first time you've ever been narky around me.'

'Oh, darlin', I'm so sorry!' Greta got to her knees and wrapped him in her arms. 'I don't know what's wrong with me.'

'I do,' said Bruno. 'You're stressed. That's the way

336

Momma behaves when she's stressed. And she has this weird look on her face too. That's the look she had on when she said she had to go and see Dannie.'

'She looked stressed?' Greta asked.

'Yeah. How do *you* say it, Greta? She looked 'up to ninety'.'

'Why can't Paloma come with us?' Rosa was hopping up and down the steps outside Dannie's house.

'Because we're staying overnight in Montpellier,' Madeleine told her, turning to Dannie. 'I'm sorry, Dannie. I should have thought to invite Paloma along.'

'No worries,' Dannie told her. 'If Daniel's been working as flat out as you say, you could probably do with what the Yanks call 'quality family time'. Have fun.'

'Thanks. I feel guilty at leaving you with sole responsibility for … you know …' Madeleine directed a meaningful look at the staircase, up which a near comatose Deirdre had been carried earlier.

'You heard what the doctor said. She'll sleep for hours. Hopefully she'll be more rational when she wakes up.' Dannie knew she was speaking in her best 'I Can Handle Anything' voice, but inside she was quailing.

'What's 'rational' mean, Mam?' piped up Paloma.

'Rational means when you're, um, being reasonable and thinking straight.'

'So does that mean Deirdre *isn't* thinking straight?'

'She's just tired, *acushla*.'

Madeleine looked up at the sky. 'Come on, Rosa – we'd better get going,' she said. 'There's bad weather forecast. Dannie – call me if you need anything.'

'Will do. Enjoy the musical.'

'We'll try.'

Dannie watched as Madeleine and Rosa moved off down the street. She was just about to turn and go back into the house when she became aware of two figures rounding the corner of the rue du Jujubier. Greta and Bruno.

'Paloma,' said Dannie briskly. 'Here's someone else for you to play with.'

'Hey – Bruno!' called Paloma. 'Come and play Kingdom Hearts with me.'

'Kingdom Hearts! Yay!' Bruno let go of Greta's hand and ran over to them, pausing to give Paloma a clumsy high-five on the step. Then the two children disappeared into the house.

Dannie had been slumped against the jamb: now she adjusted her posture, standing dignified and erect in the doorway. She knew that her body language alone would tell Greta there was no way she was crossing the threshold.

The smile that had been on the girl's lips faltered when she registered Dannie's basilisk expression and she froze in an attitude of trepidation.

'I wonder you have the nerve to show your face here,' Dannie told her peremptorily. 'I suggest you pack your bags and get out of town ASAP, Greta.'

'I – is Deirdre—'

'Deirdre knows all about you and Rory.'

Greta's hands flew to her mouth. 'Oh – ohmigod. How?'

'There's not a lot of point in talking about it, is there? The damage is done. The best thing you can do now is make yourself scarce. You've made enough mischief here.'

'But it wasn't my idea to stay on here. Rory—'

'Goodbye, Greta.'

'Wait! Please wait. Don't you think that maybe Deirdre and I should talk?'

'Deirdre is sedated. And even if she wasn't, I don't think she'd want to exchange two words with a slut like you.'

Giving the girl a brusque nod, Dannie turned, stepped back into the house and shut the door on Greta O'Flaherty's beautiful, ashen face.

22

Deirdre's limbs were leaden; there was a radio talk show gabbling in her head. She tried to open her eyes, but the lids were glued together. Her head was all cumulous grey cloud. Some strangers came and looked at her; she didn't know why. Rory was somewhere nearby and only he could help her. She called and called and called for him, but something had happened to her voice: it was like shouting against a gale-force wind. Rory didn't come.

And then she was walking with him across the market square of Saint-Géyroux. But it was Saint-Géyroux in black and white, as if someone had taken a dirty floor cloth and wiped it all over the village. The houses, shops, even the colourful little café looked besmirched. Rory had his left arm around her, his hand resting on the ribcage over her heart, but the weight of his hand was dragging at her flesh, making her feel as if her skin was on fire. She remained silent, uncomplaining: she didn't want him to disengage, feeling that she might lose him forever if he broke contact. But finally she could bear the pain no more. 'Stop!' she cried. 'Take your hand away, please! Don't you know that it's tearing at the scar tissue wrapped round my heart?'

He took his hand away. And then he was gone and Deirdre was left all by herself in the spectral grey village.

Vespers was sounding – '*Viens! Viens! Viens!*' – and obediently she headed in the direction of the church she'd only ever visited once – out of curiosity, because it was quaint, because it was *picturesque*. As she reached it, a crack of lightning ripped open the canopy of the sky.

Père Boucher was at the door.

'Father,' said Deirdre in her inadequate French, desperate to make herself understood. 'Please allow me to go inside the church and – and—' What was the word she was looking for? What was the French word for prayer? She almost certainly didn't know it, but it came to her now with perfect clarity. *Prière.* '*J'ai besoin de dire une prière,*' she told Père Boucher. I need to say a prayer.

The *curé* nodded. Unlocking the door, he pushed it open and gestured for her to pass through.

Deirdre moved past pews constructed of plain pitch pine to the far end of the nave, where a painted statue of the Virgin stood in an alcove. She was wearing a blue cloak decorated with golden stars, she had a halo of gold wire on her head and she had the face of Greta O'Flaherty. Clasping her hands together, Deirdre sank to her knees and gazed up at the mother of Christ, imploring, supplicating, begging her to undo what had happened.

But the Virgin just smiled down at her, implacably.

In the house on the rue Lamballe, Greta couldn't stop shaking. She dropped her phone twice before accessing Names, scrolling down to *S* with clumsy thumbs. Praying that Sam would pick up, Greta pressed dial.

There was a smile in his voice when he answered. 'Hey, sweetheart.'

'Sam! Oh, thank God!'

'Greta? What's up?'

'Sam, can you do me a huge favour?'

'I'd do anything for you, angel.'

'Can you run me to the airport?'

'Well, I can't run you in the car because Daniel took it into Montpellier. But I can run you in on the Harley if you don't mind getting wet. It's starting to piss down outside.'

'I don't care. I just need to get out of here.'

'What's the hurry?'

'I've been fired.'

'You've been *fired*?'

'Yes.' Greta started to cry.

'Hush, *hush*, darling!' Sam's voice over the line was all concern. 'Please hush – please don't cry. I can't bear to hear you cry down the phone.'

'I can't help it,' she sobbed. 'I've had the worst time. And I won't even be able to say goodbye to Bruno.'

She heard him suck in his breath. 'That's harsh,' he said. 'What's happened, sweetheart? What dreadful thing did you do to get yourself fired?'

'Deirdre found out that I deceived her. She's found out about me and Rory, and Dannie called me a slut, and I don't blame her.' Greta's sobs grew in volume. 'Please get me out of here, Sam!'

'OK, sweetheart. Calm down. Calm down and tell me this. How light are you travelling?'

'Pretty light. Just a backpack.'

'I'll be right over.'

There came a click on the other end of the line as Sam put the phone down. Greta stood helplessly in the middle of the kitchen floor for several moments, one leg wrapped round the other, twisting a strand of hair, then she left the room abruptly and went upstairs.

Unceremoniously, she crammed her few possessions into her backpack and stripped the bed. On the rail where her clothes had once hung, the white dress she'd worn to Bianca's *fête champêtre* looked forlorn on its wooden hanger, the filmy lace moving a little in the draft coming in through the open French windows. Greta shut them, then turned to survey the room one last time. The past's another country, she thought. This place was her past and the white dress floating on the rail appeared to her now like the ghost of a girl. Corinna.

Greta left the room and shut the door behind her, then lugged laundry and backpack downstairs and loaded the washing machine. How could she say goodbye to Bruno? She could text him, she supposed, but she'd wait until she had calmed down: she would have to think hard about how best to let him know she wouldn't be coming back. There was an A4 pad on the table alongside an un-capped marker. Tearing a page from the pad, Greta scribbled the following in big block capitals: GRETA AND MISTOFFELEES FRENDS 4EVER, and added XXX and ☺. There wasn't time for anything else.

The sound of a revving motorcycle engine came from outside. Through the window she could see Sam astride Daniel Lennox's electric blue Harley. Propping the note against the sugar bowl, Greta eased her arms through the straps of her backpack, hefted it, then exited the house through the back door, locking it behind her.

Sam was dismounting as she drew level with him, rain sluicing down his motorbike leathers.

'Don't! Don't get off,' she begged him before legging it

round to the front of the house. She stuck her keys through the letterbox, hearing them clatter as they dropped onto the tiles, then ran back to where Sam was waiting for her.

'You're clearly in a tearing hurry to get out of there,' he said.

'Yes, I am. I'm in a tearing hurry to get out of Saint-Géyroux. I just want to go home to Connemara, and my mam.' Greta knew she was running the risk of crying again, but she'd save the tears for the journey: she could weep as copiously as she liked behind the visor of a crash helmet. 'Thanks so much for coming to my rescue, Sam. I can't tell you how much I love you for doing this.'

'Have you ever ridden pillion before?'

'No,' she confessed. 'But I'll manage. I'd do anything to get out of here.'

Sam looked at her gravely. 'What about us, Greta?' he asked. 'Where do we go from here?'

'There's no time to talk now,' she told him. 'I'm terrified that Deirdre will come back and find me still here. Please, Sam – just go. We'll talk at the airport.'

'Here,' he said, handing her a helmet. 'Climb up behind me.'

She did as he asked. And as Sam and Greta took off on the Harley, a dozen pairs of eyes watched them go from behind the rain-lashed windows of the doughty sandstone houses on the rue Lamballe.

'Where's Bruno?'

Dannie was standing in the doorway of Paloma's room. Paloma looked up from her PlayStation game.

'I dunno,' she said. 'We were playing hide and seek. But I couldn't find him, so I gave up. I'm hungry.'

'I'll fix us some pasta.'

Downstairs, there was no sign of Bruno. Dannie wandered in and out of the reception rooms and into the garden, but he wasn't there either. Wherever he was hiding, he must be keeping quiet as a mouse. 'Bruno?' she called once or twice. but not too loudly. She didn't want to wake Deirdre, who was still sleeping. Back upstairs, she checked out the bedrooms, opening the door to the spare room in case he had slipped into bed beside his mam, but Deirdre was comatose solo. Feeling a little unsettled, Dannie went back into Paloma's room.

'Did you look hard for Bruno?'

'Yeah. I looked for ages.'

'And how long has he been hiding? Ten minutes? More?'

'The church bell was ringing when he went and hid.'

'Six o'clock? He went and hid at six o'clock?'

'Yes.'

Dannie checked out her watch. 'So he's been gone for forty-five minutes? Paloma! I asked you to *mind* him.'

'No. You asked me to divert him, and I did.'

'Who suggested you play hide and seek?'

'Bruno did.'

Oh, fuck. Dannie backed out onto the landing and called up to Jethro, who was in his edit suite. 'Jethro? Bruno's not up there with you by any chance, is he?'

'No. Why?'

Dannie climbed the stairs. 'Maybe he's gone back home for some reason,' she hazarded. 'He doesn't seem to be anywhere in the house.'

Jethro swivelled round in his chair and raised an eyebrow. 'In that case, you'd better get your butt round to the rue Lamballe ASAP,' he said.

Dannie ran back down the stairs, slid a pair of espadrilles on and swung through the front door. She ran the distance to Deirdre's house and arrived breathless. No one came to the door when she rang. She stood on the step for more than a minute, waiting, but the only sound she could hear was the all-pervasive sound of dripping rain. Greta must have gone already: she might have known by the expression on the girl's face when she'd dismissed her earlier that Nani Nua wouldn't hang about.

Moving round to the back of the house, Dannie tried the back door. It was locked. She peered in through the kitchen window, wiping rain from the glass. The room was empty, but someone had left a note propped up against the sugar bowl. Dannie strained to read it. She could just discern, in red capitals: GRETA AND MISTOFFELEES FRENDS 4EVER. XXX ☺.

Dannie felt something lurch in the pit of her stomach. Stepping back from the window, she cast her eyes around the garden. Could Bruno be out here? 'Bruno?' she called. 'Bruno, are you here?'

No reply came. The shed door was lying open. Perhaps he was in there? The rain had eased off, but it was still damp enough for a body to seek shelter. Dannie moved across the terrace and looked inside. Bruno was not there, but she did notice one thing. Deirdre's bike – the one that Greta had used to go cycling with Bruno – was leaning up against the far wall, but the smaller of the two bicycles was gone.

Back at the *maison de maître*, Jethro's expression was studiously impassive. The Palmer family was sitting in the kitchen having searched the house from top to bottom, just in case. They'd found Bruno's phone, but it was out of juice and there was no sign of the child himself.

'Calm down,' he told Dannie, taking her trembling hand in his. 'He can't have gone far.' He turned to his daughter. 'You might be able to help us out, Paloma. Where do you think Bruno might have gone to?'

Paloma frowned. 'Um, he might have gone to his secret place, the place that he goes to with Greta. He talks about it all the time.'

'And where is this secret place?'

'I don't know. It's a secret. It's where his fantasy friend Pluto lives. Phone Greta and ask her.'

'Shit,' said Dannie. 'Deirdre's the only one who'd have Greta's number, and I don't want to wake her.'

'I don't imagine you *could* wake her,' observed Jethro. 'That sedative could have felled a horse. Might Sam have Greta's number?'

'Sam's gone off on Daniel's motorbike,' said Paloma importantly. 'I saw him earlier. Greta was on the back and she had a backpack on.'

Dannie and Jethro looked at each other. 'He must be taking her to the airport,' Dannie said. 'What time did you see them, Paloma? Before or after Bruno went missing?'

'Before. Bruno looked dead upset when I told him.'

Dannie shot a look at her watch. It was nearly half past seven. 'In that case, they should be there by now,' she said slowly. 'How could we get hold of a number for Sam? I know – I'll try Madeleine.' Dannie reached for the phone, then paused. She didn't want to get the wind up Paloma.

'Paloma,' she said. 'I've an awful feeling I left the tap running in the upstairs bathroom. Be a sweetheart and run up and check for me, would you?'

'You gave out yards to me for doing that, Da,' said Paloma, giving her father a snooty look. 'See? I'm not the only one in this house who leaves taps running.' She pattered off into the hall, muttering something about the ecological unsoundness of wasting water.

Dannie pressed speed dial. Thankfully, in Montpellier, Madeleine picked up equally speedily. 'Madeleine – it's Dannie.'

'What's up?'

'Tell me, have you a number for Sam?'

'Haven't you tried the land line? I'm pretty sure he's at home.'

'No, it looks like he's on his way to the airport.'

'The airport? What makes you think he's going to the airport?'

'He's taking Greta O'Flaherty there.'

'What? Why?'

'It's all a bit complicated. I – I fired Greta today on Deirdre's behalf, and now Bruno's gone missing and she may be able to help us find him.'

'Bruno's missing? Sweet Jesus!' said Madeleine. 'In that case, I'd better free up the phone for you. I'll text you Sam's number right away.'

'Thanks.' Dannie hung up and looked at Jethro. 'At last we're getting somewhere,' she said. 'Madeleine's going to text me Sam's number.'

'Well, let's *hope* we're getting somewhere,' replied Jethro. 'Because if Bruno's not in the place Paloma thinks he is …'

'Don't! Don't say it! Don't even think it. Don't you know how riddled with guilt I am? I've made such a *mess* of everything.'

'Don't beat yourself up, honey.' Jethro reached for her hand.

'But I have! I *have* made a mess of everything! Bruno couldn't understand why he couldn't talk to his mam today, and he was probably worried about the fact that she was conked out in my house in the middle of the afternoon, and then his nanny disappeared without saying goodbye, and I was so distracted I did nothing to reassure him – I just told him to go off and play with Paloma. I should have known he'd be confused and upset. Oh – I'm so *stupid!* Dannie felt her face flare up, felt tears begin to burn behind her eyes. 'You were right all along, Jethro. I should never have interfered. I've been cursing myself from the moment I—'

Her text alert cut her off. The message displayed read **Sam Newman**, followed by a number. Dannie dialled immediately. The phone rang four … five … six times. 'Sam here,' she heard to her infinite relief.

'Sam! It's Dannie Palmer. Listen up. Do you have a number for Greta O'Flaherty?'

'I do,' said Sam and his voice sounded rather cold. 'But I'm not sure she'd want to talk to you after your summary dismissal of her today.'

'Oh, please, Sam! It's urgent.'

'If it's urgent,' said Sam, 'you'll be glad to know that I can put you on to the lady herself. We're waiting for her flight to be announced.'

'You're at the airport?'

'No, we're at the Daedalus and Icarus school of flying,' said Sam.

This is no time to be making flippant remarks, Dannie wanted to say, but didn't. She needed to keep Sam sweet. The next voice in her ear was the soft Connemara brogue that belonged to Greta.

'What do you want?' the girl asked.

'Greta? Can you tell me where you and Bruno go? You know, your secret place? Can you give me directions over the phone?'

'Why do you need to know?'

'Bruno's gone missing and we think that that's where he may be headed. His bike's missing too.'

'Oh, God! Let's see … it's off the road halfway between the village and the Labadou. There's a path that runs down to the river, to the left, but you don't take the fork that leads directly down. You go along a narrow trail until you get to a huge big oleander bush, and duck under that. Beyond that there's a clearing, and you have to climb—'

This was useless! 'But there are hundreds of oleander bushes between here and the Labadou! Can't you be more specific?'

'No. It's very off the beaten track.'

Dannie felt awash with despair. 'Greta, I know this is a lot to ask, but could you do me a huge favour? Could you ask Sam to bring you back here? You're the only person who can help us find Bruno.'

'I'll have to – oh!' In the background, Dannie heard the adenoidal drone of the airport tannoy. 'That's my flight being announced,' said Greta, sounding uncertain.

'Please, Greta. Please come back.' Dannie had never felt more abject in her life.

There was a pause. 'Of course I'll come back,' said

Greta. 'But you needn't think I'm doing you a favour, because I owe you nothing. I'm doing this for Bruno.'

Madeleine and Rosa were sitting on the terrace of a café in downtown Montpellier, empty sundae glasses in front of them. Rain was pelting down on the awning over their heads and the scene beyond the terrace was like a twenty-first-century version of Renoir's *Les Parapluies*. Daniel was standing at the bar, shooting the breeze with the owner of an art supply shop. He said something that made both men throw back their heads and laugh, then Daniel slapped his mate on the back and ambled back to the table to join his wife and daughter.

'Who were you talking to on the phone?' he asked as he lowered himself onto the aluminium chair.

'I was talking to Dannie,' she told him. 'There's been something of a crisis.'

'Oh? What's happened?'

Madeleine gave him a warning look, then turned to Rosa. 'Rosa, *ma puce*, will you go inside to the cash desk and tell them that we're ready for *l'addition*?'

'Can't I have more ice cream?'

'No. We don't want to be late for the theatre.'

Rosa slid off her chair and moved across the terrace, humming one of the songs from *Cats* that they had listened to on the car stereo on the way into town. Daniel had never heard any Andrew Lloyd-Webber before, and he'd announced that he'd rather listen to a dentist's drill for two hours than sit through the musical this evening.

Draining his wineglass, Daniel set it on the table. 'What's up?' he asked.

'Bruno's gone missing.'

'Holy shit. How did that happen?'

'Dannie fired Greta today, and now she needs to get in touch with her again because she thinks Greta may know where he's got to.'

'Why on earth did Dannie take it upon herself to fire Greta?'

'She's been having an affair with Rory.'

'Greta has?'

'Yes.'

Daniel looked sceptical. 'Bollocks. So where is Greta now?'

'She's en route to the airport with Sam.'

'What? Why the fuck is she going to the airport?'

Madeleine knew that what she was going to say next would scarcely be music to Daniel's ears. She shrugged. 'Presumably she's going back to Ireland,' she said.

'She can't go back to Ireland! What about my series?'

'Daniel – keep your voice down! People are looking.'

'Let them fucking look! That girl can't go back to Ireland, Madeleine – you know that. She'll have to stay on in Saint-Géyroux until the series is finished and that's going to take months!'

'Why months?'

'Because she's pregnant. I'm embarking on the *Enceinte* series.'

There was a long pause.

'How did you know she's pregnant?' asked Madeleine.

'She told me.' Jethro slammed the heel of his hand against his forehead. '*Shit*. I shouldn't have said anything. She asked me to keep it a secret.'

'It's not a secret any more. Deirdre knows, and Dannie

knows. That girl can't stay on in Saint-Géyroux, Daniel.'

'Why not?'

'Because word's bound to get out about the affair she's been having with Rory. Imagine the scandal if she stays on, once she starts to show! The rumour mongers will have a field day.'

'Pox on the rumour mongers! You think I give a fuck about them? I've been waiting for this girl to come along for years, Madeleine. I'm not going to give up on her just because of some vacuous tittle-tattle.'

'But what about Deirdre? She's our friend.'

Daniel made a dismissive gesture. 'Deirdre'll be gone by the end of the summer.'

'And what if she runs into Greta on the street or in the cafe? Can't you put yourself in her shoes? Imagine how she'd feel!'

Daniel looked a bit put out, then rallied. 'I'll think of some way round it,' he said blithely. 'Give me your phone.'

Madeleine handed it over. 'Who do you need to call?' she asked.

'Sam. I want to talk to Greta.'

'She might already have got on a flight,' Madeleine pointed out.

'In that case,' said Daniel as Rosa dropped onto the chair opposite, 'I shall just have to fly to Ireland myself and bring her back.'

In the Aéroport Montpellier Méditerranée, Greta and Sam were walking through the car park to where Sam had left the Harley when his phone rang again.

'Hey, Daniel,' he said. 'Yeah. Yeah, I'll put you on to her. It's Daniel,' he told Greta, handing her his phone. 'He wants to talk to you.'

Greta took the phone and held it tentatively to her ear. 'Hello?' she said.

'Greta! Thank Christ you're still in the country. I thought I might have to follow you to Ireland and track you down. I heard that you were leaving France.'

'I am.'

'You can't do that, Greta.'

'Why?'

'You know very well why. I need you.'

'But there's been a — a hitch, Daniel. I've been fired from my job.'

'You haven't been fired from your job as far as I'm concerned. I have seven pre-signed cheques to prove that. I'd be happy to tear them up and make them out for twice the amount. Three times the amount! Name your price, Greta.'

'Daniel, I can't. I—'

'Where are you now?'

'I'm at the airport.'

'And I understand you're going back to Saint-Géyroux to help find Bruno?'

'Yes.'

'Stay in our house tonight. Please. Just stay until I can talk to you, face to face. That's all I'm asking.'

Greta considered. She supposed she could hardly expect Sam to make the airport trip twice in the course of one evening. 'All right,' she said. 'I'll stay one more night.'

'I'll be back tomorrow around midday,' Daniel told her. 'I'll talk to you then.'

The line went dead.

'What did he want?' asked Sam.

'He wants me to stay in your house tonight,' said Greta, handing back the phone.

Sam smiled down at her. 'Talk about kismet,' he said.

23

'It's just down the road from here.' Greta indicated the gateway to a field where the car could pull over safely. She was in the passenger seat of Dannie Palmer's car, but Jethro was driving. He had volunteered to meet her and Sam at the café in Saint-Géyroux so that he could help in the search for Bruno. They'd left the Harley there, and her backpack, under the watchful eye of the proprietor. 'Did you think to bring a torch?' she asked Jethro.

'Yeah. There's one in the glove compartment.' He killed the engine and the windscreen wipers sloshed to a halt. 'I did not, however, think to bring rain gear. Although in your case it would be redundant, my dear. You're already soaked to the skin.'

'I'm used to being soaked to the skin,' she told him. 'I'm a bogger from Connemara.'

'Let's go,' said Sam from the back.

They piled out of the car into the teeming rain and Greta started moving in the direction of the path that would take them to Pluto's cave. 'This way,' she said. 'Give me the torch, Jethro.'

The path she led them down soon petered out into what appeared to be a dead end, but taking hold of the overhang of a massive oleander bush, Greta ducked under it into a kind of low, leafy tunnel. 'Careful,' she told them.

'You might get a branch in the face.'

They moved slowly, their progress hampered by low-slung branches and by the torrential rain that had turned the red soil to clay. Emerging into a clearing, Greta indicated a steep bank of earth, against which Bruno's bicycle was propped. 'Result!' she said. She shone the torch at the lowest level of the bank and pointed to where she and Bruno had scooped out a couple of rough footholds. 'It won't be easy,' she warned them. 'The footholds might give because of all the rain. I'll go first, since I'm the lightest. Hold this and keep it fixed on the bank, will you?' She handed the torch back to Jethro and he aimed it at the first foothold.

Greta wedged her right foot into it, then reached for a root that was protruding from higher up in the bank. Pulling herself up, she stuck her other foot into the second foothold, found purchase, then, with an effort, she swung her right leg up onto the top of the mound and squirmed up onto her belly.

'Made it,' she called down breathlessly. The effort had cost her: she was slightly winded.

'Are you OK?' asked Sam, his voice in the dark sounding anxious.

'Yes, I'm fine.'

'I'm coming up now,' he told her.

She heard him grunt, and then there was the sound of earth giving way and a curse from below as Sam fell back against Jethro, who promptly dropped the torch. 'Shit! The bank's collapsed,' he said.

Shadows danced as Jethro retrieved the torch, aiming the beam at the mini-avalanche of red earth. 'We're not going to make it up,' he told her. 'There's no way. If we try climbing, we'll just make it worse.'

'It's OK,' said Greta. 'Pass me the torch and I'll go on.'

'No!' said Sam. 'There's no way I'm allowing you to go on your own.'

'I know where I'm going,' Greta called down. 'It's not far, and it's all level ground from here on. There's no more crawling or climbing to be done. I'll be fine, honest.'

'You've got your phone, haven't you? I'm not running the risk of you breaking your ankle and not being able to call for help.'

'No worries.' Reaching down, she took the torch from Jethro, then aimed the beam at the two concerned faces looking up at her. 'I won't be long.'

'Good luck!' she heard Sam call from behind her as she got to her feet and turned in the direction of the river, the beam of the torch playing over the faint line of the pathway that Bruno and Greta's feet had traced in the scutch grass. Wiping rain from her eyes with a muddy hand, Greta stumbled in the direction of Pluto's cave, her progress impeded by the soaking cotton of the skirt that was clinging to her thighs.

There came the firework fizzle of lightning overhead, followed by a crash of thunder so loud it made her catch her breath. 'Bruno?' she called as she propelled herself forward through the downpour. 'Mistoffelees? Are you there?' But her voice was drowned out by the torrent and she knew that Bruno would not be able to hear her. She was approaching the entrance to the cave, when suddenly the torch went out. She clicked the switch several times, then gave up, knowing that the battery was dead. Dropping the torch, she reached into her pocket for her phone and pressed a random button. The illumination it afforded her was paltry, but it was better than nothing.

The entrance to the cave loomed like the gaping maw of some beast in a nightmare. 'Bruno?' said Greta, ducking inside and laying a hand against the wall of wet sandstone. 'Bruno? It's me. It's Greta.'

Another sudden flash of lightning lit up the interior with an eerie fluorescent glow. There, in a recess at the very back of the cave, Bruno was huddled, Pucey clutched between his hands. When he saw Greta, a look of relief spread across his face.

'Bruno!' Ducking under a stone outcrop, Greta negotiated her way across the slippery, rock-strewn floor towards the child. When she reached him, she wrapped her arms around him and held him tight against her.

'He's gone,' he said. 'Pluto's gone.' And then he started to cry. Greta rocked him and rocked him, crooning, 'There, there,' over and over again until the snuffly stage set in.

'There, there,' she said for the final time.

'You're all wet,' he told her, wiping his nose on his sleeve. 'You're like the Little Mermaid.'

'And you're like Seamus – feckin' off and leaving his family up to ninety.'

'You said 'fuck'.'

'I didn't. I said "feck". You're allowed say "feck" in Ireland.' She held him at arm's length and tried to look cross. 'Tch! What made you do it, you bold, bold boy?' she demanded. 'What made you come here all by yourself?'

'Pluto wanted to say goodbye,' Bruno told her. 'He's gone off with the Danaans forever.'

'But you must have known that people would be worried about you, Mistoffelees!'

'I wanted to tell Momma where I was going, I really did,' he said, nodding earnestly. 'But she was fast asleep and it was *urgent* that I get to say goodbye to Pluto, so I drew a picture of the cave and left it on the pillow so she'd know where I'd gone.'

There was no point in reminding him that they were the only two people in the world who knew the exact location of the cave. 'Weren't you scared to be here all by yourself in the rain and the dark?' she asked.

'No. Not really.'

Greta smiled down at his moon-pale face. 'Is it your magical powers that make you so brave, *mavourneen*?'

'No. It's because I knew you'd come and find me,' Bruno said.

In the kitchen of the *maison de maître*, Dannie lunged for the phone.

'Thank Christ,' she said into the receiver. 'Oh, thank Christ.'

She put the phone back on its cradle, set a pan of mine-strone soup on the hob and put a baguette in the oven. Hot food was a priority. Jethro and Bruno would need baths, too – and she'd better see about making up a bed for the poor wain. She climbed the stairs to the hot press, wishing that she could climb into its scented warmth and shut the door on real life. But there was too much real-life stuff still to be done. Real life … How crapper than crap real life could be: no wonder Jethro sought escape in the fantasy world of film-making.

As she rummaged for towels and sheets, Dannie found herself wondering what would have happened if she hadn't gone upstairs to Jethro's edit suite last night, hadn't seen the footage of Rory and Greta, hadn't seen the way the girl had smiled at him from her supine position on the bed … *Leave well enough alone, Dannie, can't you? Just forget about it.* The words Jethro had spoken earlier that day came back to her – dear Jesus – had it really been earlier that same day? So much had happened in that *bitch* of a day! And tomorrow would be yet another bitch of a day, when poor Deirdre would wake up to the realisation that her life had changed forever.

On her way past the spare room, second thoughts told Dannie that making up a bed for Bruno would be a waste of time. The child would want to sleep with his mother tonight. She found herself wondering where Greta would sleep and then told herself not to be an eejit. Greta O'Flaherty would no doubt be sleeping in Sam Newman's bed tonight.

The sound of a car engine idling drew her to the landing window. On the street below, Jethro had pulled up outside the front door. She could make out Sam in the passenger seat; presumably Greta and Bruno were ensconced in the back. Dumping the laundry on a side table, Dannie sprinted down the stairs and opened the front door. Jethro was getting out of the car.

'Hi,' he said, shambling up the steps. He was soaked to the skin, his hair flat against his skull. He looked wrung out. 'Is Deirdre still sleeping?' he asked.

'Yes.'

'We may have a problem.'

'*Another* one? Not *more* real-life crap!'

'Bruno doesn't want to let go of Greta,' said Jethro. 'He wants her to stay the night. He doesn't understand why she's not his nanny any more and he says he won't come into the house without her.'

'Well, there's no chance of that happening!'

'I know. She's sweet-talking him now, trying to persuade him – and it just might work. That gal could charm the birds from the trees.'

Dannie bit back the retort she was tempted to make. She may despise Greta O'Flaherty for what she'd done to Deirdre, but she owed the girl big time. If it hadn't been for Greta, Bruno might not have been found. Correction: Bruno might *never* have been found. The thought made her want to get sick.

'You'll be glad to know there's soup on,' she told him.

'Good. I'll have it when I get back.'

'Back from where?'

'I'm leaving Sam and Greta off at the café. Her luggage is still down there – Maurice said he'd mind it for her. She's staying over at the Lennoxes tonight.'

Why am I not surprised? thought Dannie tiredly. 'How's Bruno?' she asked.

'He's … OK. A little confused, and very tired. Greta did a very brave thing, you know.'

'Oh? What did she do?'

'She rescued him single-handedly. She set off in the rain and the dark on her own. That girl has some spunk.'

'Why didn't you go with her?'

'A bank of earth collapsed after she'd climbed it, so Sam and I couldn't follow her. You should have seen how she looked when she finally came back with him. Jesus! That's an image I'll have to use in a film sometime.' Jethro smiled down at her. 'They looked like orphans of the storm. Both soaking wet, with Greta holding Bruno's hand. Both baby-stepping forward with only the illumination of a mobile phone to light their way. But d'you know what the most amazing thing was?'

'What was it?' said Dannie, trying not to sound resentful.

'She was wearing this incredible smile, laughing like crazy.'

'What on earth had she to laugh about?'

Jethro gave her a curious look. 'I'd have thought that was obvious. She was just so goddamn happy to have found Bruno.'

Just then the rear door of the car opened and Greta and Bruno got out. They were both filthy, their clothes caked with mud. Greta's dress was torn and she had lost a sandal. Her hair was dripping, her face was dirty and blood oozed from a small cut on her cheekbone.

Hunkering down so that they were on a level, Greta smoothed Bruno's hair, kissed his cheek and handed him something that he slid into his pocket. 'Be off with you, back to your mammy,' she said. 'And don't be worrying her head with stories of Pluto and the Dananns and that cave.'

'What'll I do about the drawing I made her? It's on her pillow.'

'Make her another drawing of you and your sisters with big smiley faces, and leave it there instead.'

'OK. Will you text me?'

'For sure I will.'

'Goodbye, Greta.'

'Goodbye, *mavourneen*.'

Bruno appeared a little uncertain as he looked towards the doorway where Dannie was standing, then, with a last backwards look at his Nani Nua, he trundled towards the doorway.

On the street, Greta rose slowly to her feet and turned back to the car. She was just about to slide into the back seat when Dannie called her name. She saw the girl hesitate. Then she turned, apprehension writ large on her face.

Dannie steeled herself. 'Thank you, Greta,' she said. 'Thank you for bringing him back to us. I wish you a safe journey home.' And then she turned and walked back into the house.

24

In the bathroom of number one rue des Artistes, Greta lay back in a bath so peaky with foam it looked like the Pyrenees. Sam had been liberal with Madeleine's favourite bath gel and the air was redolent with Jo Malone. He was lolling in a cane-bottomed chair, watching Greta comb conditioner through her hair. In spite of the buoyancy of the scented water, Greta's limbs felt heavy with exhaustion.

'You're really going to miss that boy, aren't you?' Sam asked her.

Greta nodded. 'Yeah. He's pure honey bun. I hope he's going to be OK.'

'Now that you're gone?'

'Sure, he'll get over me,' said Greta, trying to sound more confident than she felt. 'No, I mean now that his pal Pluto's gone. He looked like someone whose favourite pet had died. D'you remember how I said to you once that it was a sign that he was growing up, once he started to let go of Pluto? Well, it was as if instead of him letting Pluto go, it was the other way round – and Pluto had been taken away from Bruno by force. Like his childhood was over, all of a sudden.'

'Well, he's had a pretty traumatic day. It must have been grim for him to have no one to mother him, and then to go back to Deirdre and Rory's house only to find you'd disappeared too.' Sam looked alert suddenly. 'Hey. Could all that climbing up banks and scrambling about in the cave have done your baby any harm, Greta?'

'Divil a bit. Sure, amn't I fit as a flea?' Greta ran her hands over her belly. 'Yes! I'm beginning to show, all right! It's exciting!'

Sam slung a leg over the arm of the chair and gave her an indulgent smile. 'Do you want a boy or a girl?' he asked.

'I know I'm meant to say I don't mind as long as it's healthy, but I've always had a *grá* for a boy babby.'

'Girls have an easier life.'

'Hey, you! That's *so* not true! My mam's fought every inch of the way and I haven't had things easy either. And now I'm going to have to go back to Dublin and find a flat and start all over again.' Greta made a face.

'You could stay in my flat.'

'In Dublin?'

'Yes.'

'That's really sweet of you, Sam, but I bet I couldn't afford to stay in your flat.'

'Why not?'

Yawning, Greta reached for the shower attachment and started to rinse her hair. 'Your flat's probably somewhere dead posh.'

Sam laughed. 'What makes you say that?'

'Because you talk posh. You're a classy piece of work, Sam Newman. Anyway, I'm not cut out to be a city girl. I think I'd much rather go back to where I belong. There's no place like home, as the auld adage goes, and home is where the heart is and I'm a bogger from Connemara at heart.'

'Hmm. Something tells me you won't be going back

to Ireland any time soon.'

'Why?'

'Daniel isn't going to give you up without a fight, Greta. He can be very persuasive.'

'You know I can't stay on here!'

'Why not?'

'*Hello?* And run the risk of bumping into Deirdre O'Dare every time I turn a corner? No way, José!' Greta stood up and wrapped herself in a bath sheet, then stepped out of the bath.

'C'mere,' said Sam. 'Let me dry you.' He held out a hand and pulled her onto his lap, then reached for a towel that was draped over a wooden clothes horse.

He started with her hair, rubbing it gently, then proceeded downwards, caressing every inch of her body with the velvety fabric. He lifted the mass of her hair and dried the nape of her neck and the scoop made by her collarbone; he dried around her breasts and under her arms; he dried the sensitive recess between her thighs and the tender place behind her knees; and he dried every single one of her toes. And when he had finished drying her, Greta was aching for him to kiss her.

He did. But the kiss he gave her was the briefest brush of her lips with his – a moth's kiss. 'Time for bed, baby,' he said, smiling at her. Then he helped her to her feet, reached for a robe for her to shrug into and tied the sash.

The room he led her to was washed in white with a high, vaulted ceiling. The only floor covering was a cream sisal runner which led directly from the door to the bed. The bed itself was a low platform draped with white linen sheets and piled with pillows. A flimsy mosquito net was suspended from a circular tester above it, lending the whole a vaguely bridal air.

Sam led Greta along the runner and when they reached the bed he undid the sash on her robe. He let it drop from her shoulders to the floor and stood gazing at the beauty of her for several moments. A sigh escaped him. Then, lifting a corner of the sheet, he gestured to her to slide beneath. Greta complied, lying back against the pillows, looking up at him with eyes that felt unfocused with desire.

She raised an arm to him in invitation, but he draped the sheet over her prone form and took a step backward. '*A demain, ma petite.* Till tomorrow,' he told her, drawing the muslin of the mosquito net around her, enveloping her in gauze, a pale butterfly encased in a chrysalis. And then he turned and left the room, shutting the door gently behind him.

The sigh Greta gave before yawning and curling herself up like a kitten was one full of regret, full of yearning. But within minutes, she was fast asleep.

She awoke the next morning from an erotic dream, feeling languorous – the personification of the cat who'd got the cream. In her dream, she had been lying on the daybed in Daniel's studio, nude but for a mass of white petticoats, a man between her legs. The man had been dressed in Regency garb and, as he slid a finger into her, she realised that he was not Jack St Ledger, nor was he Rory McDonagh …

It was Sam between her legs, kissing the intimate place he had towelled dry with such delicacy the previous night. She felt luscious, succulent, ambrosial as an apricot. Greta squirmed a little, stretched, smiled, sighed, then came.

'Oh, beautiful, beautiful girl,' said Sam, sliding up until his smiling face was looking down at her. He lowered his mouth to hers, explored it with a languid tongue: sucking, licking, tasting her as if she were some epicurean treat.

'More,' she said.

Sam made love to her as if he were learning her by heart: he was an explorer mapping a new continent, and Greta was his geography. He learned the contours of her body: the dips and valleys, slopes and declivities, the dimples and hollows and grooves and crevices; he charted the line of her spine and circled the whorls of her ears, he marvelled at the suppleness of her limbs and the curvature of breasts and buttocks and belly and the exquisite arch of her foot; and every time he happened upon a soft or a secret or a sweet-tasting place that delighted him, he made her skin sing.

When he'd finished delving the most succulent place of all, Greta turned to him and studied his face. His skin was slick with sweat, his eyes were half-closed, his mouth curved in a smile.

'You've done this before, haven't you?' she said.

'Once or twice.'

'Why didn't you do it last night?'

'Because you were a tired girl, and you'd had an upsetting day, and I didn't want to take advantage.'

'You gent!'

'I also rather liked the idea of you going through the torment of delayed gratification. You were horny as hell, weren't you?'

'Yes,' she confessed. 'Weren't you?'

'Yes. But I was OK with it. I went to Babe Station for

an hour or two after I tucked you in.'

'You dog!' She spooned herself against him, laid her head on his chest and started to play with his nipple. 'Do you want to do this again, Sam?'

'You mean right now? I don't think I'd be up to it, sweetheart.'

'No, I don't mean right now. But soon.'

'You mean tonight, maybe? And tomorrow, and the day after?'

'Mm hmm.'

'Well, yes, of course I do. Especially since we told Rosa that we were boyfriend and girlfriend. Don't you think that we'd better live up to it and do the kind of things boyfriends and girlfriends do with a modicum of style?'

God, how she loved his smile! Greta continued to circle Sam's nipple with a forefinger. 'There is one thing … that might kind of get in the way of us being boyfriend and girlfriend, you know, Sam.'

'What's that?'

She was dreading having to voice her fear. 'Well … the fact that I'm pregnant, of course.'

'Why should that get in the way?'

'You say you don't want children.'

'Correction. I said that I didn't want to be responsible for bringing a child into the world.'

'Is there a difference?'

'There's a big difference, sweetheart. But that doesn't mean I don't want a child in my life. As it happens, I'm rather partial to the little tykes.'

'So, if we are to be a – an item, you don't mind that I'm pregnant with someone else's child?'

'Sweet Greta – no, I do not mind. It's not your fault you

fell pregnant. It happens all the time in life that women get pregnant by men in circumstances that prove to be less than ideal.'

'So, say we were still boyfriend and girlfriend by the time I have the babby, would you stick around?'

'I'd be a swine if I didn't, wouldn't I?'

Greta smiled. 'You're a really nice guy, do you know that?'

'Yes. I am a really nice guy. I'm a walking example of moral rectitude.'

'Erectitude?'

'That, too.'

She reached down a hand. 'Well, *I* don't think much of your moral rectitude,' she told him in an injured voice. 'You told a big fat fib a minute ago.'

'I did?'

'Yes. You told me you wouldn't be up to it so soon again. That was a real porky pie.'

'I'm sorry.'

'Don't apologise,' said Greta, sliding a leg over him and adjusting him to a more convenient angle. 'It's nice to know you're – um – what's the big word that means horny? The ancient Greeks were always described as being it.'

'Priapic?'

'Priapic! That's it. You're very priapic, Sam Newman.'

'And you, Greta O'Flaherty,' said Sam with a smile, 'are quite exquisitely accommodating.'

Deirdre was standing on the landing of her house on the rue Lamballe, clutching the banister, listening to Greta O'Flaherty's voice drifting up the stairwell.

371

'Oh, Rory,' she heard. 'Make love to me again. Please. Make love to me as only you know how ...'

And then Deirdre didn't hear any more. She let go of the banister, missed her footing and the staircase reared up to meet her. At the bottom, she could see Greta's face beyond the shadowy outline of Rory's shoulder, her eyes shining, her hair a halo, her pretty mouth moving in slow motion. Deirdre launched herself at the girl, felt her topple, felt her pliant form give beneath her, felt her legs yield as they must have yielded for him, and then Greta's face receded far, far away as Deirdre plummeted on through darkness before landing finally on an unfamiliar bed.

There were goose-down-soft pillows beneath her head and above her stretched a canopy patterned with faded paisley swirls and spirals in shades of tawny umber. Deirdre gazed up at it, wondering where she was and why she wasn't focusing properly. Blinking sluggishly, she raised an arm to look at her watch, then realised that she was fully clothed. What was going on? Where was she, and how long had she been here?

The pattern on the canopy simultaneously pulled back and zoomed close, as though viewed through a fish-eye lens. Deirdre was in Dannie's house and life as she knew it had fallen asunder. So. This was how it felt to be cuckolded. She had toppled into hell. Her head lolled like a stone against the pillow, her limbs felt as if they'd been clamped. Sitting up with an effort, she saw – in a room that was spinning dizzily – the door to what she took to be an en suite bathroom. Exerting superhuman energy, Deirdre pulled herself off the bed, stumbled towards the door and wrenched it open. Then she crouched over the bidet and retched and retched.

Rory and Greta. Greta and Rory. She spat, then spat again. Once more, for good measure. It was no good. If she spat from now to eternity, she would never rid herself of the bile that she felt filling her up inside. Hauling herself up, Deirdre ricocheted off the basin, then clung to it, trying to steady herself. Her bare feet against the tiled floor felt as if they didn't belong to her; she didn't recognise the mad-eyed, grey-faced person staring back at her from the mirror.

I am beside myself, she thought. This is what they mean when they describe someone as being beside themselves. First-class, category A out-of-body experience was what she was going through. The person in the mirror who looked like a ghoul grimaced at her, and she wanted to shatter the glass. She clamped her eyes shut, but there was no escape. Words took shape in a spectral new font and swam behind her closed lids: *perfidy, betrayal, treachery* …

She never wanted to see either of them again. She wanted to expunge them from her life. Perfidy, betrayal, treachery. Words she'd typed just the other day …

```
INT. ELLIOT SEGALL'S OFFICE. DAY.


Elliot is leaning back in his chair in that indo-
lent fashion favoured by people who are care-
less of other people's lives. We get the
impression that he is enjoying telling it like
it is.


ELLIOT: I'm going to give it to you straight,
Dee. Do you think you can handle it?
```

DEE: I didn't employ the best divorce lawyer in LA to kid-glove me. Shoot.

ELLIOT: Being a wordsmith by profession, you'll know what the word 'draconian' means.

DEE: How do the following synonyms sound? Harsh. Intemperate. Merciless. Rigorous. Ruthless.

ELLIOT: I'm impressed. You're going to have to be all that and more. There must be absolutely no contact. No meetings, no e-mails, no telephone calls. Change your locks, change your phone number, change your e-mail address — take out a barring order if necessary. It sounds extreme, but if you want custody, you're going to need to take extreme measures.

DEE: Perfidy, betrayal and treachery constitute extreme mental cruelty, Elliot. And extreme mental cruelty warrants extreme measures.

ELLIOT: The gloves are off?

DEE: I was a tomboy when I was at school. I was the best bare knuckle fighter in Prom year.

ELLIOT: Attagirl!

CUT TO:

*

'*Midnight* – la la la la la *laa* lah …'

Madeleine, Daniel and Rosa were on their way back to Saint-Géyroux after their night spent in the Sofitel in Montpellier.

Madeleine was in the driver's seat – because Daniel much preferred riding motorbikes to driving cars – and Rosa was ensconced in the back. She was deliberately annoying her father by singing the worst songs from *Cats*.

'If you don't shut up that God-awful caterwauling, I shall punish you,' Daniel told her.

'No, you won't,' said Rosa complacently. 'You never punish me. You can't bear it.'

'You're quite right,' said Daniel. 'In that case, if you *do* shut up that God-awful caterwauling, I'll reward you.'

'What with?'

'I'll put someone new in your mural.'

Daniel had painted a mural on the walls of Rosa's bedroom. It depicted the child cavorting through enchanted forests and gardens with fabulous beasts and birds of paradise. The gardens and forests were peopled with family and friends, and every so often Rosa requested that a new person be put in. Daniel had painted Madeleine as a queen with a crown of flowers, carrying a pineapple instead of an orb – since pineapples symbolised perfection – and had executed his own likeness in the shape of an orangutan.

'Hmm,' said Rosa, contemplating. 'Who should go in? I know! I'd like you to put Sam's new girlfriend in.'

'Sam has a new girlfriend?'

'Yes,' said Rosa. 'He's going out with Bruno's nanny, Greta.'

'Is that a fact?' said Daniel. 'In that case, if *I* can't persuade her to stay on in France, maybe Sam can.'

'Why do you want her to stay on in France, Papa?'

'I'm painting her, *puce*.'

Madeleine knew there was a bad joke to be made there somewhere, but she wasn't in the humour for jokes, good or bad. The notion of Greta O'Flaherty living under her roof for the best part of half a year was, well, *testing*. She had always been resigned to accommodating Daniel's models in the past, but this was different. It was different because until now, she, Madeleine, had held a unique place in the hierarchy of Daniel's muses. She had been the only woman he had ever painted pregnant. The knowledge that he now intended to paint Greta as her baby took shape within her made Madeleine feel – well, she supposed *redundant* was the word, because Madeleine knew she had reached the age where conceiving becomes problematic. She didn't want another baby – Rosa was all the child her heart had ever desired – but it was weird to think that she might have difficulty conceiving in the event of a change of mind.

'So will you, Papa? Will you put Greta in?'

'I'd be happy to, *puce*.'

Madeleine's phone was ringing: the display told her it was Dannie.

'Can you talk?' Dannie asked when Madeleine picked up.

'Not really, I'm driving. What's up?'

'Deirdre's leaving the village. She's going back to LA and she's hiring a divorce lawyer.'

'Oh, *no*! That's tragic! When's she off?'

'Tomorrow.'

'Shit!'

'Language, Mama!' said Rosa from the back of the car.

'Sorry, sweet pea. Look, Dannie, I'll call you later, OK?'

'Sure. Talk soon.'

'*Shit!*' Madeleine muttered again, under her breath this time.

'What's wrong?' asked Daniel.

'That was Dannie. Apparently Deirdre's heading back to LA.'

'Bummer!' said Rosa. 'That means Bruno'll be gone too. He said he'd lend me his *Narnia* DVD.'

'When's she off?' Daniel asked.

'Tomorrow.'

'Oh, really? That soon?' In the passenger seat beside her, her husband started humming one of the songs from *Cats*.

Madeleine glanced at him. 'What are you so happy about?' she asked.

'If Deirdre's leaving town, there's no reason now for Greta not to stay on.'

'What do you mean?'

'Greta told me that she couldn't stay in Saint-Géyroux as long as there was a chance of meeting Deirdre. That won't be a problem any more if Deirdre's leaving tomorrow.'

'Why does Greta not want to meet Deirdre, Papa?' shrilled Rosa from the back of the car. 'Does Greta not like her any more?'

'It's a little more complicated than that,' Daniel said.

'How is it complicated?'

'Well, in a nutshell, Greta took something from Deirdre that didn't belong to her.'

'She *stole* something?'

'Maybe 'borrowed' is a better way of putting it.'

'I know what she borrowed!' Rosa sounded triumphant.

'It was that dress that she wore to Bianca's party. Greta told me herself. Is that what it was, Papa?'

'I … guess that must have been it,' white-lied Daniel.

Madeleine felt in an even worse humour now, listening to Daniel's tuneless singing while she negotiated the bends of the road that led to Saint-Géyroux. It had just hit her that the girl who was to be their house guest for the duration of her term, the girl who would be taking off her clothes for Daniel on a routine basis every single working day, the girl who had just been awarded a starring role in the cast of Rosa's mural, was the girl who had 'borrowed' the husband of one of her closest friends.

'Please,' said Daniel. 'Please stay, Greta. There's no reason for you to leave now.'

Madeleine was emptying peaches from a paper bag into a bowl on the kitchen table. She shot a look at Greta's face to see how she'd taken the news that Deirdre and Bruno were leaving Saint-Géyroux and going back to LA. There was relief there, for sure, but Madeleine was certain she saw guilt there too. Madeleine felt guilty too – as guilty if she were harbouring a criminal. Deirdre was her *friend*. She was Daniel's friend too – he adored the woman! And now they were effectively betraying Deirdre by inviting her nemesis into their house.

The Lennoxes had come back from Montpellier to find Sam and Greta having a late breakfast. They'd both been wearing bathrobes and a there was a distinctly post-coital air about them. Greta had jumped up immediately and dashed off to shower and dress, and now the girl was sitting demurely at the kitchen table while Daniel weaved his charismatic web around her. She listened attentively for several minutes while Daniel spoke about the role of the muse in cultural history: he waxed eloquent on Gala Dalí and Lizzie Siddal and Yoko Ono, and when he finished, he spread his hands in a theatrical gesture and said, 'You do realise that if you deny me the opportunity to paint you, you are denying me my creative imperative? If you absent yourself from me now, it would be akin to someone stealing Pavarotti's voice from him, Greta.'

'Or amputating Wayne Rooney's feet,' said Sam.

'Janey!' said Greta, widening her eyes. 'Well. When you put it like that, I can hardly refuse.'

'So you'll stay on?'

'I will,' she told him with a smile.

'Thank you, Greta,' said Daniel.

Madeleine noticed the look that passed between her husband and the girl. It was a look she herself had exchanged with Daniel when she'd sat for him; a look she'd last seen on the face of the Dutch girl, Marjan, who'd stayed with them. It was the look that signified the unspoken empathy between artist and model.

Greta turned to Madeleine. 'Are you sure it's all right with you, Madeleine?' she asked a little uncertainly. 'To have me staying here?'

'Of course it's all right.' Madeleine hoped her smile didn't look forced. 'If you'd said no, he'd have gone back to sculpting, and I'd have been living with Mister Grumpy Bollix again. You've saved my skin.'

The sound of the church chiming twelve came floating through the door that opened onto the garden.

Greta jumped to her feet. 'Well, if I'm to live here for the foreseeable future, I'd better earn my keep,' she said, humming as she started to stack the breakfast things on a tray. Madeleine noticed how the eyes of both Daniel and Sam followed the girl's every move until she finally disappeared into the scullery.

Daniel smiled, then reached for the paper bag and started doodling on the back of it as Madeleine drained the cafetière into his mug. 'Have you told Gilbert about the new series yet?' she asked him.

'No. I want him to sweat a bit more. I want him to earn his fifty per cent.'

'Your agent takes fifty per cent?' said Sam, aghast.

Daniel shrugged. 'It's worth it if it means I don't have to do any real-life shit.'

Unlike me, thought Madeleine. She'd had an e-mail that morning from a writer whose website she'd designed, complaining that it wasn't displaying properly, and another from a baby needs shop in Gignac saying that they wanted their web pages updated ASAP. Plus Madame Thibault had phoned in sick, so today Madeleine would have a stack of household chores to contend with. She picked up the empty cafetière and headed towards the scullery door just as Sam's mobile went off. The last thing she heard him say into his phone as she passed through into the scullery was, 'No *shit*! My dream fucking job come true!'

In the scullery, Greta had helped herself to Cif and was spraying it onto surfaces. As she reached for a cloth, she smiled at Madeleine and Madeleine found the smile so infectious that she automatically returned it. She set down the cafetière, deciding that it was time to forge some kind of alliance. If she and Greta were perforce to be house-mates, they'd have to establish some kind of a civilised *modus vivendi*.

'Is that Mitsouko you're wearing, Greta?' she asked.

'Yes. My mam wears it, and my gran. It's a kind of family tradition.'

'Is yours a big family?'

'Yes. I have four brothers and a sister. I'm the eldest.' Greta swept crumbs off the bread board, then turned to Madeleine. There was apprehension in her eyes.

'What's up?' asked Madeleine.

'It's just – now that I'm going to be living here, there's something I ought to tell you, Madeleine.'

Madeleine knew what was coming. 'Go on,' she prompted.

'I'm, um, I'm expecting a baby.'

Madeleine leaned back against a counter. 'I know,' she said.

'You *know*?'

'Greta, I'm sorry to have to tell you this, but everyone in the village knows you're pregnant. You can't keep secrets in Saint-Géyroux – especially not from the cleaning lady Mafioso. *Especially* if you leave pregnancy testing kits in your wastepaper basket.'

'Oh, shit.' Greta bit her lip. 'That was careless of me.'

'I take it the father's not part of the equation?'

'No. He's not.' Greta looked down and started rubbing at an imaginary stain on the work surface.

The emphasis she'd put on the words told Madeleine not to go there.

'When is the baby due?'

'December.'

'So it'll be Sagittarius. Or a Capricorn.'

Greta looked back up at her. 'Sagittarius is my star sign,' she said with a smile. 'That'd be a disaster, wouldn't it?

You're not meant to get on with your own star sign. Although Sagittarians are pretty easy-going. Maybe we could make it work, me and mini-me.'

Madeleine looked away. She couldn't bring herself to trust the candour in Greta's eyes – the candour that she knew masked a treacherous streak. What was that line from *Hamlet* – about smiling and smiling and being a villain? Stooping down, she started loading the dishwasher. 'By the way, Greta, have you seen a doctor yet?' she asked over her shoulder.

'No.'

'Well, you really should have by now. I'll give you the number of the local GP. He can refer you to the hospital in Gignac.'

'Thanks very much, Madeleine. But I won't be having my baby here. I want to go back to Ireland to have it.'

'That's understandable. But you'll still need to have regular check-ups and ultrasounds.'

'Ultrasounds!' Greta looked like a child who'd just been given a present. 'I can't wait for the first one! I'm dying to see what the wain looks like.'

'How are you feeling, generally?'

'Grand. Really grand.' Greta touched the wooden door of a cupboard.

Madeleine shut the dishwasher door, then got to her feet and fixed serious eyes on Greta. It was time for more questions of a personal nature. 'What about your parents, Greta? Do they know yet?'

Greta shook her head. 'I'm going to call my mam this evening.'

'And … Sam? I hope you don't think I'm sticking my nose in here, but there are some questions I'd like to ask you about him.'

Greta nodded. 'Of course.'

'I'm working on the assumption that you and he are – an item, yeah?'

'Yes. We are.'

'Does he know that you're pregnant?'

'Yes. I told him before, well, before anything *meaningful* happened between us. I couldn't have not told him, in case he had strong feelings about it.'

'And how *does* he feel about it?'

'He's cool with it.'

Madeleine nodded. 'He's a pretty cool bloke, all right.'

Just then a Red Indian whoop sounded from the kitchen.

'Was that Sam?' asked Greta uncertainly.

'It sounded like him.'

'But he *whooped!* Cool people *never* whoop.'

'In that case, I guess we'd better find out what provoked this embarrassing whoop,' said Madeleine, pushing open the door.

In the kitchen, Sam was dancing and punching the air.

'That *really* is not cool,' Greta told Madeleine in an undertone, 'unless you have Tourette's or something.'

'You're right. His street cred's seriously compromised.'

From the table, Daniel looked up at them. 'He's just heard good news about a commission he was after,' he said.

'What is it?'

'He's doing the calendar for the official sponsors of the round-the-world yacht race. Aerial shots. He'll be spending four months up, up in the air, taking photographs from a helicopter.'

'That's fantastic news!' said Madeleine.

'Yes. It is,' said Greta.

But when Madeleine looked, she saw that Greta's smile was more than a little forced.

Later, after a celebratory bottle of champagne had been cracked, Sam and Daniel went to the billiard room for a game of pool. Madeleine and Greta sat on at the kitchen table, Madeleine with a glass of fizz in front of her, Greta with a glass of fizzy water.

'Tch!' said Greta, lifting a glass and examining the paper bag that Daniel had been drawing on earlier. He had left his empty champagne flute on top of it. 'It might have got a ring on it, from the bottom of the glass.'

'It's only one of his scribbles,' Madeleine said.

'But it's a *Daniel Lennox* scribble,' Greta corrected her. 'It could be worth a small fortune.'

Madeleine shot her an amused look. 'You really are a huge fan, aren't you?'

'Yes,' said Greta earnestly. 'I have been for years. I've seen both his retrospectives in Ireland, and I even travelled to London to see the Tate Modern one.'

'Did you go to the talk he gave in Dublin back in March?'

'I – no. I missed that. I, er, had work commitments.' The girl was looking into the middle distance, eyes unfocused, as if travelling down some memory lane. 'Excuse me. I think I'll go phone my mam now,' she said, getting abruptly to her feet and leaving the room.

Madeleine took a thoughtful sip of Veuve Cliquot. What had just happened? Greta had acted almost as if she'd been *spooked*. And suddenly Madeleine found her mind doing a completely dreadful thing – one of those freaky paranoid 'what ifs?'.

What if Greta was lying? What if she *had* gone to Daniel's talk? What if – as Daniel's biggest fan – she had sought an audience with the great man? What if she had used on Daniel the Siren-esque thing that Rory and Sam had evidently found so irresistible? What if they had gone to bed together? What if it wasn't Rory's baby that Greta was carrying – what if it was Daniel's? What if – what if Daniel had *planned* this? Was *that* why he had offered Greta so much money to stay on?

Madeleine suddenly remembered the way her husband had looked at Greta on the afternoon of Bianca's *fête champêtre*, as if he were a hunter whose trophy had just wandered into his sights, and the words she'd overheard Greta say to Sam came back to her. *I never knew he was here, I promise you. If I'd known, I never, never would have come to Saint-Géyroux ...*

Had it been Daniel she'd been talking about? Had Daniel and Rory been in cahoots, the way Rory and Jethro had? Had Greta been *lured* to Saint-Géyroux? How very, very convenient it was, after all, that a pregnant muse should happen to turn up on his doorstep so soon after he'd announced his intention of painting an *enceinte* series ...

Madeleine shook her head. Too much champagne had brought on a major fit of the heebie-jeebies. Her head was paranoia central. She knocked back the remaining fizz in her glass, reached for the paper bag and looked at it. The sketch on the back was of Greta.

Upstairs in the room with the white bed, where her back-pack was waiting to be unpacked, Greta speed dialled home.

Hundreds of miles away in Connemara, her mother picked up the phone.

'Mam! How are things?' Greta said in Irish, smiling into the mouthpiece. 'I'm fine. Yes – everything's fine. It couldn't be better. No – I'm wanting to hear all your news first. All's well with you and Da? Good. Good.' Greta listened carefully as her mother filled her in on the goings-on of her da and her four younger brothers and her baby sister and her cat and the Connemara pony and the new bantam chicks, and then she took a deep breath and said, 'Mam? There's something you need to know.'

25

A velvety dusk was descending on the back terrace of the *maison de maître*. Doves could be heard settling down to sleep in the dovecote next door, candlelight cast a golden gleam over the table, lending it the appearance of a still life by a Dutch master, and the tea roses that Dannie had planted the previous year breathed perfume over the garden.

'Will you ladies excuse me, please?' said Jethro, rising from the table. 'I have work to do.'

Mr and Mrs Palmer had been entertaining Deirdre O'Dare to supper on this, her last night in Saint-Géyroux. Dannie looked up at her husband and said, 'Don't work too late,' and Deirdre said, 'Be sure to get in touch when you're back in LA.'

'Will do, ma'am.' Dannie watched as Jethro scooped up Deirdre's hand. He kept his lips pressed to her palm for several moments, and when he finally released it, he said, 'Take care of yourself, Deirdre.'

Deirdre gave a brittle laugh. 'It's funny,' she said, 'people were always saying that to me when I was a feckless youngster. But no one's said it to me for years.'

'It's heartfelt,' Jethro told her. 'And remember, I'll do anything I can to help. Goodnight, honey. *Bon voyage.*' He saluted her with a relaxed hand before turning and moving in the direction of the kitchen.

Dannie reached for a strawberry, took a sip from her wineglass. Yesterday's torrential rain had washed her garden clean of dust and it glimmered in the twilight like some fantasy movie *mise-en-scène*. The moon was peeking out from behind a cloud like the face of a beautiful woman peeking out from behind a lace curtain, Venus had just made her celestial entrance and fireflies were glimmering like fairies in the flower beds. It would have been a perfect evening if it weren't for the fact that Deirdre was so subdued.

Bruno was subdued too. Dannie had been minding him all afternoon to give Deirdre time to go back to her house on the rue Lamballe and pack. The child was clearly out of sorts about the fact that he was being dragged back to LA and upset that his Nani Nua would not be going with them. But it was also abundantly clear that he was worried about his momma. The minute Deirdre had returned earlier that evening, he had gone shooting indoors to greet her, and he'd scarcely left her side since.

Dannie looked over to where the brown-eyed boy was sitting next to Paloma on a lounger at the other end of the terrace. The pair were deep in conversation, sharing childish secrets. She'd often remarked on the astonishing resemblance Bruno bore to his mother: both had the same sparkling quality about them that bore testimony to a lust for life, and both had the same infectious smile. But neither was smiling this evening. Indeed, there was a new frigidity about Deirdre's demeanour – as if she had wrapped herself in a protective layer of emotional ice. She could not have been more different to the wild, demented Deirdre of yesterday. Dannie supposed the

Xanax the doctor had prescribed was having the desired effect.

'How did the packing go?' Dannie asked. She hadn't wanted to broach the subject of her friend's imminent departure from Saint-Géyroux until after she'd had a chance to unwind over dinner. 'Are you all set?'

'Yes. The cases are in the hall ready to go and I've booked the taxi.'

'What time's your flight?'

'Eight o'clock. We'll be in LA by tomorrow evening, their time.'

Oh, God. Everything was happening so *fast*. 'Have you really given yourself enough time to think this through, Deirdre?' asked Dannie.

'Yes. I need to get back to my girls and sort out my life ASAP. They're due back from camp soon. They're supposed to fly to Ireland next week, to see their grandpa.'

'Yours or Rory's father?'

'Rory's. I guess I can't stop them. Until I've a lawyer on my case, I can't deny him access. But I want custody.'

'What are you going to cite as reasons for the ...' Dannie could barely bring herself to utter the word. 'Divorce?'

Deirdre's expression was unreadable. 'Mental cruelty,' she said.

Mental cruelty. That just about summed up what Rory had done – installing your mot in the family home was about as cruel as it got. But those two words – 'mental cruelty' – coupled with Rory McDonagh's name just didn't ring true, somehow. Dannie knew that she was now desperate to put the brakes on this juggernaut that she had set in motion. It frightened her to the core to see how rapidly the situation was spiralling out of control. 'Are you *sure* you're not being too hasty?' she insisted.

Deirdre shook her head. 'No. I need to keep busy, otherwise I'll fall to pieces. I *love* the fact that modern technology moves things along at the speed of light. Thanks be to Christ for the internet. Thanks be to Christ for Skype and text and MSN. Can I have some more wine, please?'

'Of course.' Dannie refilled both their glasses.

Deirdre took a hit. 'It's amazing, isn't it, how quickly the fabric of an entire life can unravel, Dannie? Mine's in fucking tatters. It's like some sprinter took hold of the loose end of a sweater and ran a marathon.'

'Have you heard anything from Rory?'

'He left a couple of messages on the land line, but I deleted them without listening to them. Oh, please let me amend that – without *bothering* to listen to them. He's been calling the mobile, but I don't pick up. He sent an e-mail asking what was going on, but I just sent one back saying I was changing my e-mail account and that the next time he'd hear from me was through a solicitor.'

'That's harsh.'

'And what he did to me *wasn't*?' Deirdre's expression was fierce. 'Jesus, Dannie, I feel so *sick* when I think of what he did to me – what the pair of them did. I feel so stupid – so incredibly *stupid* that I allowed them to gull me like that. I've never wished ill on anyone before in my life, but I wish *them* ill – him and that contriving bitch with her perfect little face and her big blue eyes. Bad cess to them both! Oh, fuck! Excuse me.'

Deirdre got to her feet and Dannie watched as she blundered through the kitchen and turned left in the direction of the downstairs loo, to throw up in private. Dannie leaned her elbows on the table and put her head in her hands. In a way, she thought, it was just as well that Deirdre was out of here tomorrow, now that Greta O'Flaherty was shacked up at *chez* Lennox. Dannie had invited Madeleine to join them for this evening's farewell supper, but Madeleine had told her that she would find it too uncomfortable to sit at the same table as Deirdre, since the subject of Greta would be sure to come up.

On the other side of the terrace, Paloma and Bruno's reedy voices were infiltrating her consciousness. It took her a while to cotton on to the fact that they were talking about Greta.

'And she never finished reading you the book?' asked Paloma.

'No. But in the car last night she told me how it ended. Seamus and Eileen have to go home. They can't live with the Danaans forever.'

'Who are the Danaans?'

'They're beautiful people who have magic powers and who live in a city of white marble. And even though she said it was as difficult for her to leave me as it was for Seamus and Eileen to leave the Danaans, she said that it would make it easier if she took something of the past with her, just like the leprechaun tells Eileen to do. So she asked me to give her my friendship bracelet.'

'The one that Natasha Richardson gave to you?' said Paloma, sounding awed.

'Yes.'

'And what thing from the past did she give you?'

'She gave me a ring. Look. I have it here.' Bruno rummaged in his pocket, extracted what Dannie took to be a ring, and showed it to Paloma.

'Cool!' said Paloma.

'It's an Irish ring that friends give to each other,' Bruno told Paloma importantly. 'It's called a Claddagh ring.'

'So that's your thing from the past?'

'Yes. And she has my friendship bracelet to take home to Ireland.'

'Does she live in a city of white marble?'

'No. She lives in a place called Connemara, by the sea. She says it's her dream to live in the kind of house that Seamus and Eileen live in.'

'What kind of house is that?'

'A whitewashed cabin at the edge of the bog. One that has blue turf-smoke rising from the chimney.'

'What's turf?'

'Turf is what you burn in Ireland instead of wood. It comes from a place called the bog.'

'What's the bog?'

'The bog,' began Bruno, 'is a place where the turf-cutters live, and it's …'

And as Bruno continued instructing Paloma in all things Irish, Dannie found herself thinking about Greta and her irresistible powers of persuasion. So that was what Jethro had meant last night when he'd said that the girl could 'charm the birds from the trees'. She'd had the nous to use a fairy story as a cautionary tale. And when she'd hunkered down and smoothed his hair and kissed his cheek, she'd been exchanging tokens of friendship with the child. The ring that Greta had given Bruno had been her Claddagh ring: a ring depicting two hands clasped round a heart wrought in gold, a ring that symbolised loyalty, friendship and love.

Paloma didn't know what a Claddagh ring was. She

didn't know what a bog was, or a turf-cutter. It was time to start teaching her about her Irish heritage. She'd order some books for her from Amazon tomorrow, Dannie decided. *The Turf-Cutter's Donkey* and *The Turf-Cutter's Donkey Goes Visiting*, and books of Celtic myths and legends, and every single one of the Irish children's novels written by that author who'd won the Whitbread.

On the table, Deirdre's phone began to ring. Dannie leaned forward and checked out the display. Rory. She let it ring out. Some seven or eight seconds later came the sound of the message alert.

Dannie felt goose-bumpy. Reaching for her pashmina, she shrugged it over her shoulders. From a garden a couple of houses away, she heard a dog bark and the light laugh of a girl, and she wondered if it was Greta, messing around with Pilot and Sam in Daniel Lennox's garden. Madeleine had told her on the phone earlier that Sam and Greta were an item and were sharing a bedroom. Well – the girl certainly didn't let the grass grow under her feet! It was funny – she didn't *look* like a slapper. But maybe slapper was the wrong word? Dannie remembered that Greta's mother had been something of a hippy, a bit bohemian. Maybe the way she'd been reared had something to with Greta's … liberality?

'Sorry about that.' Deirdre dropped into the seat opposite. 'Don't worry. I'm all cried out now.' She reached for her phone, then clocked the message icon. 'Did you see the name in the display?' she asked.

'Yes. It was Rory.'

The phone started to ring again. Deirdre looked at the screen. And then she raised her hand and sent the nifty little Nokia hurtling towards the surface of the swimming

393

pool, where it sank like a stone.

She watched in silence as the ripples spread and then she turned to Dannie.

'I never want to hear his voice again,' she said.

From two gardens away came the sound of girlish laughter.

'Merci beaucoup, Madame!'

'Je vous en prie, Mademoiselle!'

Greta was multitasking – shopping, doing mental arithmetic and checking messages on her phone. There was one from her dad telling her to take care of herself and wishing her luck, there was a joke from her cousin Esther and there was a message from Bruno, signed 'Mistoffelees'. It read: Mis u greta wil send mail from la.

Greta swung through the door of the *boulangerie*, texting busily, oblivious to the looks that came her way. Some were looks of admiration, some were looks of disapproval and some were looks of speculation.

It was market day in Saint-Géyroux and Greta had volunteered to cook for Daniel, Madeleine and Sam that evening. Risotto with mushrooms, she'd decided, followed by fresh fruit salad.

On the village square, the market stalls were laden with produce, the colours the stuff of a still-life by Gauguin, the smells the gastronomic equivalent of Viagra. There were baskets piled with tomatoes and courgettes and aubergines, there were pyramids of pineapples and pomegranates and peaches, there were trugs of field mushrooms and crates of fresh fish and cartons of sweet things: biscuits and gateaux and *madeleines*. Greta bought a box of *madeleines de Commercy* for the mistress of the Lennox household and a small box of cigars for the master. For Sam, she bought a second-hand copy of *Around the World in Eighty Days*.

Sam had told her that he'd be covering the round-the-world yacht race for at least two of its laps. By the time he got back, her baby bump would be well advanced and Daniel would have almost completed his series. He'd calculated that it would take a month before he was happy with his first *Greta Enceinte*. Then there'd be a further five portraits before she took time out to go back to Ireland. The seventh portrait – to be executed on her return – would be the last. *Mère et Enfant*, he called it: Mother and Child. But every time he said it, Greta crossed her fingers. She'd never forgotten the story of tragic Lizzie Siddal – the most famous muse of all – whose baby had been born dead.

'*Merci beaucoup!*' she told the second-hand bookseller as he handed over the Jules Verne.

'*Je vous en prie, Mademoiselle!*' he said back, giving her that appreciative look that French men did so expertly. Well, not just French men, she decided. The look Sam had given her when she'd stepped out of the shower that morning had been pretty eloquent, too. She'd arranged to meet him in the café later, and the prospect of seeing him sitting there waiting for her on the terrace, with a *pression* for him and an Evian for her, made her tummy do a somersault.

As she moved between the market stalls, reaching for a nectarine from one, helping herself to a bunch of grapes from another, she remembered what he'd said to her the first time they'd met. *This is the most preposterously romantic thing that's ever happened to you. And you're hoping that maybe I'll turn out to be the kind of man you want to marry and live happily ever after with …*

As it had turned out, it *was* the most preposterously romantic thing that had ever happened to her. But was Sam the kind of man she'd want to marry and live happily ever after with? Did fairy tales come true? He'd quoted *Romeo and Juliet* to her, and look what had happened to *them*. And yet, and yet … Feck it – she'd allow herself to hope, she told herself, tossing apricots into a paper bag. She'd always been one to look on the bright side. She was a Sagittarius, after all, and Sagittarius was the most optimistic sign of the Zodiac.

'*Merci beaucoup!*'

'*Je vous en prie, Mademoiselle!*'

Greta hurried across the square, past a stall heaped with bric-a-brac and another stacked with rainbow-coloured espadrilles and another with gaudy Provençal puppets dangling from its awning. She'd buy one for Esther, she thought. And one for her mam. And her dad would love a really good bottle of wine from the local *caveaux*. She'd go back to Ireland at the end of the year laden with presents for friends and family, and for once they wouldn't be home-made. For the first time in her life, Greta O'Flaherty could afford to be *flaithiúlacht*.

She rounded a corner and there was Sam as she'd pictured him, sitting at a table with a *demi* of beer in front of him and her bottle of Evian. But he wasn't alone. Margot d'Arcy was sitting opposite him with her elbows on the table, leaning in to him and laughing coquettishly. And the searing stab of jealousy Greta felt told her that yes – she *was* in love.

She stood looking at the pair for a moment or two, registering how beautiful they looked together – for even though Margot was somewhere in her thirties, she was still remarkably foxy. Some men had a thing for older women, she knew … well, she wasn't going to stand for this! She was in love – Greta O'Flaherty was in love! – and she was going to lay claim to her man! Marching along the terrace, she made her presence felt by dropping a kiss on Sam's cheek.

'Hey, gorgeous!' he said, reaching up a hand to caress her shoulder. 'You look like something out of *Jeanne de Florette.*'

'*Bonjour*, Greta,' said Margot and Greta saw her eyes go to her tummy. So *that's* why she'd been getting some weird looks from the denizens of Saint-Géyroux! She'd read somewhere recently that a very twentieth-century morality still prevailed in provincial France, that single parenthood was frowned upon and bastard babies stigmatised.

Zut, alors! The little Irish blow-in was pregnant, and she had no ring on her finger! Did this make her a slut in the eyes of the village? Would they tch tch about the fact that she was posing for Daniel and stepping out with Sam? Would word leak out that she'd been body-double for Charlotte Lambert? Pah – let it be their problem! Let the village of the squinting windows speculate about her baby and its paternity. She wasn't going to hide herself away like some put-upon Magdalene laundry type! Greta O'Flaherty was happy, healthy and she had money in her pocket for presents.

'Can I buy you a drink, Margot?' she asked.

'Thank you, no. I have already ordered,' Margot said,

and, on cue, Maurice arrived with a tray upon which stood a *pichet* of wine and a glass. 'Please bring another wineglass, Maurice,' Margot said in beautifully modulated French.

'*D'accord, Madame. Tout de suite.*'

Margot turned back to Sam and Greta. 'I am expecting Colleen,' she told them. 'She has been labouring all day over a speech of Hecate's.'

'How's the play going?' Sam asked politely.

Margot gave a Gallic shrug. 'What can I say? It's a labour of love, *mon brave*. But what is the product of love, but a love child? It's no accident that Colleen describes the creative process as being akin to the three stages of parturition. We conceive, we gestate, we labour.' Another sideways glance at Greta's tummy; but Greta wasn't as obliging as Maurice in picking up her cues.

'I've a present for you, boy photographer,' she said, rooting in her basket. 'I found it in the second-hand bookseller.' She produced the copy of *Around the World in Eighty Days*, set it on the table in front of him and helped herself to an apricot. 'Apricot, Margot? Sam?' she said, passing round the bag.

Sam helped himself, squeezed the fruit to test its ripeness and exchanged a gratifyingly meaningful smile with her before picking up the book.

'Thanks.' Margot likewise delved a languid hand into the bag, bit into the fruit, then licked her lips, displaying pointed, feral teeth. But Sam wasn't taking in Margot's flagrant attempt to engage him in a courtship ritual. He was smiling as he registered the significance of the book's title.

'I know it's more than eighty days you'll be away,' said

Greta. 'I'm after trying to work out how many exactly. How many of those things are you doing – what do you call them? Laps?'

'Legs,' said Sam, and Greta saw Margot cross her legs ostentatiously, affording Sam a generous eyeful of thigh. 'Two.'

Greta bit into her apricot, wishing it was Margot's arse. 'And how long's a leg again?' she asked, crossing her own in retaliation.

'Not quite two months, kitten,' said Sam, and to her delight, he laid a proprietorial hand on her knee.

Result! thought Greta. 'Maths never was my strong point,' she said. 'Maybe I should do one of those countdown things that prisoners do to keep track of time – you know, making marks on a wall and scoring lines through them.'

'Aren't you sweet?' he said, leaning in to kiss her. 'Mmm. You taste sweet, too.'

As their lips met, they heard the sound of a heavy sigh. Greta looked up to see Colleen listing down the terrace. She collapsed onto an aluminium chair so dramatically that Greta feared it might buckle under her.

'*Ochone!*' pronounced Colleen, and Greta laughed. *No one* in Ireland said *ochone*, unless you were sending yourself up. Colleen clearly had a wacky sense of humour.

Margot gave Greta a reproachful look, then turned to Colleen and laid a hand on her arm. 'Finished, love?' she asked and Colleen inclined her head. 'In that case, my love, allow me to pour you a glass of wine. Where *is* that boy?' Impatiently, Margot raised a hand and clicked her fingers to attract the attention of Maurice.

Gazing at the *pichet* on the table, Colleen murmured,

O for a draught of vintage! That hath been
Cool'd a long age in the deep-delvèd earth'
Tasting of Flora and the country-green,
Dance, and Provençal song, and sunburnt mirth!

You know the poem?' She skewered Greta with her green gaze.

'Yes. It's from Keats's 'Ode to a Nightingale', isn't it?'

'Clever girl.'

Phew! She at least hadn't let herself down in front of the formidable intellect that was Colleen. Keats's 'Ode to a Nightingale' was the only poem Greta knew, now she came to think of it – apart from the *Practical Cats* ones.

Maurice arrived with another wineglass, poured and set it in front of Colleen, who murmured something about the blushful Hippocrene.

'Greta? Will you join us in a glass of wine?' asked Margot.

'No, thank you. I'm not allowed to drink.'

Colleen looked interested. 'Why, pray, is that?'

Greta decided to throw caution to the wind. She was sick of being circumspect. 'I'm pregnant,' she said cheerfully. 'I thought everyone in the village knew that by now.'

'So it *is* true!' said Colleen, throwing her arms up to heaven. 'Alleluia!'

Margot gave them the benefit of her catlike smile as Greta and Sam exchanged 'what the fuck?' glances. 'Colleen is seeking someone to play one of the juvenile female roles in our play,' she explained.

'The one about the goddesses?' asked Sam.

'Yes. We hope to stage a production in Bianca's pavilion at the end of the summer.'

'I am undertaking the role of Hecate,' said Colleen. 'Margot is playing Persephone. And we are desirous of a girl, a girl who – if we are to be true to the spirit of the Universal Mother Goddess—'

'Amen,' said Margot.

'A girl,' resumed Colleen, 'who is with child, to play Corinna.'

That name! What *was* it about that name that made it crop up again and again, wondered Greta.

'Not that ho who goes a-Maying?' said Sam.

'Ho?' said Margot, raising an autocratic eyebrow. 'I think not.'

'Chick, then.' Sam took a swig of his beer.

Margot gave him a pitying look. 'The trinity of the Universal Mother Goddess took form as Corinna the green corn, Persephone the ripe ear and Hecate the harvested corn. Since Hecate is a divinity of the underworld who deals with life and death, it stands to reason that she was petitioned for help by women having difficulty in child bearing.'

'But I can't be Corinna,' protested Greta.

'Why not?' said Sam with a wicked smile. 'You'd look great all dolled up in a mini toga like a tousle-headed Maenad.'

'What's a Maenad?'

'They were the clubbers of yesteryear.'

'Why cannot you play Corinna?' demanded Colleen.

'I'm no actress,' said Greta. 'I'd be scared stiff to stand up in public and spout a load of – lines.'

'Then no matter,' said Colleen. 'For Corinna has no

lines. She appears in dumb-show only, in a *tableau vivant*. You'd be perfect casting.'

'As the dumb blonde?' said Sam.

Greta wanted to laugh, but a magisterial look from Colleen told her that this was no laughing matter. The *ochone* thing earlier evidently hadn't been said in jest. She took another bite of her apricot.

'Who's playing Síle na Gig?' asked Sam.

'Síle will be represented in the form of an image,' said Colleen. 'We were hoping that Daniel might oblige with a sculpture.'

'I think you'll find,' said Sam, 'that Daniel has other things on his mind right now.'

'In that case,' mused Colleen, 'we might find a local artisan to fashion one out of straw, in the tradition of the Harvesters of Yore. Yes. That would perfectly complement the theme of fertility.'

'We also require an Adonis,' pronounced Margot, turning her attention to Sam. 'We had thought of you, Sam, as the Love God.'

'No can do,' Sam said urbanely. 'I'm off on an assignment.'

'Alas. In that case, we shall have to make do with the Renard boy.'

'He'd make a pretty foxy Adonis,' remarked Sam. 'But you'd want to pay him well if he's going to strut his stuff in a frock.'

'Of course we will pay well,' said Colleen. 'I like to think that I might make a financial as well as an artistic contribution to the village. We intend to employ at least a dozen young people, and pay them the Equity extras going rate.'

'You might even be able to afford Tom Cruise, now he's dipped in the popularity stakes,' quipped Sam.

But Colleen was clearly immune to jokes – even bad ones – for she was gazing at the wine-dark contents of her glass with soulful eyes. Raising the glass to her lips, she took a sip, then set it down. 'The taste of the Languedoc!' she murmured, just as Maurice whisked past, bearing a plate of *moules marinières*. 'The smells of the Languedoc!' she smiled, gesturing towards the dish. Then, cocking her head sideways, she made a wistful little moue. 'The sound of the Languedoc!'

'Actually,' said Greta, getting to her feet and checking out the display on her phone, 'that's my mobile ring tone. It's a cicada. Excuse me, please. I have to take this.'

The wicked look Sam shot her made Greta want to crease up as she trotted off down the terrace, and as she picked up the call, the big bubble of mirth swelled up inside her and burst.

'Yo, Mistoffelees!' she sang into the mouthpiece. '*Mavourneen*! How's she cutting?'

But the voice that came over the line wasn't Bruno's. It was a woman's, and her tone was Arctic Circle frigid.

'It's Deirdre O'Dare here,' said the voice. 'I'm responding to the text you sent Bruno earlier, and I just want to say that I don't want you communicating with my son ever again. Is that understood? If you try to contact Bruno again, I shall have no alternative but to take legal action.'

Greta felt as if a snake had slithered into her gut and was forcing the apricot in the wrong direction. 'But I've done Bruno no mischief,' she stammered.

'You've done everyone mischief, Greta. Everyone.

And knowing the kind of person you are, you'll probably carry on causing mischief wherever you go. I'd hazard a guess that it's a kind of hobby of yours, wreaking havoc.'

'No—'

But Deirdre breezed on, Arctic force nine. 'Before we say our final farewells, there's just one more thing you need to know. In order to be certain that you never contact Bruno again, I am going to have to employ pretty desperate measures, and I think you might need to know what they are.'

The lump of apricot in her throat had robbed Greta of the power of speech, but that didn't matter, because her erstwhile employer didn't bother waiting for a reply.

'I'm going to change Bruno's phone number,' Deirdre said conversationally. 'And I'm going to tell him you're dead. Goodbye.'

26

Deirdre had changed Bruno's phone number, but she hadn't told him that Greta was dead. She had simply encouraged him to get over her and, luckily for her, Bruno's memory was short. He even seemed to have relinquished his other half, Pluto. In LA she distracted him with all the child-friendly ammunition at her disposal: theme parks, movies, myriad outings – and of course, Melissa was there to help divert him, as well as Bruno's bossy older sisters, back from surf camp.

Deirdre vacillated over how to tell her children that her marriage was over and that she and their dad would be living in separate homes – although, of course, she allowed them access to him via telephone and internet. She supposed Aoife, being the oldest, might be able to understand the situation best – surrounded as she was by dozens of friends whose parents were on their second, third and even fourth marriages. But Aoife was such a fragile soul. Grace was more resilient, but too young. And baby Bruno had taken enough knocks recently. He was clingier than ever.

Deferring telling them was made easier by the fact that they were used to Rory being an absent father: this wasn't the first time he'd spent months away from home. Aoife had a map on her bedroom wall on which she monitored his progress around the world: Ireland, Venezuela, Moscow, London, Paris, Beijing.

Deirdre seldom allowed herself to speak of him to her children because she was scared that her tone of voice might betray her hatred of him. She hated him not just because he had betrayed her, but because he'd turned her into a person who seethed with bitterness. He'd made her toxic. He had made numerous attempts to get in touch, but she had stonewalled every single one of them. Her divorce lawyer was proving to be a formidable line of defence between her and her soon-to-be-ex husband. Not one communication came through. Deirdre had drawn a line in the sand more highly defined than the one drawn by Sir Paul McCartney when he ousted his second lady wife and, try as he might, Rory could not overstep it.

Sometimes – usually when she was weak on a Xanax and alcohol combo – she regressed and called him using the Private Caller facility, just to hear his voice. On one occasion he had picked up and said nothing for many moments. Deirdre had remained frozen, clutching the phone to her ear, not daring to draw breath, achingly conscious of a connection so highly charged it seemed almost physical. Then Rory had spoken. 'Deirdre?' he had said. She hadn't answered. She had put the phone down feeling wobblier than a newborn lamb. The last time she'd called, a woman's voice had picked up. 'Rory McDonagh's phone,' Deirdre had heard. She hadn't called him again.

Unbeknownst to Daniel, Madeleine was monitoring the progress of Greta's portraits. She had never trespassed in his studio before: she had always respected that superstition of his that decreed that *nobody* was allowed to view a Daniel Lennox painting until it received his imprimatur. But Madeleine *had* to see them: she was in the grip of a fixation, like a self-harmer who has to let blood or an alcoholic who won't be denied a drink or a heroin addict seeking the holy grail of the next fix.

The first time she had stepped over the threshold of his studio while he was out playing *boules*, she had felt as if she was committing a crime. But she had learned to live with the guilt.

The canvases were ranked with their faces against the back wall of the studio. There were now three complete portraits and one inchoate. The first portrait showed a svelte Greta lying on her back, one arm pillowing her head, the other drooping languorously over the edge of the daybed. The mass of reddish-gold hair that spilled over the pillow had been captured in the most sensuous of brush strokes: Daniel had caressed the girl's hair with paint. The second revealed Greta curled in upon herself, her hands covering her belly in a protective gesture as if safeguarding the precious cargo within.

The third portrait was the most beautiful and it was the one that Madeleine hated most. It showed Greta sprawled against dishevelled sheets in an attitude of abandon. The gentle swell of her belly was the central focus of the painting, but the eye was drawn, too, to the flush blazoning her breasts, the startlingly erect golden-brown nipples and the hectic glow of her cheeks. This Corinna was undeniably pregnant and undeniably post-orgasmic. It made Madeleine want to reach for Daniel's palette knife and stab the place under the girl's beautiful, rosy left breast.

And every time Madeleine left the studio after one of

these exercises in voyeurism, she felt as low in self-esteem as any self-harmer, any down-and-out drunk, any addict.

It wasn't just Rory's progress that was being monitored on a map: that of Sam Newman's was too. Greta charted the hovering progress of his helicopter over the Pacific every evening, picturing him hanging out of the belly of the machine like some machismo Special Ops veteran. She loved to lie in bed and sweet-talk on the phone, loved to curl up in front of the computer screen looking at the photographs he sent her, loved to idly tip-tap out besotted e-mails to him (some of which were so very soppy – or so very raunchy – they were never sent).

Greta was revelling in her pregnancy. Madeleine had driven her into Gignac for her first scan and Greta had swooned at the image on the screen, the minuscule, compact bundle of tissue and sinew and muscle that was her baby! She imagined it free-floating like a miniature moonwalker in amniotic fluid, cocooned in the cosy haven of her womb, and she occasionally felt its presence in a barely perceptible butterfly kick. She talked to it, sang to it, told stories to it, soothed it by running the reassuring palms of her hands over her tummy.

During the daytime she'd sit for Daniel, gazing into the middle distance, day-dreaming, listening to music. Occasionally – not often – he would allow her to read. During her time off, she'd cycle down to the Labadou, sometimes with Rosa to keep her company, sometimes with her sketchbook, although her painting these days was desultory, unsatisfactory, and her landscapes mostly unfinished. During the evenings she'd join the Lennox family for a meal – often one she'd have cooked herself – and then she'd take herself off to the pool in the basement for a swim before bedtime. Life was sweet: a bed of roses, a bowl of cherries.

She never allowed herself to think about Deirdre O'Dare or Bruno.

Dannie Palmer was monitoring the progress of Greta's pregnancy.

She watched sometimes from an upstairs window as the girl sashayed down the rue des Artistes, flaunting her belly without a care in the world. Greta smiled! She laughed! She radiated rude good health! Greta had about her that glow that people say all pregnant women have, but which in point of fact very few do. Most pregnant women carry the burden of work on their shoulders until the end of their term, most pregnant women have the stress and strain of other children to worry about, most pregnant women get heartburn and fatigue and backache and varicose veins and swollen ankles. But not Greta O'Flaherty. Not her! *She* was an artist's model, after all, and all she had to do was lounge around in her pelt all day, looking inspirational.

She was popular, too. The initial mistrust that the people of Saint-Géyroux had shown towards the unmarried mother-to-be had mutated into great good will. Greta had wormed her way into the collected affections of the village, and Dannie often overheard greetings on the street as the girl bowled along on her bicycle or proceeded along the footpath on bare feet (another attention-seeking affectation, Dannie decided). '*Bonjour*

Greta! Comme tu es jolie aujourd'hui!' 'Bonjour, Greta! Qu'il fait beau ici!' 'Bonjour, Greta! Comment se passe ta grossesse?'

The references to the pregnancy were what lacerated Dannie most. On the really bad days she'd go to the room she'd earmarked for the nursery, where all Paloma's old baby clothes were kept, and she'd take out the tiny white bootees with the rosebud tassels, and the soft velour sleep suit with the perky kitten's ears, and the doll-sized dress patterned with daisies, and she'd hold the items to her face until they turned damp with her tears.

Dannie hated herself when she did this. She had a child already – a bright, bonny, healthy child at that – so why did she yearn so desperately for another? She knew couples who'd made the pilgrimage across the barren desert that was IVF, so urgent was their need for children, and who had come out the other side damaged beyond repair with no baby for consolation. Was it greedy of her to want another? Was it selfish? Was there some jinx on her? Was the bad vibe she felt towards Greta O'Flaherty somehow ricocheting back on her and bringing bad cess?

'Bonjour, Greta – d'être enceinte ça te va bien!' Good day, Greta! Being pregnant certainly suits you!

Dannie got used to clamping her hands over her ears and tried hard not to think bad thoughts.

'Bonjour, Madeleine!' fluted Bianca. 'You are most welcome!' Mwah, mwah! Mwah, mwah!

'Thanks, Bianca.'

It was a blustery day in late summer. Madeleine was standing with her hostess on the balcony at the top of the flight of steps that led down to Bianca's garden.

Bianca had Dora Maar in her arms. The dog was sporting one of those laurel wreaths that the poets of ancient Greece used to wear and was smiling disconcertingly, showing teeth that reminded Madeleine of Margot d'Arcy.

'Well, this is some occasion,' observed Madeleine. 'It's not often that a gal gets an invite to the world première of a play in a sleepy French village.'

Bianca's garden was milling with people. All the invited denizens of Saint-Géyroux had turned up today, just as they had for the *fête champêtre* at the beginning of the summer – except today the only person wearing white was Bianca. So much had happened since that day, thought Madeleine. A marriage had ended, a muse had been discovered, young love had been declared, three portraits had been painted.

'Is Daniel not with you, Madeleine?' Bianca asked her.

''Fraid not. Daniel's work is pretty all-consuming right now.'

That was an understatement. The fourth portrait wasn't up to scratch, Daniel had decided. He'd stretched and primed a new canvas the previous night and started work on it that morning. Today, Saturday afternoon, should have been Greta's day off, but she was sequestered in his studio again, experimenting with new poses for him. The knowledge made Madeleine feel nauseous. It was time to change the subject.

'I understand that Colleen and Margot are off back to Ireland tomorrow?' she said.

Bianca drooped and made a little moue. 'Yes, indeed. I shall miss my Creatives. But they have promised to return. They have become such dedicated Francophiles that they've decided they wish to spend Christmas here in Saint-Géyroux. I intend hosting a proper French Christmas with a goose, of course, and a *bûche de Noël* and *Messe de Minuit* on Christmas Eve. Ah! Dannie! You are welcome, to be sure!'

Dannie joined them on the balcony. She observed the greeting ritual, as Madeleine had done before her.

'Jethro sends his regrets, Bianca,' said Dannie. 'He's just jetted off to LA.'

'That Jethro!' tched Bianca. 'He needs to slow down!'

Dannie looked tired, Madeleine thought. She'd lost weight, and it didn't suit her. There was a pinched look about her face and a haunted look in her eyes.

Come to think of it, Madeleine hadn't been that impressed by her own appearance when she'd checked herself out in the mirror before leaving the house that afternoon. She was convinced that the lines around her eyes were more deeply etched than they had been only a few months earlier and the skin on her throat had acquired the texture of crêpe paper.

These days, Madeleine wanted to scribble on the faces that looked up at her from the pages of women's magazines. She wanted to scribble on Sharon Stone, who told her that Dior's Capture Totale would make her more beautiful today than she'd been at twenty. She wanted to scribble on the smug face of the model extolling the benefits of the age-defying, youth-reviving, life-enhancing, non-surgical solutions available to her. She wanted to scribble on the stupid, vacuous smile of the blonde who had electrodes stuck to her face, the blonde who promised her that *her* product would treat frown lines, laughter lines, problematic breasts, abs, buttocks, pelvic floors, hands and cellulite. But more than anything, she wanted to scribble on the beautiful face that gazed out at her from the canvases in her husband's studio.

'Help yourselves to drinks,' Bianca told them. 'I must just go and see how my Creatives are getting on. Calm their stage nerves! Colleen was pacing her room like a big cat earlier.'

Madeleine and Dannie watched as Bianca and Dora Maar bustled off, meeting and greeting and *souhait*-ing as they went.

'Cheers,' said Madeleine, relieving a passing waiter of two glasses and handing one to Dannie. 'How's life?'

'Not great,' admitted Dannie. 'How's yours?'

'Ditto.'

Exchanging mirthless smiles, they turned to face the garden, leaning their elbows on the parapet of the balcony. Below them, the saplings in Bianca's arboretum were doing Mexican waves in the strengthening wind.

'What's your problem?' asked Madeleine.

'Greta O'Flaherty,' said Dannie. 'I can't hack the way she flaunts that baby bump of hers. What's *your* problem?'

'Greta O'Flaherty. I can't hack the way she flaunts that beautiful body in front of my husband every day.'

This time Dannie's smile was a little less mirthless. 'Well, I have to say it comes as something of a relief to know that I'm not only one who's bitter and twisted and eaten up with jealousy.'

Madeleine looked down at Valérie Poiret, who was wandering across the lawn below, her new baby in her arms. 'You know what our real problem is, Dannie? We're getting old.'

'Old? Arra, come on, Madeleine – isn't it a fact that life begins at forty? And neither of us have got there yet. Unlike Bianca,' Dannie added in an undertone.

'Bianca's never forty!'

'Don't tell her I told you. She let slip a reference to her sister's fortieth birthday party last week, and I know for a fact that her sister's younger than her.'

'Well, fair play to her. She obviously looks after herself.'

'So do you,' said Dannie loyally. 'You look great.'

'Thanks. You're sweet to say so.'

'I'm not being sweet. I mean it.'

Madeleine sagged. 'Oh, Dannie – it's such bloody hard work! I'm so bone weary of all the *pressure* to stay looking young! All that time spent peeling and exfoliating and oiling. The money I invest in creams and lotions and anti-ageing serums could keep a Third World country afloat for a year. And now there's all that nip-tuck stuff to contend with. Soon anyone who *hasn't* had surgery will look like an alien from the planet Zog. And the worst thing of all is having to watch beauty go upstairs to the beast's studio every day.'

'Really? You once told me you didn't have a problem with Daniel painting beautiful women.'

'I lied.'

'In that case, you're one feck of a liar,' said Dannie. 'You had me convinced.'

Madeleine smiled, then looked back down at the garden. 'Bianca's done it again,' she said. 'The place looks fabulous.'

Bianca had pulled out all the stops for the world première of *Síle na Gig in the Temple of Hecate*. The struts supporting the roof of the yoga pavilion where the play was to be staged were garlanded with white gardenias, the stage floor was polka-dotted with white petals and the rear of the pavilion had been swagged with white muslin. A giant corn dolly Síle na Gig had pride of place on a white-painted plinth. Speakers were suspended from tree branches, garden chairs were scattered here and there and rugs had been spread on the lawn. There was a profusion of food and drink laid out on the white linen cloth that covered the trestle table on the terrace and waiters glided among the guests looking as if they were on castors. Madeleine had never been to Glyndebourne, but she imagined that this might be it in miniature.

'What's this play about, I wonder?' she asked.

'I did some Googling. Hecate was the great goddess of fertility, apparently. She had control over life and death and she had the power to bestow – or withhold – from mortals any gift she chose.'

Dannie had printed out a web page that reproduced a prayer to the goddess by some ancient scribe. She kept it in her wallet and took it out from time to time, wondering if she shouldn't start making sacrifices to Hecate rather than petitioning God for a baby. It went:

Come infernal, terrestrial, and heavenly Hecate, friend and lover of darkness,
Thou who doest rejoice when the bitches are howling and warm blood is spilled,
Thou who art walking amid the phantom and in the place of the tombs,
Thou whose thirst is blood, thou who doest strike chill and fear in mortal hearts,
Cast a propitious eye on our sacrifice.

'She was also known as Bombo,' Dannie told Madeleine.

'Bombo?' Madeleine laughed. '*Síle na Gig in the Temple of Bombo* doesn't have quite the same ring to it, somehow. Uh oh,' she added, returning her attention to the garden.

'What's wrong?'

'That muslin backdrop's billowing about rather tempestuously. I hope it doesn't come adrift.'

'I've just realised there's another thing to go "uh oh" about,' remarked Dannie.

'What's that?'

'The wind's coming straight down from the north-west. You know what that means.'

The two women exchanged ominous looks. In the past five minutes, the wind had really got up. Guests wearing hats were holding on to them and girls with full skirts were keeping their arms pinned rigidly to their sides. The petals that had been scattered on the stage were eddying, caught up in miniature whirlwinds, and water from the fountain was being whisked in the direction of those members of the audience who stood to its immediate left, causing them to shuffle away from the stage area.

Whoooh!

'What's that?'

Whoooh!

'It sounds like some kind of a trumpet.'

Whoooh!

It was indeed a trumpet. A Tibetan one. Bianca was making her way across the lawn to the yoga pavilion, wearing a solemn expression and blowing into the intricately carved human thigh bone she'd picked up in a souk in Tangier. When she reached the pavilion, she stopped and turned to the assembled company.

'*Monsieur le Maire*, ladies and gentlemen, *mesdames et messieurs, copains et copines,* I am very happy to welcome you here today, to share with you a unique theatrical experience. Since I constructed my Sanctuary for Creatives, I have been blessed to have harboured within its walls one of the most illustrious luminaries the country of Ireland has ever produced. Ireland – *Irlande* – that land renowned for its saints and scholars, its writers, artists, poets and playwrights – has lent us – nay, has *bestowed* upon us – her grande dame of literature, and I am thrilled that this play by the renowned Colleen will be performed for the first time in my Sanctuary for all of you assembled here this afternoon. Ladies and gentlemen, I give you: *Síle na Gig in the Temple of Hecate*!'

Applause rang out as Bianca gestured theatrically to the door in the garden wall through which now trudged a troupe of local people wearing Grecian tunics and sheepish expressions and carrying – rather fittingly, Madeleine thought – sheep crooks. The girl who'd been cast as Corinna was the heavily pregnant fishmonger's daughter who had the unfortunate appearance of a petrified trout, while poor Joel Renard – who'd been roped in as Adonis – resembled one of the cast members of *Dumb and Dumber*. There was a snigger and a smart remark from some wag in the audience, and then silence descended as Colleen and Margot brought up the rear of the procession. Colleen was battering her bodhrán with a little wooden mallet and Margot's fingers were fluttering nimbly over the silver stem of her tin whistle. They were both attired in silk gowns so diaphanous they might as well have been naked.

There was a fidgeting among the audience and one or

two embarrassed coughs, and then Colleen stepped onto the platform and adopted a Junoesque stance. 'Persephone, come!' she said, raising an imperious arm, and as Margot joined her on the platform, there came two or three wolf whistles. The strains of an Irish lament started to wail through the speakers and Colleen and Margot surged together in a ritualistic dance, silken robes shimmering and fluttering around them. As the dance progressed, the shimmering got more shimmery and the fluttering more fluttery, until suddenly the wind snatched rudely at the muslin backcloth and ripped it away from its moorings. One of the shepherds tried to hook it with his crook, but the length of muslin evaded him and took off over the roof of Bianca's house like Casper the Friendly Ghost. The fountain redirected its jet straight at the stage, dousing the leading actresses with water, and the Mexican wave of the saplings in the arboretum became even more animated.

'Merde!' shouted a shepherd as his skirt blew up, and 'Le mistral!' shouted a hapless shepherdess, watching as her coronet of white silk daisies went spinning across the lawn. It landed on top of an outraged-looking Dora Maar, whose laurel wreath had wound up round her neck and whose fur looked as if it was being blow-dried backwards on the highest setting.

In a couple of heartbeats, everything was pandemonium. Síle na Gig tumbled off her plinth and fell flat on her fanny. Trays of glasses being borne aloft by waiters went crashing to the ground. The linen cloth beat its wings so wildly round the trestle table that big splotches of food spattered the surface, like a bad Jackson Pollock. The garden swing was to-ing and fro-ing as if some poltergeist was having a go and ornamental ferns in pots were keeling over like targets on a shooting range. People were running in all directions, colliding into each other, gardenias were pelting down from the sky and speakers were falling out of trees. Colleen's bodhrán had escaped custody and was bowling along a pathway, rumbling loudly as it went, and Bianca was flapping around in ever-diminishing circles like the White Queen in *Alice in Wonderland*, ineffectually trying to restore order and shrieking, 'Don't panic! Don't panic! *Ne paniquez-pas!*'

And then came the dust storm. This was no ordinary dust – this was the dust that accompanied a mistral, the kind of dust you don't mess with. Madeleine and Dannie ducked back into the house through the French windows, and as they did, Madeleine caught over her shoulder a last glance of Colleen and Margot on the platform of Bianca's yoga pavilion.

It was clearly a case of 'the show must go on', for despite being drenched by the fountain, Margot and Colleen were still performing the Dance of the Goddesses. The silk of their robes was now completely transparent and had moulded itself tight against their bodies, infiltrating every nook and cranny. To an uninitiated eye, the pair would appear to be completely starkers.

The last lines of the bedtime story she'd read to Rosa last night came back to Madeleine. With a smile, she turned to Dannie.

'Well, there's no adage like an old adage,' she said.

'What do you mean?'

'The emperor's wearing no clothes,' said Madeleine.

27

```
INT. GEORGIA'S HOUSE
BATHROOM. DAWN.

FADE IN

We are CLOSE on Georgia's face. Her phone is
clamped to her ear. As the CAMERA pulls back,
we see that she is lying on the floor. BLOOD is
pooling onto the tiles.

GEORGIA: Stephen? I've lost the baby. Stephen?
I think I'm dying.
```

Deirdre's agent, Blake Parker, looked up from the script, a frown on his face. 'It's certainly different.'

'That's the idea,' Deirdre told him.

'It's hardly the rom com I expected.' Blake set the screenplay down on the restaurant table. They were having dinner on the terrace at the Sunset Tower, and the purple haze over LA seemed to stretch to infinity. 'What happened, Deirdre? What made you decide to take a detour to the dark side?'

Deirdre shrugged. 'I didn't make any conscious decision. The characters dictated the action. That's always been the way – you know that. My screenplays have always been character rather than plot driven.'

'Maybe – but your characters have always been upbeat, a little quirky. I don't see Kate Hudson playing Dee, somehow.'

'Who do you see playing her?'

He considered. 'Angelina.'

'Perfect!' Deirdre smiled.

'That's something else that's different about you, Deirdre. Your smile.'

'What about it?'

'To use a screenplay cliché, it don't reach your eyes no more.'

'Well, you know what they say, Blake,' said Deirdre, pouring herself a very politically incorrect liberal glass of wine, not bothering to wait for the sommelier. 'They say the eyes are the windows of the soul. And my soul hasn't been doing much smiling lately.'

'Things are still bad between you and Rory?'

'Yeah. They're terminal.'

'Have you spoken?'

'No. It's all being handled by our legal people.'

'Nasty.' Blake leaned back in his chair and pushed the bar of his designer sunglasses further up the bridge of his nose. The label on the jacket he'd hung ostentatiously over the back of his chair announced that he was sporting Ozwald Boateng, his manicure was impeccable, his watch was Patek Philippe and Deirdre felt a sudden surge of hatred for all things LA. Los Angeles was like the swimming pool that lay beyond the sliding glass walls of the restaurant: smooth, diamantine, seductive. But what lay beneath the surface of the city was murky and shark infested, with a lethal undertow. 'Will you get custody of the kids?' Blake asked.

'I'm sure to. It's all about strategy, like a game of chess.'

'How are they taking it?'

'Not great. But kids are resilient. I heard Grace trying to explain it to Bruno last night. She said she knew that he wanted Dad and Mom to stay together forever, but they couldn't because "Dad broke up Mom's heart".'

Blake gave a low whistle. 'No more rom com, then?'

'No more rom com,' said Deirdre with mock jocularity. 'It's sex, death and revenge from now on. Life is earnest, Blake. Life is real. Life is not an idle dream.'

'Who said that?'

'I don't know. It was a favourite saying of my ... soon-to-be ex-father-in-law.'

Blake gave her a sympathetic look, then raised his glass to her. 'Here's to moving forward,' he said.

'Here's to the screenplay,' Deirdre amended, raising her glass back. 'Here's to *Wreaking Havoc*.'

'To *Wreaking Havoc*. It's a good title.'

'I wanted to call it *Love Lies Bleeding*,' said Deirdre. 'But someone else got there first.'

'Look at you! You look so beautiful! You look, well, the word 'swell' springs to mind!'

Greta laughed at Sam's bad joke. 'And you look like some kind of hero,' she told him.

They were standing in Arrivals, feasting their eyes on each other. It was true that Sam looked like some kind of action hero. He was wearing fatigues and a camera jacket, his hair had been bleached a shade of white gold by sun and sea spray and his tan was what once might have been described as Bondi Beach before the Australians began to observe the slip slap slop rule. There, on the concourse of the Aéroport Montpellier Méditerranée, Greta O'Flaherty felt herself tumble head over heels in love with Sam Newman all over again.

'How've you been keeping?' Sam asked.

The question was a little redundant. He knew well how she'd been keeping: they'd phoned and e-mailed every day. But she supposed he wanted confirmation in the flesh.

'I'm fine, the baby's fine.'

'You look blooming.' Sam reached out a hand and caressed the swell of her belly. 'More blooming than a flower. Will we still be able to make the beast with two backs?'

'If you don't find my belly a turn-off.'

'A turn-off? Jesus, no. You look like the epitome of womanhood. You're desire personified. Your breasts have got bigger as well.'

'And my ass is vast. The received wisdom is doggie style, by the way.'

Sam sucked in his breath. 'Oh, man,' he said, trailing his eyes over her body. As they lingered on her breasts, Greta felt a great wave of lust wash over her.

'I was going to say let's go for something to eat,' she told him. 'But I don't think I can wait to get home. The traffic's bogging, and the Navette from Montpellier took forever to get here.'

'How did you get into Montpellier?'

'Bus.'

'So it's going to be a bitch of a long journey home. That will be exceeding uncomfortable, since I'm nursing the mother of all erections.' Sam looked down at his crotch, and so did Greta.

She gave him a delighted smile. 'I can see I'm in for a treat,' she said.

'Necessity is the mother of invention.' Sam grabbed her hand and started unceremoniously leading her towards the exit. 'And I'm having a bright idea.'

'Where are we going?'

'The airport hotel. They say that they're designed for busy commuters who are forever jumping on flights, but that's not their real function.'

'What *is* their real function?'

'They're for people like us,' Sam said, 'who've been apart for too long and who can't wait to jump each others' bones.'

The airport hotel was just that: bog standard airport hotel. But for Greta, as she stripped off her clothes and stood naked in front of an awestruck Sam, it was the most romantic place on earth.

He took her fast, first, bending her over an armchair and making her utter the kind of sounds you hate to hear other people make in the hotel room next door. And then he lay her across the bed and worshipped her. The ceremony lasted nearly three hours. Sam Newman and Greta O'Flaherty – golden of skin and golden of hair – were the stars of a *tableau vivant* of their own making: Adonis and Corinna in their very own temple of Hecate.

Later, ravenously hungry, they ordered room service.

'God, I missed you,' said Sam, laying into a bowl of *frites*.

'You missed me, or you missed the sex?'

'Both, of course.'

'I'm glad to hear it. That means you weren't tempted by some sexy lone yachtswoman. God, I wonder how *they* manage without sex? Eleven months is a long time to be celibate.'

'Strictly speaking, the word 'celibate' shouldn't be used in relation to not having sex.'

'Why not?'

'Because 'celibate' means being unmarried, and loads of unmarried people have sex.' Sam stuffed a chip into his mouth and looked her directly in the eye. 'I'm sick of being celibate,' he said.

'You mean you're sick of not having had sex for so long or you're sick of being unmarried?'

'The latter.'

'You're sick of being unmarried.'

'Yes.'

'Oh.' Greta reached for a chip and dipped it in mayonnaise.

'Have you worked out the implication yet?' Sam asked.

'It's a tough one,' she said slowly, 'since English isn't my first language, but I think that – in a very roundybouty way – you might be asking me to marry you?'

'Go straight to the top of the class!' said Sam. 'And if you come up with the right answer to my question, you will most definitely be teacher's pet.'

Greta started making a pattern with the chip in the mayonnaise, glooping it up into little peaks. 'The right answer?' she said. 'The right answer for you, or the right answer for me?'

'Hopefully one size fits all.'

'The right answer for you – would that be 'yes'?'

'For sure it would.'

Greta looked up at him with agonised eyes. 'Oh, Sam! I'm sorry. That's the wrong answer for me.'

There was a pause, then Sam said, 'You don't want to marry me?'

'I do! I *do* want to marry you. But I can't.'

'Why not?'

'Because of the baby.'

'Jesus, Greta! That should be a good reason to say yes! If you marry me, the baby will have a father.'

Greta shook her head. 'But don't you see? The baby will never have brothers or sisters. I know this sounds dead selfish, but I want a big family, Sam. I want more than one baby, and I want more than anything to go back to Connemara and be near my mam and my brothers and sisters. You probably wouldn't be able to understand because you're an only child and a city person, and city people are different, but to rear a family is all I've ever really wanted. And you don't want to have babies, Sam.' Greta's eyes went back to the pattern in the mayonnaise. It looked like the surface of one of Daniel's gloopier paintings.

'I've changed my mind.'

'What? Why?'

'I had a long talk with Daniel before I went away. A bottle-of-whiskey-up-till-four-in-the-morning-no-holds-barred kind of talk. He told me that if I wanted to take things a stage further with you, I'd have to be able to give you babies. He said the baby thing was your *raison d'être* – more so even than your painting. He said that if I wasn't going to give you babies, there was no point in continuing the relationship. He said that when you talked about having children, you became completely alive. He said that he deliberately encouraged you to talk about them when you were sitting for him, because when you did, your face became luminescent – like Lizzie Siddal's in that portrait of her by Rossetti. What's it called?'

'The *Beata Beatrix*?'

'That's the one.'

Greta was feeling very, very dazed and confused now. 'But that's the reason you split up with Perdita, Sam. Because you didn't want children.'

'I didn't want children until I met you. Until I met you – and watch it, here comes the lecture – I was cynical and jaded and sick to death of the human race. I despised it for destroying this planet, and I certainly didn't want to propagate it. I was a top-of-the-range misanthropist. But I never dreamed that I would meet a girl who was as good and pure and generous of spirit as you are, Greta O'Flaherty.'

Greta felt her face go very red as tears threatened. 'I'm not good,' she said.

'Yes, you are. You told me you were born on a Sunday.'

'What's that got to do with it?'

'You know the rhyme. "The child that is born on the Sabbath day is bonny and blithe and good and gay." Well, let's strike the gay bit.'

Greta snuffled a bit through the tears that had started to course down her pink cheeks.

'*And* you're a sunny Sagittarius,' continued Sam. 'And you're a girl.'

'What's so great about being a girl?'

'You're made of sugar and spice and all things nice. I should know. I've tasted enough of you.' He gave her a wicked smile.

427

Greta shook her head vehemently. She was crying in earnest now. 'No, Sam. I'm not all nice. I do awful things too, just like everybody else.'

'All right. 'Fess up. Apart from producing copious amounts of snot, what awful things do you do? Here, mucky pup!' Sam reached for a paper napkin and handed it to her so that she could blow her nose.

'I send people to the Bin of Fire,' she said.

'They're getting married,' said Madeleine.

'Sam and Greta are?'

'Yes.'

Dannie looked astonished. 'And he doesn't mind that she's pregnant by another man?'

'Evidently not. He's completely besotted with her.'

Madeleine and Dannie were sitting in the kitchen of Madeleine's house, having coffee. Well, Madeleine was having coffee; Dannie was on green tea because she was looking after her body. She'd cut out alcohol, was eating lots of fruit and leafy green vegetables and was on a course of folic acid. She'd was religiously keeping the diary that told her the optimum baby-making days in her cycle and she'd invested in a thermometer to help track ovulation.

Jethro and she had made love the previous night because she was ovulating. Although 'making love' was a bit of a misnomer. The white-hot, spontaneous sex they used to enjoy had cooled to a degree that could only be described as tepid: sex for them these days had become a kind of drill. She continued to dress provocatively for him, but only when there was a chance of making a baby.

For Dannie, the art of erotic dressing had now become a means to an end. She did it to arouse Jethro, not for fun. She knew that she was treating her husband like a sperm bank, but this was no time for emotional pussy-footing.

'What do you think?' Madeleine asked her.

'About Sam and Greta?' Dannie took a sip of green tea and considered. 'I think she's on to a good thing. Sam's quite a catch, after all.'

Madeleine raised an eyebrow. 'Don't you think you're being a bit cynical?'

'Not at all. Let's itemise. Good looking? Check. Related to a world-famous artist? Check. Successful in his own right? Check.'

'I think she's genuinely stuck on him.'

'Madeleine, get real! Genuine isn't a word I'd associate with Greta O'Flaherty.'

Madeleine shrugged, then leaned back in her chair. 'It's weird, you know, Dannie. I've tried not to like her because of what she did to Deirdre. But I can't. There's something so – artless about her.'

Dannie didn't want to talk about Greta. Deftly, she changed the subject. 'Speaking of Deirdre, I had e-mail from her this morning. Did you get it? She CCed it to you.'

'I haven't checked mail today.'

'She's going to be spending Christmas here. She's coming with Bruno.'

'Oh? What about the girls?'

'They're going to Rory's family, in Ireland.'

'Oh, fuck. So they're spending Christmas apart. How sad.'

'And she's decided to put the house on the market.'

'The house in LA or the house here?'

'The house here.'

'No! Oh, *no*.'

'Looks like they're ready to divvy up the spoils.' Dannie reached for the teapot and topped up her mug. 'That's when things could get really nasty.'

Madeleine gave her a thoughtful look. 'What was the name of that film Rory was working on when the break-up happened? The one he made with Charlotte Lambert?'

'*Love Lies Bleeding.*'

Madeleine sucked in her breath. 'Kinda sums it up, doesn't it?'

'It certainly does.'

A morose silence fell, then Madeleine said, 'Jethro's worked with her a couple of times, hasn't he?'

'Charlotte Lambert? Yes.'

'Did you see that interview with her on Sky last week?'

'No. Was it any good?'

'Yeah. She seems really sweet. She had a big cancer scare recently and had to have a length of her bowel removed. She was actually really funny about it, in a gallows humour kind of way. I'm full of admiration for people who can crack jokes about their near-death experiences.'

'Who's had a near-death experience?' Daniel strolled into the kitchen. He was wearing his painting overalls and his hands were covered in pinky-gold paint. Dannie suspected he'd been working on flesh tones.

'Charlotte Lambert.'

'Who's she?'

'She's an American film star, darling,' explained Madeleine.

'Would I have seen her in anything?'

'She played Lizzie Siddal in that biopic about Rossetti.'

'Oh, yeah. That was a shocking film. But she was easy on the eye. Looks a lot like Greta, come to think of it.'

Daniel headed towards the scullery and came back with a cold chicken leg.

'Have you finished work for the day?' Madeleine asked him.

'Yeah. Greta asked for the afternoon off. She wants to go cycling with Sam.'

'Cycling!' exclaimed Dannie. 'Is that wise, in her condition?'

Daniel shrugged. 'Those copper-haired Celts are hardy.'

Hardy, hale and blooming with good health, Dannie sneered inwardly. *Oh!* Oh, how she hated herself! She was sourer than a crab apple, more venomous than a viper, more acidic than heartburn. She was turning toxic. No wonder no babies were queuing up to be confined in the poisonous environs of her womb. No wonder Jethro had rolled off her last night and turned his back to her once he'd done his 'duty'. No wonder Paloma had made that fiendish face at her the other day when she'd given out about the state of the child's room. She didn't deserve another baby! She was a bitter and twisted hag. But she was learning to disguise what lay beneath. 'How are the portraits going?' she asked Daniel pleasantly.

'They're good.'

'I hear Greta's going back to Ireland to have her baby?'

'Yes. But she'll come back here once it's born.'

This was news to Dannie. 'Oh? Why?'

'Because the final portrait of the series is to be of mother and child,' said Daniel.

Mother and child. *Mother and child.* Sweet Jesus! What crime against heaven had Dannie committed that a girl like Greta O'Flaherty could produce a baby and she couldn't? 'Excuse me,' she said, rising to her feet. 'I must just nip to the loo.'

Outside in the hall, Dannie leaned her hands on the console table, trying to control her breathing. *Mother and child.* Greta was coming back here to Saint-Géyroux with her baby! Was it not bad enough that she paraded her pregnant belly through the village without having to watch her flaunt her real live flesh and blood sprog all over the place? *Mother and child.* Dannie looked at herself in the fly-blown, gilt-framed mirror that hung above the table. Her reflection gazed back at her, hollow-eyed, pinch-cheeked, pursed of mouth. She looked as barren as she felt.

The sound of feet clattering on the staircase made her turn.

'Are you *sure* it's safe for you to ride a bicycle?' It was Sam's voice.

'Arra, never a bother. Didn't my mam cycle up to the ninth month in all her pregnancies? And all her wains were fine and dandy.'

Oh, Christ. Dannie couldn't bear it. She didn't want to meet the golden couple on the stairs. Crossing the hallway, she ducked into the doorway under the stairwell, the one that led to the swimming pool. Out of the corner of her eye, she saw Sam reach for his inamorata and swing her into his arms.

'C'mere, beautiful,' he said.

'Why?'

'I want to kiss you.'

'*Again?*'

'You're the most kissable person I know.'

There followed excruciating kissy noises before Sam's voice came again.

'Oh, darling. Feel that.'

'Janey, Sam, you're the horniest man I've ever met!'

'Didn't we decide that the *mot juste* was priapic?'

'Pria-*prick*, more like. You're insatiable.'

'You're succulent.'

'You're stiff as the Dublin Spire.'

'You're soft as cotton candy.' A pause. 'And you're wetter than Venus rising from the waves.'

'Sam! Don't do that! Someone might come.'

'I hope it's you.'

'Stop it now, you bold boy, and get on your bike. I need my exercise.'

'I'll give you all the exercise you need in bed. Let's go back upstairs.'

'No, Sam. I'm dying for a cycle.'

'We could go for a swim.'

'But I want fresh air!'

'Greta, please. I've got to have you now. I want to have you in the pool.'

'The pool?' Dannie heard a languorous sigh. 'We can't, Sam!'

'Why not?'

'What if someone else decides they want a swim? Like Rosa?'

'Luckily, Daniel came up with a solution to that years ago. There's a bolt on the door. Come along, kitten. Come on. You know you want to.'

Footsteps. No! Dannie cast around wildly for some way out. There was only one. Her heart thumping, she slipped behind the door to the basement and fumbled with the bolt, sliding it home seconds before the handle turned.

'What's up?' It was Sam's voice. 'It looks like there's someone in there already. Hello? *Hello?* Is there someone in the pool?'

Dannie took a deep breath, then unbolted the door and opened it.

'Hi, there,' she said, with an excessive display of casualness. 'Call me impulsive! I just felt a sudden overwhelming urge for a swim.'

Greta and Sam stood looking at her curiously.

'Cool,' said Sam. 'So did we.'

'Well, fire ahead,' said Dannie. 'It's all yours now.'

'Thanks.'

Greta and Sam passed through the door and shut it behind them and Dannie heard the sound of the bolt being shot. She stood there motionless with her back to the door for several more moments, feeling too shaky to move. And then she heard, in Greta's subdued tones, 'That's weird. She couldn't have been swimming. Her hair wasn't wet. I sometimes wonder about that woman, Sam.'

'What do you mean?'

'I don't think I've ever seen her smile. She seems to take no *joy* in anything. I wonder what her problem is.'

Sam laughed. 'Maybe she's not getting laid enough.'

'Tch! You and your one-track mind.'

'C'm on. Let's have that swim.'

'Her hair *definitely* wasn't wet.'

On the other side of the door, Dannie started to cry.

28

Greta was enjoying her sessions with Daniel more than ever. He never talked much while he was painting, but he didn't seem to mind when she did. She told him about her family and growing up in Connemara; she told him how her passion for painting had been inherited from her mother; she told him about her cousin Esther and how she'd encouraged her to enrol in NCAD; she told him about the children she'd chaperoned; and she told him about that bastard Jared Kelly, who – Esther had informed her via e-mail – had buggered off back to the States. Sometimes she felt that this is what it must be like to go to a shrink, when you lie on a couch and pay someone to listen while you tell them your life story. Except she wasn't paying Daniel: he was paying her.

And then one day he said, 'It's done.'

'You've finished?'

'I've finished.'

Greta clapped her hands. 'Yay! Can I see it?'

Daniel smiled at her and tapped his nose. 'No. Not until the series is complete. You should know the rules by now.'

'Describe it for me then,' she said, reaching for her frock and pulling it over her head.

'It's pure soul.'

'Pure soul? That sounds like one of those compilation CDs you can buy on the shopping channel.'

'There's actually such a thing as a *shopping* channel?' Daniel sounded appalled.

'Yes, Mr Luddite, there is. I'll take you on a guided tour some day, if you like.'

'I'm not sure I would like it.'

'D'you know something? Until I met you, I thought my parents were the only Luddites in the world.'

'They're signed up members of Luddites United too?'

'Yep. They refuse to keep a computer in the house. We don't even have a television at home in Connemara.'

'Really?'

'Scouts' honour.'

Daniel smiled. 'I haven't heard that expression for years.'

'My brothers were all Scouts. They had to have *something* to do with no television in the house.'

'What did you do?'

'I painted.'

Daniel gave her a look of consideration. 'Tell me this, Greta. Have you ever heard of a very old-fashioned expression, when a person is described as being "the soul of honour"?'

'My grandpa used to say it. It means that a person's good, doesn't it?'

'It means more than that. It means that a person is absolutely incapable of a dishonourable action. That's you, Greta. You have the most candid eyes of anyone who's ever sat for me. Your soul lights up your face, and makes it lambent with goodness.'

'What's lambent mean?'

'Shiny.'

'Why didn't you just say shiny, then?'

'Because "your soul lights up your face and makes it shiny with goodness" doesn't have the same ring to it, somehow.'

Greta laughed, then started piling her hair into a makeshift chignon. 'I wonder is sending people to the Bin of Fire a dishonourable action?' she mused.

'What's the Bin of Fire?'

'It's when you click on someone in your organiser and drag the envelope icon down to the bin and – oh. Of course – you don't do computers. I can tell by your expression that you haven't a clue what I'm talking about, you big gom.'

Greta bit her lip. What had she just done? She'd just called Daniel Lennox, major artist of international repute, a big gom. That was overstepping the mark: that was way too smart of her. Should she apologise?

But there was no need, because Daniel just smiled and said, 'I'll miss you, Greta O'Flaherty.' He moved to the battered wooden desk where he kept his cheque book and uncapped his fountain pen. 'Has Sam booked the car yet?' he asked.

'Yep. Me and Sam will be driving out of the village in style the day after tomorrow. I can't wait for my mam to meet him.'

'Christmas in Connemara. You're a lucky girl. I spent a winter there once when I was a young man, painting. I couldn't get enough of that landscape.'

'It's kind of addictive, isn't it? No wonder Irish emigrants dream about going home. Ooh.' Greta sucked in her breath and Daniel looked up sharply.

'Are you all right?' he asked.

'Yeah. It's just heartburn,' said Greta, padding on bare feet to the fridge on the other side of the room. Madeleine had recommended celery for heartburn and Daniel had taken to keeping a head of celery in the studio for her. He also kept a supply of Jelly Babies, for which Greta had developed a craving – apart from the green ones. She saved those for Sam. 'Isn't heartburn a stupid name for it?' she said, opening the fridge door and helping herself to a celery stick. 'Since it's got feck all to do with the heart. It's a weird thing, being pregnant. I've never suffered from heartburn before.'

'How are you feeling, generally?'

'A bit tired, a bit of backache. But d'you know what the worst thing is?'

'What?'

'These horrible, horrible thick ankles. I hope you haven't put them in the portrait. Maybe you could paint on ruffled socks, to disguise them.'

Daniel laughed, signed the cheque with a flourish and handed it to her.

'What's this for?'

'It's your Christmas bonus.'

'Do muses get Christmas bonuses?'

'This one does.'

'Well, that's really sweet of you, Daniel. Thank you.' Moving back to the daybed, Greta sat down and started chewing away happily on her celery stick. 'D'you know what? Maybe I shouldn't cash this cheque. I'd say that the signature alone is worth a fortune. Remember that story about how Picasso used to sign cheques in restaurants and then the restaurant owner framed them instead of— Daniel?'

'What's up, sweetheart?'

'You made a mistake. You put in too many noughts.'

'No, I didn't make a mistake.'

'What do you mean? You've made this out for way too much.'

'I've made it out for what I think you're worth.'

'I'm not worth this!'

'Yes, you are. You've inspired the most stunning series of portraits I've ever painted, Greta, and you deserve proper remuneration. We both know there's a reciprocal thing going on here: we know that artist and model give and take in equal measure.'

'But – but—'

'But me no buts. Think of the prices these paintings will command.'

Greta's eyes went back to the cheque. 'But – *this*! I could put a down payment on a small house with this!'

'Go ahead!' said Daniel with a laugh. 'Put a down payment on a cottage in Connemara and go there and live with Sam and the baby. I should like to think of you doing that.'

'Daniel, I can't accept this.'

Daniel gave her a warning look from underneath his eyebrows. 'If you don't, you'll live to regret it.'

'Why so?'

'I'll slash the canvas.'

'Ha, ha.'

'I mean it.' Daniel moved to the table and helped himself to a Stanley knife.

'You wouldn't do that!'

'How many months have you been sitting for me, Greta?'

'Five and a bit.'

'So I'd hazard a guess that you know me pretty well by now?'

Greta frowned. 'I suppose I do.'

'In that case, you'll know I'm a man of my word. I'll say it again. If you don't accept that cheque, I will slash the canvas.' Daniel unclipped the safety catch on the knife and slid out the blade.

'But – but—' Greta was inarticulate again.

'You think I'm joking, don't you?' Daniel took a step towards the easel and Greta saw the blade glint as he raised his left hand.

As it came down in slow motion, she struggled to her feet. 'OK, OK, you win!' she cried, clutching her belly and gripping the edge of the daybed. He smiled and she sent him a filthy look before sinking back down onto the pillows. 'Jesus, Daniel – you might have made the baby come!'

'You will cash the cheque, then?'

'Cash it? Are you mad? No. I'll lodge it to my account.'

Daniel took a step back from the canvas. 'Is that a promise?' he said.

'It's a promise. I'll do it tomorrow.' She looked at the cheque in her hand again. 'This is an *insane* amount of money. And oh, you big bastard! You gave me such a fright.'

Daniel picked up a rag and started the post-sitting ritual of cleaning his brushes. 'It's called *quid pro quo*. I've given you some financial security, but you've given me something astonishing in return. You've given me the most beautiful portraits I've ever made.'

You've given me the most beautiful portraits I've ever made.

On the other side of the studio door, Madeleine paused on the landing. She'd climbed the spiral staircase because Daniel needed to talk to Gilbert Blatin before the agent left Paris for some Sotheby's event in London, and Daniel had asked her to remind him to make the phone call.

You've given me the most beautiful portraits I've ever made ... Oh, God! Moving to the window, Madeleine rested her hands on the ledge. In the glass, her spectral reflection gazed back at her, the fine lines around her eyes reminding her of how much older she was than the girl in Daniel's latest paintings.

'Try to avoid UV light, pollution and stress: they're all ageing accelerators', she'd read that day in yet another anti-ageing magazine article. Anti-ageing! How could you be 'anti' something that was inevitable? You couldn't hold back the advance of time any more than King Canute could hold back the waves. *Fight lines and wrinkles! Shave a decade off your looks! Achieve instant rejuvenation!* Who did the magazines think they were kidding? *How* could you avoid stress anyway if you were confronted with page after page of features telling you that ageing was unacceptable and persuading you to part with unfeasible amounts of money for products pushed by pharmaceutical multinationals?

From behind the studio door came the tinkling sound of laughter. Greta O'Flaherty might be leaving Saint-Géyroux in a day or two, but she'd soon be back with her baby. Or would she? Would she bother to keep her side of the bargain, now that she had an 'insane' amount of money to take home to Ireland with her? Was Dannie right about the girl? Was she duplicitous and manipulative, hypocritical and ingratiating? Had she more faces than the hydra? And had Daniel really given her all that money simply in return for her 'inspirational' qualities, in return for just lounging around on a daybed? An *insane* amount of money – for that?

She did the maths again. Daniel had definitely been in Dublin around the time that Greta had conceived her baby, giving his talk at IMMA. *Could* they have met then? Could he be paying her off for the baby? Those words came back to her, the words that she'd heard Greta speak to Sam shortly after she'd arrived in France. *I never knew he'd be here, I promise you. If I'd known, I never, never would have come to Saint-Géyroux …*

Or could it be the other way round? Could Greta be blackmailing Daniel? Could – *oh, stop it! Stop being so suspicious and evil-minded!* No wonder Madeleine was worried about ageing when she harboured such toxic thoughts. They say you get the face you deserve by the time you hit forty, and the way things were going, before the decade was out, Madeleine was going to have the face of a bitter and twisted hag.

Turning abruptly away from the window, she stapled on a smile, then knocked on the studio door.

'Daniel?' she said. 'May I come in?'

'You may,' he replied. 'We're all done.'

Madeleine opened the door and went through. 'You wanted me to remind you to phone Gilbert.'

'Oh, yeah. Thanks.'

'I'm free to go, so, am I?' Greta asked him.

'You are free as a bird until we see you in the New Year. Where are you off to today?'

'The market,' she said, moving across the studio floor. 'I want to do a shop for a big farewell feast. I'm cooking

442

dinner tomorrow as a way of saying thank you to you for being so good to me. You two are the most generous people I've ever met.'

And Greta sent Madeleine a big smile as she passed her by and descended the staircase, singing.

I'm not generous, thought Madeleine. I'm not generous at all. I'm the most mean-minded sow on the face of the planet.

She looked across the room. Daniel was standing in front of his easel, gazing at the portrait he'd just finished.

'The soul of honour,' he said. 'Beautiful.'

There were scrummy cooking smells coming from the kitchen of number one rue des Artistes. Madeleine had been upstairs in her study, working on a flash animation. It had worked better than she'd expected and she felt like celebrating.

Another reason for celebrating was that Daniel had made love to her that morning. It had been a while since they'd had sex and Madeleine felt like Scarlett O'Hara the day after being ravished by Rhett. Today she was untrammelled by insecurities, today her self-esteem was good, and tomorrow Greta O'Flaherty was going back to Ireland with Sam.

In the kitchen, Greta was sliding potatoes off a chopping board into a pot, Sam was uncorking a bottle of wine and Pilot was sniffing the air like a cartoon dog.

'What are you cooking?' Madeleine asked. 'It smells fantastic.'

'Irish stew,' said Greta. 'My gran's recipe. The secret is to add the lamb bone.'

'Wine, Madeleine?' Sam asked.

'Thanks.'

Sam poured two glasses, then sat down at the table and activated his laptop. 'Come and see this,' he said. 'Greta and I found it on the internet.'

Madeleine sat down beside him and watched as a photograph of a cottage shimmered onto the screen. It had a red-painted front door, geraniums in window boxes and a wisp of blue smoke plumed from the chimney.

'We've been looking for a place to live.' Sam angled the screen for her so that Madeleine could study the web page. 'And we think we may have found it.' Madeleine read on.

Charming stone-fronted lakeside cottage. On 1.5 acres of meadows with direct access down to the shores of Lough Corrib; fully fitted kitchen, open plan living/dining room with fireplace, three large bedrooms (one en suite), bathroom with free-standing Victorian claw-foot bath, playroom/study. This beautiful property is situated on the eastern shore and is secluded but not remote. Your horizon is dominated by the dramatic mountains of Connemara and islands are within easing rowing distance. As you listen to the lapping of the lakeshore, the words of the poet W.B. Yeats will murmur to you. Here, 'Peace comes dropping slow ... Midnight's all a-glimmer and noon a purple glow.' The 1.5 acres boast a garden planted with meadow flowers, well-established timbers and romantic walkways. There is an outhouse and plenty of room in the daisy-strewn paddock on which to tether a Connemara pony, build a henhouse or establish a beehive!

'What do you think, Madeleine?' Greta had turned away from the stove and was wiping her hands on a tea towel.

'It's a pretty des res, all right,' said Madeleine. 'Are you really thinking of buying it?'

'We're going to take a gander when we're over there. It's my dream cottage!' Greta smiled over her shoulder as she passed through to the scullery.

'So you'd sell up your flat in Dublin, Sam?'

'In a heartbeat.'

'What about a dark room for you?'

'There's that outhouse. Although I'm not sure how much time I'll have free for developing photographs. All that running around after ponies, hens, bees and babies will have me bushed.'

Madeleine smiled. 'You should acquire a couple of goats too. Start making your own cheese.' She took another look at the description. '"Secluded but not remote." Are you sure you can handle seclusion? It's a big change, you know – moving from the city to the sticks.'

'You managed it pretty well. Weren't you the ultimate city slicker before you downshifted here?'

Madeleine shrugged. 'I guess I was.'

'Then you should also know that change is what life's all about, Auntie. Change is to be embraced, not avoided.'

'Oh, Sam! You've just succeeded in making me feel middle-aged and unadventurous.'

'Middle-aged? You? I'd never describe my sexy aunt as being middle-aged. You're in your prime, Madeleine Lennox. You're a babe!'

'Sexy!' scoffed Madeleine. 'It's a long time since anyone called me sexy.' Well, she thought, strictly speaking that wasn't true, because Daniel had called her sexy in bed that very morning. Smiling, she raised her glass in a toast. '*Santé*,' she said. 'Here's to your dream cottage, Sam Newman!'

Later that evening, as they sat around the dinner table, Daniel proposed another toast.

'*Bon voyage* tomorrow, you two,' he said.

'*Bon voyage!*' echoed Madeleine, with some feeling. It would be nice to have her husband all to herself again for a while.

'Thanks,' said Greta. 'D'you know, I'm desperate to see my mam. And she's pure desperate to meet Sam. I sent her a photograph and she says he looks like one of those surfer dudes on Tallabawn Strand in County Mayo.'

'How did you send a photo?' asked Rosa, giving Greta a puzzled look. 'You told me that you lived in a Days of Yore house that had no computers.'

'I printed it out, *mavourneen*, and sent it the old-fashioned way, by snail mail.'

Daniel nodded approvingly.

Rosa reached for a hunk of bread and started mopping up the juices on her plate. 'Mama, did you know that Greta's mum and dad don't even have a television?'

'Is that true?' Madeleine was intrigued.

'Yeah. They're a bit hippy-ish, my parents.'

'Wasn't it harsh, growing up without a television?'

'Not really. It just meant that I painted more.'

'Did you have a radio?' asked Rosa. 'Or a CD player?'

'Yes, we had a radio. And yes, we had a CD player.'

'Did you have a phone?'

'Ah, yeah. But no mobiles. My mother nearly threw a

fit when I told her I'd bought a mobile phone. She was convinced I was going to contract some deadly form of brain cancer.'

'So are they dead strict, your parents?' asked Rosa.

'Divil a bit! They let me fly free as a bird. I had a brilliant childhood.'

'But will Christmas there be fun with no television?'

'Christmas without television,' said Sam, 'will be a blessed relief.'

Rosa looked thoughtful. 'When you come back after Christmas,' she said, pushing away her plate, 'when the baby is out of your tummy, can I play with it?'

'The baby will be too small for playing with,' Greta told her. 'And babies that young are dead boring. All they do is eat and sleep and poo.'

'All the better for painting them,' said Daniel.

'You sound like the wolf in Red Riding Hood, Papa,' said Rosa. 'Greta, will you read me my story tonight?'

'I'd be glad to. Which one do you want?'

'*The Little Mermaid.*'

Madeleine saw Greta raise an eyebrow at Rosa and the child meekly added 'please'. *The Little Mermaid*, she thought, taking a sip of wine. The beautiful fairy tale princess who behaved so honourably, the heroine who sacrificed her soul to save her prince. What had Daniel called Greta yesterday? *The soul of honour.*

'*The Little Mermaid* is a done deal,' Greta told Rosa. 'But you've to promise me that you won't keep me up too late reading to you. Sam and I have to be up at the crack of dawn tomorrow.'

'To head off in the limo?' asked Rosa.

'Well, strictly speaking, it's not a limo,' said Greta.

'Limos have chauffeurs, and Sam's going to be doing the driving.'

'You should sit in the back and make him wear a cap like the one Lady Penelope's driver wears.'

Greta smiled as she rose awkwardly from the table and started to clear away dishes. 'I'd rather sit in the front and keep him company.'

'Hey! Let me clear those away,' said Sam.

'Thanks, angel.' Greta helped herself to a celery stick from the jug on the table. 'I've a touch of heartburn. I feel like a big bloated toad.'

'Is the celery helping at all?' asked Madeleine.

'It is, thanks. Well, it's either that or the Jelly Babies. Excuse me. I'll be back in a minute.'

Greta headed for the kitchen door and Madeleine felt a rush of sympathy for her. She remembered how it felt, in the final trimester, to have that bump up against your ribcage and the discomfort after an evening meal. And while Greta bore absolutely no resemblance to a big, bloated toad, Madeleine knew what she meant. She must be longing for the baby to come.

Daniel handed Sam his plate, stretched and yawned. 'Madeleine tells me that you and Greta might have found a place to live,' he said.

'We're going to check out a cottage. It looks ideal. Three bedrooms, playroom, big garden – perfect for kids.'

'And this from the man who swore he was never going to propagate the species!'

Sam gave an abashed smile. 'The love of a good woman,' he said, 'can work miracles.'

Daniel reached for the wine bottle and topped up

glasses. 'You will make sure she comes back to me, won't you?' he said. 'Once the baby's born.'

The look Sam gave him was borderline incredulous. 'Greta's given you her word she'll come back. She wouldn't renege on it. Don't you know that the name O'Flaherty means 'lordly in action'?'

'You're right,' conceded Daniel. 'She's far too honourable to renege.'

That word again! *Honourable!* This was the girl who had had a torrid affair with Rory McDonagh, right under his wife's nose! But Madeleine could hardly remind her husband of that in front of Rosa.

Daniel burped, then took a cigarette from his pack.

'Papa!' said Rosa crossly. 'You are not to smoke in front of Greta.'

'She's not here.'

'It doesn't matter. And think of me, your beloved daughter, who is being made to be a passive smoker. Go outside and smoke your stinky cigarettes.'

'It's raining,' said Daniel mutinously.

'I don't care.'

'All right. You win,' said Daniel, putting the cigarette back in the pack. 'You've no idea what it was like when you were away, Sam – to be the only man living in a house surrounded by bossy bloody women.'

'I think I could live with that,' said Sam as the door opened and Greta came through, 'if they were all as gorgeous as these three.'

Greta held up a clear plastic bag, inside which were some gaudily wrapped packages. 'These are for Christmas,' she said. 'They're only—'

'Presents!' squealed Rosa, jumping up and dancing

across the kitchen floor. 'Can I open mine now?'

'Well, strictly speaking, you should wait until Christmas Day. What do you think, Madeleine?'

Rosa turned entreating eyes on her. 'Please, Mama! Please let's open them now!'

Madeleine considered. 'OK. It's nice to able to say thank you personally, and it means I won't have to nag you to write a thank you letter.'

Greta handed Rosa her present. 'It's only—'

'Yay!' yelled Rosa, tearing off the wrapping paper. 'Look!' she said. 'A lion! Oh, he's so *cute*! Look at his velvetiness! And his mane! I'm going to call him Riff-Ruff. And there's something else! Oh – it's a picture of Pilot. *Oh!* He looks like the king of all dogs.' Rosa gazed at the portrait, then looked in awe at Greta. 'Did you paint this, Greta?' she asked.

'I did.'

'Wow. It's awesome! It's better than any of my dad's. No offence, Papa,' she added hastily.

Greta laughed. 'Oh, I'm not in the same league,' she said. 'But maybe some day I'll be able to put the initials RHA after my name.'

'What's RHA mean?'

'It stands for Royal Hibernian Academy,' Greta told her. 'They're a posh crowd of artists.'

'What's 'Hibernian'?'

'It means 'Irish'.'

'Why don't they just put Irish then?'

'Because 'Hibernian' sounds better. A bit like saying 'lambent' instead of 'shiny'.'

Madeleine saw Greta and Daniel exchange a glance of amusement so private she had to look away.

'What's 'lambent'?'

'Janey! You're like what's his name on *Mastermind* today, Rosa! Lambent means shiny – like my face.'

'Bend down so I can kiss your lambent face,' said Rosa. Greta complied. 'Papa! Mama! Open your presents!' came the command.

Greta handed a package to Madeleine and another to Daniel. Sam said, 'Hey! Do I not get anything?'

'You,' Greta told him, 'will be getting yours on Christmas Day in Connemara. And I'd better warn you that my brothers will insist on playing that woegeous Slade song about wishing it could be Christmas every day.'

'Holy shit! Christmas every day sounds like the worst kind of Groundhog Day,' said Sam.

'Would they not rather play 'Frosty the Snowman'?' asked Rosa. 'That's my favourite.'

'No. They like punching the air too much. You can't punch the air to 'Frosty the Snowman'.'

Madeleine unwrapped her package to find a box. Inside, nestled in tissue paper, was a necklace of beads strung together by a network of silver filigree. The beads were exquisite, handmade and decorated with tiny whorled pink rosebuds against a blue and silver background, like miniature Fabergé eggs.

'They're Venetian glass,' said Greta. 'I found them in an antique shop in Montpellier, and I just thought they were so you, Madeleine. I hope you like them?'

Madeleine smiled up at Greta's apprehensive face. 'I love them,' she said. 'They're beautiful. Will you do the honours, Daniel?'

Daniel rounded the table, took the beads from Madeleine and fastened the clasp at the nape of her neck.

'They really *are* you,' he said, standing back to admire her. 'How clever of you to find them, Greta.'

'Open yours, Papa!'

As Daniel fiddled with ribbon, Rosa started making like a cheerleader, punching the air and singing 'I Wish it Could be Christmas Every Day'. Sam groaned and put his hands over his ears. 'Now look what you've done,' he told Greta. 'I want ear plugs for Christmas.'

Discarding the ribbon, Daniel peeled the paper off to reveal a picture frame. He stood appraising it for several moments, and Madeleine saw him smile before he raised his eyes to Greta's. She was looking pink with embarrassment.

'It's good,' he said. 'You have a gift. You really have. This is worth many thousands of words.'

'Thank you,' said Greta.

'No. Thank *you*,' said Daniel.

'Let's see, Papa?' Rosa reached out a hand and took the picture frame from him. 'Oh, Mama!' she cried. 'You look so beautiful! And Papa looks a bit like Riff-Ruff.'

Setting the picture down on the table in front of Madeleine, Rosa leaned against her mother so that they could study it together. Greta's painting showed Madeleine and Daniel lounging together on a recliner in the garden. They were both barefoot, Madeleine in a sarong, Daniel in loose linen trousers and a T-shirt. Madeleine was gazing into the middle distance, an expression of profound contentment on her face, while Daniel was looking down at his wife with eyes that were eloquent with adoration.

A painting's worth a thousand words. So that was what Daniel had meant by this being worth many thousands!

It was a testimony, exquisitely wrought in oils, of a couple still very much in love.

'Thank you,' Madeleine said. 'What a thoughtful present. It's really, really beautiful.'

'She's talented, my missus-to-be, isn't she?' said Sam. 'I lent her my camera to take the photograph that inspired that painting. She came running into the house one day, going, "Sam! Sam! Give me your camera, quick!" She'd just seen the pair of you in the garden, and knew it would make an unforgettable image. And wasn't she right?'

Madeleine looked back up at Greta and smiled. 'Thank you,' she said again.

And suddenly she felt overwhelmed with shame. Greta had clearly gone to a great deal of time and trouble to find presents that were perfect for each member of the family. And she, Madeleine, had not bought the girl anything.

That night, Daniel and his wife made love again.

When Madeleine came downstairs the next morning, Greta and Sam had gone. But there was a note on the kitchen table. It read:

> I have been so privileged to live in your house for the past five months. I have learned so much from you, Daniel – and you, Madeleine, have been so kind and good to me. And Rosa, you have kept me company like a little sister. I will never forget these days that Sam says are called halcyon days. Thank you from the bottom of my heart, and

I look forward to seeing you in the new year with my BABY!!!

☺ With lots of love from Greta. XXX ☺

PS: Please give Pilot the lamb bone and a big kiss from me.

29

It was still dark when Sam and Greta drove out of Saint-Géyroux. They drove through Limousin and Poitou and Bretagne and spent a night in the pretty seaside town of Roscoff before boarding the ferry that would take them to Rosslare. From Rosslare the Merc sped smoothly north-west to Connemara.

When Daniel had asked Greta all those months ago if she would like a strong and silent type or a cheerful and chatty type to drive her home to Ireland, she had opted for the latter. But she and Sam spoke little on the journey. He was concentrating on unfamiliar roads and she just wanted to listen to reggae. She could feel her baby moving lustily inside her and she knew it was responding to the rhythm. The skin over her belly was drum-skin tight when she laid a hand on it: she could feel a tiny foot sticking out of her side.

Midway across Ireland, as Greta stuggled to make herself comfortable in the passenger seat, she felt a twinge, then another. A Braxton Hicks contraction: the contractions that she'd been told were for 'practice'. She'd learned about Braxton Hicks in her antenatal classes in Gignac, before she'd given up going to them because she'd hated them so much. Greta rarely took 'agin' anything, but she'd taken agin the antenatal stuff with a vengeance. She'd loathed breathing practice – all that *hah-hah-hah*-ing and *fuh-fuh-fuh*-ing – she'd loathed the feckin' exercises and she'd especially loathed the way she was expected to bond with complete strangers just because they had a physical condition in common.

She supposed all the loathing had something to do with her fluctuating hormones and the fact that it was difficult to understand the rapid French of the no-nonsense midwife who taught the classes. But Greta hated being told what to do and what not to do. She just wanted to be allowed to go with the flow and do as her body told her. And right now, as they flew through County Offally, it told her she needed rest. Pressing the recline button, Greta made a pillow of her arms and shut her eyes. Within minutes, she was asleep.

When she woke, they were passing Galway University Hospital. Greta was almost tempted to ask Sam to stop, but she knew the doctor would pack her off home with the words 'Braxton Hicks' ringing in her ears. Instead, she unreclined her seat so that she could watch Connemara unfurl as the Merc glided along the road heading west.

Outside of Galway city, the scenery became more beautiful with every mile they travelled. There were the Twelve Bens, their purple peaks dusted with icing-sugar snow; there was Kilrowan harbour, its ruffled surface diamantine; there was Lisnakeelagh Strand, a vista of gold and turquoise; there was home.

And as Greta stepped out of the car and caught the first glimpse of her mother at the door, she felt the baby start to come.

*

Madeleine had invited Jethro and Dannie for Sunday lunch. She'd served up a platter of mezze to start, followed by guinea fowl with root vegetables, and now they were laying into *tarte tatin*. Paloma and Rosa were in fits of giggles, exchanging silly jokes about dogs, making Pilot the star of each one.

'What did the cowboy say when the bear ate Pilot?' Paloma asked Rosa.

'I give up. What *did* the cowboy say when the bear ate Pilot?'

'Well, doggone!'

There ensued titters of merriment.

'What's the difference between Santa Claus and Pilot?' Rosa asked Paloma.

'I give up. What *is* the difference between Santa Claus and Pilot?'

'Santa Claus wears a whole suit, Pilot just pants.'

The titters turned into snorts.

'How do you stop Pilot from smelling?' asked Daniel.

The girls looked at each other and raised their eyes to heaven. 'Put a peg on his nose,' they said in unison.

Daniel shrugged. 'I've always wanted to do stand-up,' he said.

'Can we get down?' asked Rosa. 'I want to show Paloma the painting that Greta made of Pilot.'

'Yep. Off you go.'

'Come on, Pilot!' Rosa called as they slid off their chairs. Pilot was lying on the rag rug by the stove with his nose on his paws. 'Come on, lazybones! We're going to teach you a new trick today.'

Yawning, the dog got to his feet obediently and shambled across to the door, claws clicking against the terracotta tiles.

'Why is Pilot such a crap dancer?' Paloma asked.

'I give up. Why *is* Pilot such a crap dancer?'

'Because he has two left feet.'

Spluttering with laughter, the girls left the room.

As the door shut behind them, Madeleine turned to Dannie and smiled. 'I was going to ask them to clear the table, but I didn't think I could take any more of those jokes,' she said, pushing away her plate. 'God, I'm stuffed.'

'So am I,' said Dannie. ''Replete' is the word.'

Madeleine reached for her glass, sipped and savoured the sweet, smoky taste of Daniel's favourite local wine, the Mas de Daumas Gassac that he claimed tasted of burnt apple and fig. The kitchen was warm from the stove; the aroma of baking still hung in the air; a CD of piano music was playing softly in the background; a light drizzle was falling beyond the glass doors to the garden; and a lovely Sunday-afternoon laziness prevailed. On the other side of the table, Daniel and Jethro were looking at some newsworthy item in a back copy of *Le Monde*, muttering imprecations.

'Have you heard from Deirdre recently?' Madeleine asked Dannie.

'Yeah, I got an e-mail yesterday.'

'When's she due to arrive?'

'Day before Christmas Eve.'

Madeleine looked thoughtful. 'Christmas'll be strange in that house without Rory and the girls.'

'Well, there's no *way* he could come here.'

'It's still a complete stand-off then?'

'Yeah.'

'It's so sad,' said Madeleine, shaking her head.

From somewhere above came the sounds of riotous shrieks. Dannie looked ceiling-ward. 'Poor Pilot,' she said. 'I suppose we'll get a demonstration later of his new trick.'

'As long as they don't dress him up. I always feel so sorry for him when they do that,' said Madeleine. 'Rosa found a website for pampered pets the other day and wanted me to order a pink bunny suit for him.'

'You can buy pink bunny suits for dogs on the internet?' An incredulous Daniel looked up from *Le Monde*.

'Oh, yes. And fairy princess costumes and leopard-print frocks and jewellery and quilted red velvet pillbox hats.'

He narrowed his eyes at her. 'Are you winding me up?'

'Not at all.' Madeleine gave him an amused look. 'They even have dog home gyms and dog chaises longues and dog buggies.'

'Dog *buggies*! You mean people take their dogs out for walks in *buggies*?'

'You see it all the time in LaLa Land,' Jethro told him. 'Or else they carry their pets around in little designer tote bags.'

'Fuck,' said Daniel. 'The world's gone mad.'

'Any chance of more wine?' asked Jethro, draining his glass.

'Sure.' Daniel got to his feet and slid another bottle of Mas de Daumas from the wine rack. 'The world's gone mad,' he said again, shaking his head mournfully.

'Jethro, you didn't happen to run into Rory when you were in LA last, did you?' asked Madeleine.

'No. He was on location in London, filming the Pixie Pirelli movie.'

'I wonder how he is?'

'There's a rumour,' said Jethro, looking a bit sheepish, 'and you know I don't subscribe to rumours, but the one currently circulating is that he's hooked up with Charlotte Lambert.'

'*No!*' said Madeleine.

'You didn't tell me that!' said Dannie.

Jethro shrugged. 'Like I said, I don't do gossip.'

'But – Charlotte *Lambert!*'

'Why shouldn't Rory hook up with Charlotte?' asked Jethro. 'She's a really sweet person.'

Madeleine and Dannie exchanged dubious looks.

'I dunno,' said Madeleine. 'There's something … not quite right about it.'

Dannie nodded. 'I know what you mean,' she said.

'What *do* you mean?' asked Daniel.

'Well, after the whole thing with Greta …'

'Pah,' said Daniel, drawing the cork on the wine bottle. 'I never believed that outlandish rumour.'

Madeleine shot him a look. 'Well, seeing as how you're so besotted with the girl, Daniel, I can see why you wouldn't want to believe it.'

'I am not besotted with the girl,' said Daniel indignantly. 'I just have a very special relationship with her. You know—'

The phone shrilled.

'Excuse me,' said Madeleine, reaching for it. She was glad that the phone had interrupted what might have become an unseemly bickering match: there was nothing worse than a couple having a domestic in front of friends. ''*Allo,*' she said, picking up French fashion, noticing abstractedly that an unfamiliar number was displayed.

460

'Madeleine!' It was Sam's voice.

'Sam! Where are you calling from?'

'I'm calling from the hospital in Clifden. Greta's had her baby!'

'Oh!' Madeleine covered the mouthpiece with her hand and turned to the assembled company. 'Greta's had her baby!' she announced. 'Is she OK?' she asked Sam.

'No worries at all. They're both doing fine.'

'Boy or girl?'

'Boy. Eight pounds, two ounces. He's beautiful. He's taken to her breast straight away, no problem.'

'What's she called him?'

'Lennox.'

Lennox? But of course, Madeleine told herself – of *course* she would name her baby after her idol. 'Oh. Daniel will be well chuffed to hear that. I'm glad to hear they're both well. How long was the labour?'

'Not long. About five and a half hours. She started just as we arrived at the house in Kilrowan, so we just drove straight on into Clifden with her parents following in their car.'

'Was it tough going?'

'Well, she did an awful lot of shouting and yelling and cursing and blinding.'

'Did she opt for an epidural?'

'No. She just had a little gas and air towards the end.'

'Brave girl. How are *you* feeling?'

'A bit wrung out. But I'm looking forward to siring some of my own.'

'Polyphiloprogenitive.'

'Come again?'

'It's a big word that means 'stud'.'

'Me to a T!'

'Will you send a picture?'

'Unlikely. Kilrowan is a broadband-free zone.'

'Use your phone.'

'No can do. That's why I'm calling from the hospital land line. My phone's out of juice, and when I asked Greta's mother if she had a charger she looked at me like I was barking. Greta was right when she said that her parents were as dyed-in-the-wool Luddites as Daniel. He'd be right at home here. Oh – I'd better go, Madeleine. My money's running out and I've no more change. I'll call again from—'

The line went dead.

Madeleine set the phone down. 'A little boy,' she told the room, 'called Lennox. Eight pounds two ounces. Mother and child are both doing fine.'

She took a look around the kitchen, at the expressions on the faces of the three people gathered round the table.

Daniel looked as proud as if he'd fathered the baby himself; Jethro looked inscrutable. And poor Dannie looked utterly bereft.

'Deirdre?' It was Blake Parker on the phone. 'I have news, and I'm afraid it's the kind you'd only want to hear from a friend.'

Deirdre slumped. 'Fuck. Not *more* fresh hell. I don't think I can take any more, Blake. I'm up to ninety as it is, waiting for feedback on the script.'

'Listen. I'm going to advise you not to pick up the phone to anyone before you leave for France. You're going at the beginning of next week, yeah?'

'Yeah.'

'Your phone's going to start hopping, Deirdre, and you're not going to want to talk to anyone.'

'I see.' She took a deep breath. 'Bring it on, then.'

'The *Enquirer* has been in touch.'

'Oh, Jesus.'

'They were looking for a quote. They wanted to know how you'd reacted to the news that – oh hell, Deirdre, there's no easy way to tell you this. The word is that Rory is seeing Charlotte Lambert.'

For a long moment, Deirdre didn't speak. 'Thanks, Blake. I'm glad it came from you,' she said, putting the phone down without waiting for a response.

She sat motionless for several moments before getting up from her desk and moving from the study to the landing. From the playroom below came the strident strains of the Scissor Sisters and the sound of Bruno's laugh. 'Melissa?' Deirdre called over the din. 'Can you come here for a sec?'

'Sure.'

Melissa emerged from the playroom and made for the stairs. Halfway up, registering the expression on Deirdre's face, she stopped.

'What's wrong?' she said, all concern. 'Deirdre, what's happened?'

Deirdre leaned her elbows on the balustrade, then put her face in her hands. 'You're going to hear it soon enough, Melissa, and so are the kids. The world and his wife are going to know this soon. Rory's seeing Charlotte Lambert.'

'Oh. Oh, God, Deirdre – I'm so sorry! I'm – oh, God. I don't know what to say.'

'You don't have to say anything. I'd just like you to get rid of the kids for a while, OK? I need some head space.'

Melissa sounded dubious. 'Are you sure that's wise, Deirdre? Don't you think—'

From below, the Scissor Sisters did that screechy thing they did so well and Deirdre flinched.

'Please,' she said. 'Take them to the movie theatre, take them for something to eat. I just need a few hours on my own to get my head around this. As someone once famously said, "If you're going through hell, keep going." I've got to keep going.'

'Well ... if you're really sure?'

'I'm sure.'

Turning away, Deirdre crossed the landing to her study. As she pulled the door shut behind her, she heard Melissa say, 'Take care, Deirdre.'

Take care. She should take care. She didn't want to fall apart. She didn't want to fall apart *again*. Reaching into a drawer, Deirdre helped herself to one of those tiny little white pills that would turn the blue sky beyond her window the colour of lead, the blue water the colour of slate. There was vodka in the mini-fridge. She poured herself a shot and washed down the pill that would numb the pain and make life monochrome.

Crawling to the divan, Deirdre curled up and waited for the drug to kick in and her breathing to steady. Perfidy, betrayal, treachery ...

The bastard. The bastard. The fucking, fucking *bastard*. What was Rory *at*? Was he doing this deliberately? Rubbing her nose in it? Fucking first Greta, then Charlotte? Or had he had a thing going on with Charlotte all along? Is that why he'd hired her look-alike as a nanny, so that he could fuck her vicariously? How long had Rory been cheating on her? Had there been others? She'd believed him when he'd told her that sex was the last thing on his mind when he had to do raunch; she'd believed him when he'd moped on about his dad – when he'd come out with all that guff about the kids' Irish heritage and how they really should hire an Irish-speaking nanny; she'd believed him when he and Greta had professed not to have met before. How they must have laughed! How pathetically easy she had been to gull! She hated, hated, *hated* herself for being so naïve.

The land line rang. She turned the answering machine off, stuck the phone in the safe and shut the door on it. She switched her cell phone off, then set the vodka bottle down on her desk and sat down in front of her computer.

Let him have it! Let the fucker have it!

EXT. DEE'S DUPLEX. POOLSIDE.

DEE is talking on her phone. She is leaving a message on STEPHEN'S answering machine.

DEE: Hello, fuckwit. Well, whaddya know – I've just heard about the hardcore video of you and your whore on the internet. What impeccable timing – just as your son turns sixteen. Great birthday present, fuckwit. Now listen up. If I read one word about you and your whore in the paper if I read *one more word*, fuckwit – you will *never* see your son again. Never. He came home crying from school today, having been subjected to the vilest bullying from the kids who'd seen that sick video. Put your prick away what are you trying to prove, you stupid fuck?

One – just one more word, one more picture and
you will *never* see that boy again, and mark this
– neither will his grandfather. Fuck, fuck, fuck
you, you stupid fucking fuckwit. I hope you and
your prick and your jailbait fucking whore rot
in hell forever.

DEE throws the phone in the pool, reaches for
the vodka bottle.

CUT TO:
INT. STEPHEN'S HOUSE

STEPHEN and GEORGIA are listening to the
message.

GEORGIA: Nor hath hell any fury like a woman
scorned.

Deirdre leaned back in her chair, reread the dialogue,
pressed save, then poured herself another shot of liquid
anaesthetic.

In Saint-Géyroux, Dannie had just taken delivery of the
Christmas present she'd ordered for Jethro. Or rather, for
her to wear for Jethro's delectation. She unwrapped the
package to find the following: a pair of darling knickers,
polka-dotted and trimmed on each hip with a miniature
geyser of multicoloured ribbons; a bra in watered silk with
teeny bows on the straps and a rosebud for a clasp; a pair
of French directoire knickers in hummingbird hues, a
butterfly wing of a camisole, a wisp of a suspender belt
and several pairs of gossamer stockings.

Once upon a time she wouldn't have bothered waiting for Christmas: she wouldn't have been able to resist putting on the sexiest of the garments there and then and shimmying up to the edit suite to seduce her husband as he worked. But she knew that if she did that now, he'd simply assume that it was baby-making time of the month.

She put the lingerie away in the chest where she'd hidden other Christmas gifts: books and clothes and toys, bottles of excellent wine and boxes of handmade chocolates, and she remembered how Paloma had asked her just that morning what she, Dannie, wanted most for Christmas. Dannie had told her that she'd have to think about it. That had been a lie, of course, because she hadn't had to think about it. But she could hardly tell her only child that what she wanted most for Christmas was a baby.

Every night, her dreams were full of babies – chuckling, roly-poly, sweet-scented babies – and every night, the babies were taken away from her by mysterious hands, leaving her sobbing and crumpled and crying out for them to be restored to her.

But the worst nightmare of all was the one in which Jethro came to tell her he was leaving her for Greta O'Flaherty. In this dream, Dannie would prostrate herself at his feet and beg him not to go, asking him over and over again why he was abandoning her. And Jethro would look down at her with an expression of unconcealed contempt and say, 'I'm leaving you because you can't give me babies and Greta can. The baby she's nursing is mine, Dannie.'

'Bye!' mouthed Deirdre, stapling on a bright smile as she waved to her girls. 'Have a wonderful Christmas!'

Aoife, Grace and Melissa were disappearing through the departure gate in LA airport while Deirdre and Bruno stood hand in hand, watching them go. Melissa had made all the arrangements and done all the liaising with Rory, who was meeting up with them in Heathrow.

Deirdre felt a big bubble of misery swell up and threaten to overwhelm her as she turned and scanned the flight details on the illuminated display. Her Air France flight was due to leave from the same terminal in two hours' time. Two hours in the airport would be akin to spending two hours in Hades. Jolly Christmas music was blaring relentlessly from every retail outlet, ubiquitous Santas were ho-ho-hoing and Deirdre was hungover again from a toxic combination of vodka and Xanax. But at least initial feedback on her screenplay had been good. The verdict from the director was a big thumbs up and copies of the script had been biked to Angelina, Brad and Nicole.

'C'mon, sweet pea,' she said to Bruno. 'We'll check into a more comfortable place and wait there till our flight's announced.'

In the sanctuary of the VIP lounge, Deirdre took an airport novel from her cabin bag and settled down to read while Bruno cuddled up beside her with Dr Seuss.

Opposite them, a girl with hair extensions and expensive nails was chewing gum and reading a tabloid. The tabloid was the *National Enquirer*, and the headline – in a lurid red and yellow font – read: 'Stud-Muffin McDonagh Dates Co-Star Lambert! Photos show how CLOSE they are!' The words were juxtaposed alongside a grainy photograph of Rory and Charlotte, emerging hand in hand from a restaurant.

The gum-chewing girl cocked her head as a flight was announced. Then she checked her watch, rose to her feet and discarded the paper.

Deirdre couldn't help it. She reached for the rag. Angling it so that Bruno couldn't see the headline, she turned to the main story.

Sex-on-legs Irish-born star Rory McDonagh was spotted last week leaving this London eatery with his *Love Lies Bleeding* co-star, Charlotte Lambert.

An eyewitness told The ENQUIRER that the couple seemed 'very loved-up'. According to the source, they 'dined in a secluded booth and couldn't take their eyes off each other. They behaved in a way that only couples very much in love would. There were lots of intimate smiles, and when they rose from the table, Rory escorted Charlotte to the door of the restaurant in a gentlemanly fashion, resting his hand on the small of her back.

Meanwhile, the actor has reportedly moved out of the beach house he shared with soon-to-be ex-wife, screenwriter Deirdre O'Dare, and their kids Aoife, Grace and Bruno. He is in London to film *Hard to Choos*, a film based on the popular novel by chick-lit writer Pixie Pirelli.

Love Lies Bleeding, in which Rory plays notorious hell-raiser Jack St Ledger and Charlotte plays his lover, Lucy, Duchess of Rutland, is due to be released early next year. Advance reports say that

> the screen chemistry between the two stars is
> incendiary, and the sex scenes steamier than a
> morning fog in Malibu!

There were three photographs accompanying the article. Two of them were blurred paparazzi shots of Rory and Charlotte leaving the restaurant, the third was of Deirdre and Rory at some Hollywood bash. They were both wearing big smiles and the caption read: 'Rory and his wife Deirdre in happier times.'

Deirdre stood up, moved to the waste bin and dropped the paper in it. Then she went to the rest room to clean her teeth, spritz her face and wash her hands.

Nor hath hell any fury …

It was a shame, she thought, that she hadn't seen the *Enquirer* article sooner. If she had, she would never have allowed her girls to jet off to Ireland to spend Christmas with their father and grandfather. Still, there was St Patrick's Day, and Easter, and Father's Day. To deny Rory access on Father's Day would be the cruellest cut of all, and since the gloves were clearly off now, Deirdre had no qualms about using every weapon in her arsenal to wreak havoc.

Dee's speech came back to her.

> One just one more word, one more picture and you
> will never see that boy again, and mark this
> neither will his grandfather. Fuck, fuck, fuck
> you, you stupid fucking fuckwit. I hope you and
> your prick and your jailbait fucking whore rot
> in hell forever.

30

On New Year's Day, a powder-blue Merc pulled up outside number one rue des Artistes. Sam emerged, then moved round to the passenger side to open the door for Greta and baby Lennox.

'Thanks,' she said, shivering as she stepped out into the bitterly cold Saint-Géyroux morning. 'Jesus! I hope Daniel remembered to put the heating on high in the studio. I don't want my darling babby catching cold.' Sam hauled their luggage out of the boot, then opened the door to the courtyard. They passed through into the house and Greta smiled. 'Sure, he has the place like a furnace for me!'

'Hello?' called Sam, dumping the bags on the hall floor. 'Is there anyone home?'

A moment or two of silence followed, then the kitchen door opened and Pilot loped through, followed by Daniel.

'Yo, Pilot!' exclaimed Sam as the dog jumped up and put his paws on his chest. 'Yo, Daniel!' he said as Daniel gave him an avuncular punch on the arm.

Then Daniel turned to Greta. He moved towards her, laid his hands on her shoulders and dropped a kiss on her forehead. 'Welcome home,' he said, 'and happy New Year.'

'This isn't my home,' said Greta with a smile.

'It's your home until the final portrait's painted,' Daniel told her, taking a step back. 'May I see the baby?' he asked. 'Let me have a look at Lennox Junior.'

Greta carefully adjusted the bundle in her arms and tweaked the pale blue cashmere that swaddled her son so that Daniel could see his face.

Daniel looked at the child, then looked back at Greta and smiled.

'He's beautiful,' he said. 'He's perfect.'

She smiled back at him. 'Didn't I tell you he would be?' she said.

'Where's Rosa?' asked Sam. 'And Madeleine?'

'They've gone to a New Year's Day champagne brunch at Bianca's house. Colleen and that Margot are hosting it. You're both invited, but I had hoped, Greta, that you might allow me to do some preliminary sketches? The studio's warm, and I got things in for the baby – little toys, you know, teddies and suchlike. I know he's too young to play with them, but I just thought that it would make him feel more at home if there was baby stuff around. And there's a cot for him to sleep in from time to time if you get too uncomfortable holding him.'

Greta laughed. 'Aren't you the thoughtful auld yoke, Daniel!' she said. 'And no worries, I'd be perfectly happy to sit for you. I've missed the smell of linseed oil and I wouldn't wonder that Lennox has, too. The last thing I feel like doing is going to a champagne brunch.'

'I'll stroll on down to Bianca's then,' said Sam. 'A glass of champagne is *exactly* what I need after that drive.'

'Was it a bitch?' asked Daniel.

Sam shrugged. 'It wasn't too bad. The roads were

clear and we broke the journey in Limoges.'

'And you're quite certain you're ready to go to work, Greta?' Daniel asked solicitously.

'I'm sure I'm ready,' she said. 'Didn't I sleep all the way from Limoges?' She looked down at her baby, all wrapped up in layers of cashmere. 'What about you, snuggly bunny?' she said. 'Are you ready to go to work? Do you realise what a lucky boy you are, to have your portrait painted by a posh Hibernian artist? Will you be a good boy for your namesake, for Mr Famous Painter Lennox?' She looked back up at Daniel. 'Did you get the camomile tea I asked for?'

'Yes. It's in the kitchen. Shall I make a flask for you?'

Greta nodded. 'That'd be good. I'll go on up, so.' Leaning into Sam, she kissed him and ran a hand down his face. 'Don't drink too much champagne,' she told him, 'and stay away from that foxy Margot. She has the hots for you, handsome, you know that?'

'I certainly will stay away from foxy Margot,' Sam told her. 'She scares me to death. And don't allow Daniel to work you too hard.'

Greta turned towards the staircase and made her way up. Taking the right fork, she moved down the corridor and ascended the spiral staircase at the end that led to Daniel's studio.

The studio was like a hothouse, bombarded as it was by winter sun streaming in through the skylights and the heat generated by the ornate old-fashioned radiators. Setting her baby on a rug on the floor, Greta surveyed the room. It was as it had always been, apart from the cot that had been set up in a corner. Greta crossed to it, ran a hand over soft flannelette sheets. The sheets were topped with a hand-worked quilt, over which a veritable zoo of velour animals had been scattered: rabbits and teddy bears and penguins and kangaroos and dinosaurs. A mobile featuring lions and tigers rampant had been strung up over the cot and a hand-painted frieze that was clearly the work of Rosa hung on the wall. It bore the legend 'Welcome Baby Lennox' worked in silver and gold stars and a self-portrait of Rosa in crayon had a speech bubble coming out of her mouth: 'Be Good and Try not to Wriggle when You are Sitting.'

Smiling, Greta wandered back across the floor, breathing in the smell of linseed with a kind of languorous relish. She divested herself of her coat and scarf and hung them over the bentwood chair. Her sweater followed, then her T-shirt, skirt, shoes, woolly stockings, pants and nursing bra.

Next, she stooped to pick up baby Lennox and proceeded to unwind him from his cashmere swaddling. He blinked open sleepy eyes as Greta peeled away his baby-gro and removed his – thankfully clean – nappy, which she dropped into the swing-bin that Daniel had prudently provided.

Then she sat down on the daybed and put her baby to her breast.

'Hush, little baby,' she sang in a soft lilt, 'don't say a word. Momma's going to buy you a mockingbird. And if that mockingbird don't sing, Momma's going to buy you a diamond ring.'

That reminded her. She removed the solitaire that Sam had given her for Christmas and lobbed it into her discarded shoe before resuming her lullaby.

The sound of the door opening made her look up.

Daniel was standing on the threshold of the studio, a flask in his left hand. They exchanged that look: the look that signified the unspoken, quintessential empathy between artist and model, and then Daniel smiled.

'Beautiful,' he said. 'Perfect.'

In Bianca's house, Madeleine was making small-talk with the local chat show host, who had trapped her in a corner and who was chatting for the Olympics. She kept looking at his disconcertingly white teeth, which she found incredibly distracting. What procedure had he undergone to get them so white? she wondered. Was it painful? Was it expensive? Should she make enquiries about having it done?

On the other side of the room, a disconsolate-looking Deirdre O'Dare was knocking back rather a lot of champagne and talking desultorily to Monsieur Verdurin. Madeleine had seen Deirdre on a number of occasions since she'd arrived back in Saint-Géyroux, but not once had either woman mentioned the fact that Rory and Charlotte Lambert were being outed by the most vicious gossip mags. Nor had Madeleine told her that Greta O'Flaherty was due to return to Saint-Geyroux that day, with Sam and her new baby. She just hoped that neither of them would happen to bump into each other before Deirdre was due to fly back to LA, never to return to the village.

Deirdre had told Madeleine that she had left instructions for her solicitor to put the house on the market in the New Year, contents and all – apart from the portrait that Daniel had painted of her, which she had decided to put out on loan to the Irish Museum of Modern Art.

As she watched the gleaming teeth of the chat show host, Madeleine found herself wondering if Greta and Sam and the baby were back yet, and just as the thought entered her head, there was Sam, rounding the door into Bianca's dining room, looking beleaguered. Madeleine saw him lunge for a glass of champagne like a drowning man lunging for a lifebelt.

'Excuse me,' she told the chat show host. 'I've just seen my nephew come in. I must go and wish him a happy New Year.'

'And a happy New Year to you, too,' grinned the host.

Madeleine struggled across the room and laid a hand on Sam's arm.

'Hey, beautiful Auntie!' he said, slinging an arm round her shoulders. 'Happy New Year!'

'And the same to you.' Madeleine stood on tiptoe to kiss his cheek. 'How long have you been here?'

'About an hour. I got stuck with that Margot d'Arcy. She wants me to do a shot of herself and Colleen for the jacket of their play script.'

'*Síle na Gig and the Temple of Hecate*?' said Madeleine.

'The very opus.'

'Where's Greta and the baby?'

'Back at home. Daniel couldn't wait to get his mitts on her and Lennox.'

'You mean they're sitting for him already?'

'They are.'

'He's that keen?'

'So it would seem. But you can hardly blame him. He's been waiting for this moment for years. Jesus.'

'What's wrong?'

'I've just got a load of Deirdre O'Dare. She looks rough.'

Sam raised a hand to attract Deirdre's attention and Madeleine said in an urgent undertone, 'Whatever you do, don't say anything to Deirdre about Greta being back with her baby.'

Sam gave her a puzzled look. 'What? Why not?'

'She's going through the mill with Rory.' Oh, God. Gossipy Madame Bouret was in earshot.

'But what's that got to do with—'

'Did I hear you say that our darling Greta's—' began Madame Bouret.

But Madeleine pretended not to have heard her and practically dragged Sam across the room to where Deirdre was reaching for yet another glass from the tray of a passing waiter.

'Hi, Deirdre! Happy New Year,' Sam said heartily.

'Ha! Bit of an oxymoron, that, isn't it?' Deirdre presented her cheek so that Sam could kiss it. 'For some of us, a new year is not a thing to be celebrated.'

Madeleine noticed that Deirdre was slurring her words. Madame Bouret was looking over at them, eyes aglitter with curiosity. 'Sam?' said Madeleine. 'Would you take Deirdre out into the garden? I'm sure she'd love to see Bianca's new water feature.'

'What?' Sam just looked at her blankly.

'I think she could do with a little fresh air,' Madeleine murmured, clenching her teeth in a smile.

'Oh. Oh, sure.' Sam took hold of Deirdre's forearm and started guiding her across the room.

'Where are we going?' Deirdre asked him.

'Apparently Bianca has a fabulous new water feature,' came Sam's reply.

And the last thing Madeleine heard as Sam escorted Deirdre from the room was, 'I don't want to see some poxy fucking water feature! You think I give a fuck about water features when my life is ...' Her voice faded away like dialogue in a radio play.

Madeleine looked round at the all-smiling, all-chatting happy New Year faces. Bianca Ingram was flirting with Jethro Palmer; Margot d'Arcy was sending predatory smiles towards the chat show host; Dannie Palmer was laughing at some story of Monsieur Prévoste; and Colleen was admiring Valérie Poiret's baby. *Daniel couldn't wait to get his mitts on her and Lennox* ... Abruptly, Madeleine was seized by an overwhelming urge to see Greta's baby. She moved into the hall just in time: Rosa's red and white Christmas socks were disappearing up the stairs.

'Rosa?' she called. 'Let's make a move.'

'Aw, Mama, no! I'm having too much fun. I don't want to go home yet. Can't I stay on for a bit and go home with Sam?'

'Oh, all right. But please don't make yourself sick by guzzling any more of those meringues.'

Madeleine helped herself to her coat from the cloakroom, then let herself out of Bianca's house. She covered the distance between the Sanctuary and the rue des Artistes feeling vaguely unsettled. There was no one else around. Everyone was either at the party, enjoying the regal munificence of Colleen and Margot, or they were snugly ensconced at home, watching New Year's Day television in front of the fire. Madeleine's breath was coming fast as she hurried, little puffy clouds escaping from her mouth.

In the hall, she took off her coat, then crossed to the kitchen.

Daniel was pouring water from a kettle into a flask. 'Was that fun?' he asked, glancing up at her.

'Not really. Where's Greta?'

'She's upstairs in the studio. I'm making more herbal tea for her. She's addicted to this camomile stuff. It stinks.' Daniel sniffed, then made a face. 'Why don't you go up and say hello?'

'I'll do that.'

Out into the hall she went, heels tip-tapping on the terracotta tiles. Up the stairs, right fork, down the corridor, *tap, tap, tap*: up the spiral staircase; *tap, tap, tap* at the studio door.

'Come in,' came Greta's voice.

Madeleine pushed the door open. Greta was sitting on the daybed wearing a silk kimono, her back to the door. She stood up as Madeleine passed through into the room.

'Happy New Year, Greta,' said Madeleine.

'Happy New Year!' Greta turned. Her mass of strawberry blonde hair was tumbling over her shoulders, her skin looked more translucent than ever, her candid blue eyes were shining. The folds of her kimono were open to the waist, and she was holding a baby to her creamy white breast. 'Come and meet Lennox, Madeleine,' she said. 'Come and meet the most beautiful baby boy in the world.'

Greta smiled down at the infant she was suckling, ran a hand over his head of downy hair, trailed a finger along the curve of his cheek.

And Madeleine saw that baby Lennox, two-week-old son of Greta O'Flaherty, was as dark-skinned as his mother was fair.

Greta raised her smiling eyes to Madeleine. 'Isn't he beautiful?' she said.

Dannie was walking home from Bianca's party, wishing everybody she passed a Happy New Year. She was feeling bubbly: she'd relaxed her ban on alcohol and allowed herself a glass of champagne today. Jethro had linked her right arm, Sam her left, and Paloma and Rosa and Bruno were cantering ahead, the girls wearing festive antlers. Burnt-out fireworks – testimony to last night's celebrations – still littered the market square and the Christmas lights that ticker-taped the village were flickering into life.

'Where's Madeleine going to in such a hurry?' remarked Jethro as Madeleine Lennox swung round a corner, heading in the direction from which they'd just come.

'Hey, Auntie!' Sam called across the square. 'Where are you off to?'

'Oh! There you are.' Madeleine turned and crossed the square to them. 'I thought you might still be at Bianca's, Dannie. The answering machine picks up on your land line and your mobile just rings out.'

'That's because I left the mobile at home,' Dannie told her. 'What's up? You look a bit wired.'

'Um.' Madeleine gave her an uneasy look. 'I'd love a 'chat'.'

Dannie could tell by the way Madeleine had put inverted commas around the word that actually, something a lot more meaningful than a 'chat' was what she wanted. She could also tell by the way her friend shot a look at the kids that she didn't want them earwigging.

'In that case, can we come back to your house?' Dannie asked. 'There's a problem with our heating and the fire's bound to have gone out by now. I didn't mean to stay so long at Bianca's, but I was having fun.'

'Sure,' said Madeleine. 'Our house is like a furnace because of the baby.'

The 'B' word. Ow. If Dannie went to the Lennoxes, she'd have to admire the baby.

'OK,' she said, trying to sound chipper. 'Jethro was going to drop in to you anyway to borrow some book of photographs that Sam was raving about. You don't mind if the kids come?'

'Of course not. Rosa'll be thrilled to be able to show off her presents again. The novelty hasn't worn off yet.'

'Allow me, Auntie.' Sam offered Madeleine his free arm and together all seven of them straggled off towards the Lennox residence.

'Deirdre was a bit the worse for wear, I thought,' Dannie observed in an undertone as Madeleine unlocked the gate to the courtyard and held it open for the kids to pass through. 'That's why I offered to take Bruno off her hands for a while.'

'Mmm. I noticed. Did she get home OK?'

'Yeah. We walked her there. I said I'd drop Bruno back to her later. I got the feeling she needed some time on her own. I suppose it's a bit like going through a bereavement.'

'That's kind of what I wanted to talk to you about.'

'Oh?' Dannie took a look at Madeleine's expression. 'Has something awful happened, Madeleine?'

'I – I don't know. Come on through to the kitchen. I'll make you a cup of tea.'

'Thanks.'

In the hall, they divested themselves of coats and scarves, then Jethro and Sam took a left towards the stairs. 'Join us later for a glass of wine, Jethro,' Madeleine called after him.

'Thank you kindly, ma'am,' Jethro told her. 'I'm clean out of Mas de Daumas and I'd be glad to help myself to some of Daniel's stash.'

Following Madeleine into the kitchen, Dannie sat down at the table while Madeleine flicked a switch on the kettle and helped herself to a bottle from the wine rack.

'You need a large one, by the look of things, Madeleine Lennox,' Dannie said.

'I'd get through a bottle no problem, the way I'm feeling,' admitted Madeleine, pulling the cork and pouring. 'Camomile OK for you?'

'Camomile would be grand.'

'We got some in for Greta. It's her latest thing.'

Dannie watched as Madeleine slung a teabag into a mug and poured boiling water over it. She looked completely distracted, as if she was trying to work out some conundrum. Then she set the mug down in front of Dannie, took a seat opposite and fixed her with a grave look.

'Has this got something to do with Greta?' asked Dannie.

Madeleine nodded.

'Sam said that Daniel had started painting her already. Is that what you're upset about?'

'No. Dannie, I know this is an awful thing to say, but I had always half-expected – well, *more* than half-expected, to be honest – that Greta's baby would have a look of Rory.'

'It's not an awful thing to say, Madeleine. That's what I expected, too.'

'The fact is - it doesn't.'

'The baby doesn't look like Rory?'

Madeleine shook her head, then took a big slug of wine. 'The baby is very cute,' she said, setting down her glass, 'but he doesn't look like Rory at all.'

Oh, God, thought Dannie. She remembered that Greta had named her baby Lennox. Could it be – was it possible that it was *Daniel's* child? Was that why Madeleine was looking so harrowed? Or – dear God forbid – might it even be Jethro's? Was that what Madeleine was trying to tell her? That ferocious nightmare – the one in which Jethro told her with such scathing contempt that he'd sired a child with Greta – had recurred more than once recently, and she knew it was because the baby's conception date nagged her so. And Greta's words came back to haunt her, those words that Madeleine had repeated: *If I'd known he'd be here, I never would have come to Saint-Géyroux.* Could it have been Jethro she was talking about? 'Who does the baby look like then?' she asked, fearful of the answer.

'Greta's baby's black, Dannie.'

'He's black?'

'Yes.'

'So … who's the father?' Dannie asked stupidly.

'I haven't a clue.'

Dannie sat, trying to digest this information. Greta's baby was black, ergo Rory was not the father. Did that mean that there had been no affair between Greta and Rory? But that was impossible – all the evidence indicated otherwise! There was the film footage she'd seen that night in Jethro's edit suite. There was the whole contrived Irish nanny thing. There was the fact that Rory and Greta had concocted an elaborate tissue of lies and had even gone so far as to enlist Jethro's help in covering up their acquaintance – their *intimate* acquaintance. There *had* to have been something going on between them!

Because, Dannie realised now, if there hadn't – *if there hadn't* ... Oh, sweet Jesus. If there had been no affair between Rory and Greta, then she, Dannie, had done something so monumentally bad that it was understandable that God was punishing her by not giving her a baby. Oh, sweet Jesus ...

The kitchen door opened and Jethro and Sam came through. Jethro was leafing through a book of David Doubilet's marine photographs and Sam was talking arcane photography talk.

'Sam?' Dannie asked when he'd finished.

'Yo.'

'Madeleine tells me Greta's baby is – beautiful?' She was trying hard to sound casual, but she could hear the tremor in her voice.

'Yes. He is.'

'Have you a photograph?'

'I've loads on my camera upstairs. But there's a few on my phone as well.' Sam took his phone from his pocket and started going through photos. 'Let's see, which is my favourite? Ah. Here we go.'

Sam handed Dannie his phone. There, displayed, was a picture of a golden Greta propped up against pillows in a hospital bed. She was smiling beatifically to the camera, holding her brand new baby in her arms. Helping himself to a couple of glasses, Sam began pouring wine.

'Sam?' said Dannie. 'D'you know who the baby's father might be?'

'The father,' said Sam, 'is a bastard drummer in a rock band who left Greta for another woman and then fucked off to the States.'

Dannie and Madeleine exchanged frightened looks.

'What's wrong?' asked Sam, registering their expressions.

'I know what's wrong,' said Jethro. He was standing leaning up against a kitchen counter, and the way he was looking at Dannie made her feel even more frightened.

'Did – did you know, Sam, that Greta knew Rory McDonagh before she came to France?' asked Dannie.

'Sure I knew. She stood in for Charlotte Lambert on *Love Lies Bleeding*. She was devastated when she realised who she was working for, you know. That's why she tried to keep it a secret.'

'Why did she want to keep it a secret?'

'Well, it's obvious, isn't it? How would you feel if you found out you were working for the wife of a man with whom you'd had to fake sex scenes? 'Body double' is hardly the class of thing you put on your CV when you're applying for a job as a child-minder.'

He was right. Oh, God, he was right. *What had she done?*

Dannie had wreaked havoc, that's what she'd done. She hadn't just made mischief: she'd made mayhem, created chaos. She'd taken an emotional Sabatier to the marriage of two of her dearest friends. And she was now going to have to work harder than nimble-fingered Arachne at stitching up the bloody wound she'd inflicted.

*

Daniel took a bottle of champagne from the fridge in the studio, then reached for a couple of glasses.

'No champagne for me, thanks,' said Greta.

'Are you sure? Not even a small one to celebrate Lennox's first day as an artist's model?'

'Not even a small one. The alcohol passes through into the mother's milk and I don't want my babby getting tipsy.'

'I'll have a glass on my own then before I come down.'

Daniel popped the cork and Greta tried to remember the last time she'd drunk champagne. Of course! It had been on the morning of her last day as Charlotte Lambert's body double, when champagne had been all there was to drink in the fridge in the flat she'd shared with Esther. She remembered how Fuchsia, the girl in the flat next door, had been passing and heard the pop of the cork, and she'd poked her head round the door to check out the early morning party action. Greta had never forgotten – would never forget – the look on Fuchsia's face when she got a load of the dude who was standing in her kitchen. She'd been invited in, of course, and the three of them had shared the bottle, and when Rory went to take his leave, Fuchsia had dashed into the next-door flat to grab her copy of *Heat* magazine so that he could autograph his Torso of the Year So Far page for her. Acting on a similar impulse, Greta had asked him to sign the jokey note he'd given her, the one that read: 'To 'Corinna'. Thanks for some of the best vicarious sex I've ever had. XXX'

Picking her baby up, Greta moved to the door. 'I'll see you later, Daniel,' she said.

'You will.' Daniel raised his glass at her, then reached for one of his paint rags. 'You'll be glad to know that I'm cooking tonight,' he said.

'In that case,' Greta told him with a smile, 'I'll know to steer well clear of the kitchen.'

She descended the stairs, humming lullabies to her baby. She was feeling tired now, and hungry. A *tartine* would be good, with maybe some apricot conserve: she loved the Bonne Maman stuff. There were voices coming from the kitchen: the door was not quite closed.

'I have to say that the response struck me as being a bit OTT.' It was Sam's voice. 'You'd have thought that Greta had been having an actual *affair* with Rory, the way things were handled.'

'That's because,' said a woman's voice, 'we *did* think that Greta and Rory were having an affair.'

Greta stopped, frozen in her tracks in the hall.

'What? Where on earth did you get that idea from?' Sam's voice, again.

'It was my fault. I jumped to conclusions,' said the woman's voice, and Greta recognised the Connemara accent. It was Dannie Palmer speaking, the woman who'd taken it upon herself to dismiss Greta. 'I put two and two together,' she was saying, 'and convinced myself that they had to be having an affair. When I told Deirdre my suspicions, that's when everything went pear shaped.'

'Jesus! You honestly thought that Greta was the kind of girl who'd have an affair with the husband of the woman who's employing her?' Sam's voice dripped contempt.

Oh, how I love you Sam Newman! thought Greta. I love your chivalrous soul, I love your respect for women,

I love your faith, I love your trust, I love your candour. I've loved you from the moment I met you. You are my hero, my soul mate, my redeemer and I'll love you till the day I die and give you all the babies you could ever want, ever.

'Yes. I did think that.' Dannie's voice came again: it was Greta's cue. In the silence that followed, she moved towards the door, took hold of the handle and pushed.

Sam was standing on the other side of the kitchen. He looked at Greta and she could tell at once from his expression that he knew she'd heard, for Dannie's outrageous announcement had brought tears to Greta's eyes and sent blood coursing to her cheeks. Turning cold eyes on Dannie, Sam crossed the room and said: 'I wonder what Greta would make of that? Perhaps you should try asking her.'

'What do you mean?'

'She's right behind you.'

Greta saw Dannie turn a stricken face towards the door, then felt Sam's comforting presence beside her as he slipped an arm around her waist.

'Have you anything to say, sweetheart?' he asked.

Greta looked down at Dannie. What had this woman *done*? She had wrecked heads and destroyed lives. She had jumped to conclusions, she had stirred things up, she had made mischief. She had gossiped – and Greta's mother had always told her that gossip was the most invidious form of injury. Greta's mother had taught her to be a good girl; Greta's mother had taught her to be the soul of honour. That this woman could have imagined for a moment that she, Greta, had been having an affair with Rory McDonagh while living under the same roof as his wife and child was a sick, sick, *monstrous* thing.

'What have you done?' she asked Dannie. 'What havoc are you after wreaking?'

The older woman's eyes were brimful with tears, but Greta didn't care. She remembered what Esther had said to her on the night they'd sent Jared to the Bin of Fire. *Well hey! This is a Greta O'Flaherty I have never seen before.* And how she, Greta, had replied: *I don't like bad manners Esther, and I don't like injustice. I know I'm a walkover usually, but I have a steely side, too.* A stainless, steely side.

'Shame on you,' Greta told Dannie. They were the three most hurtful words her mother had ever said to her when she was a child; it was the ultimate put-down, the biggest begetter of guilt, the admonition that cut to the bone.

In her arms, baby Lennox stirred, blinked, unclenched tiny starfish hands and started to make mewly noises. 'There, there, baba,' said Greta. 'There, there, my little man.' She dropped a kiss on his forehead, then looked back at Dannie. '*Shame on you,*' she said again.

Turning away, Greta went back up the staircase, leaning on Sam for support.

31

Dannie rose to her feet.

'Where are you going?' asked Madeleine.

'I'm going to right some wrongs,' Dannie told her. 'I'm going to see Deirdre.'

Moving to the kitchen door, Dannie went through and crossed the hall, grabbing her coat on the way.

Outside, the street was deserted. It was dark now and beginning to rain, but Dannie didn't feel the wet or the cold. She was remembering the night all those months ago when Greta had gone to the rescue of Bruno: the night the girl had returned Deirdre's boy safe and sound to her. She remembered the way Greta had looked as she'd stood on the street outside Dannie's house – the street where Dannie had dismissed her earlier that same day, calling the girl a slut because that's what Dannie had believed her to be. Greta's hair had been dripping wet that night, her face had been covered in grime and blood, her eyes had been like those of a hunted animal. Dannie had looked at an angel of mercy and seen a whore.

How had she got it so wrong? How had she made such a grotesquely distorted character assessment? How had she managed to jump to conclusion after grossly inaccurate conclusion? Oh, God, God, she prayed, please let everything be all right. Please let me try and make things better. I don't care if Greta hates me, I don't care if Deirdre and Rory hate me, I don't care if Jethro hates me – just let everything be OK. If everything is OK, then I don't care if I never have another baby. Please God, just let everything be OK.

She was on the rue Lamballe now. There was no light from the McDonagh-O'Dare house. Deirdre was probably sleeping – and if Dannie thought her own nightmares were bad, what must Deirdre's be like? She, Dannie, had been responsible for putting her friend through living hell.

Dannie tried the bell and waited. No one came. She tried again and waited again. No one came. Feeling panicky, she tried a third time, keeping her finger pressed against the button for at least a minute. But still Deirdre didn't come.

In mounting panic, Dannie ran round to the back of the house. She misjudged a step and went over on her ankle, landing heavily on the path and feeling pain shoot through her. She was glad it hurt: it served her right. She hoped she'd fall again – she'd welcome more pain. Whatever physical pain Dannie suffered would be Ha'penny Place stuff compared with the mental agony Deirdre had gone through – was still going through.

The back of the house was in darkness too. Dannie rapped her knuckles hard against the door, then harder still. More pain. Good. And then she thought: You feckin' eejit. Try the door.

It was unbolted.

Dannie passed through into the kitchen. The house was very quiet.

'Deirdre?' she called. But no answering call came.

Oh, Jesus. Moving across the floor, Dannie switched on the light. The panicky flutterings in her chest were coming faster now.

The kitchen was messy: dishes stacked in the sink instead of in the dishwasher, damp laundry spewing into a basket, the remains of a baguette on the table. An empty bottle of wine.

Dannie moved into the hall and called Deirdre's name again. No response. From the sitting room, she could see the light of an answering machine, its blink like a blood-shot eye. She went in and turned up the dimmer switch. More mess: Bruno's toys, scattered magazines, discarded DVD cases. Another bottle of wine, half empty this time. A blister pack of pills. Xanax.

Dannie lunged for the door, took the stairs two at a time. She dived through the first door, into Deirdre and Rory's bedroom. The sheets on the bed were rumpled, but there was no one in the bed and no one in the en suite bathroom. Deirdre's portrait on the wall looked back at Dannie, locking eyes with her. But the expression was no longer come-hitherish – it appeared accusing.

The next room – Aoife and Grace's – was empty, the undisturbed beds forlorn looking.

Dannie slammed through a third door, the door to the room that she knew to be Bruno's. On the bed, Deirdre lay curled up in a foetal position, a mobile phone clutched in her hand, a T-shirt pressed against her face. Dannie had seen that T-shirt before. Jethro had one, Rory had one and Bruno had one too. The legend it bore read: *Love Lies Bleeding.*

'Deirdre?' said Dannie. 'Deirdre?'

As she moved to the bed, she felt as if her limbs had

been dislocated: they didn't seem to belong to her. Reaching out a hand, she touched Deirdre's face, knowing that if the face she touched was cold, she, Dannie, was not just guilty of the sins she'd already heaped up: she was also guilty of manslaughter. Thank God! Deirdre's face was warm.

'Deirdre!' said Dannie again, lowering herself onto the bed and taking her friend by the shoulders. 'Deirdre! Wake up. Wake up! For the love of God, Deirdre, will you wake the fuck up!'

Deirdre's brow puckered. She scrunched her eyes shut tighter, then raised a listless hand as if Dannie were some irritating insect that she wanted to swat away.

'Deirdre! You've got to wake up!'

'No,' Deirdre's voice was querulous. 'G'way. I'm cosy here.'

'Deirdre! Listen to me. You've got to listen to me.'

Deirdre wrapped the T-shirt round her head and Dannie tore it away.

'My T-shirt!' wailed Deirdre. 'Give it back.'

'No. I'm not giving it back until you sit up and listen to me.' But Deirdre just curled in on herself even more. 'Sit up and listen!'

No response. There was nothing else for it. Dannie smacked Deirdre hard across the face. Deirdre yelped, and for the first time her eyes opened. She rubbed her cheek and gave Dannie an aggrieved look.

'What did you do that for?' she said. 'I never did anything to hurt you. You're horrible.'

'Yes. I am horrible. Now sit up. Sit up, Deirdre, and listen to me. Do as I say or I'll hit you another dig.' Dannie dragged Deirdre up until she was slumped against the pillows. 'Good girl,' she told her. 'You can have your shirt back now.'

Dannie handed Deirdre the shirt. She watched as her friend folded it, stroking it with a slack hand before holding it up to her face. Dannie was reminded of the way she did that with Paloma's baby clothes, and she found herself wondering whether it was Bruno's T-shirt that Deirdre was using as a comfort blanket, or Rory's.

'Now. Are you listening?' Deirdre's eyes above the cotton of the T-shirt looked mutinous, but she nodded. 'How many pills did you take, Deirdre?' Dannie asked.

Deirdre shrugged. 'I dunno.'

'How *many*?'

'I wasn't counting.'

Dannie reached for the phone.

'What are you doing?'

'I'm calling an ambulance.'

'No!' Deirdre made an ineffectual lunge for the phone. 'No,' she said again in a pleading voice. 'No ambulance, Dannie. Please.'

'Deirdre, see sense. You may need to have your stomach pumped.'

'No! I promise you, Dannie, I don't need my stomach pumped. I didn't take an overdose – I just took maybe one too many Xanax and washed it down with too much booze. I've been – I've been doing that a lot lately.' Deirdre started to cry as the words came pouring. 'If you call an ambulance, word will get out that I tried to kill myself, and after all I've been through, I couldn't handle that. Just think what the *Enquirer* would have to say – suicide's the worst crime a mother can commit. And then Rory would look for custody, and if he took my babies away from me I would die. My heart would break again, and it's been broken so many times that it won't stand another chance. My heart will never mend, Dannie.'

'Oh, Deirdre!' Dannie flung her arms around her friend and held her tight. Tears were streaming down her face too. 'Oh, Deirdre, I'm sorry. I'm so, so sorry.'

For many minutes, the women just sat there on the bed, clinging to each other and weeping copious tears, Dannie rocking Deirdre in a feeble attempt to comfort her. And then the phone rang.

'Don't pick up!' said Deirdre.

Dannie checked out the display. 'It's Bruno,' she said.

'Bruno!' whimpered Deirdre. 'Oh, God. I can't talk to him, Dannie. I'm not able.'

'I'll take it.' Dannie wiped her nose on her damp sleeve. 'Yo, Bruno!' she said, investing her voice with great jocularity. 'How's it going?'

'Fine.' The child sounded a little perplexed. 'Is that Dannie?'

'It is!'

'Is Momma there?'

'She's in the shower, *acushla*.'

'Oh. Can you tell her that I've been asked to spend the night here in the Lennoxes'?'

'Sure. A slumber party? That'll be fun!'

'Yeah! Paloma's staying too, and Madeleine says we can stay up late because it's still the holidays – and guess who else is here, Dannie? Greta! And she's got her baby with her.'

'Well. Isn't that something else! I'll pass the message on to your ma, darlin'.'

There was a kerfuffly noise on the other end of the

line and then Bruno said, 'Oh – hang on, Dannie, Madeleine wants to speak to you.'

The next voice Dannie heard was Madeleine's. 'How are things?' she asked.

'I can't talk now,' said Dannie. 'I'll call you tomorrow. I'm going to stay the night here. Will you tell Jethro?'

'Sure.'

'Thanks, Madeleine.'

'Listen,' said Madeleine. 'I'm going to ask the kind of questions that only need monosyllabic answers, OK?'

'OK,' said Dannie, shooting a look at Deirdre. She was still slumped with her eyes shut, but she had stopped crying.

'Is she in a bad way?' Madeleine asked.

'Yeah.'

'Does she need medical help?'

'No.'

'Thank God. Is there anything I can do?'

'No.'

'Have you said anything to her yet – about the Greta thing?'

'No.'

'I guess it's not a bad idea to leave that till the morning. Maybe she'll be feeling better then – more able to handle it.'

'Yes.'

'Phone me if you need me, Dannie – any time.'

'I'll do that. Thanks, Madeleine.'

'Good luck, Dannie.'

Dannie set the phone down on Bruno's bedside table, noticing abstractedly that the book by his bed was *The Turf-Cutter's Donkey*. 'Bruno's staying over at the

Lennoxes',' she said, taking Deirdre's hand. 'Is that cool with you?'

Deirdre nodded. 'I'm glad. I would have hated it if he'd come home and found me in a state.'

'You're still in a state,' Dannie told her. 'Come down to the kitchen. I'm going to get gallons of black coffee into you. But first I want you to go to the bathroom and make yourself puke.'

'Oh, fuck.' Deirdre buried her face in the shirt. 'Do I have to? How totally sordid.'

'It beats having your stomach pumped. You should have a cold shower as well while you're in there.'

Oh, how efficient she was! Dannie thought as she helped Deirdre to the bathroom and set out fresh towels and pyjamas for her. How good at dispensing advice! Dannie the proficient, Dannie the plain-speaker, Dannie the bullshit-free agony aunt.

Going back into Bruno's room, she picked up Deirdre's phone and the *Love Lies Bleeding* T-shirt. She'd say nothing to Deirdre tonight, she decided as she trailed into the bedroom that Deirdre and Rory had once shared and laid the shirt on the pillow. She'd allow her a decent night's sleep before she broke the news that one of her best friends had become the emotional equivalent of a weapon of mass destruction. How many lives had Dannie been responsible for fucking up? Rory and Deirdre's, Aoife, Grace and Bruno's. Greta O'Flaherty's. Actually, strike that: substitute 'suicide bomber' for 'weapon of mass destruction'. For Dannie Palmer had succeeded brilliantly in fucking her own life up as well. What a brilliant career she had forged as a home wrecker, morale annihilator and mind-body-spirit terminator.

Hey! She rocked as the Arnold Schwarzenegger of the emotional world.

Discarding her wet clothes, Dannie helped herself to sweats from a chest of drawers – a pair of Rory's by the cut of them. Then she went downstairs, put the kettle on and started tidying up.

Tomorrow she'd lose her friend forever, she thought as she pulled damp laundry from the washing machine and set about loading the dryer. Tomorrow she'd feast on crow and humble pie. Tomorrow she'd have a taste of what it must have been like to be Greta O'Flaherty before the village had been won round by her curiously old-fashioned Pollyanna-ish ways, back in those early days when Greta had been cold-shouldered, ostracised and looked at sideways.

And now Dannie remembered the contempt she'd heard in Sam's voice earlier this evening, remembered the way Jethro had looked at her with that resigned 'I told you so' expression. And worst of all, she remembered the words that Greta had fired at her with the precision of a knife-thrower. *Shame on you.*

An occasional laugh came from the playroom upstairs, but otherwise the atmosphere in the Lennox household was subdued. Greta and Sam were ensconced in their room with baby Lennox, Daniel was in his studio and Madeleine was trying to read a book by the fire in the sitting room. Outside, the rain was bucketing down.

Madeleine couldn't concentrate. What a horrible, *horrible* day it had been. And presumably it was still being a horrible day for Dannie and Deirdre. She would never,

ever forget the look on Dannie's face when Greta had wished shame upon her. *Shame on you*. What made those words so emotive?

Madeleine realised now that Greta was quintessentially shame*less*. She wondered why it was considered insulting to be called shameless – as in a 'shameless hussy'. How much more laudable to be shameless than shame*ful*! Greta had conducted herself shamelessly when she'd worked as a body double, she'd conducted herself shamelessly when she'd posed naked for Daniel and she'd conducted herself shamelessly when she'd walked the streets of the village of the squinting windows with her pregnant belly proudly on display. She wasn't ashamed of her body. To be free of shame was clearly something devoutly to be wished for: hadn't the original woman, Eve, been shameless before she'd eaten the apple and started covering herself up with fig leaves? And every soul in Saint-Géyroux should know now that there was no shame – no shame at all – that could be attached to Greta O'Flaherty.

The phone rang. It was late, nearly midnight. Who would call at such an hour? Dannie. Of course. Madeleine grabbed the cordless without bothering to check the display.

'Dannie! Is everything all right?' she said.

'Madeleine?' It was a man's voice. 'It's Rory.'

'Rory!'

'I'm sorry to be phoning so late. No one's picking up in the Palmer house and I didn't know of any other way to get through to Deirdre. She won't take my calls.'

'Oh, God – Rory! It's all so horribly tragic.'

'I know.'

But it needn't be! Madeleine thought. There was hope now – now that Dannie's monumental mistake had been uncovered. She had to tell Rory, had to let him know what had happened. She felt brimful with exultation suddenly. There was a way to save Deirdre's marriage after all!

'Rory, oh, Rory – I'm so glad you rang!'

'Madeleine, I—'

But Madeleine was intent on being the bearer of glad tidings – nothing was going to get in the way of that: she was on a mission. She forged on with blithe disregard.

'Listen, Rory, there's something you need to know. It was all an appalling mistake – Deirdre and you and the thing with Greta. It was all a truly dreadful mistake. You see, Deirdre thought that you were having an affair with Greta – she even thought that Greta's baby might be yours. But of course, it's not, and Dannie fessed up just this evening to having jumped to the wrong conclusion, and after that the whole thing just snowballed and spiralled out of control, and Dannie's with Deirdre now, and she's in a bad way.'

'Deirdre's in a bad way?'

'Yes. Oh, Rory – maybe you could try ringing her tomorrow, once Dannie's—'

'Madeleine. I'm in a bad way too.'

'Oh. I'm sorry, Rory, of course you are. But things could be good again between you two, and—'

'Madeleine, I'm sorry, but I'm not really taking this on board. I'm in a bad way because my father died today.'

'Oh. Oh, God. Oh, Rory, I am *so* very sorry.'

'That's OK. Thanks. You might pass the news on to Deirdre. She was fond of my da. But don't disturb her tonight if she's not well.'

'As you wish ... I'll go round there tomorrow.'

'Thank you, Madeleine. Tell me – what's your e-mail address?' Madeleine dictated it, then Rory said, 'I'll e-mail you the funeral arrangements when we know them. Being a bank holiday today, we were a bit stymied. Perhaps you'd let Deirdre know the details as soon as they arrive?'

'Of course I will.'

'Thanks, Madeleine. Goodbye.'

Madeleine was on the verge of saying goodbye back when she was hit by a sudden thought. 'Rory? Bruno's here – he's staying the night. Would you like to talk to him?'

There was a pause and Madeleine heard a catch in Rory's voice when he spoke again. 'Thank you. I would like to talk to him. I'd like that very much. But ...' There was another pause, another struggle for breath before Rory resumed. 'But I won't say anything to him about his *dadóg*. That'd be better coming in person from Deirdre.'

'Of course,' agreed Madeleine. 'I'll just run upstairs with the phone. The kids are all sleeping in the playroom.'

She got up from her chair, swung into the hall and sped up the stairs. In the playroom, the children had improvised a big bed out of oversized cushions and beanbags. The three of them were lying snuggled under a king-sized duvet. Greta was reading to them from a storybook and baby Lennox was asleep in his carry cot.

Greta looked up at Madeleine and smiled. 'They're nearly asleep,' she said, indicating with a nod the lolling heads and half-closed eyes. Closing the book, she got to her feet, picked up the carry cot and strolled soundlessly across the floor.

'Good night, Madeleine,' she said on her way past. 'Sweet dreams.'

'Same to you.'

Madeleine moved to the bed. 'Bruno?' she said, leaning over him. 'Your dad's on the phone. He wants to talk to you.'

Bruno smiled sleepily and reached out a hand for the cordless. 'Pops!' he said into the mouthpiece. '*Athas an Bhlian Nua Dhuit!* Happy New Year!'

Madeleine tiptoed from the room.

The last thing she heard Bruno say was, 'Big hugs! I love you so, so much. Yes. I miss you too. Don't cry, Pops. Please don't cry.'

Madeleine just managed to shut the door to the playroom before her own tears started to come.

32

'I've done it. I've told her. Will you come over now?'

'Yes,' Madeleine told Dannie. 'I'll come straight away. How did she take it?'

'It was awful,' said Dannie. 'I think she's in shock – I'm not quite sure she really took it in. I was kind of hoping that she might go ballistic, like she did that time when I told her about – you know. But she didn't. She just went all quiet.'

'Why did you want her to go ballistic?'

'Because I deserve to be hated, Madeleine.'

'No you don't! Don't be daft, Dannie. Anyone could have made the mistake you made.'

'Maybe. But that doesn't stop me feeling like shit.'

'Oh, come *on*. Beating yourself up isn't going to achieve anything. And Deirdre's going to need our help more than ever now.'

'Oh, Christ. Don't tell me something else awful's happened?'

'Rory phoned last night to tell me that his father died yesterday.'

Dannie's voice on the phone sounded stricken. 'Oh, *no*! Oh, *shit*.'

'I think it had been on the cards – he was in a hospice.'

'When's the funeral?'

'Friday. I got an e-mail with the details this morning. Deirdre's going to have to travel over with Bruno, and you and I are going to have to make all the arrangements. So listen up, Dannie. You are not to waste any more energy feeling sorry for yourself, OK?'

Madeleine knew she was sounding harsh, but if Dannie were to carry on weeping and wailing over the milk she'd spilled, she'd be no use to anyone.

There was a pause. 'I'll organise everything. It's what I'm good at,' Dannie said.

'That's what I like to hear. Chin up, Ms Palmer. I'll be with you in five minutes.'

Madeleine put the phone down, then moved to the kitchen table and picked up the printout of the e-mail she'd received from Rory earlier that morning.

Dear Madeleine,

Here are the details of my father's funeral, as they will appear in tomorrow's *Irish Times*:

'McDonagh, Joseph: (Clarenbridge, Co. Galway) January 1, 2008 (peacefully), in Galway Hospice. Loving father of Emer and Rory. Sadly missed by his children, his daughter-in-law, Deirdre, son-in-law, Michael, and grandchildren Aoife, Bruno, Constance, Fergal and Grace. Removal to Oranmore church, Galway, arriving at 5 o'c on Friday 3rd. Funeral mass at 11 o'c on Friday followed by burial in Renville Cemetery. Donations if desired in lieu of flowers to Safe Home Ireland. The family are deeply grateful to the staff of the Galway Hospice for their care of Joseph. *Bás in Éireann.*'

I'd be really grateful, Madeleine, if you could help Deirdre get here in time. If she's under the weather, she may need someone to travel with her. Might you or Dannie be generous enough to volunteer?

Dad was sorry not to have seen Bruno before he died. I would have sent for him, but because Dad was in pain for the last few days, I decided against it. It's better that Bruno's memories are of a grand-father in the full of his health. He was also sorry not to have seen Deirdre. He had a real soft spot for her. For some reason, he always associated that W.H. Davies poem with her – you know the one that has the line 'No time to turn at beauty's glance, and watch her feet, how they can dance.' He said she had the dancingest eyes of any woman he'd ever met. I guess they're not dancing so much these days.

Thanks for helping out. I hope all's well with you and Daniel.

Big hugs, Rory.

'Morning, Madeleine.'

Greta wandered into the kitchen, looking a little dozy. She was wearing the kimono she slipped into during her work breaks and baby Lennox's head was lolling against her shoulder. He was bleary eyed too and a little drool was dangling from his rosebud mouth. As Greta rubbed his back he brought up some wind and Greta smiled approvingly and said, 'Good baba.'

'Greta?' Madeleine asked her. 'My Irish was crap at the

best of times, and it's practically all gone now, apart from *céad míle fáilte*. What does *Bás in Éireann* mean?'

'It means 'May you die in Ireland',' Greta said. 'It's a favourite blessing of the Irish emigrants. Their dream is that they can return home to Ireland to die. Some people think it's morbid, but I think it's kind of lovely.'

'It is,' said Madeleine. 'It is lovely.'

And then she remembered something Rory had said to her last summer, during the few brief halcyon days he'd enjoyed in Saint-Géyroux. He'd told her that he wanted his kids to have an Irish-speaking nanny because he'd love them to be able to talk Irish to their grandpa. Aoife and Grace had never had a chance to learn the language – unlike Bruno, who had picked up a smattering when Greta had been living at *chez* McDonagh-O'Dare. But it had been too late for Bruno. Rory's father was lying dead in a hospice, and poor Bruno McDonagh-O'Dare had never had the chance to speak to his grandpa *as Gaelige*.

Madeleine had been planning on giving a copy of the e-mail to Dannie and Deirdre. Now, on rereading the printout, she decided against it, copying the funeral details onto a Post-it instead. She knew that if Deirdre read the stuff about Rory's dad being sorry that he hadn't been able to see his grandson before he died, it would devastate her, and if Dannie read it, it would make her feel even guiltier than she already did.

And Madeleine knew that Dannie needed to be strong now if she was to right her wrongs and make amends.

Bruno had coped with the news of his grandfather's death in the same way as most children of his age do when they've been bereaved of someone they don't know that well. He'd boo-hooed on his mother's lap for several minutes, and then, when Rosa had arrived with a new PlayStation game, he'd been right as rain and raring to go.

Dannie had organised everything. She'd stayed overnight at Deirdre's so that she could keep her friend company and so that she could oversee housekeeping and mealtimes and Bruno-minding; she'd booked their flights; she'd packed for both Deirdre and her boy; she'd driven them to the Aéroport Montpellier Méditerranée and left her car in the long-term car park; and she'd arranged for a driver to collect them from the airport in Galway. Because there were no direct flights to Galway from Montpellier, they had to go via Heathrow.

Deirdre seemed glad to be told what to do. Dannie sensed that she was fragile as a China doll and needed all the kid-gloving she could get. And Dannie was happy to give as much as it took to try to make it up to her friend.

In Heathrow, Dannie checked them in, then settled Deirdre and Bruno at a booth in one of the myriad cafés while she went off to fetch coffee and sandwiches and juice for Bruno. As she queued at the cash desk with her tray, she looked over to where her charges were sitting. Bruno was dancing his little black-and-white velour cat on the tabletop to the rhythm coming from his iPod and Deirdre was gazing into the middle distance.

Deirdre wore a slightly bewildered look these days, as if she didn't really know what was happening to her. Dannie suspected it was the Xanax, and while she was glad the drug was helping her through this bad time, she hoped Deirdre would stay off the drink. Xanax and alcohol clearly did not mix. But to her reasonably certain

507

knowledge, Deirdre had consumed no alcohol since that awful night in the house in rue Lamballe.

Dannie smiled over at her and Deirdre smiled back vaguely. She had even assumed the look of a China doll, thought Dannie. She'd lost a lot of weight since the summer and her complexion had a pallor that was most un-Deirdre. She was wearing a little black suit today with a boxy jacket and a fitted skirt with plain black heels. She sat upright on the banquette, feet together, her gloved hands clutching the handle of the bag on her lap. She looked like a widow, Dannie realised.

As she slung her change into her purse and picked up the tray, Dannie noticed a couple of blokes in leather jackets loitering with intent behind the booth in which Deirdre and Bruno were ensconced. One of them had a digital recorder in his hand, the other was wielding a camera. Suddenly they rounded the booth: one adopted a threatening attitude, shoving the recorder into Deirdre's face, while the other aimed his camera straight at her, the *click click click* of the shutter sounding like small arms fire, the flashgun drawing the attention of rubberneckers.

Encumbered as she was by the tray, Dannie could only watch as Deirdre stretched out her arm to pull Bruno in to her so that his face was concealed by her shoulder.

'Ms O'Dare?' Dannie heard the man with the microphone bark. 'Would you care to share with us your feelings about your husband and Charlotte Lambert?'

'Please go away,' came Deirdre's reply. 'That is none of your concern.'

'When will your divorce be finalised?'

'Please go away. That is none of your concern.'

'Do you know if Rory and Charlotte have any plans to

marry after your divorce goes through?'

'Please go away. That is none of your concern.' Deirdre's face was paper white now. Dannie could tell from her expression that she was struggling to remain impassive, but her eyes were full of terror.

Abruptly, Dannie lost it. She yelled something inarticulate, dropped the tray she was carrying, heard it crash to the floor and saw startled faces turn in her direction as she rounded on the paparazzi to let them have it.

'Fuck off!' she screamed, clenching her fists. 'Fuck off back to hell, you fucking fuckers! Leave my friend alone! She's on her way to a fucking *funeral*, for fuck's sake! Don't you think she has enough on her plate without bastards like you – you pair of fucking *hyenas* – invading her space and giving her grief? Fuck – hyenas is too good a name for yiz – hyenas only feast on dead flesh. You bastards scavenge for living, breathing flesh and devour feckin' hearts whole. You fucking scandalmongers! *Shame on you!*

'Hey! Cool it, babe.' The bloke with the recorder spread his hands in a defensive fashion. Then he laughed, shrugged and said, 'It's only a job.'

'Whooh! Fei*sty*!' remarked the geezer with the camera, turning to her. 'Say cheese, sweet tits!' he added, letting his flashgun off in her face.

The pair grinned at her, then ambled off, mumbling something that was evidently filthy, because the paparazzo leered back over his shoulder at Dannie and waggled his tongue at her.

Dannie was practically hyperventilating when she sat down on the banquette beside Deirdre. 'Darlin', are you all right?' she said. 'And Bruno? How are you?'

Bruno blinked at her. 'Hey, Dannie!' he said. 'You were

legend! You were like the Terminator!' He gave her a wan smile of approval before plugging himself back into his iPod.

'Yeah, you were,' said Deirdre with a tremulous smile. 'Well done, you. You said everything I wanted to say, but couldn't. I had to be grace under pressure.'

'You were that, all right! I admire your *sang-froid*.'

Deirdre shrugged. 'It's not easy. But you learn a lot from LA publicists. Could you imagine if they'd got a shot of me waving my arms around like a madwoman? And just think of the copy: "When we asked Ms O'Dare for a comment, she said. 'Fuck off back to hell, you fuck-ing fuckers!'" Except they would have substituted aster-isks for the 'fucks'. And they would have twisted it to make it look as if I was telling Rory and Charlotte to fuck off to hell. Thanks, Dannie, for doing the needful for me.'

'You're more than welcome.' Dannie looked ruefully over at the tray she'd dropped. The bus boy clearing up the mess of spilled coffee and broken crockery was sending her murderous looks. 'Sorry!' she mouthed at him.

Deirdre nodded towards the departures notice. 'Our flight's been delayed by twenty minutes,' she remarked. 'The change came up while you were in the queue.'

'Good,' said Dannie. 'That means we've still got time for coffee. I'll try again, will I?'

Getting up from the banquette, she headed towards the self-service counter, aware that people were giving her curious looks after her Terminator speech. As she helped herself to a tray, a text alert stopped her in her tracks. She fished out her phone. The envelope icon told her the mes-sage was from Jethro and she opened it to find the following:

Have jst spken 2 charlotte lambert. She says stuff in enquirer
piece of shit. She and rory jst gd frnds. She marrying childhood sweetheart nxt yr. Tell Deirdre. XX

Dannie reread the text, then searched for Deirdre's
number and pressed forward. Some minutes later, as she
rejoined the queue for the cash desk, her laden tray provoking apprehensive looks from the hovering bus boy, she
saw Deirdre take her phone from her bag and check out
the display.

For the first time in days, something flickered in her
expression. Then Deirdre put the phone back into her
handbag, resumed her straight-backed posture and
continued her scrutiny of the middle distance.

Dannie watched as Rory cast the last shovelful of earth.
He set the spade down, then straightened up and surveyed
the assembled mourners.

'Joseph would have hated it,' Rory said, 'if I kept you any
longer from celebrating his life at his wake. So I'll be brief. I
just want to recite a couple of verses of my father's favourite
poem. It's from William Blake's 'The Divine Image'.'

Thrusting his hands in his pockets, Rory looked down
at the freshly dug grave. Then he raised his head and
looked directly at where Deirdre was standing, all three of
her children grouped around her.

> To Mercy, Pity, Peace, and Love,
> All pray in their distress,
> And to these virtues of delight
> Return their thankfulness.

For Mercy has a human heart,
Pity, a human face;
And Love the human form divine
And Peace the human dress.

A lone piper took Rory's place as he moved to his family. Dannie saw him hold out his hand to Deirdre. Deirdre took it and Rory intertwined his fingers with hers. Then he took a step closer to his wife, raised his other hand and drew her head against his shoulder.

Together the couple stood by the graveside with tears on their cheeks, lamenting Rory's lost father, lamenting lost love.

Later, in the Great Southern Hotel, Dannie and Deirdre went back to their respective rooms to change. Rory had stipulated that he wanted no black to be worn at his father's wake since it was to be the celebration of a life, not the mourning of a death.

Deirdre emerged into the foyer wearing a pretty dress in layered scarlet chiffon. Dannie noticed that she'd stuck a rose from one of the hotel displays in her hair and that she'd freshened up her make-up and spritzed herself with scent, and she felt something like hope flutter in the pit of her tummy. *Please, God, please, God, please please ...*

'Hey! You look lovely!' Dannie told her and Deirdre flicked indifferent eyes over Dannie's silk jersey wrap dress and gave her an automatic, 'Thanks – so do you,' in return.

Together they took the lift to the function room where the party was being held and – to Dannie's great relief – Deirdre refused the glass of wine proffered by the waiter standing sentinel at the door.

Over by the stage that had been set up for the dance band, the girls and Bruno were mingling with their Irish cousins. Deirdre had told Dannie that Constance was the same age as Grace, and Fergal just a little younger than Bruno, so chances were they'd get on all right, despite the fact that they lived on opposite sides of the ocean.

On spotting Deirdre, Aoife came over like a heat-seeking missile and wound an arm around her mother's waist and Dannie heard her say, 'Mommy, Mommy. Pops has missed you an awful lot and Christmas was no fun without you and Bruno, especially since *dadóg* was so sick.'

Please, God, please, God, please please …

'And *I've* missed *you*,' Deirdre told her. 'Maybe experimenting with a new kind of Christmas wasn't such a good idea after all.'

Please, God, please, God, please please …

The room filled up. There was much roistering and toast-making and singing of songs – as there always is at any halfway decent Irish wake – and then the band started up. They played the usual diddley-eye suspects: 'My Wild Irish Rose' and 'She Moved through the Fair' and 'Carrickfergus', and then came the bass notes, the opening eight that introduced Van Morrison's 'Brown Eyed Girl'.

On the other side of the room, Dannie saw Rory get to his feet. His eyes searched the crowd and fell at last upon Deirdre. Excusing himself from the knot of people he was with, he moved across the floor until he stood facing her. Looking down at her with sad eyes, he seemed at a loss for words. Then he clicked his heels together and executed an ironic, military-style bow. 'They're playing what used to be our song,' he said. 'May I?'

Deirdre took the hand he extended and rose from her chair, and Dannie watched her disappear into the throng of dancers, chiffon drifting round her in a blur.

Aoife was regarding her curiously. 'Why are you crying, Dannie?' she asked. 'Is it because of *dadóg*?'

'I never knew your *dadóg, acushla*. I'm crying because I'm remembering a fairy tale I once heard about a prince and a princess who were very much in love.'

'Tell me the story!'

'Well, a wicked witch cast a spell over the prince and the princess and gave them each an awful sickness and sent them off to live in different kingdoms. But after a while, the witch repented of her wickedness and worked very hard indeed to weave a new spell that would bring them back together again and make them better.'

'And did it work?' asked Aoife.

Dannie caught a glimpse of Rory and Deirdre in the crowd. Rory's right arm was curved around his wife's waist, his left hand supported her right, but they weren't looking at each other. They were both looking into middle distance.

The healing would take time, Dannie knew. No marriage could recover overnight from the kind of damage that had been inflicted on Rory and Deirdre's. But Dannie was convinced it *could* happen. It *must* happen.

Please, God, please, God, please please … And then Dannie realised that, for the first time in years, she wasn't pleading with God to give her a baby. She was pleading with him to right the wrong she had done; she was pleading with him to reunite her two dear friends.

'Did it work, Dannie?' asked Aoife again. 'Did the spell work?'

'I don't know,' said Dannie, smiling down at Aoife's sweet, inquisitive face. 'I never heard the end of it. But it's a fairy tale, isn't it? And how do fairy tales always end?'

'Happily ever after, of course' said Aoife.

'That's right,' said Dannie. 'Happily ever after.'

Under cover of the silk jersey of her dress, Dannie crossed her fingers.

EPILOGUE

Madeleine knocked at the door to Daniel's studio. She'd just had a phone call from Sam to tell her that he and Greta had bought their dream cottage and she wanted to let Daniel know. She'd been in the shower when the call had come through, but she'd taken the call regardless because she was aching to know if the couple's bid had been successful. The minute she put the phone down, she'd slung on her kimono and climbed the spiral staircase.

'Come in, Madeleine,' she heard from the other side of the door.

She turned the handle. Daniel had just that morning had the *Greta Enceinte* series crated so that the paintings could be delivered to the gallery in Paris. Now he was priming a fresh canvas.

'Hell's teeth, Daniel! You're not starting work on something else *already*?' Madeleine asked crossly. 'You've been working flat out for seven months, for heaven's sake! Don't you think you should take a break?'

'Nope,' he told her. 'Not when there's a muse to be obeyed.'

Madeleine felt something curl up in her gut.

'You've found a new muse?'

'No. My muse – the one and only original – never went away.'

Madeleine was confused. 'But Greta's been gone for weeks.'

'I'm not talking about Greta, Madeleine. I'm talking about you.'

'Me?'

'Yes. You're the inspiration for my new series.'

'Me?' repeated Madeleine, feeling flummoxed. 'You don't want to paint a thirty-something with cellulite, Daniel!'

'Oh yes, I do. I have an idea for a brand new series.'

'You do? What is it to be?'

'I'm calling it *Madeleine, Arrivée à Maturité. Madeleine in her Prime.*' Daniel raised his eyes from the canvas and looked directly at her. She knew that look. 'When do you want to start sitting?' he asked her.

Madeleine moved slowly across the floor, loving the feel of the silk brushing against her bare skin. When she reached the daybed in the centre of the studio floor, she stopped and stood quite still. Man and wife regarded each other levelly, exchanging that look of equals; that look that signifies the unspoken empathy between artist and muse.

Then Madeleine smiled. Slowly, she undid the sash of her kimono, parted the lapels and let the silk slide to the floor.

'There's no time like the present,' she said.

That night, Madeleine wrote her first sonnet for many, many months.

> I've got my voice back! This sonnet's for you –
> My darling Daniel, husband, lover, friend ...
> Some danse macabre it was to apprehend
> The prospect of our union going askew.
> You took a flight path inspired by your muse
> While I trailed down some sunless avenue,
> So threatened by this seeming parvenu
> That all I thought of daily was 'J'accuse!'
>
> I'm settled now. So glad to know the truth:
> So pleased that Greta's no usurping minx;
> So thrilled that 'prime' is sexier than youth;
> So reassured the plot's ironed out its kinks ...
>
> Here's to the future of our treasured friends!
> And as for Hecate? May she make amends ...

A solemn-looking Dannie Palmer was studying her reflection in a cheval glass. She was wearing – for the very first time – the underwear that she'd bought for Christmas. The bra in watered silk with teeny bows and rosebud clasp; the matching pair of French knickers; the wisp of a suspender belt; a pair of gossamer stockings.

She turned away from the mirror as the door to the bedroom opened and Jethro walked in. He looked knackered – he'd been working in the edit suite until late every night that week – and when he got a load of the get-up Dannie was wearing, he looked even more knackered.

'Hell, Dannie,' he said. 'Is it that time of the month again? I'm not sure I'm going to be able to get it up for you tonight, darlin'.'

Dannie said nothing. She took Jethro by the hand and led him to the bed. He sat down heavily, then slumped back against the mattress.

'You're a persistent gal,' he said.

Dannie straddled him, took his face between her hands and smiled down at him.

'I'm very glad that I'm a persistent gal,' she told him, 'because they say that persistence pays off.'

'Is that a fact?' Jethro tried unsuccessfully to stifle a yawn.

'It is, to be sure.' Dannie reached down a hand.

'Then we must be the exception that proves the rule.'

'The exception that proves the rule. I've never understood that saying. What on earth does it mean?'

'I haven't a clue. I've never understood it either.'

'Persistence pays off. The exception that proves the rule. Absence makes the heart grow fonder. Out of sight, out of mind. A good man is hard to find. A hard man is *good* to find. Hmm. I thought you said you weren't going to be able to get it up tonight?'

'How could I resist you in that garb, Madame Palmer?' Jethro hooked a thumb round the cup of her bra and tugged, exposing a nipple. Then he rolled Dannie over so that she was lying on her back. He took hold of her bra strap and rubbed the fabric between finger and thumb. 'Was this stuff expensive?' he asked.

'It was *very* expensive.'

'Your predilection for fancy underwear will be the ruination of me.' Jethro smiled at her. 'I suppose I should just look on it as an excellent investment.'

'Investment?'

'In terms of baby-making.'

'In that case, you'll be glad to know it's already paid off, Monsieur Palmer.' Dannie smiled back at him.

'What do you mean, Sphinx?'

'I'm pregnant.'

Deirdre had been asked to rewrite her screenplay. Although the creative team loved it, the money men weren't happy with it – they thought it was too dark, too bleak and twisted, and they were insisting on a happy ending. They especially hated the loss of Georgia's baby, so the baby had been restored to her. The scene where Georgia had collapsed bleeding on the bathroom floor had been cut in its entirety – as had Dee's rant on the phone – and the character of the divorce lawyer had become a marriage guidance counsellor. Deirdre secretly thought that this new version was a little too anodyne, but you couldn't argue with the money men. And anyway, she'd rather the story ended up on a screen in front of the viewing public than sit on the hard drive of her computer forever. She had done a lot of wrestling with her manuscript and had come to the all-important final scene.

```
INT. DEE'S DUPLEX.

KITCHEN. NIGHT.

We are CLOSE on Dee's face. She is sitting at
the counter, sipping wine and listening to the
sound of the children's boisterous LAUGHTER
coming from upstairs. Her expression is tabula
rasa. We cannot know what she is thinking.
Picture Greta Garbo as Queen Christina.
```

```
As the CAMERA pulls back, we see that there is
another, half-full wineglass on the counter.
Stephen enters the room, leans against the door
jamb. They look at each other. There is no need
for dialogue.

DISSOLVE TO:

FINAL CREDITS
```

In Connemara, Greta and Sam were returning from a
ramble. Sam had been taking photographs of the beautiful mountains known as the Twelve Bens and Greta had
been making little line drawings of baby Lennox in her
sketch book.

It was a cold spring day, one of those astonishing
Matisse-blue days when the only clouds in the sky are the
barely perceptible brushstrokes of vapour trails. On days
like this, Connemara seems as magical a place as any in a
fairy tale.

Greta lifted her face to the sky and shut her eyes. The
faint smell of turf smoke came to her on the wind, that
most evocative of all smells – more evocative by far, she
was sure, than Proust's stupid cake. In the sling strapped
against her front, she felt Lennox stir. She looked down
at his cherub face, wondering what he was dreaming of,
then turned to Sam, who was bolting the five-bar gate at
the top of the path.

'There's nothing on telly tonight,' she told him. 'But
there's a radio documentary on about your uncle. It's a re-
peat. But I wouldn't mind listening to it again – especially
now that I know Daniel's bark's much worse than his

bite.' She gave Sam her loveliest smile. 'We could sit by the fire, listening to the radio like Days of Yore people, and toast marshmallows.'

'Sounds good to me,' said Sam.

He held out his hand, pulled her in to him and kissed her, and then they turned away from the gate.

There was the turf pile, and there the road to home. They could see the whitewashed cottage at the edge of the lake and the blue turf-smoke rising from the chimney.

In all the wonderful past, they had not seen anything more lovely.

a KATE THOMPSON novel

'Utterly charming, and deliberately sassy,
if this book were food it would be a gooey
chocolate muffin! Delicious!'

Irish Independent

Whether it's shopping by proxy for Coco de Mer
lingerie, being set upon by a gang of goats in a
classy country house hotel, wearing ill-advised shoes or
sending out all the wrong signals to all the wrong men,
hapless Charlotte Cholewczyk just can't seem to win.
Until she finds herself winging her way to Paris,
where she discovers that it's wickedly hard tochoose
between love, sex and friendship...no, strike that,
and make it *fiendishly* hard!

'A book that will inspire you to appreciate
the finer things in life, including romance'

Irish Times

www.pixiepirelli.com

ISBN 978-1-905494-07-1